BIRTHRIGHT: BOOK THE SECOND

BECAUSE IT IS MY BLOOD

GABRIELLE ZEVIN

SQUARE
FISH

Farrar Straus Giroux
New York

Thank you to Marie-Ann Geißler and Stephanie Feldman Gutt for their assistance with the German and Spanish translations. All mistakes should be considered the author's however.

BECAUSE IT IS MY BLOOD. Copyright © 2012 by Gabrielle Zevin.
All rights reserved. Printed in the United States of America by
LSC Communications, Harrisonburg, Virginia.

Library of Congress Cataloging-in-Publication Data
Zevin, Gabrielle.
Because it is my blood / Gabrielle Zevin.
p. cm.—(Birthright ; bk. 2)
Summary: In 2083, seventeen-year-old Anya Balanchine seeks a way to make
Balanchine Chocolate legitimate, and although a trip to Mexico gives her new
insights and ideas, escaping her mobster family's legacy of violence may
prove impossible.
ISBN 978-1-250-03422-9 (paperback) / ISBN 978-0-374-30674-8 (e-book)
[1. Organized crime—Fiction. 2. Chocolate—Fiction.
3. Celebrities—Fiction. 4. Violence—Fiction. 5. Family life—New York
(State)—New York—Fiction. 6. New York (N.Y.)—Fiction. 7. Oaxaca
de Juárez (Mexico)—Fiction. 8. Mexico—Fiction. 9. Science fiction.] I. Title.
PZ7.Z452Bec 2012   [Fic]—dc23   2011036991

Originally published in the United States by Farrar Straus Giroux
First Square Fish Edition 2013
Square Fish logo designed by Filomena Tuosto

3 5 7 9 10 8 6 4 2

AR: 4.5 / LEXILE: 640L

To my beautiful mother, AeRan Zevin,
who always sends me home with second supper
and who makes life beautiful

IN THE DESERT

In the desert
I saw a creature, naked, bestial,
Who, squatting upon the ground,
Held his heart in his hands,
And ate of it.
I said, "Is it good, friend?"
"It is bitter—bitter," he answered;
"But I like it
Because it is bitter,
And because it is my heart."

—Stephen Crane

CONTENTS

Casa Marquez Hot Chocolate

1 red chili pepper
½ vanilla bean
1 cinnamon stick
3 or 4 crushed rose petals
2 cups milk
*2 or 3 squares bittersweet chocolate without nuts**

Pick up your machete and split the chili pepper down the middle.
Remove seeds. Are you still holding your machete? If not, what is
wrong with you? Abuela advises you should never let your guard
down in the kitchen. *Okay.* Still holding your machete, split the
vanilla bean the long way. Break up the cinnamon stick. This will
be hard—your anger will be an advantage in this task. Crush the
rose petals with your fists like a teenage girl with a broken heart.
(You know about that.)

Drown the chili pepper, vanilla bean, cinnamon-stick pieces,
and crushed rose petals in the milk. Heat the milk until it is
simmering. Let it simmer for no more than 2 minutes. Any longer,
the milk turns bad, and Abuela says that the whole thing will
surely be a disaster.

Shave chocolate into thin strips, then whisk into milk mixture
until chocolate is melted.

Remove from heat and let rest for 10 minutes. Strain, and heat
again. Some like it warm, but not you, Anya.

Serves 2. As your own nana—*que en paz descanse*—used to say,
"Share it with someone you love."**

---

*Balanchine Bittersweet is preferred but you can use whatever you have on hand.
**WARNING: This is not sweet. Drink at your own risk.

I

I AM RELEASED INTO SOCIETY

Cᴏᴍᴇ ɪɴ, ᴀɴʏᴀ, have a seat. We find ourselves in the midst of a situation," Evelyn Cobrawick greeted me, parting her painted red lips to reveal a cheerful sliver of yellow tooth. Was this meant to be a grin? I certainly hoped not. My fellow inmates at Liberty Children's Facility were of the universal opinion that Mrs. Cobrawick was at her most dangerous when smiling.

It was the night before my release, and I had been summoned to the headmistress's chambers. Through careful adherence to rules—all but one, all but once—I had managed to avoid the woman for the entire summer. "A situ—" I began.

Mrs. Cobrawick interrupted me. "Do you know what I like best about my job? It's the girls. Watching them grow up and make better lives for themselves. Knowing that *I* had some small part in these rehabilitations. I truly feel as if I have thousands of daughters. It almost makes up for the fact that the former Mr. Cobrawick and I were not blessed with any children of our own."

I was not sure how to respond to this information. "You said there was a situation?"

"Be patient, Anya. I'm getting there. I . . . You see, I feel very bad about the way we met. I think you may have gotten the wrong impression about me. The measures I took last fall may have seemed harsh to you at the time, but they were only to help you adjust to life at Liberty. And I think you'll agree that my conduct was exactly right, because look what a splendid summer you've had here! You've been submissive, compliant, a model resident in every sense. One would hardly guess that you came from such a criminal background."

This was meant as a compliment so I thanked her. I snuck a glance out Mrs. Cobrawick's window. The night was clear, and I could just make out the tip of Manhattan. Only eighteen hours before I would be home.

"You are most welcome. I feel optimistic that your time here will serve you well in your future endeavors. Which brings us, of course, to our situation."

I turned to look at Mrs. Cobrawick. I very much wished that she would stop referring to it as "our situation."

"In August, you had a visitor," she began. "A young man."

I lied, telling her that I wasn't sure whom she meant.

"The Delacroix boy," she said.

"Yes. He was my boyfriend last year, but that's done now."

"The guard on duty that day claimed that you kissed him." She paused to look me in the eyes. "Twice."

"I shouldn't have done that. He had been injured, as you

probably read in my file, and I suppose I was overcome to see him well again. I apologize, Mrs. Cobrawick."

"Yes, you did break the rules," Mrs. Cobrawick replied. "But your infraction is understandable, I think, and human really, and can be overlooked. It probably surprises you to hear an old gorgon like me say that, but I am not without feelings, Anya.

"Before you came to Liberty in June, acting District Attorney Charles Delacroix gave me very specific instructions regarding your treatment here. Would you like me to tell you what they were?"

I wasn't sure, but I nodded anyway.

"There were only three. The first was that I was to avoid any unnecessary personal interaction with Anya Balanchine. I don't think you can disagree that I followed that one to the letter."

That explained why my stay had passed in such relative peace. If I ever saw Charles Delacroix again (and I hoped I'd have no reason to), I'd be certain to thank him.

"The second was that Anya Balanchine was not to be sent to the Cellar under any circumstance."

"And the third?" I asked.

"The third was that I was to contact him immediately if his son came to visit you. Such an event, he said, could possibly necessitate a revision to both the quality and length of Anya Balanchine's stay at Liberty."

I felt myself shudder at the word *length*. I was well aware of the promise I had made Charles Delacroix regarding his son.

"So, when the guard came to me with the news that the

Delacroix boy had been to see Anya Balanchine, do you know what I decided to do?"

She—horrors!—smiled at me.

"I decided to do nothing. 'Evie,' I said to myself, 'at the end of the year, you're leaving Liberty and you don't have to do everything they say anymore—'"

I interrupted the conversation she was having with herself to ask, "You're leaving?"

"Yes, it seems I've been forced into early retirement, Anya. They're making a huge mistake. Not anyone can run this kingdom of mine." She waved her hand by way of changing the subject. "But as I was telling you before . . . 'Evie,' I said, 'you don't owe that awful Charles Delacroix a thing. Anya Balanchine is a good girl, albeit one from a very bad family, and she can't help who does or doesn't visit her.'"

I offered cautious thanks.

"You're very welcome," she replied. "Perhaps someday you'll be able to return the favor."

I shivered. "What is it you want, Mrs. Cobrawick?"

She laughed, then took my hand in hers and squeezed it so hard one of my knuckles cracked. "Only . . . I suppose I'd like to be able to call you my friend."

Daddy always said that there was no commodity more precious or potentially volatile than friendship. I looked into her dark, red-rimmed eyes. "Mrs. Cobrawick, I can honestly say that I won't ever forget this act of friendship."

She released my hand. "Incidentally, Charles Delacroix is an incredible fool. If my experiences working with troubled girls have taught me anything, it's that no good ever comes from keeping young lovers apart. The more he pulls, the more the two of you will pull back. It's a Chinese finger trap, and the finger trap always triumphs."

Here, Mrs. Cobrawick was wrong. Win had visited me that one time. I had kissed him, then told him that he should never come again. To my great annoyance, he'd actually obeyed me. A little over a month had passed since that encounter, and I hadn't heard from or seen Win since.

"As you're leaving us tomorrow, this will also serve as our exit interview," Mrs. Cobrawick said. She opened up my file on her slate. "Let's see, you were brought here on . . ." She scanned the file. "Weapons-possession charges?"

I nodded.

Mrs. Cobrawick put on the reading glasses she wore on a brass chain around her neck. "Really? That's it? I seem to remember you shooting someone."

"In self-defense, yes."

"Well, no matter. I am an educator, not a judge. Are you sorry for your crimes?"

The answer to that was complicated. I did not regret the crime I had been charged with—having my father's gun. I did not regret my actual crime either—shooting Jacks after he shot Win. And I did not regret the deal I had made with Charles Delacroix that had ensured both my siblings' safety. I regretted nothing. Of course, I could sense that saying this would have been frowned upon. "Yes," I replied, "I'm very sorry."

"Good. Then, as of tomorrow"—Mrs. Cobrawick consulted her calendar—"the seventeenth day of September in the year 2083, the city of New York considers Anya Balanchine to be successfully rehabilitated. Best of luck to you, Anya. May the temptations of the world not lead you to recidivism."

It was lights-out by the time I got back to the dormitory. As I reached the bunk bed I had shared with Mouse these past eighty-nine days, she lit a match and gestured that I should come sit by her in the bottom bunk. She held out her notepad. *I need to ask you something before you go,* she had written on one of her precious pages. (She was only allotted twenty-five per day.)

"Sure, Mouse."

They're letting me out early.

I told her that was great news, but she shook her head. She handed me another note.

After Thanksgiving or even sooner. Good behavior, or maybe I use too much paper. Point is, I'd rather be here. My crime makes it so I can't ever go home. When I get out, I'll need a job.

"I wish I could help, but—"

She put her hand over my mouth and handed me yet another prewritten note. Apparently, my responses were just that predictable.

DON'T SAY NO! You can. You're very powerful. I've thought a lot about this, Anya. I want to be a chocolate dealer.

I laughed because I couldn't imagine that she was in earnest. The girl was five feet tall in socks and completely mute! I turned to look at her, and her expression told me that she hadn't been kidding. At that moment, the match burned out, and she lit another one.

"Mouse," I whispered. "I'm not involved in Balanchine

Chocolate that way, and even if I was, I don't know why you'd want that kind of a job."

I'm seventeen. Mute. Criminal. I have no people, no $, no real education.

I could see her point. I nodded, and she passed me one last note.

You are the only friend I've made here. I know I'm small, weak, & mousy, but I am not a coward and I can do hard things. If you let me work with you, I will be loyal to you for life. I would die for you, Anya.

I told her that I didn't want anyone to die for me, and I blew out the match.

I climbed out of Mouse's bunk and went up to my own, where I quickly fell asleep.

In the morning when she wrote and I said goodbye, she didn't mention that she had asked me to help her become a chocolate dealer. The last thing she wrote before the guards came for me was *See you around, A. My real name is Kate, by the way.*

"Kate," I said. "It's nice to meet you."

At eleven a.m., I was taken to change out of the Liberty jumpsuit and back into my street clothes. Despite the fact that I had been booted from the school, I had worn my Trinity uniform the day I had surrendered myself. I was so used to wearing the thing. Even three months later, as I was pulling the skirt over my hips, I could feel my body wanting to go back to school, and specifically to Trinity, where classes had started without me the previous week.

After I'd changed, I was brought to the discharge room. A lifetime ago, I had met Charles Delacroix in this same room, but today, Simon Green and Mr. Kipling, my lawyers, waited for me instead.

"Do I look like a person who has done hard time?" I asked them.

Mr. Kipling considered me before he answered. "No," he said finally. "Though you do look very fit."

I stepped out into the muggy mid-September air and tried not to feel the loss of that summer too much. There would be other summers. There would be other boys, too.

I breathed in, trying to get all that good exterior air into my lungs. I could smell hay, and in the distance, something rotten, sulfurous, maybe even burning. "Freedom smells different than I remember," I commented to my lawyers.

"No, Anya, that's just the Hudson River. It's on fire again," Mr. Kipling said with a yawn.

"What is it this time?" I asked.

"The usual," Mr. Kipling replied. "Something to do with low water levels and chemical contamination."

"Fear not, Anya," Simon Green added. "The city's nearly as run-down as you left it."

When we arrived back at my apartment, the elevator wasn't working, so I told Mr. Kipling and Simon Green that they needn't see me to the door. Our apartment was on the penthouse level—the thirteenth floor, which the building elevator superstitiously referred to as the fourteenth floor. Thirteenth or fourteenth, it was a long trek up, and Mr. Kipling's heart was still weak. My heart, however, was in terrific shape as I'd spent the summer doing Liberty's strenuous athletic drills three, sometimes four times a day. I was lean and strong and I was able to race up the stairs. (*Aside: Is it too much to add that, while my heart the muscle was in terrific shape, my heart the heart had certainly been better? Oh, probably, but there it is. Don't judge me too harshly.*)

Having left my keys (and other valuables) at home, I was forced to ring the doorbell.

Imogen, who I had left in charge of my sister, answered it. "Anya, we didn't hear you come up!" She poked her head into the foyer. "Where are Misters Kipling and Green?"

I reported the condition of the elevator.

"Oh dear. That must have just happened. Maybe it'll fix itself?" she said brightly.

What, in my life, had ever fixed itself?

Imogen told me that Scarlet was waiting for me in the living room.

"And Natty?" I asked. She should have been home from genius camp four weeks ago.

"Natty's . . ." Imogen hesitated.

"Is something wrong with Natty?" I could feel the *thrum* of my heart.

"No. She's fine. She's spending the night at a friend's." Imogen shook her head. "A project for school she needs to work on."

I tried very hard not to let my hurt feelings show. "Is she angry with me?"

Imogen pursed her lips. "Yes, a bit, I imagine. She was upset when she found out you'd lied about going to Liberty." Imogen shook her head. "You know teenagers."

11

"But Natty's not—" I had been about to say that Natty wasn't a teenager, but then I remembered that she was. She had turned thirteen in July. Yet another thing I had missed thanks to my incarceration.

A familiar voice came from down the hallway. "Is that the world famous Anya Balanchine I hear?" Scarlet ran up and threw her arms around me. "Anya, where did your boobs go?"

I pulled away from her. "Must have been that really nourishing Liberty food."

"When I saw you at Liberty, you were always in the navy jumpsuit, but in your old Trinity uniform, it's more obvious to me that you look . . ."

"Awful," I filled in.

"No!" Imogen and Scarlet said in unison.

"It's not like the last time you went to Liberty," Scarlet continued. "You don't look sick. You just look . . ." Scarlet's eyes drifted to the ceiling. I remembered from my first year of Forensic Science that when a witness looked up that way, it meant that she was in the process of inventing. My very best friend was about to lie. "You look changed," she said gently. Scarlet took me by the arm. "Let's go into the living room. I have to catch you up on everything that's been happening. Also, I hope you don't mind, but Gable's here. He really wanted to see you and he is my boyfriend, Anya."

I did kind of mind, but Scarlet was my best friend, so what could I do.

We went into the living room, where Gable stood by the window. He was leaning on crutches, and there was no wheelchair in sight. In other respects, he was also much improved.

His complexion was beyond pale, nearly white, but there was no obvious scarring where the skin grafts had been. Black leather gloves covered his hands so I couldn't see what had become of his mangled fingers.

"Arsley, you're walking again!" I congratulated him.

Scarlet applauded. "I know," she said. "Isn't it great? I'm so proud of him!"

With some difficulty, Gable maneuvered himself toward me. "Yes, isn't it wonderful? After months of physical therapy and countless painful surgeries, I can now accomplish what most two-year-olds manage much better. Aren't I a miracle of modern medicine?"

Scarlet kissed him on the cheek. "Don't go into that dark place, Gable. Stay in the light with Anya and me!"

Gable laughed at Scarlet's joke, and then he kissed her, and then she whispered something in his ear, and he smiled, and she helped him over to the love seat where they both sat down. *OMG*, as Nana would have said, Scarlet and Gable might actually be in love! For a moment, I almost felt jealous of them. I didn't want to be with Gable again—certainly not! After everything Scarlet had done for my family, I could not begrudge her a boyfriend. The plain truth was, I missed being in a couple.

I curled into the familiar burgundy chair.

"Seriously, Gable," I said. "You look amazingly good."

"You look awful," Gable replied.

"Gable," Scarlet admonished him.

"What? She looks like a little boy or a long-distance runner. Didn't they feed you anything in there?" Gable continued. "And your hair is scary."

My hair was indeed tangled and frizzy. There hadn't been conditioner or gel or even a proper hairbrush at Liberty. As soon as Gable and Scarlet left, I would begin addressing the situation.

"How's Trinity?" I asked by way of changing the subject. Gable was repeating his senior year because of how much of the previous one he'd missed.

"Boring now that you're not there," Gable said with a shrug. "No one's been shot or poisoned for months."

One of Gable's qualities was his sense of humor.

"Gable Arsley," Scarlet said with a furrowed brow, "you are being awful and you are making me regret having brought you today."

"Apologies, Anya, if I caused offense."

I told him that he hadn't, that I was pretty hard to offend these days.

Scarlet stood up. "We should go. Imogen made us promise that we wouldn't stay long." She gave Gable her hand, and he rose somewhat awkwardly to his feet. That was when I remembered the elevator. Gable had trouble walking across the room. He was never going to be able to make it down thirteen flights on crutches.

Upon consulting with Imogen, who then consulted with the building superintendent, it was determined that the elevator wouldn't be repaired until the next morning. Gable would have to spend the night, a scheme that did not thrill me. If Gable was staying, Scarlet's parents wouldn't allow her to, and the last time Gable Arsley had almost spent the night in this apartment, it had not gone well.

I decided that Gable should sleep on the couch. I didn't want him in Leo's old room.

After these arrangements were made, I was finally able to slip away to my bedroom. I had been meaning to clean myself up, but instead I fell asleep on my bed. When I awoke, it was two in the morning, and the apartment was silent. I slipped out of my room and went down the hall to the shower.

I didn't care how much water cost these days. I figured I was owed three or four showers. Of course, I lavished extra attention on my hair. O conditioner—an ugly word for such a beautiful thing!

After my shower, I detangled my hair and gave it some proper product and when I looked in the mirror, I thought I looked almost normal again. I wrapped my flowered bath towel around myself and went back to my bedroom.

The light was on. I wondered if I had forgotten to turn it off.

When I opened the door, Gable was sitting in the chair by my bed. He was dressed in a pair of Leo's pajamas that Imogen must have lent him, and his crutches were propped by the dresser.

"Arsley," I said, checking that my bath towel was secured under my arms. "You shouldn't be in here."

"Oh, Anya, don't be so paranoid," Gable said. "I heard you were awake, and I was awake, too, so I thought I'd keep you company."

"I don't want company after I get out of the shower, Arsley."

"I . . . I won't try to do anything to you, Anya, I swear. Just

15

don't make me get up yet. My leg swells at night. Let me sit here a bit. I promise I'll keep my eyes closed while you change."

"I've been in prison, Arsley, and if you try anything, so help me . . ." I opened my closet door so that I could discreetly put on my pajamas from behind it, and then I sat cross-legged on my bed. "So," I said.

"I was thinking of the last time we were alone together in this room," Gable said. "I know you think I behaved badly and I'm sorry for that. I did want to sleep with you that night, but I never would have forced you."

I shook my head. "Is this you apologizing?"

"Yes, I guess it is. I'm almost glad the elevator broke because otherwise I never would have gotten you by yourself and I've wanted to say that to you for such a long time. It's sweltering in here by the way." Gable took off his leather gloves and I could see that he had three silver fingertips in place of his amputations. He looked like a robot.

"Arsley, your fingers!"

Gable laughed at me. "You're supposed to pretend not to notice them."

"But they're kind of amazing."

He waved them. "Would you like to touch them, Anya?"

I kind of did, but I didn't think it was a good idea for me to touch any parts of Gable, even his bionic ones.

"Come on, Anya. Shake my hand. Friends can shake hands, can't they?"

We were not friends.

"Don't be boring, Anya," Gable said. "Do you know what school you're going to yet?"

16

"Wherever will have me, I suppose."

"It's stupid them not letting you come back," Gable said. "You saved Win Delacroix's life."

It had not escaped my notice that Scarlet had stealthily avoided the subject of Win the entire afternoon. I did not want to hear news of Win from Gable Arsley of all people. Still, I would take what I could get. "Is Win"—I tried to make my voice casual—"back at Trinity this year?"

Gable rolled his eyes. "Oh, I can see exactly how much you don't care about him. You've always been the world's worst liar, Anya. Aren't you talking to him anymore?"

"We aren't allowed."

"That wouldn't stop me." Gable ran his metal fingers through his hair. "He doesn't eat lunch with Scarlet and me this year, which is fine. I always found him annoyingly earnest. How you could go for him after me, I'll never understand."

I wanted to ask more, but I didn't want to have to ask, if you know what I mean. Luckily, Gable was delighted to volunteer information. "Listen, Scarlet said we shouldn't tell you this yet, but you'll find out soon enough anyway. Win's with Alison Wheeler."

I inhaled and tried not to feel anything. "I know who she is." Win had taken her to the Fall Formal last year. He'd said he was just friends with her, but that didn't seem likely now. No wonder I hadn't seen him in so long.

"What do you mean 'I know who she is'?" Gable demanded. "Of course you know who she is. We've been going to school with her for years."

I had been trying to avoid saying something more revealing about the matter. "How did it happen?" I asked.

"Boy meets girl. She was helping out on his dad's campaign, I guess. Something like that. She's not bad-looking though. I'd do her."

I narrowed my eyes at him. "You mean if you weren't with Scarlet."

"That is presumed, Anya."

"You should go now," I told him.

"Why? So you can cry into your pillow over Win? Come here. I'll let you cry on my shoulder."

"Go," I told him.

"Help me up, would you?"

I offered him my hand, and as he was getting to his feet, he whispered in my ear, "You're prettier than Alison Wheeler, and Win Delacroix is an idiot."

Gable was loathsome, but even a loathsome person can make a girl feel better sometimes. "Thank you," I said.

I'd finally bounced him from my room when he turned. "Say, do you have any chocolate around?"

"I can't believe you're even asking me that!"

"What? I haven't had any in months," Gable replied. "Besides, it wasn't chocolate that made me sick. It was Fretoxin. You should know better than anyone that there's nothing wrong with chocolate."

I told him it was too late for me to know anything for certain. "Do you want my help out to the living room or can you manage it yourself?"

18

"It's more fun if you come," Gable said.

"Not for me." I closed my bedroom door, turned off my light, and got into bed. Even though it was stuffy in my room, I pulled the covers over my head.

I could imagine a pretty little scenario in which Win was with Alison Wheeler just to distract his father from the fact that he was seeing me. The only problem with that theory was the fact that Win was *not* seeing me. As I have already mentioned, he hadn't seen or contacted me in over a month. The logical thing to conclude was that Win really was seeing Alison Wheeler.

Maybe it was for the best, though? If I were still with Win, I would put Natty and Leo in danger. It was easier this way, right? Charles Delacroix's and my plan had been a success. That moment in August had been an anomaly. Maybe it had really been goodbye.

So, good. Everyone had moved on. No one had gotten hurt. (Much.) I had served my time. I was a free woman. And Win, obviously, was a free man.

I wished Nana were here. She would have told me to embrace my freedom. Or maybe she would have told me to have a bar of chocolate.

In the morning, I was woken by the sound of laughter. I pulled on my bathrobe and went out to the living room. I expected that Scarlet had arrived early to escort her boyfriend home, and I was thankful to her. I was more than eager to be rid of my houseguest.

Gable was seated on the couch. He was gesturing with his silver-tipped hand as he said, "Wait, wait, you're laughing before I'm even at the good part."

I looked over at the burgundy chair. A woman sat there, but it wasn't Scarlet.

"Annie!" Natty stood up and threw her arms around me. In shoes, she was slightly taller than me and this was disturbing. "I told myself I was going to give you the cold shoulder, Annie, but I can't. Why did you lie to me about going to Liberty?"

"I just wanted you to have a good time at genius camp," I told her.

"I'm not a little kid anymore. I can handle things, you know," Natty informed me.

"Yeah," Gable added. "She's definitely not a little kid."

I told Gable to shut up. "She's only thirteen. And you have a girlfriend." And yet Gable was right. The change in my sister was undeniable. I held her at arm's length so that I could look at her. Over the summer, Natty had grown, maybe four inches, and her skirt was too short. The legs that used to be spider legs had a definite curve to them. She had breasts and hips and a pimple on her chin. She was only thirteen but she looked about twice that. I didn't like the way Gable was looking at her. I debated whether to hit him over the head with a lamp.

At that moment, Scarlet arrived. "Your hair looks much improved," she said as she kissed me on the cheek. "Good morning, Natty darling! Doesn't she look so grown-up, Anya?"

"Indeed," I said.

"It's a good thing, too, now that she's skipped into tenth," Scarlet continued.

"Wait, what's this?" I asked.

"I told Imogen I wanted to tell you myself," Natty explained to me.

Scarlet nodded. "Come, Gable. The elevator is working again. We should go before you're stuck here another night." Scarlet turned to me. "I hope he behaved himself."

"Don't lie, Anya!" Gable said.

I told Scarlet that Gable had behaved exactly as I'd come to expect, a remark Scarlet chose to take at face value.

Scarlet helped her appalling boyfriend to his feet, and finally they were gone.

I turned to my sister. "You skipped two grades?"

Natty worried the pimple on her chin with her pinkie. "Miss Bellevoir and the people at genius camp thought it was a good idea, and, well . . ." Her voice turned cool. "You weren't around to discuss it."

My baby sister, a sophomore at Holy Trinity?

I sat down on the couch, which still reeked of Gable's cologne. After a bit, Natty sat down next to me. "I missed you," she said.

"Did you have nightmares this summer?" I asked.

"Only one or two or three or four, but when they'd start, I'd pretend I was you. Brave like you. And I'd say, 'Now, Natty, you are just having a dream. Go back to sleep.' And it worked!" Natty put her arms around me. "I honestly hated you when I found out you'd gone to Liberty. I was so mad, Annie. Why did you do it?"

I explained to her in the simplest terms possible the deal I had made with Charles Delacroix to protect her and Leo. She wanted to know if ending my relationship with Win had been part of that deal. Yes, I told her, it had been.

"Poor Annie. That was the hard part, I bet," Natty said.

I smiled. "Well, I'd wager that Liberty isn't as fun as genius camp. It doesn't help that everyone keeps telling me how horrible I look."

Natty studied my face. She held my cheeks in her hands, hands with disarmingly long fingers. "You look strong, Annie. That's all. But then you've always been strong."

She was a good girl, my sister. "Arsley said that Win has a girlfriend?"

"He does," Natty admitted. "But I don't know, Win's so different. He seems angry all the time. I tried to talk to him the first day of school. I wanted to know if he'd heard from you, and he kind of blew me off."

I reminded her that she'd promised to hate Win Delacroix for the rest of her life.

"That was before I knew you'd lied about Liberty," Natty said. "Anyway, his leg seems to have healed. He's still got a cane, but he's not like Gable or anything."

"Natty," I said, "tell me honestly. You weren't flirting with Gable this morning, were you?"

"That is gross, Anya," Natty said. "We're in the same math class. He was telling me a story about the teacher. I was laughing to be polite."

"Thank God," I said. I didn't think I could handle Natty

flirting with Gable Arsley. Later, after I had been home a while longer, Natty and I would need to have a serious discussion about boys.

Natty stood and offered me her hand. "Come," she said. "We need to go to Saturday market. We're out of just about everything. And Imogen says thirteen is still too young to go by myself."

"She's right," I said.

"You went at thirteen, didn't you?" Natty insisted.

"I was almost fourteen. And that was only because no one could take me."

Natty and I rode the bus down to the market at Union Square. You could purchase or trade for just about anything there. Toilet paper or T-shirts. Turnips or Tolstoy. Things that start with T and every other letter of the alphabet. As usual, it was a madhouse. Tables and tents everywhere. Every possible space was filled with a human being, and all those human beings wanted and they wanted now. Or actually, a week ago. Occasionally, someone died in a stampede. Nana once told me that when she was young, there had been grocery stores where you could buy anything you wanted, whenever you wanted. Now, all we had were irregularly stocked bodegas. Your best bet really was the Saturday market.

That day, our list included: laundry detergent, hair conditioner, dried pasta, a thermos, fruit (if we could find it), a new (longer) wool kilt for Natty, and a paper book for Imogen (it was her thirty-second birthday the following week).

I handed Natty a pile of cash and ration coupons. Then I

assigned her the book and the kilt. The price was usually the price on those items, so you didn't have to be an experienced marketer. I would take care of everything else. I had come armed with several bars of Balanchine Special Dark, which I had been surprised to find while taking stock of our mostly barren pantry. Though I had lost my taste for chocolate, it could still be useful when negotiating.

As I made my way through the crowd to where the household chemicals stand usually was, I passed a group of college students who were demonstrating. (Political activity was common at the markets.) A malnourished-looking girl with greasy brown hair and a long flowered skirt jammed a pamphlet into my hand. "Take one, sister," she said. I looked down at the pamphlet. On the front cover was a picture of what I thought was a cacao pod and the words *Legalize Cacao Now!* "All the stuff they tell you about chocolate is a lie," she continued. "It's no more addictive than water."

"Trust me, I know," I said as I slipped the pamphlet into my bag. "Where'd you guys get the paper for the pamphlets?"

"The paper shortage is a lie, friend," a man with a beard replied. "They're just trying to control us. Always plenty of paper for good old American dollar bills, ain't there?"

These were the kind of people who thought everything was a lie. Best to be on my way before one of these pro-chocolate folks noticed who I was.

I lucked out and was able to get everything but the fruit and the pasta at the first chemicals stand I visited. I found a pasta vendor a couple of rows down, and he gave me a good deal on penne after I threw in a meat ration coupon and a bar of chocolate. I traded a woman selling flowers two chocolate bars for a bouquet of roses—it was extravagant but I longed for something sweet-smelling and colorful after the summer I had had. The only thing left was the fruit. I'd just about given up on getting anything except the canned stuff when I spotted a sign that read:

Jane's Citrus
Oranges Grown Right Here in Manhattan

I walked up to the stand. Oranges were my absolute favorite, and they weren't the kind of thing they served at Liberty.

Win's mother noticed me before I noticed her. "Anya Balanchine," she said breathlessly. "Yes, I thought it was you. It's Jane Delacroix."

I took a step back. "I should go," I said. If her husband was around, there could be a scene.

"Anya, wait! Charlie isn't here. He's campaigning in one of the boroughs. I didn't want all my summer oranges to go to waste, so I'm here. My husband would rather I wasn't, but I argued that it was fine. I'm a farmer not a politician's wife. Besides, real people do market. We're trying to look like real people, don't you know?" Jane Delacroix's pretty face was more lined than the last time I had seen her.

"Oh," I said.

"Please take one. Win once told me you liked them. He'll be back any moment, by the way. He's gone to trade for more sacks. People have their own bags, of course, but the oranges need to breathe. You can't toss them in anything. Stay," she ordered.

Win was here? I scanned the crowd: countless faces, but none of them was his.

She held out the fruit, and as I went to take it, she clasped my hand in hers. "How are you?"

I considered the question. "Happy to be free, I guess."

Jane Delacroix nodded. "Yes, freedom is a very good thing." Win's mother had tears in her eyes. "Take two oranges, please. Take a whole sack," she said. She let go of my hand and started filling her last red mesh bag with oranges.

I told her I was blocking her line. Which I was. There was no time for emotional exchanges at the market, and Jane Delacroix had a valuable commodity.

She thrust the bag of oranges at me. "I will never forget that you saved my son's life." She grabbed my face and kissed me on both my cheeks. "I'm sorry for everything. I know you are a good girl."

Over her shoulder, I saw Win enter through the back of the fruit stand. He was carrying mesh sacks in a variety of colors.

I took a deep breath, reminding myself that Win had a girlfriend and that I was not she.

"I should go," I said. "I have to meet my sister!" I pushed my way through the crowd, away from Win.

I found Natty at the paper books stand, which was called 451 Books. Unlike the chemicals, pasta, or citrus stands, it was empty, except for Natty. She held up two books to me. "What

26

do you think, Annie? Which would Imogen prefer? *Bleak House*, by Charles Dickens, or *Anna Karenina*, by Leo Tolstoy? One's about, like, a lawsuit, I think, and the other's a love story maybe? I'm not sure."

"The one about the lawsuit," I said. My heart was beating like mad. I put my hand on my chest as if that could stop it.

"*Bleak House* it is," Natty said, moving away to pay for the book.

"Wait, let's get both. One from each of us. You'll give her the love story. I'll do the lawsuit."

Natty nodded. "Yes, she is good to us, isn't she?"

I took a deep breath, making sure that I had all my parcels. Detergent, check. Conditioner, check. Pasta, check. Flowers, check. Thermos, check. Oranges . . . Blast! I'd somehow left the oranges in Win's mother's booth. No way I was going back for them either.

We left the books booth, and despite the fact that she was way too old for it, I took Natty's hand. "Were you able to get any fresh fruit?" she asked.

I told her that I hadn't been. I must have looked truly wretched when I said this because Natty felt the need to comfort me. "It's fine. We still have canned pineapple," Natty said. "Maybe even some frozen raspberries."

We were almost out of Union Square when I felt a hand on my shoulder. "You left these," he said. I turned, but I already knew who it was. Of course it was Win. "My mother insisted I find you . . ."

What was wrong with Win's mother?

"Hello, Natty," Win continued.

27

"Hello, Win," she said coolly. "You don't wear hats anymore. I liked you better with hats."

I took the sack of oranges and said nothing.

"I almost didn't catch up with you two. I'm not as fast as I used to be, I guess," Win said.

"How is your leg?" I asked.

Win smiled. "Still hurts like heck. How was the rest of your summer?"

I smiled, too. "Awful." I shook my head to steel myself against him. "I heard you're seeing Alison Wheeler."

"Yes, Anya, I am," Win replied after a pause. "Word moves quickly."

And hearts even more so. "I once told you that you'd get over me faster than you thought, and I was right."

"Anya . . ." he said.

I knew I sounded bitter, and what was the point of that? The truth was, any wrong he might be doing me now, I probably deserved. It was an accomplishment really—to have turned someone as devoted as Win so quickly.

I told him I was happy for him. I didn't mean it, but I was trying to pretend like I was a grownup. (Didn't grownups tell lies like that?) He looked as if he might have wanted to explain about Alison, but I didn't really want to know. Usually, I wanted to know everything about everything, but in this case, I was fine being left in a forgiving patch of darkness. Win had made things easy for me, hadn't he? Instead, I leaned in to hug him for what I imagined would be the last time. "Take care of yourself," I said. "I probably won't be seeing you around."

"No," he agreed. "Probably not."

I guess I was sentimental back then. I had one bar of Balanchine Special Dark left and I gave it to him. I made him promise that he wouldn't show his dad. He took the bar without a word or a wisecrack about it being poisoned. I was grateful for that. He just slipped the bar into his pocket and then he disappeared into the crowd. He did have a limp, and it occurred to me that I was glad to have left him with something other than that limp. He probably counted himself luckier than Gable Arsley.

Natty and I got on the bus with our parcels. "Why Alison Wheeler?" Natty asked after we'd been on the bus a couple of minutes. "He loves you."

"I broke up with him, Natty."

"Yes but—"

"And I got him shot."

"But—"

"And maybe he's tired of me. Of our family. Of how difficult it all is. Sometimes I get tired of me, too."

"Not Win. No," Natty said in a soft but resolute voice. "It doesn't make sense."

I sighed. Natty might have looked twenty-five, but her heart was still so very twelve (thirteen!) and this was comforting to me. "I can't think about him anymore. I have to find a school to go to. I have to see Cousin Mickey. I have to call Yuji Ono. But from now on, we're going to the market at Columbus Circle," I said. "I don't care if we do have to cross the park!"

———◇———

As we entered the apartment, the phone was ringing. I heard Imogen answer it. "Yes, I think Anya's just come in. Hold on a moment."

I went into the kitchen to unpack my bags, and Imogen held out the phone to me. "It's Win," Imogen said with a dopey grin on her face.

"See," Natty said with an annoyingly knowing look in her eyes.

Imogen put her arm around Natty. "Come, dear one," she whispered. "Let's give your sister some privacy."

I took a deep breath. As I crossed the kitchen to the telephone, it felt like the blood in my veins had begun to warm. I took the phone. "Win," I said.

"Welcome back, Anya." The voice was familiar, but it definitely wasn't Win's.

My hands turned to ice. "Who is this?"

"It's your cousin," he said after a pause. "It's Jacks. Jakov Pirozhki."

As if I knew another Jacks. "Why are you pretending to be Win?" I demanded.

"Because you wouldn't talk to me otherwise. And we do need to talk," Jacks said.

I told him we had nothing to talk about. "I'm hanging up now."

"If you were going to hang up, you would have just done it."

He was right, but I said nothing. My silence must have made him nervous because when he next spoke, his manner was more contrite. "Listen, Annie, listen. I don't have much time. I only get one phone call a week, and they ain't free, you know."

"How is prison life, Cousin?"

"It's unspeakable in here," Jacks replied after a pause.

"I hope it's Hell."

"Please, Annie. Come see me at Rikers. I have things I want to tell you that I can't say over the phone. You never know who's listening."

"Why would I ever do that? You poisoned one of my boyfriends and shot the other when you were trying to shoot my brother. I was expelled from school and sent to Liberty because of you."

"Don't be naïve," he said. "Those things were in motion long before me. I don't have the *syvasi*. Please. In your heart, you can't honestly believe that I . . . Things are not what they appear . . . I've already said too much. You must come see me." He lowered his voice. "I believe that you and your sister are in terrible danger."

For a second, I felt fear in my heart, but then it passed. Who cared what Jacks said? He would have said or done anything to get what he wanted. Wasn't this the exact technique he had used to manipulate Leo? Telling him that Natty and I were in danger as a way of controlling him? "It seems to me, Jacks, that the person who has put my family in the greatest danger has been you. And you, dear cousin, are in prison for the next twenty-five years. Personally, I've never felt safer in my entire life. Please don't call here again," I said. As I hung

31

up the phone, I thought I might have heard him say something about my father, but I couldn't make it out. He really would have said anything.

In the living room, Imogen and Natty waited for me. "What did Win say?" Natty asked with happy, dancing eyes.

I looked at Natty. I couldn't protect her from this. "It wasn't Win. It was Jacks."

Imogen stood up from the couch. "Anya, I apologize. He did say he was Win, and I guess I don't know Win's voice well enough to tell the difference."

I assured her that it wasn't her fault.

Natty shook her head. "That was incredibly mean of him. What did he want anyway?"

I couldn't exactly repeat what Jacks had said about the two of us being in terrible danger. I sat down next to Natty and put my arms around her. I would do anything to keep her safe and I wondered how I could even have allowed myself the indulgence of lamenting Win. Natty was the love of my life, not him. At that moment, the love of my life extricated herself from my embrace—was she getting too old for such things?—then she asked me a second time what our ne'er-do-well cousin had wanted.

Here, I told a pretty lie: "To welcome me home."

I COUNT MY BLESSINGS

SUNDAY MORNING, Natty and I went to church. The new priest was an incredibly boring speaker, but the homily was not without interest to me: it was about how we focus too much on the things we don't have instead of the things we do. I was certainly guilty of such behavior. To pass the time, I decided to count my blessings:

1. I was out of Liberty.
2. Natty and Leo, as far as I knew, were safe.
3. Win had made it easy for me to keep my bargain with his father.
4. We had money and health.
5. We had Imogen Goodfellow, Simon Green, and Mr. Kipling . . .

By the time I had reached six, we were standing to receive the host.

On our way out of church, someone called my name. I turned: it was Mickey Balanchine and his wife, Sophia. "Hello, cousins!" he greeted Natty and me warmly. Mickey kissed us both on our cheeks.

"Since when do you go to this church?" I asked Mickey, having never seen him there before. Natty and I attended a Catholic church because our mother had, but everyone on my father's side of the family went to an Eastern Orthodox church if they went at all.

"Since he married a Catholic," Sophia Balanchine replied in that strange accent of hers. Though she spoke English very well, it was obviously not her native language. "Good morning, Anya. Nataliya. We met, but only briefly, at the occasion of my marriage. It is good to see you both looking so well." She, too, kissed us on our cheeks. "It's hard to tell which of you is the older sister."

Mickey pointed a finger at me. "You were supposed to come see me as soon as you got out."

I told him that I'd only been home since Friday afternoon and had planned to visit him that week.

"Mickey, you must give the girl room," Sophia said, and then she did just the opposite, hooking arms with Natty and me, and insisting that we join them for brunch. "You have not eaten," she accused us, "and we live only blocks from here. We should cease making spectacles of ourselves on the front stoop of this cathedral." She wasn't Russian, but something about her reminded me of Nana. I took a moment to consider Sophia Balanchine. I remembered that I had thought her plain at

34

the wedding but maybe that had been harsh. She had brown hair, brown eyes, a large, rather horsey nose. Indeed, everything about her was large—her hands, her lips, her eyes, her cheekbones—and she was several inches taller than her husband. (Mickey was so short I had always suspected him of wearing shoes with lifts.) Sophia Balanchine seemed powerful. I liked my cousin somewhat better knowing he was married to this woman.

Though Natty and I tried to demur, Sophia insisted we come to brunch and somehow we found ourselves at their town house on East Fifty-Seventh Street, not far from where Win's family lived.

Sophia and Mickey occupied the bottom two floors of a three-story brownstone. The top floor was used by Mickey's father, Yuri Balanchine, and his nurses. Any day now, they expected Yuri to die, Sophia Balanchine informed me. "It will be a mercy," she said.

"It will be," Natty agreed. I'm sure she was thinking of Nana.

Over lunch, we stuck to innocuous subjects. I found out the source of Sophia's unusual accent—she had a German father and a Mexican mother—and Mickey and Sophia asked me about my plans for the following school year. I told them that I wasn't sure what I was going to do. The third week of the semester was about to start, and I feared that I wouldn't be able to find a suitable school that would also find me suitable. Considering my criminal record, I mean.

Natty sighed. "I wish you could just go back to Trinity."

On some level, I was glad not to be going back to Trinity. It was a chance to make a break from old routines, old people. That was what I told myself, at least.

"After what you have been through, it is good to make a change, I think," Sophia said, echoing my own thoughts. "Though it is also difficult to have to go to a new school in your senior year."

"It's an insult," Mickey said. "Those bastards had no cause to throw you out."

He was wrong. The administration had had perfect cause: I had brought a gun to school.

The discussion then turned to Natty's time at genius camp, a subject I had heard very little about myself. She had spent the summer working on a project to strip water from garbage before it left people's houses. As she described her work, Natty sounded smart, impressive, genuinely happy, and I knew all at once that I had done the right thing in making sure she had made it to camp. I was proud that this was my sister and even a little proud of myself for having done right by her. My throat closed up. I stood and offered to help clear the table.

Sophia followed me into their kitchen. She told me where to set the dishes and then she touched my elbow. "You and I have a mutual friend," she said.

I looked at her. "We do?"

"Yuji Ono, of course," Sophia said. "Perhaps you did not know that he and I went to an international high school together in Belgium. Yuji is my oldest and dearest friend in the world."

It made sense. They were both the same age, twenty-four, and in point of fact, they did have a similar manner of speaking. And that was why he had been at her wedding, not merely to keep tabs on my family. I wondered how much she knew about the role her oldest and dearest friend had played in Leo's escape. The thought of it made me uncomfortable. "It was Yuji," she continued, "who introduced me to my husband."

I hadn't known that.

"He told me to give you his regards when I saw you."

Hadn't our meeting at the church been accidental? "But you didn't know you would see me today?" I said after a pause.

"I knew I should see you eventually," she explained without missing a beat. "My husband had visited you at Liberty, had he not?"

Who was this Sophia Balanchine anyway? I tried to remember her maiden name. Bitter. Sophia Bitter. I wished Nana were still alive so that I could consult with her. She knew everything about everybody.

Sophia laughed. "Yuji thinks so well of you that, at times, I have been jealous. I have been dying to meet Anya the Great."

I reminded her that we had, in fact, met.

"The wedding? That is not really meeting!" she protested. "I want to *know* you, Anya." She stared at me with her dark, dark eyes.

I asked her what she thought of me so far.

"The only impression I can have of you is physical, and physically, you are attractive enough but your feet are freakishly large," Sophia said.

"And what do physical impressions really matter anyway?"

"You say that because you are pretty," she replied. "I assure you that they matter very much."

Sophia Balanchine was an odd woman.

"Were you and Yuji ever boyfriend and girlfriend?" I asked.

She laughed again. "Are you asking me if I am your rival, Anya? I am a married lady, don't you know?"

"No, Yuji and I aren't that way." I could feel the blush spread across my face. "I just wondered. I'm sorry if it was rude," I said.

She shook her head, but there was a smile on her face. "That is a very American question," she said. I suspected I was being insulted. "I love Yuji very much. And all that interests him interests me as well. This is to say that I hope you and I will be very great friends."

My sister and Sophia's husband joined us in the kitchen. "My brilliant little cousin says she needs to get home to study," Mickey informed us. "I wondered, Anya, if you'd like to say hello to Dad before you go."

"You'll come see me next week after you've got this school business sorted out," Mickey said as we walked up the two flights of stairs to where my uncle Yuri was dying. "He had another stroke over the summer so he is difficult to understand," Mickey continued. "He may not even be awake, and if he is, he may not recognize you. The doctors have him on so much medication."

I was used to dealing with the dying and infirm.

The curtains were drawn, and the room smelled sweet and fetid, much like Nana's had in the year before her death. Yuri's eyes were open, though, and they seemed to light up upon seeing me. He held out one of his arms to me. "Ahhhhnuh." He said my name with a tongue that was too thick. As I got closer to see him, I could see that half of his face was paralyzed and one of his hands was permanently flexed into a fist. He waved his good hand toward Mickey and the nurse who was in the room. "Goooo! Ahhhloh."

Mickey translated this for me. "Dad says he wants to talk to you alone."

I sat in the chair by Uncle Yuri's bedside. "Ahhhhnuh." His mouth was working furiously. "Ahhhhnuh, goooooooooo theeeeee ahkkkkkk."

"I'm sorry, Uncle Yuri. I don't know what you want."

"Theeeee okkk." My face was coated in spit, but I didn't want to insult him by wiping it away. "Mahhhh pohhh boooooooi. Theeeeeee yahkkkkk. Yakkkk!"

I struggled to make sense of this. I shook my head. There was a slate by the bed. I set it in front of him. "Maybe you could write it?"

Yuri nodded. For several moments, he occupied himself with moving his finger around the slate but when I looked down, it was a maze of scribbles. "I'm sorry, Uncle. Maybe we could get Mickey. He understands you better than I can."

Uncle Yuri shook his head vigorously. "Ahhhhnuh, ohffffffeeee ohh noooo!" Uncle Yuri grabbed my hand and held it to his heart. He was perspiring and there were tears of frustration in his eyes. "Luuuuuuuuuuuufffffffffffff."

"Love?" I asked. I still had no idea what he was trying to say, but he nodded with relief that I had at least translated that one word. With my free hand, I grabbed a tissue from the nightstand and blotted his forehead with it.

"Luuuufff," he repeated. "Thhhhhaaaaaaaaaahhhrrrr."

I felt his hand weaken and his body relax. At first I worried he was dead, but he was only asleep. I set his hand on his chest and then I slipped out of the room. For the moment, I had escaped death again.

On the two-mile walk home, I added more blessings to my list:

6. I was young enough to correct any mistakes I had made.
7. I was strong and could go wherever my legs could carry me.
8. Anything I wanted to say to anyone living, I could still say.

"You haven't said a word since we left. What are you brooding about, Annie?" Natty asked.

We had just reached the southern edge of the park. (It was undeniable that the park was somewhat safer since Charles Delacroix had come to town with his policy of prosecuting even small crimes.) I turned to look at my sister. Though I hadn't had a stroke like Uncle Yuri, it was still difficult for me to express what was in my heart. I wanted to tell her that I loved her, that she was the most important person in the world to me, that I was truly sorry for having lied to her about Liberty. Instead, I asked her what she wanted for dinner.

"Dinner already?" she asked. "We just ate brunch."

Monday, while Natty and all other nondelinquents were at school, I went about the business of finding a new school for myself. Mr. Kipling had thought I should wait until after I was out of Liberty to formally begin the process. His theory had been that it was better for me to appear to have put my incarceration behind me.

According to Simon Green's preliminary research, there were a dozen private schools comparable to Holy Trinity, and of that number, eight didn't admit incoming seniors. That left a grand total of four schools that would even consider me. A further issue was that I was, in Simon Green's words, "The infamous Anya Balanchine—sorry, Anya, but it's true." The media would likely find out about any school that admitted me, which would lead to bad publicity for the school. After making several inquiries, Simon Green had only come up with one real option, the Leary Alternative School, in the East Village, within walking distance of my cousin's speakeasy. I had an interview scheduled with them that afternoon. Mr. Kipling would accompany me.

I usually just wore my Holy Trinity uniform everywhere, but I didn't think that would be appropriate for an interview at another school. I decided to wear the suit I had worn to Mickey and Sophia's wedding.

So, Leary. It was kind of artsy, if you know what I mean. No one wore uniforms. A lot of the classrooms didn't have desks; kids sat in circles on the floor. Many of the male teachers had beards. One female teacher I saw wasn't wearing any shoes. There was a distinct aroma to the place—clay? herbs? Obviously, it wasn't what I was used to but I told myself that that wasn't necessarily a bad thing.

Mr. Kipling gave my name at the front desk and then we were pointed in the direction of a cluster of beanbag chairs. "Interesting place," Mr. Kipling said to me while we waited. He lowered his voice. "Do you think you could see yourself making a go of it here, Anya?"

What other choice did I have? There were public schools, but any good one had a long waiting list and many of my credits might not even count. I could end up in high school until I was twenty.

After about a half hour, the headmaster, a curly-haired man in a brown corduroy suit, emerged from his office. "Come in, Anya. Stuart." I bristled at hearing Mr. Kipling referred to by his first name. "Sorry to keep you folks waiting. I got a late start to my afternoon meditation. I'm the headmaster here, Sylvio Freeman. Everyone calls me Syl."

We went into his office, where there was a thick kilim rug in reds and oranges, and no furniture. "Have a seat." Headmaster Syl indicated the rug.

Syl poured us cups of licorice rooibos tea. "I've read all about you, Anya. Your academic record is perfectly drizzly though you should know we don't give letter grades here." He paused. "Forensic science. That's your thing, right?"

I nodded.

"We don't offer that subject, but there's always independent study. In any case, I'd love to take you on."

"Oh, that's wonderful," Mr. Kipling said.

"I ran the idea by my Board of Overseers," Headmaster Syl continued. "The chocolate-daughter thing wasn't a problem for them. We have kids from many different backgrounds. Unfortunately, well . . . See, we're all about peace here. And the gun possession. Well, that's a bit of a deal breaker. My board doesn't want that kind of thing at Leary."

"We had to come down to hear this?" Mr. Kipling asked.

"I wanted to meet Anya myself. And it's not without hope, Stu. The folks on my board agreed that next year, when more time has passed, they'd be happy to reconsider her application." Syl smiled at us. "Take a year off, Anya. Volunteer somewhere. Maybe take some classes in forensics at the university. Then come back to us."

A year was an eternity. All my friends would have graduated, even Gable Arsley. I stood and thanked Headmaster Syl for his time. Mr. Kipling was still struggling to get up from the floor, so I offered him my hand.

On my way out the door, Headmaster Syl grabbed my arm. He lowered his voice to a conspiratorial whisper. "I'm involved with the pro-cacao movement. Maybe you'd like to speak at one of our rallies. I'm sure you'd have some superdeep insights."

At last, the real theme of this meeting. The real reason Mr. Kipling and I had been forced to drag ourselves downtown just for me to be rejected. This man was no better than my old history teacher Mr. Beery.

"I'm trying to avoid making a public spectacle of myself these days, Mister . . . Uh, Syl," I said.

"Understood," he said. "Though I wonder . . ." Syl furrowed his brow. "You are known, for better or for worse, and that's power, my friend. If you've got a chess set, why play checkers?" Syl offered me his hand, and I shook it. "Perhaps I'll be seeing you again someday, Anya Balanchine."

I doubted that very much.

"I didn't think that place was right for you anyway," Mr. Kipling said as we walked back to his office. There was a light rain, and Mr. Kipling's bald head was shiny with mist. "No letter grades. And that weird smell. And what kind of head-master doesn't have any furniture?" We stopped to wait for a walk signal. "Don't worry, Anya. We'll find a school for you. A far better one than that."

"Honestly, Mr. Kipling, if Leary Alternative doesn't want me, what school will? There isn't a school in the city that has a reputation for being more liberal than Leary, and even they think I'm damaged goods. And they're probably right." I was standing on a street corner at one thirty in the afternoon on a Monday, and I didn't want to be. I wanted to be at Trinity. I wanted to be pretending to fence or complaining about tofu lasagna. I hadn't realized how much of my identity was wrapped up in that uniform, in that school. I felt as if I belonged no-where. Despite my resolution to count my blessings, I was start-ing to feel very sorry for myself.

"Oh, Annie. I wish I could make this easier for you." Mr. Kipling took my hands in his. The rain had picked up, and the traffic light had turned, but neither of us moved. "All I can say is that this, too, shall pass."

I looked at my longtime adviser. If he had a weakness, per-haps it was that he loved me too well and expected the rest of the world to conform to his opinion. I kissed him on his bald head. "Thank you, Mr. Kipling."

Mr. Kipling blushed a deep scarlet. "For what, Annie?"

"You always believe in me. I'm old enough to appreciate that now."

Back at Mr. Kipling's office, we were joined by Simon Green, and the three of us went over my options. "As I see it," Simon Green said, "there are still a handful of other schools in Manhattan we could try—"

I interrupted him. "But don't you think the others are even more likely to have the objections that Leary Alternative had about me?"

Simon Green took a moment to consider this. "I'm not a mind reader, and of course, I'm not saying I agree with them, but yes, I do."

"Maybe that hippie headmaster was right," Mr. Kipling said. "You could take a year off—"

"But I don't want to take the year off!" I protested. I'd be practically nineteen when I graduated and that was dangerously close to twenty, i.e., ancient. "I want to graduate with everyone else."

"So, we look at schools outside New York," Simon Green suggested. "People won't know who you are there. Finishing schools in Europe, college-prep programs, even military schools."

"A military school! I . . ." I couldn't even complete the thought.

"Simon, Anya is not going to a military school," Mr. Kipling said softly.

"I was only brainstorming," Simon Green apologized. "I thought that a military school might be liberal about admittance after the semester had started. Even considering Anya's . . . history."

My history. Naïvely perhaps, I had thought the worst of this would be over once I had served my time at Liberty, but that wasn't turning out to be the case. I walked over to the window. Kipling & Sons had a view of Madison Square Park. After dark, all the chocolate dealers hung out there. I'd gone with Daddy when I was a little kid. You could get just about any kind of chocolate there—Belgian, bittersweet, baking, and of course, Balanchine. That was when chocolate had been my favorite flavor in the world and before it had taken away almost everyone I loved, and ruined my life. I rested my temple on the glass. "I hate chocolate," I whispered.

Simon Green put his hand on my shoulder. "Don't say that, Anya," he said gently.

"Why shouldn't I? It's brown, ugly, altogether aesthetically unappealing. It's unhealthy, addictive, illegal. It's bitter when it's good and too sweet when it's cheap. I can't honestly understand why anyone bothers with the stuff. If I woke up tomorrow and the world had no chocolate in it, I would be a happier person."

Mr. Kipling put his hand on my other shoulder. "You can hate chocolate today if you want. But I wouldn't make a policy of it. Your grandfather was chocolate. Your father was chocolate. And you, my girl, are chocolate."

I turned around to face my lawyers. "Look into all the

options for schools, bearing in mind that I really can't leave Natty. If we don't find anything, maybe I'll get a job."

"A job?" Simon Green asked. "What skills do you have?"

"I have no idea." I told them we'd talk later in the week and then I headed out the door.

I was still waiting at the bus stop when Simon Green caught up with me. "Mr. Kipling says I'm to accompany you home."

I told him I would rather be alone.

"Mr. Kipling is very worried about you, Anya," Simon Green continued.

"I'm fine."

"I'll get in trouble if I don't come with you."

The bus arrived. On the side was a screen advertising: CHARLES DELACROIX (D) FOR DISTRICT ATTORNEY. His aging-superhero face dissolved into his campaign slogan: Great cities require great leaders. The whole thing made me sick. I would have waited for another bus but the schedules were erratic. The Charles Delacroix Express was what it would have to be.

Simon Green sat next to me on a seat toward the back of the bus. "Do you think Delacroix will win?" he asked.

"Haven't honestly put much thought into it," I said.

"But I thought you and he were such great friends," Simon Green joked.

I could not bring myself to laugh.

"I think it's been a harder campaign than he thought it would be. But I tell you, I don't think he's awful," Simon Green said after a pause. "I mean, I think his heart is in the right place."

"Heart?" I scoffed. "That man has no heart."

"The truth is, Anya, I think he could be very good for us. He's talking a lot about how a safe city needs to have laws that make sense."

"I don't care."

"You should, though," he remonstrated me. "I'm sorry you lost your boyfriend in all this, but there are greater matters at hand here. Charlie Delacroix is more than just Win Delacroix's father, and assuming he prevails here, no one thinks district attorney is the last stop for him. He could be mayor, governor, president even."

"How wonderful."

"Someday, I might like to get into politics myself," Simon Green said.

I rolled my eyes. "You really think the best way to go about that is acting as legal counsel to the first daughter of organized crime?"

"Yes," he said. "I do."

"You'll have to explain that to me sometime."

Simon Green's laughter was drowned out by a sickening scream followed by an ominous thud. My head was thrust forward into the seat in front of me. There were more screams, and then the bus came to a stop. Simon Green grabbed my arm. "Anya, are you all right?"

My neck hurt a little but other than that, I felt fine. "What just happened?"

"We must have hit something," Simon Green said in a dazed voice. I turned to look at him. There was a gash on his right temple where his glasses had pierced his skin. "Mr. Green, you're bleeding!"

"Oh dear," Simon Green said weakly.

I ordered him to hold his head back. Then I took off my jacket so that I could use it to sop up the blood.

"Everyone stay on the bus!" the driver barked. "There's been an accident."

Obviously. I looked out the window. In the middle of Madison Avenue, a girl of about my age was lying unconscious. Her limbs were contorted into catastrophic angles. The worst part was her head, which had nearly twisted off her neck. Only a small band of skin was keeping her from being decapitated.

"Simon," I said. "I don't think she's going to live."

Simon leaned over me to examine the scene. "Oh dear," he whispered just before he passed out.

At the hospital, I waited while they examined Simon Green. The doctors determined that, aside from blood loss, there was nothing seriously wrong with him. They stitched up the gash on his temple. Because he had passed out, they were making him stay the night for observation.

I had called Mr. Kipling, who assured me he was on his way. Simon Green and I watched the news on his slate while we waited for Mr. Kipling to arrive. The lead story was about the bus accident. "In Midtown today, several were injured when a city bus bearing a Charles Delacroix campaign advertisement struck a pedestrian."

"Ooh," Simon Green said, "bad publicity. The Delacroix people must be furious."

The news cut to a man-on-the-street interview. "The girl—she must have been sixteen, seventeen—she was crossing in the middle of the street when *boom*. And next I know, she's lying there on the ground with her head nearly cut off. Poor thing. You can't help but feel for the parents in cases like this."

The reporter broke in. "The teenager was pronounced dead at the scene. The other injured passengers were taken to Mount Sinai Hospital. In an unusual coincidence, Anya Balanchine, the daughter of notorious crime boss Leonyd Balanchine, was also a passenger on the bus and is believed to be seriously injured."

"That is so annoying!" I yelled at the screen. "I'm not injured. I'm fine!"

Simon Green shrugged.

"They have no right releasing my name," I grumbled.

"Last spring, Anya Balanchine was arrested for the shooting of her own cousin, who had been trying to shoot Anya Balanchine's boyfriend at the time, William Delacroix, the son of acting District Attorney Charles Delacroix."

"His name is Win!" I objected.

"Although Charles Delacroix initially led in the polls, in the last month his major challenger, the Independent Party candidate, Bertha Sinclair, has narrowed the gap to five points. It's too early to see how this latest incident will impact voters."

"Like it's his fault a bus with his picture on it hit that girl," Simon Green commented.

A nurse knocked on the doorframe. "There's a man here for you," she said to me. "Is it okay if I let him in?"

"Yes, we're expecting him."

The nurse went to fetch Mr. Kipling.

I sat down on the side of Simon Green's hospital bed. This whole day had been ridiculously frustrating and yet, I had to count my blessings. That girl had been my age and I'm sure she hadn't woken up this morning thinking she was going to die. Blessing number nine: At least I haven't been hit by a bus and decapitated. Despite everything, I started to laugh.

"What's funny?" Simon Green asked.

"I'm just glad—" I started to say, and then Simon Green cut me off.

"Hey, that's not Mr. Kipling!" he said.

I turned. Through the window in Simon Green's hospital room, I saw Win. He was wearing his Trinity uniform. Win waved at me.

"I'll only be a moment," I said to Simon Green. I stood up, straightened my skirt, and went out to the hallway.

"You look pretty good for a gal who's seriously injured," Win greeted me. His voice was casual. "You wore that to your cousin's wedding."

I looked down at my jacket, which was stained with Simon Green's blood. "I'll never be able to wear it again." It would not be the first (or the last) of my clothing to meet such an end. I offered him my hand to shake but he embraced me instead. It was a hard embrace, one that hurt my still sore neck, one that lasted too long. "I was on the bus but they got everything else wrong," I said.

"I can see that."

"Why are you here?" I asked.

Win shook his head. "I was nearby when I heard about the accident. And I wanted to make sure you weren't dying. We're still friends, aren't we, Anya?"

I didn't know if we were friends. "Where's your girlfriend?"

Win told me she was in the lobby.

"And she doesn't mind that you're here?"

"No, Allie knows that you are important to me."

Allie. The l's replaced the n's, and it was like I had never existed. "You shouldn't be here," I told him.

"Why?"

"Because . . ." I couldn't make myself say all the reasons. Because we didn't belong to each other anymore. Because it hurt me to be near him. Because I had promised his father. Because his father had the ability to make my life very difficult if I didn't keep my promise.

"Anya, if you thought I was dying, wouldn't you come?" Win asked.

I was still considering this question when Mr. Kipling arrived. Upon seeing Win, Mr. Kipling looked more than a little nonplussed. "Why are *you* here?" Mr. Kipling spat at him.

"I'm going now," Win said.

"Be careful how you leave, son. The paparazzi have just arrived. They're probably looking for a shot of an injured Anya Balanchine, but I bet they'd settle for a shot of the acting district attorney's son. And you know what would really drive everyone mad with delight? A shot of you and Anya together."

Win said that he had learned a secret way out of the hospital from when he'd stayed there last spring and that that was how he and Alison would go. "No one will ever know I was here."

"Good. Do that. Now," Mr. Kipling ordered. "Anya, I'm going to go see how Simon is doing but I don't want you to go home without me. I should be there to shield you from the reporters." Mr. Kipling went into Simon's room.

"Well," Win began once we were alone. He stood up straight and took my hand in both of his. "I am relieved that you are well," he said in a strangely formal way.

"Um, okay. I am relieved that . . . you are relieved."

He released my hand. As he turned away, he stumbled a bit over his cane. "I was hoping for a more elegant exit," he said.

I smiled, reminding myself that I didn't love him one bit, and then I went back into Simon Green's room.

It was almost nine by the time Mr. Kipling and I were finally in the elevator and on our way out of the hospital. "I've got a car waiting for us. If there are any reporters still out there, let me do the talking," Mr. Kipling said.

"There she is!"

There were probably only a handful of cameras, but the flashes were still blinding in the darkness.

"Anya, are you glad to be out of the hospital?" one of the reporters called.

Mr. Kipling walked in front of me. "Anya is happy to have

escaped serious injury," he said. "She's had a very long day, folks, and she just wants to go home." He led me by my elbow toward the curb, where the car was parked.

"Anya, Anya, how was Liberty?" another reporter yelled.

"Give us a quote about Charles Delacroix! Do you hold him accountable for the bus accident? Do you think he'll win the election?"

Mr. Kipling had gotten into the car, and I was about to follow him when something stopped me. "Wait," I said. "I do have something I want to say."

"Anya," Mr. Kipling whispered, "what in the world are you doing?"

"The girl who died today. She was my age," I said. "She was crossing the street and then she was gone. I am sorry for her friends, her family, and especially her parents. It is a tragedy. I would hope that the fact that an infamous person was riding on the bus wouldn't take away from that."

I got into the car, then pulled the door shut.

Mr. Kipling patted me on the shoulder. "Well done, Annie. Your Father would be proud."

When I got home, Imogen and Natty were waiting for me, and no small amount of tears was shed over my safe homecoming. I told them they were making too much of it, but it was nice to know that my absence had not gone without notice. It could not be denied that I had been worried over. I was missed. I was loved. Yes, I was loved. And in that, at least, I was blessed.

I I I

I RESUME MY EDUCATION;
MY PRAYERS ARE ANSWERED; MONEY
MAKES THE WORLD GO 'ROUND

BY THE FOLLOWING MONDAY, Charles Delacroix was down two points in the latest Quinnipiac polls, officially putting him in a dead heat with Bertha Sinclair, and I was still no closer to finding a school. Mr. Kipling and I discussed both these issues in our daily phone call. We kept the calls pretty short to manage costs, but their profligate regularity was a sign of just how worried about me Mr. Kipling was.

"Do you think it was the bus?" I asked.

"That and—you won't like hearing this, Anya—the fact that you were on the bus allowed the Sinclair people to dredge up the old story about you and Charles Delacroix and his son. There are some people who think your sentence to Liberty was too light and showed favoritism, and the Sinclair campaign is playing right into that."

"Too light? Obviously they've never stayed there," I quipped.

"True, true."

"You know, Simon likes him. Charles Delacroix, I mean."

Mr. Kipling laughed. "Yes, I think my young colleague has a bit of a crush. Ever since he talked to him last September to arrange your release from Liberty.

"Anya, I hope you won't think this is an invasion of your privacy, but I had a question I wanted to ask you." He inhaled. "Why was Win at the hospital?"

I told him I had no idea.

"If you're still with him, as your attorney, that's something I should know."

"Mr. Kipling," I said, "Win has a new girlfriend, though I do think he has the tragically misguided idea that we should still be friends." I told him about Alison Wheeler and how they had rekindled a romance while working on Charles Delacroix's campaign.

"I am sorry, Anya, but I can't pretend to be anything but relieved."

I had wrapped the phone cord around my wrist. My hand was starting to turn white for lack of blood.

"Onward! Let's talk schools," Mr. Kipling said brightly.

"Did you find something?"

"No, but I had an idea I wanted to run by you. What would you think of homeschooling?"

"Homeschooling?" I repeated.

"Yes, you'd finish up your senior year at home. We'd hire a tutor or *tutors* even. You'd still take your college entrance exams . . ." Mr. Kipling rambled on about homeschooling, but I had stopped listening. Wasn't homeschooling for the socially maladjusted? The outcasts? But then, I suppose I was well on my way to being both. "So?" Mr. Kipling said.

"Kind of feels like giving up," I replied after a pause.

"Not giving up. Just a little retreat until we can come up with something better."

"Well, on a positive note, I guess I'd graduate top of my class."

"That's the spirit, Annie."

Mr. Kipling and I said goodbye and then I hung up the phone. It was only ten in the morning, and I had nothing to do for the rest of the day except to wait for Natty to come home. I couldn't help but think of Leo after he'd lost his job last year. Was this how he had felt? Forgotten, discarded, outcast?

I missed my brother.

Natty and I hadn't made it to church on Sunday, so, lacking other plans, I decided to go.

If I haven't mentioned it before, the church Natty and I went to was St. Patrick's Cathedral. I loved the place even if it was falling apart. I'd seen pictures of it from one hundred years ago, back when it still had turrets and there hadn't been a hole in the ceiling. But I was fond of that hole actually. I liked to be able to see the sky when I was praying.

I put some money in the basket for the campaign to restore St. Patrick's and went into the nave. The kind of people in a church in a decaying city in the middle of a Monday morning were a pretty sad lot—aged, homeless. I was the only teenage girl there.

I sat down in a pew and crossed myself.

I said my usual prayers for my mother and father in Heaven.

I asked God to watch over Leo in Japan. I thanked Him that I had been able to keep us safe to this point.

And then I asked for something for myself. "Please," I whispered, "let me figure out a way to graduate on time." I knew it was kind of a silly thing to want, considering the more complex problems in my life and in the world in general. For the record, I also thought it was cheap to use prayer in this way—God wasn't Santa Claus. But I had sacrificed a lot and well, the heart wanted what it wanted, and sometimes what the heart wanted was to walk down the aisle at its high school graduation.

When I got back from church, the phone was ringing.

"This is Mr. Rose. I'm the school secretary at Holy Trinity. I'd like to talk to Anya Balanchine."

So Trinity had finally hired a new school secretary. That had only taken two years. "This is she."

"The headmaster requests an audience with you tomorrow morning at nine. Are you free?"

"What is this about?" I asked. It could, for instance, have been something to do with my little sister.

"Headmaster prefers to discuss the details in person."

I did not tell Natty or Scarlet about my meeting nor did I wear my Trinity uniform. I did not want to presume what I so desperately hoped—that somehow, somehow, the administrative board at Holy Trinity had revised their decision, that they were taking pity on me and were allowing me to return for my senior year.

Mr. Kipling offered to come to the meeting, but I thought

it was better that I go alone. I didn't want to remind Headmaster that I was the kind of girl who had a lawyer where a proper parent should have been.

Since the last time I had been at school in May, metal detectors had been installed at the main entrance. I could only assume that had had something to do with me. Way to leave a mark on the place, Anya.

I went straight to Headmaster's office, where I was greeted by Mr. Rose. "Nice to meet you," Mr. Rose said to me. "Headmaster will be with you in a moment."

The familiarity of that office was almost unbearable. It was where I had found out my brother had shot Yuri Balanchine. It was where I had been accused of poisoning Gable Arsley. It was where I had met Win.

Headmaster poked her head out the door. "Come in, Anya."

I followed her into the room, and she closed the door behind me.

"I was glad to hear you weren't injured in that bus accident," Headmaster began. "And I must compliment you. You did acquit yourself very nicely in the short interview I saw on the news."

"Thank you," I said.

"We've known each other a long time, Anya, so I'm not going to beat around the bush here. An anonymous donor has made a significant financial contribution to Holy Trinity. The only stipulation is that Anya Balanchine be allowed to continue her education."

"I . . . That's news to me."

The headmaster looked me in the eye. "Is it?"

I returned her gaze. "Yes."

"The donor, if I am to believe that it isn't you or someone from your family, claims he or she saw your interview on the news and was impressed with your, I believe the word was *grace*. The donation is so sizable that the board and I feel we cannot merely ignore or return it without talking to you first. As you know, no one wants you with your guns and your drugs back on this campus."

I nodded.

"Have you found another school yet?" Headmaster asked me warily.

"No. The places I tried feel the same way about me that you do. Also, I'm a senior, so . . ."

"Yes, I imagine that does make things more difficult. We don't admit incoming seniors here either." Headmaster leaned back in her chair and sighed. "If I was to let you return, your freedom here would have to be seriously curtailed. I have parents to answer to, Anya. Each morning, you would have to stop by my office so that Mr. Rose could search through your bag and frisk you. In addition, you could not participate in after-school activities, social or extracurricular. Do you think you could live with that?"

"Yes." I would have agreed to almost anything at this point.

"Any violation of rules would result in your immediate suspension."

I told her I understood.

The headmaster furrowed her brow. "It's a public relations fiasco. If you were me, what would you tell the parents?"

"That Holy Trinity is first and foremost a Catholic school. And that Catholic schools have to practice forgiveness. That you showed me charity when no other schools wanted me."

Headmaster nodded. "Seems sensible. Don't mention the donation at all."

"Exactly."

"Would you even want to come back here?" Headmaster asked me in a kinder voice than the one she'd heretofore been using. "These haven't exactly been happy years for you, have they?"

I told her the truth. "I'm sorry if I ever made it seem otherwise but I love Holy Trinity, Headmaster. It has, despite everything, been the one good and consistent place in my life."

"We'll see you tomorrow, Anya," Headmaster said after a long pause. "Don't make me regret this."

When I got back home, I called Mr. Kipling to find out if he'd made the donation to Holy Trinity.

"I don't know anything about it," Mr. Kipling said. "I'm putting you on speaker so Simon can hear."

"How are you feeling?" I asked Simon Green.

"Much better," Simon answered. "Did your headmaster say how big the donation was?"

"Only that it was sizable."

"Anya, I would tread carefully here. Someone may have an ulterior motive," Mr. Kipling warned.

I asked Mr. Kipling if he was advising me not to go back.

"The fact is, we still don't have any other viable options." Mr. Kipling sighed a hurricane wind. "No, I just want you to keep your eyes open for anything that might seem strange. Someone wants you back at Trinity, and it makes me more than a little nervous that we don't know who or why."

"I'll be careful," I promised.

"And it goes without saying that you should keep your distance from Win Delacroix," Mr. Kipling added.

I swore that I would.

"Are you happy, Anya?" Simon Green asked. "You'll get to graduate with your class."

"I think I am," I said. And, for the first time in a very long time, I allowed myself to be, if only just a little bit.

That night, I called Scarlet to tell her I was coming back. I had to hold the phone away from my ear. *(Readers, I swear you could hear Scarlet's screams all the way to Brooklyn.)*

And then I was back at Trinity. Aside from the daily frisking—Mr. Rose and I were developing quite the intimate relationship—it was as if I had never been gone.

All right, there were a few changes, some for the better, others less so. Scarlet had definitely improved at fencing without me to lean on. Natty now took her classes in the upper-school building, so I got to see her several times a day. Win was in my FS III class, but his partner there, as everywhere else, was Alison Wheeler. He was friendly to me, but kept his distance. At lunch, I ate with Scarlet and Gable and tried not to feel like a third wheel. But, well, there were definitely worse things in life than being a third wheel. Mr. Beery announced that the school play would be *Romeo and Juliet*. When Scarlet suggested I audition, I was happy to inform her that the school had forbidden me to participate in extracurricular activities. It was no great sacrifice. Despite my triumph the prior year as chief witch in *Macbeth*, I was no actress and besides, I had had more than enough drama for one life.

I kept my promise to Mr. Kipling to be vigilant for evidence of conspiracy but I saw nothing. Perhaps I did not wish to see anything. I have, as you may recall, been guilty of such behavior in the past. I ignored messages from Mickey Balanchine that I probably should not have ignored. In my defense, I had missed a lot of work and my thinking was that there would be plenty of time to assume the mantle of my birthright.

I had been back at school almost two weeks when Alison Wheeler cornered me in the library, where I had been spending my lunch hour taking a makeup test. The library was one of the few places where they still had paper books, though no one ever used them. They were really there for decorative purposes.

Over the summer, Alison had cut off her red storybook hair and now she wore it in a pixie cut that made her green eyes look unnaturally large. She sat down in the seat across from me. In all the years we had known each other, I couldn't remember us ever having had a conversation.

"That's wrong," she said, indicating a response I'd given on the test. (You may recall that she was ranked the number-one student in my class.)

Instinctually, I pulled my slate closer to me. I didn't want to get thrown out for cheating.

"You're hard to get alone," Alison commented. "Always

with Scarlet or Gable or your sister, or in the main office getting searched—that's what they're doing to you, right?"

I didn't reply.

"What I think," Alison Wheeler said to me, "is that sometimes the reason things don't make sense is because they don't make sense." Her green eyes looked at me in a level way.

I turned off my slate and put it in my bag.

"I think Win and I should eat at your table with Scarlet and Gable Arsley. I think that is what we should do."

"Why? So I can have a front-row seat to the boy I used to love with his new girlfriend?"

Alison cocked her head and studied me. "Is that what you think you'd be seeing?" she said after a moment.

"Yes, I do."

Alison nodded. "Of course. I must be very cruel."

I said nothing.

"Or maybe I think it good that Win should have his friends. His father's campaign is very hard on him, Annie."

I would rather she didn't call me Annie. I was starting to really dislike Alison Wheeler.

The next day, I got a B on my test, and Win and Alison joined us at the table.

Though I had tried to discourage Alison Wheeler, lunch was livelier than it had been with just Gable and Scarlet. Scarlet was less boring, Gable less sullen. Alison Wheeler was odd but dry and smart, too. And Win, well you know how I felt about him as I have exhaustively and probably pathetically detailed those emotions. Suffice it to say, it was the closest

Win and I had been since that day at the hospital, and you might think that would be torturous for me but it wasn't. Seeing Win with his new girlfriend was easier than imagining it had been.

I did not even get him by himself until that Friday. Everyone else had left lunch early for one reason or another, and Win and I found ourselves alone, separated only by picked-over trays of lasagna and a gnarled wooden table.

"I should go," he said, but he didn't move.

"Me, too," I agreed, but I didn't move either.

"You must—" he began.

"How is—" I said at the same time.

"You first," he said.

"I was going to ask about your father's campaign," I said.

Win chuckled. "That wasn't what I was going to say at all, but since you asked, I think Dad's going to prevail." He looked me in the eye. "You probably despise him."

My feelings about Charles Delacroix were nearly as complex as the ones I had for his son. On some level, I admired Win's father. He had been a worthy adversary. But I hated him, too. That seemed a rude thing to say to someone's son however. I decided to keep my mouth shut.

"I wish I could hate him but he is my father," Win said. "And I think, despite everything, that he'll be a very good district attorney. Campaigns . . ." His voice trailed off.

"Yes?"

"They seem like they last forever, but they don't, Annie." Suddenly, he reached across the table and took my hand, which I immediately pulled back.

"Are friends not allowed to shake hands?" Win asked.

"I think you know why I can't shake your hand."

I stood up and grabbed my tray. I slammed it down on the conveyor belt that led to the kitchen and a little bit of sauce ended up on my sweater.

The bell rang. As I was leaving the cafeteria, I felt a hand on my shoulder. I turned. It was Dr. Lau, my Forensic Science teacher. She was the only member of the faculty who had spoken up in my defense last spring and, not coincidentally, the only one who seemed glad that I had returned. "Anya," she said. "I wouldn't."

"Wouldn't what?" I asked innocently.

I made my way to Twenty-First Century History, where we had just begun studying the events that had led up to the second prohibition. I was familiar with several of the boldface names.

I V

I AM SURPRISED; I AM
SURPRISED AGAIN

Friday night, I was planning to stay in, but Scarlet insisted that I come out with her and Gable. "You haven't gone out once since you've been back from Liberty," she said to me on the ride home from school. "You can't spend the rest of your life at home with Natty and Imogen. We'll get dressed up and go to one of our old places. How about your cousin Fats's?"

There was nowhere I wanted to go less except possibly Little Egypt.

"Or maybe you'd prefer Little Egypt?" Scarlet asked.

"Fats's is fine," I said.

"I thought you'd say that. Meet us there at eight. And, Anya?" she added just before we parted, "Don't wear your school uniform!"

Around seven thirty, I changed per Scarlet's instructions, then took a bus downtown.

"Hey, kid," Fats greeted me. "Your friends are in the back room."

Fats had lost quite a bit of weight since I'd last seen him. "You're skinny," I said.

"Gave up sugar," he informed me.

"Cacao, too?"

"No, never cacao, Annie."

"Maybe we should stop calling you Fats."

"Nah, it's got a nice bit of irony now."

I went into the back room.

"Surprise!"

The place was packed, and it took me a second to realize I knew everyone there. Scarlet, Gable, Natty, Imogen, Mickey and Sophia Balanchine, Mr. Kipling and his wife, Simon Green, Chai Pinter, and several other of my classmates. Even Alison Wheeler was there, though she had come solo.

As you already know, I was a fan neither of surprise parties nor of parties in particular. Still, I could not help but appreciate that so many people had come out for me. Scarlet came up and kissed me on the cheek. "What kind of best friend would I be if I let you come back to Trinity without a party?"

I made the rounds, talking to everyone, thanking them for having shown up.

"Win really wanted to come," Alison Wheeler whispered in my ear.

In the back of the room, a bit separate from everyone else, stood Mickey and Sophia Balanchine. They were talking to a third person. How could I not have noticed him before?

"Yuji Ono!" I exclaimed, throwing my arms around him in

a manner I'm not entirely sure was dignified or appropriate. But, well, he had saved my brother's life.

He smiled at me in his shy way.

"What are you doing here?"

"Business, of course," he said.

"Had you returned any of my calls, you would have known this," Mickey Balanchine remonstrated me.

Yuji Ono gave me a look. I could tell he was disappointed in me.

"It took me longer to resolve my high school situation than I would have liked," I explained. Even as I was saying this, I knew how pathetic it sounded.

I turned to Yuji Ono. I wanted to ask about my brother but not in front of Mickey and Sophia. "Will you come see me at the apartment tomorrow?"

"I don't know if I will have the time," he said. "I am only in town for three days and my schedule is inflexible."

"I could come see you, then. Where are you staying?"

"I will try to come to you," Yuji said coolly. It annoyed me that he didn't trust me enough to tell me where he was staying when I had trusted him with my whole life.

"Give the child a break, Yuji," Sophia teased him.

I didn't like being referred to as a child. "Come or don't come," I said. I turned to Mickey. "How is your father?"

"Any day now," Mickey said glumly. Sophia took his small hand in her large one.

I thanked the three of them for coming and then I went to talk to Simon Green, who had not managed to integrate himself into the rest of the party.

"You look utterly miserable," I said to him.

Simon Green laughed. "Parties aren't really my thing."

"Mine neither," I said. "What's your reason?"

Simon Green took off his glasses and wiped them on his sleeve. "I'm afraid I had a very lonely childhood. Never got used to being with people."

"The opposite for me. Everything was too crowded. Middle-child syndrome I think they call it."

Simon Green nodded toward the corner of the room. "Is that Yuji Ono?"

"Yes." I didn't want to talk about him.

"And who's that?" He was pointing at Alison Wheeler, who was dancing with a girl from my history class.

"Ah, that would be my ex-boyfriend's new girlfriend. We're friends. It's all very grown-up and civilized."

"Her?" Simon Green's tone was one of utter incredulity. "We're talking about the redheaded girl with the pixie cut?"

"Yes, her." I paused. "Why not her?"

"Just not what I expected." I tried to convince him to elaborate, but Simon Green would go no further.

I continued my rounds. Before I knew it, it was 11:20, and the only ones left were Scarlet and Gable. Scarlet told me to go home, but I stayed. I knew Gable wouldn't be much help cleaning up.

"It wasn't awful, was it?" Scarlet asked me. "You weren't hating me the whole night?"

"Of course not, you silly duck." I kissed Scarlet on the cheek. "No one has ever been a better and more loyal friend to me than you have."

70

"How completely touching," Gable said sarcastically. "Can we please go home now?"

I asked Scarlet if she wanted to ride the bus back with me. She informed me that she was planning to spend the night at Gable's.

"Scarlet!" The Catholic schoolgirl in me was scandalized.

"No, it's fine," she insisted. "Gable doesn't like me traveling uptown at night and his parents don't mind if I use the spare room."

As it was late—ten minutes until city curfew—my cousin Fats insisted that he see me back to the Upper East Side.

We were waiting for the bus when a black car pulled up to the stop. The door opened. For a second, I wondered if I was about to be shot, if this was how it was all going to end. *(But we are only on page seventy-one of the second volume of my life, so surely this could not be the end.)*

Fats reached into his pocket. Just in case he had to shoot, I suppose.

Yuji Ono leaned out of the car. "A ride, Anya?" I nodded to Fats to let him know I was fine and then I got in the car.

I had had several cups of coffee that night to aid in the illusion that I was in possession of a sparkly party personality. As soon as I sat down, I started feeling the effects of the caffeine in my body. My heart beat like a hummingbird's. I was flushed, too bold, too sharp. More like Scarlet than myself. "I thought you were mad at me," I said to him.

"I am," he said. "Outraged." I couldn't tell if he was serious.

"How is my brother?" I asked.

"Very well," Yuji promised me. "I have a present for you,

but only after you tell me why you've been neglecting Mickey Balanchine."

Daddy used to say that the only people who made excuses were failures. "It was harder coming back from Liberty than I thought it was going to be."

"You mean finding a secondary school?" Yuji Ono made a face. "Why do you even need a high school diploma?"

"You would rather me be uneducated? A fool?"

"That is not what I am saying. But the things you need to learn, you cannot learn in school."

"Every time I see you, you lecture me," I complained.

"That is because I am counting on you, Anya. I think you will agree that I have gone to great lengths for you."

"Of course, Yuji."

"You are my investment."

"I don't belong to you though."

The car was just passing the southeastern edge of the park. Yuji reached into his pocket. He took my hand and pried it open. On my palm, he placed a small wooden lion.

"Did Leo make this?" I asked quietly.

"Yes, he has taken up carving."

I looked at the lion, my miniature miracle. Leo had touched this. Leo was safe. I smiled at Yuji and tried not to cry. "He's good at this."

I turned to thank him. I was about to kiss him on the cheek when the car passed over a pothole and I ended up kissing him on the mouth. It was not romantic in the least. His teeth knocked against mine. "I'm sorry," I said. "I was aiming for your cheek. Potholes, you know. This city!"

Yuji blushed. "I know, Anya." He turned his dark eyes on me. "You would never try to kiss an old man like me on the lips."

"Yuji, you're not old," I protested.

"Compared to you, I am." He turned to look out the window. "Besides, I have heard that you are secretly with your old boyfriend. The politician's son."

I twisted in the seat. "What? That absolutely isn't true! Who said that?"

"Mickey and Sophia suspect it."

"They barely know me! They should keep their mouths shut."

"You are back at your old school, are you not?" Yuji asked me.

"Only because nowhere else would have me. Yuji, it is impossible for me to be with Win. And you should know that even the suspicion of that could be disastrous for me."

Yuji shrugged. He might have been the most infuriating person I had ever known.

"Was Sophia Bitter your girlfriend?" I asked.

Yuji smiled at me. "Is tonight the night for archaeology?"

"That isn't an answer."

"Mainly she was my school friend," Yuji said after a rather long pause. "She was my best school friend."

"Why didn't you tell me that when we were at the wedding?" I asked.

"It wasn't relevant."

"Neither is my personal life then."

We traveled up Madison Avenue in silence.

I closed my hand around the lion, letting its edges and imperfections etch themselves into my flesh. Yuji put his hand around my fist. "So you see. Our lives are interconnected."

His hand was ice around mine, but the sensation was not entirely unpleasant.

The car stopped on East Ninetieth Street, where I lived, and I opened the car door.

"I am sorry that we argued," he said. "I . . . The truth is, I see you as . . . part of myself. I should not, though."

I got out of the car and went upstairs. I went into Natty's room. She had already fallen asleep, but I woke her up anyway.

"Natty," I whispered.

"What?" she asked drowsily.

I held out my palm so that she could see the wooden lion.

"Leo? It's Leo, isn't it?" Her eyes were bright and alert.

I nodded.

She took the wooden lion and kissed it on its head. "Will we ever see him again?"

I told her that I hoped so and then I went to bed myself.

I had barely slept at all when I awoke to a banging on the apartment door. "Police!"

The clock read 5:12 a.m. I pulled on my bathrobe and went to the door. I looked through the peephole. Indeed, two uniformed police officers stood there. I opened the door, but left the security chain on. "What do you want?"

"We're here for Anya Balanchine," one of the police officers said.

"Yes. That's me."

"We need you to open the door, ma'am. We're here to take you back to Liberty," the officer continued.

I ordered myself to stay calm. I could hear Natty and Imogen stirring in the hallway behind me. "Annie, what's happening?" Natty asked.

I ignored her. I had to stay focused. "On what grounds?" I asked the officer.

"Violations of the terms of your release."

"What violations?" I demanded.

The officer said that he didn't have that information—just instructions to bring me back to Liberty. "Please, ma'am, we need you to come with us."

I told him I would come out, but that I needed a moment to change.

"Five minutes," the officer said.

I closed the door and walked down the hallway. I tried to consider my options. I couldn't run; there was no other way out of the apartment, except suicide. Besides, I didn't want to run. For all I knew, this could have been some sort of clerical error. I decided to go with the police officers and figure out the rest later. Imogen and Natty stood at the end of the hallway. Both seemed to be awaiting my instruction. "Imogen, I need you to call Mr. Kipling and Simon Green."

Imogen nodded.

"What should I do?" Natty asked.

I kissed her on the head. "Try not to worry."

"I'll say a prayer for you," Natty said.

"Thank you, sweet."

I ran to my bedroom. I took off my necklace and changed

75

into my school uniform. I went into the bathroom, where I took a second to brush my teeth and wash my face. I looked at myself in the mirror. You are strong, I told myself. God doesn't give you anything that you can't bear.

I heard more banging on the door. "*It's time!*" the officer called.

I returned to the foyer, where Natty and Imogen looked at me with shell-shocked faces. "I'll see you soon," I said to them.

I walked to the door, unchained it, and pushed it wide open. "I'm ready," I said.

The officer was holding a pair of handcuffs. I knew how this went. I held out my wrists.

At Liberty, I wasn't brought to the intake room as I had been the previous two times I'd been there. They didn't even have me change into the Liberty jumpsuit. Instead, I was delivered to a Liberty guard, one I didn't recognize, then led down a hallway.

A hallway that led to several flights of stairs.

I knew this route, and it could mean only one thing.

The Cellar.

I had been there once before and it had nearly killed me, or at least driven me crazy.

I could already smell the excrement and the mold. Fear crept into my heart. I stopped short. "No," I said. "No, no. I need to talk to my attorney."

"I have my orders," the guard said without emotion.

"I swear on the graves of my dead mother and father, I haven't done anything wrong."

The guard pushed me and I fell to my knees. I could feel them scrape against the concrete. It was already so dark and the stench was terrible. I decided that if I didn't stand up, then they couldn't make me go down there.

"Girl," the guard said, "if you don't stand up, I will knock you out and carry you myself."

I clasped my hands. "I can't. I can't. I can't. I can't." I was begging now. "I can't." I grasped the guard's leg. I was past having dignity.

"*Assistance!*" the guard called. "*Prisoner is noncompliant!*"

A second later, I felt a syringe go into the side of my neck. I did not pass out, but my mind went blank, and it felt as if my troubles were behind me. The guard tossed me over her shoulder like I weighed nothing and carried me down the three flights of stairs. I barely felt it when she placed me in the kennel. The cage door had only just closed when I finally did lose consciousness.

When I awoke, every part of me hurt, and my school uniform was ominously damp.

Outside my tiny cage, I could see a pair of crossed legs in expensive wool pants attached to a pair of feet in recently shined shoes. I wondered if I was hallucinating—I had never known there to be any lights in the Cellar. A flashlight beam moved toward me. "Anya Balanchine," Charles Delacroix greeted me. "I've been waiting near ten minutes for you to wake up. I'm a very busy man, you know. Dismal place here. I'll have to remember to have it shut down."

My throat was dry, probably from whatever drug they'd given me. "What time is it?" I rasped. "What day is it?"

He pushed a thermos through the bars, and I drank greedily.

"Two a.m.," he told me. "Sunday."

I had been asleep almost twenty hours.

"Are you the reason I'm here?" I asked.

"You give me too much credit. How about my son? Or you yourself? Or the stars? Or your precious Jesus Christ? You're a Catholic, are you not?"

I did not reply.

Charles Delacroix yawned.

"Long hours?" I asked.

"Very."

"Thanks for taking time out of your busy schedule," I said sarcastically.

"All right, Anya, you and I have always been able to be candid with each other, so here it is," Charles Delacroix began. He took a slate out of his pocket and turned it on. He turned it toward me. The photograph was of Win and me in the Trinity cafeteria. Win was holding my hand across the table. It had been taken Friday. How long had he held my hand? Less than two seconds before I had pulled away.

"It isn't what it looks like," I said. "Win was shaking my hand. We're trying to be . . . friends, I guess. It wasn't even a moment."

"I do believe you, but unfortunately for both of us, this indiscretion was long enough for someone to get a picture," Charles Delacroix said. "On Monday, a news story will run with this picture and the headline 'Charles Delacroix's Mob

Connections: Who He Knows and What That Means to Voters.' Needless to say, this is not ideal for me. Or for you."

Yes, I could see that.

"That generous, anonymous donation to Trinity—"

"I had nothing to do with it!"

"Anya, I already know that. Haven't you ever suspected who did make that donation, though?"

I shook my head. My neck was sore where they had injected me. "The truth is, Mr. Delacroix, I didn't care. I just wanted to go back to school. I tried to find another school, but none would have me with the weapons charges."

Charles Delacroix clucked sympathetically. "Our system does make it challenging for parolees to follow the straight and narrow."

"Who did make the donation?" I asked.

"The donation was made by"—he paused for dramatic effect—"the Friends of Bertha Sinclair."

"Bertha Sinclair?" The name was familiar, and had my head not been pounding, I might even have been able to place it.

"Oh, Anya, I'm terribly disappointed. Aren't you following the campaign at all? Ms. Bertha Sinclair is the Independent Party candidate for district attorney. She might even beat me the way things are going."

"Good."

"It hurts me to hear you say that. Now you're just being cruel," Charles Delacroix said.

"Which of us is the one in a kennel not even fit for a dog?"

"But back to the Friends of Bertha Sinclair. Lovely Bertha's campaign first started gaining some real momentum after that unfortunate bus accident. Glad to see you're well, by the way. And do you happen to know from whence this momentum came?"

I nodded slowly. It was as Mr. Kipling had said. "Because the news linked your name and mine and Win's all over again. And our relationship makes you seem corrupt. And you are supposed to be Mr. Incorruptible."

"Bingo. You are the cleverest seventeen-year-old I know. And so those Friends of Bertha Sinclair, not being a stupid lot, came up with a plan that would throw you and my hapless boy together again. They were just waiting for pictures of the two of you. A kiss. A date. But you and Win didn't deliver those so they took what they could get. A second of indiscretion when Win grabbed your hand across a lunch table."

My cheeks burned with the memory. I was grateful for the low light.

"I am, frankly, amazed he resisted that long. Win is not known for his restraint. The boy is his mother—all heart, no sense. Alexa, his sister, she was the one like me. Brave and sensible. She was like you, too. Probably why the boy finds you so compelling, actually."

I said nothing.

"So, to conclude. Every time the story of you and Win is reported, the media gets to imply I'm corrupt and the Sinclair people don't have to say a darn thing."

"But it's over now," I protested. "The picture runs tomorrow. And that's the end of it. You'll take a small hit and then everyone will forget about it."

"No, Anya. It's only the beginning. They will wait for you every day after school. They will try to get pictures of you in class. Your peers, because they are young and thoughtless, will find ways to provide them. Win won't even have to be holding your hand for them to run this same story. He can be standing near you. He can be reported to be in the same building as you. This picture is a game changer, don't you see?"

"But Win has a girlfriend! Can't you just tell them that?"

"They'll say that pictures don't lie and that Alison Wheeler is a ringer."

"A ringer?"

"A fake. A fraud. Someone my campaign has employed to make it look like you're not with Win."

"But I'm *not* with Win!"

"I believe you. And if the polls were better . . ." Charles Delacroix looked at me with tired eyes. "I've thought about what to do, and I could only come up with one thing that puts an end to this story."

"Throwing me back in here? But I didn't violate our agreement! And you can't lock someone up for dating your son. I'll have Mr. Kipling go to the media, and you'll look like a monster."

Charles Delacroix seemed not to have heard me. "But you have broken several laws since getting out of Liberty, haven't you?"

He turned his slate toward me. First, a picture of me bartering with chocolate in Union Square. Then, a picture of me drinking coffee at Fats's. Finally, a picture of me getting out of Yuji Ono's car. The photo was time-stamped, 12:25 a.m. Past

81

curfew, in other words. All of these were minor infractions. Unfortunately, I was sitting across from the King of Enforcing Minor Infractions.

"You've been having me followed!"

"I needed insurance in case you didn't honor our arrangement. You are, rightly or wrongly, considered a delinquent. And, as you well know, the light, three-month sentence you received only holds if you don't continue in your delinquency. If I put you in Liberty for a year, say, it solves two of my problems. No one can say I showed you favoritism, and no more stories about you and Win."

"I can't stay here for a year," I whispered.

"How about six months. The election will be completely over by then."

"I can't." I would not cry in front of Charles Delacroix. "I just can't."

"In exchange, I can promise you that no one will bother with your little sister, if that's your concern."

"Are you threatening me?" I asked.

"Not threatening, bargaining. We're bargaining here, Anya. Don't forget, I do have legitimate reasons for returning you to Liberty. Chocolate possession. Caffeine consumption. Curfew infraction."

I felt like a trapped animal.

I *was* a trapped animal.

I wanted to talk to Mr. Kipling although, on some level, I knew he couldn't protect me from this. I had been unlucky, yes, but I had also been incredibly foolish. "The election is over the second week of November. Why not let me out at Christmas? That's three months."

Charles Delacroix considered my offer. "Let's say four. The end of January has a nicer ring to it. It could have the appearance of impropriety if you're out the month after the election."

I nodded. Charles Delacroix reached his hand through the bars, and after a moment, I shook it. My wrist felt incredibly sore, and I winced.

Charles Delacroix rose. "I'm sorry about this. I'll make sure you aren't sent down here again. I only wanted to ensure we were able to speak to each other without being observed."

"Thank you," I said weakly. But I knew he was lying. Sending me to the Cellar had been a very specific form of intimidation.

He was about to leave when he turned and kneeled down so that we were face-to-face. "Anya," he whispered, "why couldn't you have just made both our lives easier and disappeared for a year? Visited your relatives in Russia? I know you have friends in Japan. A girl like you probably has friends in all the kingdoms of the world."

"New York is my home, and I wanted to finish high school," I said lamely.

"Your lawyer should never have let you go back to Trinity."

"Mr. Kipling didn't want me to. Everything that happened, I caused myself. I should have been more vigilant."

"Not the bus accident," Delacroix said. "That was just unlucky. For both of us, I mean."

"And especially for that girl who was killed."

"Yes, you are right, Anya. Especially for her. Her name was Elizabeth." Charles Delacroix reached through the bars to touch my cheek. "This place is run atrociously. There are holes. If you happen to slip down one in a week or two, I doubt you would be missed."

"You're trying to scare me."

"The opposite, Anya. I'm trying to help you."

I was beginning to see his meaning. "How would I ever come back?"

He stood up, taking his thermos with him. "You have a friend who is going to be the new district attorney in New York. A friend who thinks that the prohibition laws are incredibly wrongheaded and have done nothing but ruin lives. A friend who remembers that you did save his son's life. A friend who will be better able to help you once this blasted campaign is over."

"We are not friends, Mr. Delacroix."

Charles Delacroix shrugged. "At the moment, perhaps not. But when you have lived as long as I have, you become comfortable with the notion that last year's enemy may be this year's friend. The reverse is true, too. Good night, Anya Balanchine. Be well."

About fifteen minutes after Charles Delacroix had left, a guard arrived to lead me to the intake room. Even though it was nearly three in the morning, Mrs. Cobrawick and Dr. Henchen were waiting for me. "I am sorry to see you back here, Anya," Mrs. Cobrawick said. "But I can't say that I am surprised."

Mrs. Cobrawick looked at my file on her slate. "My, my,

my. Multiple parole violations. You were a very busy girl. Caffeine consumption, curfew infraction, and chocolatiering."

I said nothing.

"Won't you ever learn to follow the straight and narrow?"

Still, I said nothing. I was so very tired. I thought I might collapse.

"We may as well get started. Anya, please remove your clothes for decontamination," Mrs. Cobrawick ordered. She turned to Dr. Henchen and said, "I fear these cannot be salvaged. They are so covered in filth."

I bent down to take off my skirt. As I was bending, I felt a strange pain in my chest and then I fell to the floor, banging my head on the tiles. My abdominal muscles convulsed wildly and I threw up. Dr. Henchen ran to my side. "Her heart is racing and she's turning blue. We need to get her to the clinic."

The next thing I knew, I was on a gurney being wheeled across Liberty Island to the medical area. I had never been there before but it was surprisingly clean and modern-looking compared to the rest of the place. A doctor cut off my Trinity uniform, and then they put sensors on my naked chest. I did not even bother to feel embarrassed. And then, for the second time in less than twenty-four hours, I passed out.

When I awoke the next morning, I tried to sit up, but my wrist was handcuffed to the bed rail.

A doctor came into the room. "Good morning, Anya. How are you feeling?"

I considered the question. "Sore. Exhausted. But overall, not that bad."

"Good, good. You had a heart episode last night."

"Like a heart attack?"

"Almost, but much more minor. There isn't anything wrong with your heart. You had an allergic reaction. It could have been something you ate, or it's possible that someone slipped you something, though luckily it wasn't in a quantity high enough to kill you. We won't know any of this for sure until the toxicology reports come back. The cause could be as simple as stress. I imagine you have been under some stress lately."

I nodded.

"But in case it is something more serious, you'll need to stay here for at least the next several days, for monitoring."

"I was given a sedative early Saturday morning by the guards at Liberty. Could it have been that?"

The doctor shook his head. "I doubt it—the timeline really wouldn't make sense—though that's good to know. So, rest up, Ms. Balanchine, and take it easy. You have several visitors in the hallway who are dying to see you. If it's all right with you, I'm going to tell them they can come in now."

I sat up in bed as best I could and adjusted my hospital gown so that all my important bits were covered.

Mr. Kipling, Simon Green, Scarlet, Imogen, and Natty came into the room. They had been told the official story—that I had broken the terms of my release with those petty crimes. As was to be expected, Natty cried a little and Scarlet cried a lot, and then I asked everyone except Mr. Kipling and Simon Green to leave. After I had relayed the highlights of my conversation with Charles Delacroix to them, Simon Green sighed, and Mr. Kipling stood up and banged his fist on the table.

"That makes a lot more sense, though. I wondered why they were bothering you about coffee and curfew," Simon Green said. "So, what do you want to do, Anya?"

"I think I should leave New York." I decided this as I was saying it.

"Are you sure?" Mr. Kipling asked.

"I can't stay at Liberty. Who knows how long it will suit Charles Delacroix to leave me here. He's saying January now, but I don't trust him anymore. Not to mention, I don't know if I'll survive it. Someone may have tried to poison me last night. I have to go. There is no other way."

Mr. Kipling nodded to Simon Green. "Then we will help you come up with a plan."

Simon Green lowered his voice. "In my opinion, our best chance for getting you out is while you're still in the hospital. After that, you'll be too entrenched at Liberty, and we'll have less access to you."

"Basically, we'll need to do two things. Determine the best way to get you out of here. And then figure out where you're going to go," Mr. Kipling said.

"Japan?" Simon Green suggested.

"No. Definitely not." I didn't want to lead the rest of my family straight to my brother.

"The Balanchines have many friends all over the world. We will find something suitable," Mr. Kipling said.

I nodded. "I need to arrange for Natty and Imogen, of course."

"Of course," Mr. Kipling said. "I promise that Simon Green or I will check on them every day that you are gone. But the truth is, I see no reason that things should change."

"But what if my relatives or the press become interested in Natty's welfare once I'm gone?"

Mr. Kipling considered this. "I could become Natty's legal guardian if you'd like."

"You would do that for me?"

"Yes. A long time ago, I worried it would complicate our business arrangement but I've been thinking about this possibility since Galina's death, and I think it is the best way I can help you. I would have made the same offer last year but everything progressed so rapidly after Leo shot Yuri Balanchine. And then it didn't seem as if there would be a need once you had resolved things with Charles Delacroix. But maybe this would be the best way to settle things once and for all."

"Thank you," I said.

Simon Green looked at Mr. Kipling. "The other thing we could do is send Natty to a boarding school out of state or country. This might be simpler in the short term. Forgive me, Stuart, but you have a bad heart and the timing of the application itself might raise eyebrows."

A nurse came into the room. "Ms. Balanchine needs to rest now."

Mr. Kipling kissed me on the cheek. "I am very sorry I did not advise you better."

"You tried, Mr. Kipling. You told me not to go back to Trinity. You told me to avoid Win. I didn't want to listen. I always think I'm being so smart, but then later, it turns out I've made so many mistakes."

Mr. Kipling took me by the handcuffed hand. "This isn't completely your fault, Anya. Nowhere near it."

"When will I stop being so wrong all the time?"

"You have a good heart. And a good brain, too. But you are young and a human being, after all, and so allowances must be made."

I TAKE MY LEAVE

I SPENT THE NEXT FIVE DAYS handcuffed to a bed while I planned my escape from Liberty. In the hospital, my visitors weren't really restricted and this came in incredibly handy. Someday, I would have to thank whoever had poisoned me. Perhaps someday, I would. *(Yes, readers, I had been poisoned and, had I had the time to reflect on the matter at all, the source would have been completely obvious.)*

My time was spent in the following manner: Tuesday morning, the first person who came to visit was Yuji Ono. "How is your heart?" he asked by way of greeting.

"Still beating," I told him. "I thought you were meant to be gone on Monday."

"I found reason to extend my stay." He bowed, then genuflected by the side of my bed so that his lips landed by my ear. He whispered, "Simon Green tells me that you wish to leave

New York. This is good. I think you should go somewhere you can learn the business."

"I can't go to Japan," I said.

"I know that, though for my own reasons, I wish it were otherwise. I think I have an alternative for you. Sophia Bitter's family has a cacao farm on the west coast of Mexico. You will be able to take a boat there and the connection to Balanchine Chocolate is not so obvious that anyone will think to look for you."

"Mexico," I said. "I'm a city girl, Yuji." A Mexican farm sounded so far from everything and everyone I had ever known.

"Don't you think your father would have wanted you to see where cacao is grown?" Yuji asked.

I had no idea what Daddy would have wanted and I wasn't even sure that I cared.

"Would you yourself not like to know what the source of all this misery is?" Yuji waved his gloved hand around the gray hospital room.

I told him I had never thought much about it.

"Do you trust me, Anya?" He took my handcuffed hand. "Do you believe that I, of all people, want what is best for you?"

I thought about this. Yes, I decided, I did trust him as much as I trusted anyone.

"I trust you," I said.

"Then know I do not say this lightly when I tell you that this is where I want you to go. You will be better able to run

Balanchine Chocolate someday if you know a bit about how cacao is grown. And this will make you a superior partner for me. A superior business partner, I mean." He dropped my hand and moved in even closer to me. "Don't be frightened, Anya."

"I'm not." I looked him in the eye. "Nothing frightens me anymore, Yuji."

"The warmth and sunshine will be good for you, and you will not be lonely, as Sophia's family is very kind. If it matters to you, it will be easy for me to invent reasons to come and see you."

What difference did it make where I went, really? I was leaving the only home I had ever known. "I don't speak Spanish," I said with a sigh. I had taken Mandarin and Latin in school.

"Many people will speak English there," Yuji said.

And so it was decided. I would take my leave in the pre-dawn hours of Sunday morning.

Tuesday afternoon brought Scarlet and she was crying again. I told her that if she wept every time she saw me, I wouldn't want her to come anymore. She sniffled and declared dramatically, "I've had to end things with Gable!"

"Scarlet, I'm sorry," I said. "What happened?"

She held up her slate. On the screen was the picture of Win and me in the dining hall underneath the headline Charles Delacroix had shown me two days earlier: "Charles Delacroix's Mob Connections."

"I'm the one who's sorry, Annie. Gable took this picture, and worse, he sold it!"

"What do you mean?"

"He got a long-lens camera phone for his eighteenth birthday," Scarlet began. *(NB: You may recall that minors weren't allowed to have camera phones.)* "And when I saw the picture yesterday morning, I knew someone from our school had taken it. And I doubted it was one of the teachers, so that only left the kids over eighteen. I turned to Gable. 'Who would do such a thing to Annie?' I asked. 'Who would be so low? Doesn't she have it hard enough?' And he wouldn't really answer me. And I knew, I just knew! And then I pushed him as hard as I could. So hard he lost his balance and fell to the ground. And I stood over him, screaming, 'Why?' And he's saying, 'I love you, Scarlet. Don't do this!' And I'm like, 'Answer the question, Gable. Just tell me why.' And finally, he sighs, and he says it wasn't anything against you or Win. He'd done it for the money. Someone had approached him weeks ago, saying they would pay big bucks if he could deliver a picture of Anya Balanchine and Win Delacroix in a compromising situation. And then Gable tried to justify his actions by saying that you owed him this money because of how much he'd lost because of you, like his foot and his good looks and such. And then he said someone else would have taken that picture anyway, if not him."

At this point, Scarlet started to cry again. "I feel like such an incredible fool, Annie!"

I told her that it wasn't her fault. "I wonder how much money he got."

"I don't know. But I hate him. I hate him so much!" She was by the door, bent over and sobbing. I wanted to comfort her, but I didn't have much mobility on account of the handcuffs.

"Scarlet, come over here."

93

"I can't. I disgust myself. I let that snake back into your life. You warned me about him. I just never thought you would be the one to get hurt."

"The truth is, Scarlet, I shouldn't have let myself get into that situation with Win."

"What situation? You were eating lunch." Scarlet always took my side in everything.

"Win shouldn't have taken my hand, and I shouldn't have let him. I should probably never have gone back to Trinity either. And Gable is right about one thing. Someone else would have taken that picture, trust me. It was coming with or without Gable Arsley's involvement. Someday, I'll be able to explain all of it better."

Scarlet approached my bedside. "You have to know I had nothing to do with this."

"Scarlet, I wouldn't even think that!"

She lowered her voice. "I never told him about what we did for Leo."

"I didn't think you would have."

Scarlet smiled weakly. Suddenly, she ran across the little hospital room to the bathroom, where she threw up. I heard the toilet flush and the water come on. "I think I'm getting the flu," she reported once she'd returned.

"You should go home," I told her.

"I'll come see you as soon as I'm feeling better. I love you, Annie. I'd kiss you but I don't want to get you sick."

"I don't care. Kiss me anyway," I said. In case she didn't make it back to Liberty before Sunday, I wanted to know that we had said a proper goodbye.

94

"Okay, Annie. As you like it."

She kissed me, and I grabbed her hand. "Don't blame yourself for any of this, Scarlet. I am only sorry that the tragedies that dog me have caused you grief, too. What I said after the party . . . You really have been the most loyal and true friend anyone could ever ask for. When I think about these last couple of years, I can't even imagine how bleak things might have gotten for me without you."

Scarlet flushed the color of her name. She nodded, and then she was gone.

The rest of the week passed quickly, with visits from just about everyone and with plans for my escape.

By Thursday, Simon Green and I had settled the arrangements. I was to be released from the hospital on Sunday morning. On Saturday night / early Sunday morning, well after the last nurse had checked on me, I was to get out of my bed and improvise a way out of the hospital, then past the fence that encircled Liberty Island. At that point, a rowboat would transfer me to Ellis Island. On Ellis Island, I was to be met by another boat that would take me to Newark Bay, where I would take a shipping vessel to the west coast of Mexico. In the morning, when the nurses came to transfer me back to the dormitory at Liberty, I would be long gone.

Simon had left me with a copy of the handcuff key, which I stuffed into the side of the mattress under the sheet. The only thing we hadn't figured out was how I was to get past the guards at the end of the hallway. "Do you have anyone here who can provide a distraction of some sort?" Simon Green asked. Reluctantly, I thought of Mouse and her assertion to me that she could do "hard things." Even though I needed her help, I didn't want her to get into more trouble on my account, and yet I lacked other options.

I got a message to her to come see me, and that afternoon, she did. She had a black eye. I asked her what had happened.

She shrugged. Then wrote, *Elbow to the face. Rinko.*

I told her what I needed. She nodded. Then she nodded some more before putting pencil to pad. *I'll come up with something. I am honored that u came to me, A.*

"Once I'm gone, they'll probably figure out you helped me. You understand that means you won't get out in November, right?"

I do. Don't care. Nowhere to go. Better to have friends in a year or 2 than b friendless, homeless, & penniless in Nov.

"I feel selfish asking you to help me," I said. "Asking you to stay here longer when I'm trying to avoid the same thing."

Mouse shrugged again. *Our situations are diff. I am a criminal. U are a name. Besides, they are stupid here & they might not figure it out & then u will owe me anyway. I will bet on u, if u will bet on me. Around 2 a.m., right?*

"Yes. Go see my lawyer Simon Green when you're free. He will help you with whatever you need."

She made an "okay" sign.

"Thank you, Kate," I said.

She bowed, then slipped out of the room. No one had seen her come in, and no one had seen her leave. I wondered if I could count on a girl so quiet to make enough of a distraction.

Saturday morning, Natty and Imogen came to see me. They knew nothing of my plans, and so I tried to keep the mood light. I did hug Natty extra tight. Who knew when I'd be able to see her again.

Simon Green and I had decided that I shouldn't have any visitors in the afternoon. I needed to rest for the long night ahead.

Still, I couldn't sleep. I was anxious and I couldn't even walk around to calm myself. I was starting to wish we hadn't told everyone not to come.

I looked at the clock. It was 5:00. Visitors weren't allowed after 6:00 anyway.

I closed my eyes.

I had fallen into a sort of half sleep when someone came into the room.

I rolled over. A tall boy with longish blond dreadlocks and thick black glasses. I didn't recognize him until he spoke. "Annie," Win said.

"You look ridiculous," I told him, but I couldn't help smiling. "Where's your cane?"

He walked over to me, and I struggled to sit up in bed and tugged at his ropy wig.

"I didn't want anyone to figure out who I was."

"You didn't want to make things worse for your father."

"I didn't want to make things worse for you!" He lowered his voice. "Dad said you were being transferred from the hospital tomorrow. That if I insisted on seeing you, today would be the best day. And that if I needed to behave so foolishly, I should at least wear a disguise. Thus, the wig."

I shook my head and wondered how many of my plans Charles Delacroix had guessed. "Why would he do that?"

"My father is a mystery."

He pulled a stool over to the bed. He rubbed at his hip.

"Arsley was the one who took the picture," I told him.

"I know," Win said, bowing his head. "I shouldn't have done that. Taken your hand, I mean. Not in such a public place." As he said this, he stroked my fingertips with his own.

"You couldn't have known how it would all turn out."

"I did know, Annie. I did. I had been warned. By my father. By my father's campaign manager. By Alison Wheeler. By you, even. I didn't care."

"What do you mean, 'by Alison Wheeler'?"

Win looked at me. "Anya, haven't you guessed?"

I shook my head.

"I was the one who asked Alison to go to you in the library."

"Why would she do that?"

"Well, she didn't want to but she knew I wanted to be near you. And I convinced her that lunch would be safe enough since Arsley and Scarlet and Alison would be there, too."

I was still confused. "Why would your girlfriend do that?"

"Anya! Don't tell me you didn't suspect!"

"Suspect what?"

"Alison is my friend but she also works for my father's campaign. They asked her if she would pretend to be my girlfriend during the campaign season so it would appear that I had put my relationship with Anya Balanchine—*you*—behind me. It was July—we weren't together—and, despite everything, I wanted to help my father. How could I say no? He is my father, Anya. I love him. As I love you."

Had Anya Balanchine—*me*—not been handcuffed to the bed, she would have run out of the room. I felt like my brain was exploding and my heart, too. He reached over the bed rail and wiped my cheek with his sleeve. I suppose I was crying.

"You really didn't suspect?"

I shook my head. My throat was thick and useless. "I thought you had tired of me," I said in a voice about as intelligible as my uncle Yuri's.

"Annie," he said. "Annie, that could never happen."

"We won't see each other for a really long time," I whispered.

"I know," Win whispered back. "Dad told me that might be the case."

"It could be years."

"I'll wait," he said.

"I don't want you to," I told him.

"There's never been anyone else for me but you." He looked over his shoulder to see if anyone was watching us. He leaned over the bed and put his hand on the back of my head. "I love your hair," he said.

"I'm cutting it all off." Simon Green and I had thought I would be less recognizable when I was traveling without my mane. Shears would be waiting for me on Ellis Island.

"That's a shame. I'm glad I don't have to see that." He pulled my head closer to him and then he kissed me, and even though it was probably pressing my luck, I kissed him again.

"How can I stay in touch with you?" he asked.

I thought about this. E-mail wasn't safe. I couldn't give him the address of the cacao farm, even if I knew it. Maybe

Yuji Ono could deliver a letter to me. "In a month or two, go to Simon Green. He'll know how to get to me. Don't go through Mr. Kipling."

Win nodded. "Will you write me?"

"I'll try," I told him.

He reached over the bed rail and set his hand on my heart. "The news said this almost stopped."

"Sometimes I wish it would. What good is it, you know?"

Win shook his head. "Don't say that."

"Of all the boyfriends in the world, you are the least suitable one I could have picked."

"Same to you. Only *girlfriend*, I mean."

He rested his head on my chest and we were quiet until the time for visiting was over.

As Win walked to the door, he adjusted his absurd wig.

"If you meet someone, I'll understand," I told him. We were seventeen years old, for God's sake, and our future was uncertain. "We shouldn't make any promises that are too hard to keep."

"Do you really believe that?"

"I'm trying to," I said.

"Is there anything I can do for you?" he asked.

I thought about this. "Maybe check in on Natty every now and again. She adores you and I know she'll be lonely without me."

"I can do that."

And then he was gone.

All I had left to do was wait.

100

Around 1:55 a.m., I heard nurses and guards running down the hallway. I called out to one of the nurses. "What's happened?" I asked.

"There's been a fight in the girls' dormitory," she told me. "They're bringing over a half dozen badly injured girls. I have to go!"

I nodded. *Thank you, Mouse.* I prayed she wasn't too hurt.

It was time. I slipped the key out of the mattress and unlocked the handcuff. My wrist was sore, but there was no time for that. Shoeless and still dressed in an open-backed hospital gown, I walked down the hallway and slipped through the door marked Fire Stairs. I ran down the stairs with legs stiff from the prior week's inactivity. On the ground floor, I poked my head out into the hallway. A guard was directing gurneys down the corridor. It was now or never but I didn't know how to get past the exit without being observed by the guards or the girls on the gurneys. From one of the gurneys, Mouse poked her head up. She had two black eyes, a gash on her forehead, and her nose looked like it might be broken. With her less swollen eye, she looked at me. I waved. She nodded and mouthed something that looked like "Now." A second later, she screamed. I had never even heard Mouse's voice before and here she was screaming for me. Mouse's body began to writhe and convulse. Her arms flailed in a seemingly random pattern, but from my vantage point I could see her design. Mouse was managing to strike the other girls and anyone else who happened to be in the vicinity.

"This girl is having a seizure!" a guard called.

As all attention turned to Mouse, I was able to slip past everyone.

I ran outside on bare feet. It was late October now and maybe 50° out but I barely noticed the cold. I had to get to the gate. Simon Green had promised to bribe the guard who watched the gate, but just in case, he had given me a syringe with one dose of tranquilizer at the same time as he'd given me the handcuff key. I hoped I wouldn't have to use the syringe, but if I did, I knew to aim for the neck.

I ran through a dark patch of grass, trying not to wince as burrs pierced my feet.

Finally I reached the cobblestoned driveway that led to the gate. Someone had left the gate wide open. I looked in the guard's station. No one was there. Perhaps Simon's bribe had worked or maybe the guard had simply been called to the girls' dormitory.

I was almost to the shore when a voice called my name. "Anya Balanchine!"

I turned. It was Mrs. Cobrawick.

"Anya Balanchine, stop!"

I debated whether to run back and try to tranquilize her or just take my chances and keep moving forward. I looked up and down the shoreline. The rowboat that was to take me to Ellis Island wasn't there yet, and I must confess that the idea of tranquilizing that woman appealed to me.

I turned around. Mrs. Cobrawick was running toward me. I heard the sizzle of a Taser.

"Stop!"

Her Taser would trump my syringe.

I started running for the water.

"You'll drown!" Mrs. Cobrawick yelled. "You'll freeze to death! You'll get lost! Anya, it isn't worth it! You think you're in a desperate situation, but all of it can still be worked out."

I could see the floodlights of Ellis Island. I knew that it was over a half mile away, and having lived in a time of extreme water restrictions, I was not the most experienced swimmer. I knew enough about swimming to know that a mile in the water was going to feel like ten miles on land. But what choice did I have? It was now or never.

I dove.

Just before my head hit the water, I thought I heard Mrs. Cobrawick wish me luck.

The water was freezing. I could feel my lungs constrict.

The way my hospital gown was billowing out, it felt like it was drowning me. I untied it. With nothing but underwear on, I started to swim in the darkness.

I tried to remember everything I had ever read or heard about swimming. Breathing was important. Keeping water out of your lungs. Swimming straight, too. Nothing else was coming to mind. Hadn't Daddy ever said anything about swimming? He'd said something about every other subject in the world.

I ignored the cold.

I ignored my lungs and my heart.

I ignored my aching limbs.

And I swam.

Breathe, Anya. Go straight. I kept repeating this to myself as I paddled my arms forward and kicked my legs.

I was almost three-quarters of the way to Ellis Island and completely exhausted when Daddy's voice popped into my head. I don't know if this was something he'd actually said to me or if I was just losing my mind. What the voice said was: "If someone throws you in the pool, Annie, the only thing to do is try not to drown."

Swim.

Breathe.

Don't drown.

Swim.

Breathe.

Don't drown.

And what felt like an hour later, I was there.

I coughed when I hit the rocks. But I had to keep going. At this point, I knew I was probably behind schedule and I didn't want to miss my second boat. I used my rubbery arms to scale the rocky cliff. I could feel my limbs and naked stomach getting cut on the sharp stones, but somehow I made it.

When I tried to stand, my legs were slick and useless. There was a sick, wet feeling in my throat and lungs. And yet I was alive. I ran across the shore until I found the boat that would deliver me—a motorboat with the name *The Sea Quill* painted on the side.

The sailor averted his eyes upon seeing my partial nudity. "Sorry, miss. There're clothes for you in the bag. I didn't know you'd come upon me nekkid, though."

The sailor started the boat and we headed for New Jersey. "Worried we missed each other," the sailor said. "I was about to leave."

In the canvas bag that had been provided for me, I found boys' clothing—a dress shirt, a newsboy cap, a pair of gray pants with suspenders, and an overcoat—and then I found a large piece of gauze, a pair of round spectacles, a fake ID for one Adam Barnum, some money, a mustache and spirit gum, and finally, a pair of scissors. I put on the clothes first. I twirled my hair into a bun and concealed it under the newsboy cap. It didn't feel right. I asked the sailor if he had a mirror. He nodded toward the cabin down below. I descended, taking the scissors, the gauze, and the mustache with me.

The illumination in the cabin consisted of a single bulb, and the mirror was only six inches in diameter and pitted from the sea air. Still, it would have to do. I applied the spirit gum to my upper lip and stuck on the mustache. I looked less like myself, but I could still see that my current disguise was unconvincing. The hair would have to go.

I spread out the bag so that it would catch the clippings. I rarely had my hair cut, and I had certainly never cut it myself. I thought of Win's hands on my head, but only for a second. There was no time for sentimentality. I picked up the scissors and in less than three minutes all I had left was one inch of wavy hair. My skull and neck felt naked and cold. I looked at myself in the mirror. My head looked too round and my eyes too large, and if anything, I looked more babyish. I donned the hat again. The hat, I felt, was going to be key.

In the hat, I did not look like Anya Balanchine. And if

I squinted I could even see where I looked a bit like my brother.

I tried on the glasses. Better.

I backed up in an attempt to see more of myself in the tiny mirror.

The clothes were boyish enough, but something was off.

Ah, breasts.

I unbuttoned my shirt so that I could wrap the gauze tight around my chest—the bandage stung against the places where the rocks had lacerated my skin—and then I buttoned myself back in.

I studied myself.

The effect was not awful, but it disturbed me. It might seem silly, but I had spent most of my life as someone people had called pretty. I was no longer "pretty." I was not even handsome. I was somewhere between homely and ordinary. I thought I would pass as—what was my new name?—Adam Barnum.

I wondered if I should keep this up the whole time I was in Mexico or if I should only try to do this while I was in the process of escaping. I suspected the disguise worked best if you didn't consider me too closely.

I climbed the ladder back up to the main deck. I threw my hair clippings overboard.

Upon seeing me, the sailor started. He picked up his gun.

"Captain, don't shoot. It's just me."

"My word, I didn't recognize you! You were such an attractive little thing ten minutes ago and now you're plain as mud."

"Thank you," I said.

I crossed my arms over my chest.

At Newark Bay, there were hundreds of shipping containers and boats. For a second, fatigue set in, and I despaired of being able to find the right ship. But then I remembered Simon Green's instructions—row three, cargo ship eleven—and I quickly found the shipping vessel that was supposed to take me to Puerto Escondido, Oaxaca, on the west coast of Mexico.

Simon Green and I had decided on the shipping vessel for three reasons: (1) because the authorities, if they bothered to look for me, would probably go to the airports, the train stations, or even the passenger-ship docks, (2) because my family had many connections with exporters, which made it easy to find a shipping vessel that would harbor me, and (3) security was notoriously lax on cargo ships—I kept my head down and no one even asked to see Adam Barnum's ID.

The only problem with this plan was that a passenger on a cargo ship was basically cargo. The first mate pointed me to a room set up in an opened rusty metal container with a cot and a bucket and a box of old-looking fruit—still, it was fruit!— and no windows.

"Not exactly luxury," she said.

I took in the room. It looked slightly more commodious than the Cellar at Liberty.

The first mate eyed me suspiciously. "Have you no luggage?"

I lowered my voice to what I thought was a plausibly boyish register and informed her that my things had been shipped in advance. They hadn't, by the way. I was a person without a single possession.

"What takes you to Mexico, Mr. Barnum?"

"I'm a student naturalist. There are more plant species in Oaxaca than anywhere else in the world." Or so Simon Green had told me.

She nodded. "This boat doesn't actually have docking privileges in Puerto Escondido," she told me. "But I'll have the captain stop the boat and one of my crew will row you the rest of the way there."

"Thank you," I said.

"The journey to Oaxaca is about thirty-four hundred nautical miles, and assuming a vessel pace of fourteen knots, we should be there in approximately ten days. Hope you don't get seasick."

I had never been on an extensive sea journey so I didn't yet know if I was prone to seasickness.

"We should depart in about forty-five minutes. Gets pretty boring out there, Mr. Barnum. If you want to come play cards with us, we do Hearts in the captain's quarters every evening."

As you might expect, I did not know the rules to Hearts, but I told her I would try to play.

As soon as she was gone, I closed the door to my container and lay down on the cot. Though I was exhausted, I could not sleep. I kept waiting for the sirens that meant I would be discovered and returned to Liberty.

Finally, I heard the ship's horn. We were leaving! I lay my shorn head on the flat bag of feathers that must have once been a pillow and quickly fell asleep.

VI

I AM AT SEA; BECOME FAR TOO ACQUAINTED WITH THE BUCKET; WISH FOR MY OWN DEATH

FOR THE TEN DAYS OF MY JOURNEY, I did not have opportunity to play Hearts or any other game, aside from a game I affectionately dubbed Race Across the Container to the Bucket. *(Yes, readers, I was seasick. I see no need to trouble you with the details except to mention that, once, I threw up so hard I sent my mustache flying across the room.)*

This current plague did not allow me to sleep very deeply, but I did have hallucinations or, I suppose, waking dreams. One vision I had revolved around a Christmas pageant that was being staged at Holy Trinity. Scarlet was the female lead, of course. She was dressed like the Virgin Mary and she was holding a baby with Gable Arsley's face. Win stood by her side, and he was supposed to be Joseph, maybe; I couldn't tell. He was wearing a hat again and instead of his cane, he had a staff. To one side of him was Natty, carrying a box of Balanchine Special Dark, and next to her was Leo with a pot of coffee and a lion on a leash. Somehow I was the lion. I knew this because of my shorn mane. Natty scratched me between the ears, then offered me a piece of chocolate. "Eat one," she said. And I did, and a second later, I was awake and running across the room again, to reacquaint myself with the bucket. I had no idea what I was throwing up at this point—I hadn't eaten much of anything for days. My abdominal muscles hurt and my throat was terribly sore. It was lucky I had cut off all my hair because there was no one to hold it back for me. I was friendless and a fugitive, and I suspected there was no one more dejected and wretched in the whole world than Anya Balanchine.

VI

I BEGIN A NEW CHAPTER;
AT GRANJA MAÑANA

Aɴ ᴇɴᴅʟᴇss ᴛᴇɴ ᴅᴀʏs ʟᴀᴛᴇʀ, we arrived in Oaxaca, where, along with a sailor named Pip, I was transferred into a small dinghy.

As we approached the shoreline, my seasickness began to resolve itself only to be replaced by a homesickness such as I had never known before. It was not that the coast of Oaxaca lacked charms. The rooftops were dotted in promising shades of orange, pink, turquoise, and yellow, and the ocean was bluer and better-smelling than any water you'd find in my hometown. In the distance, I could make out mountains and forests, green, so green, with icy swirls of white. Were these swirls clouds or mists? I did not know—the icy swirl was not a meteorological phenomenon that we city girls were familiar with. The temperature was 67°, warm enough that the chill I had experienced since swimming to Ellis Island ten days ago at last began to fade. Still, this was not my home. It was not the place where my sister lived or where my grandmother and parents had died. It was not the place where I had fallen in love with the planet's most inappropriate boy. It was not the land of Trinity and of buses with my boyfriend's father's picture on the side. It was not the land of chocolate dealers and drained swimming pools. No one knew me here and I knew no one— i.e., Mr. Kipling and Simon Green's plan had worked! Maybe the plan had worked too well. I could die in this boat, and no one would care. I would be a mysterious body with a bad haircut. Maybe, at some point, a local cop would get the idea to use that tattoo on my ankle to identify me. But that was the only thing that identified me, this body, as Anya Balanchine. That regrettable tattoo was the only thing separating me from oblivion.

I wanted to cry, but I feared appearing unmanly to the sailor. Though I had not yet seen myself in a mirror, I could sense how awful I looked. I could see (and smell) the flecks of vomit on my one suit of clothes. My hair I did not wish to consider. I did feel my much abused mustache slipping off my face. I would discard it as soon as the sailor and I parted company. If I were to pass as a boy—I didn't yet know what story had been told Sophia's relations—it would have to be one without facial hair.

We were nearly to the shore when the sailor said to me, "They say the oldest tree in the world's here."

"Oh," I said. "That's . . . interesting."

"I mention it because Captain said you were a student botanist."

Right. That whole lie. "Yeah, I'm going to try to see it."

The sailor studied me curiously, then nodded. We had reached the beach of Puerto Escondido, and I was glad to be quit of that boat and of boats in general.

"You got someone meeting you?" the sailor asked.

I nodded. I was supposed to meet Sophia's cousin, a woman named Theobroma Marquez, in the Hotel Camino, which was supposedly in a shopping area called El Adoquin. I was unsure of how to pronounce any of this, of course.

I thanked him for the ride.

"You're very welcome. Word of advice?"

"Yes," I said.

"Keep your hands in your pockets," the sailor said.

"Why?"

"Boys' hands don't look like that."

Well, this boy's do, I wanted to say. I mean, what if I really had been a boy? What business was it of his? I felt outraged on slightly effeminate student botanist Adam Barnum's behalf. "Which way to El Adoquin?" I asked in my most imperious voice.

"You're almost there. El Adoquin runs parallel to Playa Principal." He pointed me in a direction, then rowed away. As soon as he was gone, I ripped off my mustache and stuffed my incriminatingly girly hands into my pockets.

I walked toward the town square. My clothes were heavy, appropriate for autumn in New York, and I began to feel light-headed from the humidity. The fact that I hadn't eaten anything aside from a past-prime apple in several days may also have contributed to my light-headedness. My stomach was acidic and hollow, and my head throbbed.

113

It was Wednesday morning, and despite my disheveled appearance, no one much noticed me.

A funeral procession traveled down the street. The coffin was covered in red roses, and a puppet skeleton controlled by sticks was held in the air. The women wore black lace dresses to their ankles. An accordion was wailing, and everyone sang a discordant song that sounded like musical weeping.

I crossed myself and kept walking. I passed, of all things, a chocolate store! I had never seen one out in the open like that. In the window were stacks of small, puck-like disks of chocolate wrapped in waxy papers. The exterior was paneled in rich mahogany, and inside were red stools and a bar. Of course, it made sense. Chocolate was legal here. As I was looking in the window, I caught sight of my own reflection in the glass. I pulled my hat farther down over my head and resumed looking for the hotel.

I quickly identified the Hotel Camino, as it was the only hotel in the area, and went inside. At this point, I could tell that if I didn't sit down, I was going to pass out. I went into the hotel bar and scanned the room for Theobroma Marquez. I looked for a girl who resembled Sophia, though aside from her height, I found I could barely remember anything about her. The bartender had not yet come on duty. The only one there was a boy around my age.

"*Buenos días,*" he said to me.

I really was on the verge of fainting—rather Victorian of me, I know—and so I sat down at one of the tables. I took off my hat and ran my fingers through my hair.

114

I became aware that the boy was staring at me. It made me self-conscious so I put my hat back on.

The boy came over to my table. He was grinning, and I felt as if I were the punch line to some great joke. "Anya Barnum?" That settled it. I was relieved to know that I was a girl, but not a Balanchine. This seemed a fine compromise. He offered me his hand. "Theobroma Marquez, but everyone calls me Theo." The name was pronounced *Tay-oh*. I was also relieved that Theo spoke English.

"Theo," I repeated. Though he was short, Theo looked sturdy and strong. He had eyes so brown they were almost black, and dark eyelashes like a horse's. He had stubble that indicated the beginnings of a beard and mustache. It was sacrilegious to say it, but he looked a bit like a Spanish Jesus to me.

"*Lo siento, lo siento.* I did not recognize you at first," he said. "They said you would be pretty." He laughed as he said this, not in a mean way, and I didn't feel all that offended that I'd just been called ugly.

"They told me you were going to be a girl," I replied.

Theo laughed at that, too. "It's this *estúpido* name of mine. A family name, though, so what can I do? Are you hungry? It's a long drive to Chiapas."

"Chiapas? I thought I was staying at a cacao farm in Oaxaca."

"You cannot grow cacao in the state of Oaxaca, Anya Barnum." He said this in a patient voice that indicated he was dealing with someone impossibly ignorant. "Granja Mañana is in Ixtapa, Chiapas. My family supplies to and has chocolate factories in Oaxaca, which is why I am the one who has to get you today."

Oaxaca or Chiapas. It didn't matter either way, I supposed.

"So, are you hungry or not?" Theo asked.

I shook my head. I was hungry but I was also eager to get to my destination. I told him I needed to use the bathroom, and then we could be on our way.

In the bathroom, I took a moment to consider myself in the mirror. Theo was right. I wasn't pretty anymore, but luckily, I wasn't all that vain either. Besides, I had a boyfriend, sort of, and I wasn't in the mood for seducing boys anyhow. I washed my face, paying special attention to the sticky residue that the mustache adhesive had left on my upper lip, and slicked back my hair. (*Readers, how I did miss that mane of mine!*) I threw the necktie into the trash, rolled up the sleeves of my shirt, and went back out to join Theo.

Theo studied me. "You are less hideous already."

"Thanks. That's the nicest thing anyone's ever said to me."

"Come, the car's over here." I followed him out of the bar. "Where are your things?"

I told the same lie about them being shipped.

"No matter. My sister will lend you whatever you need."

Theo's "car" was a green pickup truck. On the side, GRANJA MAÑANA was painted in gold, and beneath that was a grouping of what I thought at the time were leaves in fall colors.

As it was a big step up to the truck, Theo offered me his hand. "Anya," he said with a furrowed brow, "don't tell my sister I said you weren't pretty. She thinks I have no manners already.

116

I probably don't, but . . ." He smiled at me. I suspected that smile got him out of (and into) all sorts of trouble.

We drove out of the town of Puerto Escondido and onto a strip of road that had a wall of green mountains and rain forest on one side and ocean on the other. "So, you're friends with Cousin Sophia?" asked Theo.

I nodded.

"And you're here to study cacao farming?"

I nodded again.

"You have a lot to learn." He was probably thinking of the apparently hugely embarrassing gaffe I had made in thinking that cacao was grown in Oaxaca.

Theo gave me a sidelong glance. "You're from the United States. Is your family in chocolate?"

I paused. "Not really," I lied.

"I only ask because many of Sophia's friends are in chocolate."

I didn't know if Theo or the Marquezes could be trusted. Before I'd left New York, Simon Green had told me that he thought it would be best if I kept my history to myself as much as possible. Luckily, Theo did not pry any further on this point. "How old are you?" he asked. "You look like a little baby."

It was the hair. I lied again, "I'm nineteen." I had decided that it would be better for me not to be seventeen, and saying eighteen sounded more fake to me somehow.

"We're the same age," Theo informed me. "I'll be twenty in January. I'm the baby of the family, and that's why I'm so spoiled. Circumstance has turned me into a petted, silly lapdog."

"Who else is there?"

"My sister Luna. She is twenty-three and very nosy. Like with me, you can say, 'Oh, Theo, my family, they are *not really* in chocolate,' and I won't press. Your business is your business. But with her, you should have a better answer, so you know. And then there's my brother, Castillo. He is twenty-nine. He is at home through the weekend but usually he is off studying to be a priest. He is very serious, and you won't like him at all."

I laughed. "I like serious people."

"No, I am kidding. Everyone falls in love with Castillo. He is very handsome and everyone's favorite. But you shouldn't like him better than me, just because I am not serious."

"I'll probably like him better than you if he manages not to call me ugly in the first minute of my knowing him," I told him.

"I thought we were over all of that. I explained! I apologized!"

"You did?"

"In my head, *sí, sí*. My English is not that good. *Lo siento!*"

His English seemed fine to me. I decided then and there that Theo was lovable and awful and that most of what he said was going to be nonsense. Theo turned the truck onto a different road that led uphill and away from the ocean. He continued, "I have another sister, Isabelle, who is a married lady and lives in Mexico City. And then there is Mama, Abuela, and Nana. Mama runs the business. Abuela and Nana know all the secret recipes and they do the cooking. They will think you are too skinny."

I felt sad at the mention of the name Nana. "Abuela is your grandmother, right? So, who is your nana?"

"My *bisabuela*," he replied. "Great-grandmother. She is ninety-five years old and as healthy as can be. She was born in the 1980s!"

"People live a long time in your family," I commented.

"The women, *sí*. They are strong. The men, not so much. We have weak hearts." An old woman was pushing a cart filled with a yellow fruit that looked like an overgrown apple down the side of the road. Theo pulled the truck over. "Excuse me, Anya. Her house is not far, but I know her back bothers her when it rains. I will return in less than ten minutes. Don't drive off without me." Theo got out of the truck and ran over to the woman. She kissed him on both cheeks, and he began pushing the cart down the road and then disappeared with the woman into an opening in the forest.

Theo returned to the truck with a piece of the fruit in each hand. "For you," he said, placing one of the large fruits in my hand. "*Maracuyá*. Passion fruit."

"Thank you," I said. I hadn't ever had or even seen one before.

Theo restarted the truck. "Do you have a great love, Anya Barnum?"

"I don't know what you mean."

"A great love! A grand passion!"

"Do you mean a boyfriend?" I asked.

"*Sí*, a boyfriend, if you favor such a boring word. Is there someone who you'll weep for and who weeps for you back at home?"

I considered this. "Does it count if it's hopeless?"

He smiled at me. "It especially counts if it is hopeless. The

119

woman I was helping. She is the *abuela* of the girl I love. Sadly, the girl has told me she can never love me back. Yet still I am pulling over to help her grandmother. Can you explain this?"

I could not.

"Can you imagine the kind of girl who is so heartless as to resist someone so lovable as me?"

I laughed at him. "I'm sure there is a story."

"Oh yes, it is very tragic. Why does everyone always like love stories? What about absence-of-love stories? Aren't they much more common?"

Out my window, there was a large stacked-stone structure. "What's that?"

"Mayan ruins. There are even better ones in Chiapas on the Guatemalan border. My ancestors are Mayan, you know."

"*Theobroma*? Is that a Mayan name then?"

Theo laughed at me. "You do have a lot to learn, Señorita Barnum."

The road was bumpy, and I was starting to feel carsick. I leaned my head on the window and closed my eyes and soon I fell asleep.

I awoke to the sound of a bleating goat, and to Theo shaking my arm. "Come on. I must get out and push the truck. I will leave her in neutral and you try to steer." I looked out the window. It had started to rain, and the rain had caused mud to run over part of the road. "You know how to drive, right?"

"Not really," I admitted. I was a city girl, which is to say I was well versed in bus schedules and walking shoes.

"Not a problem. Just try to stay in the center of the road."

Theo pushed the truck, and I steered, too little at first but then I got the hang of it. About twenty minutes later, we were back on the road. That was my first lesson in cacao farming, I suppose. Everything took longer than you thought it would.

As we continued driving up the mountain, it got darker and darker as the forest became increasingly dense. I had never in my life been somewhere so wet or so green, and I couldn't help saying this to Theo. "Yes, Anya," he said in what I would later come to know as his "very patient" voice. "That's what it's like when you live in a rain forest."

We came to a metal gate with the word MAÑANA on it. A second gate was open, and as we drove past, I could see that it said GRANJA.

We drove down a long dirt road. "This is the farm," Theo said.

The trees were about twice the height of the workers who tended them. For grooming the trees, the men used flat swords that were over a foot long.

"They're pruning the trees," Theo informed me.

"What do you call the tool they're using?" I asked.

"A machete."

"I thought those were used for killing people," I said.

"*Sí*, I am told they are good for that, too."

Finally, Theo pulled up to the main house of Granja Mañana. "*Mi casa*," Theo said.

Theo's *casa* was as big as a small hotel. It was two epic stories, both a faded yellow with gray stonework around the windows and arches. The ground floor had a blue-and-white tiled porch, the second level, a series of sociable stone balconies, and the roof was covered in festive terra-cotta tiles. The house was undeniably massive but not, to my eye, unfriendly.

When I got out of the truck, Theo's mother was standing on the porch. She was wearing a white blouse, a coral necklace, and a khaki skirt, and her dark brown hair grew past her waist. She said something to Theo in Spanish and then she hugged him as if she hadn't seen him in weeks. (It turned out that he'd only been gone a day.)

"Mama, this is Anya Barnum," Theo introduced me.

Theo's mother hugged me. "Welcome," she said. "Welcome, Anya. You are my niece Sophia's friend here to learn about cacao farming?"

"Yes. Thank you for having me."

She looked at me, shook her head, clucked something else in Spanish to Theo, and shook her head again. She looped her arm through mine and escorted me inside.

The house was even more colorful indoors. All the furniture was in dark wood but the walls and the pillows and the rugs were in every hue of the rainbow. Over the mantel was an almost childish painting of what I thought at the time was the Virgin Mary in a field of red roses. (I would later learn that this depiction of the Virgin is known as Our Lady of Guadalupe.) There were several thick blue glass vases with orchids in them. (The orchids were native to the orchard. My own nana would have loved them.) A spiral staircase in blue-and-white tiles like those on the porch took up the center of the main room. It was a lot to take in, though I imagine it wasn't the decor but the humidity and the fact that I hadn't eaten in so long that made me feel light-headed.

"Call me Luz," Theo's mother said.

"Luz," I said. "I'm . . ." I'd had some practice fainting in the last several weeks, and I could feel myself starting to slip under. I tried to edge toward one of the sofas so that my head wouldn't end up slamming against those picturesque, though let's face it, pretty unforgiving-looking tiles. I began to fall backward. I saw Theo running toward me, but there wasn't time. As I was about to hit the floor, I landed in someone's arms.

I looked up. Above me was a very square face with a big chin and a wide nose. His eyes were light brown and very serious, and his mouth was stern somehow. He had stubble enough that it could reasonably be called a beard, and extremely thick eyebrows. "Are you hurt?" he asked in Spanish, though somehow I knew what he was saying. His voice was deep and sounded the way an oak tree might sound if it could talk.

"No. I just need to lie down," I said. "Thank you for catching me. Who are you, by the way?"

I heard Theo sigh heavily. "That is my brother, Castillo, Anya."

Luz shouted instructions and next thing I knew I was installed in a bedroom on the second floor.

When I awoke the next morning, a pretty girl with thick hair like my sister's was seated by my bed. The girl looked nearly identical to Luz, only twenty or so years younger. "Oh good," she said. "You're awake. Mama wanted us to watch you in case you took a turn for the worse and we needed to take you to the hospital. She thinks you're probably just malnourished and unaccustomed to the humidity. She says you will live. Stupid Theo. He should have taken you for lunch. We all

123

yelled at him—'Theo, what kind of host are you?'—and now he feels pretty awful. He wanted to come in here to apologize to you but Mama is traditional. No boys in the girls' rooms. Even grownups. I'm twenty-three." I had thought she was so much younger. "You're nineteen, right? You look like a baby! Back to Theo. He never thinks about anyone but himself because he is the baby of the family and ridiculous and we spoil him terribly. It's no use yelling at him really. I'm Luna, by the way." She paused to offer me her hand to shake. Luna and Theo were both fast talkers. "You're not bad-looking but you need a better haircut."

I self-consciously clutched at my hair.

"I can do it for you later if you want. I'm very artistic and I'm good with my hands."

At that moment, two older women entered the room behind Luna. They looked alike except the first was old and the second was really, really old. I realized they must be the grandmother and great-grandmother that Theo had mentioned in the truck. The older of the two, Theo's nana, pushed a ceramic mug into my hands. "Drink," she said. When she smiled at me, I could see she was missing one of her top teeth.

I took the mug. The beverage was brown with a reddish hue, and thick like wet cement. I didn't want to be rude to my hosts, but the substance didn't look all that promising.

"Drink, drink," Theo's nana repeated. "You feel better." The two older women and Luna were staring at me in anticipation.

I raised the mug, then set it down. "What is it?" I asked.

Luna laughed at me. "It's only hot chocolate."

I reported that I had had my share of hot chocolate.

"Not like this," Luna assured me.

I took a cautious sip and then a larger one. Indeed, it wasn't like any hot chocolate I had had before. It was spicy and not all that sweet. Cinnamon was involved but also something else. Paprika, maybe? And did I detect something citrusy? I drank the rest of the cup. "What's in this?" I asked.

Bisabuela shook her head.

"*Secreto de familia*," Abuela said.

I didn't know much Spanish, but I certainly understood about family secrets.

Bisabuela took the mug from me, and then the grandmothers were gone. I sat up in bed. I was already feeling better and I told Luna so.

"It's the chocolate," she said. "It's a health drink."

I had heard chocolate called many things in my lifetime but never a "health drink."

"Nana says it's an ancient Aztec recipe. They used to give it and nothing else to the soldiers before they went out to battle." Then she told me that if I was interested I should ask one of the older women or Theo, who was interested in all that chocolate folklore.

"Is it folklore or is it fact?" I asked.

"A little of both," she said. "Come, Anya, I put some clothes for you in the closet."

She pointed me in the direction of the shower. Wanting to be a good houseguest, I asked her if there were any water restrictions. Luna made a face. "No, Anya," she said patiently, "we do live in a rain forest."

In the afternoon, Theo took me on a tour of their farm. He showed me the huge nurseries where they grew the cacao saplings, and the open-air buildings that were used to store the wooden boxes where they would ferment the mature beans, and on the sunniest side of the plantation, the patios that were used to dry out the beans before they were sold. We went out to the orchard last. It was quite shady and moist, as it was located under a rain forest canopy. Theo told me that cacao required both the shade and the moisture of the rain forest to grow. Obviously, I had never been in a cacao orchard and I had certainly never seen a cacao pod up close. Some of the cacao leaves were purplish but many had begun to change to green. Tiny white blossoms with pinkish centers grew in clusters along the branches. "Cacao is one of the only plants with flowers and fruits at the same time," Theo informed me. The pods themselves were slightly smaller than the palm of my hand, but the thing that surprised me the most was their color. I'd always known chocolate as brown, but some of the cacao pods were maroon, almost purple, and others were gold and yellow and orange. They looked fantastical to me. Magical, I suppose. I wished Natty could see them, and for a second, I wondered if I should have tried to arrange for her to come out here with me. Of course, that would have been impossible for many reasons. "They're so pretty," I couldn't help but say.

"They are pretty, aren't they?" Theo agreed. "In less than a month, they'll be ready to cut from the trees so that they can begin the fermentation process."

"What are the farmers doing today, then?" The farmers

had the same machetes that I had seen yesterday and at their feet, wicker baskets.

"They're cutting off any pods that show signs of having been infected with fungus. That is the irony of cacao—it craves water, but can also be destroyed by it. The fungus is called *Monilia*, and even just a little bit of it can spoil an entire crop if it is not checked." He expertly scanned the nearest tree, and pointed out a green-yellow cacao pod that was black at the tip with radiating specks of white. "Do you see? That is what the beginning of pod rot looks like." He took his machete out of his belt and handed it to me. "You slice it off. It'll be harder than you think, Anya. Cacao farming is not woman's work. These trees are strong." Theo made a muscle with his arm.

I informed him that I was no weakling. I took the weapon from Theo. It was heavy in my hands. I lifted it up to swing at the plant, then stopped myself. "Wait. How do I cut it? I don't want to mess it up."

"At an angle," Theo told me.

I lifted the machete and sliced off the infected pod. My cut looked jagged. The plant really was tough. Doing this all day would probably be pretty exhausting.

"Good," Theo said. He took the machete from me then recut the incision I had just made.

"I thought you said I was good."

"Well, you will get better," Theo said with a grin. "I am encouraging you."

"Maybe I need my own machete?"

Theo laughed at me. "It's true. The selection of a machete is a deeply personal matter."

"Why don't you have machines to do this?" I asked him.

"*Ay, dios mío!* Cacao resists machines. She likes human hands and caresses. And she needs human eyes to spot the *Monilia*. She hates pesticides. Attempts to genetically modify her beans have all been complete failures. She needs to struggle or the cacao produced will not be the richest. She needs to face certain death over and over again. *Mi papá* used to say that growing cacao in the 2080s was identical to growing it in the 1980s or the 1080s—that is to say, she has always been impossible to grow, and she is still impossible to grow. That is why it became illegal in your part of the world, you know. I am fairly sure that it was the cacao that sent my father to an early grave." Theo crossed himself and then he laughed. "But I love it anyway. Everything worth loving in this world is difficult." Theo kissed one of the pods with a big smack of his lips.

I walked away from Theo, down one of the orchard rows, scanning each tree for signs of fungus. The light was low, so it was not the easiest work. "There!" I exclaimed when I finally found one. "Give me your machete."

Theo handed it over. I imitated the swift swinging motion I had seen him use, and the cut I made was, I thought, respectably clean.

"Better," Theo said, but he still recut it.

We continued walking through the orchard. I'd scan for signs of *Monilia*, then I'd point it out so that Theo could cut it off. Theo was very serious about the cacao, and he talked much less than on the drive to Granja Mañana the previous day. He was a different person on the farm, and I found him much easier to be with than the boy in the truck. As we headed toward the rain forest side of the plantation, it grew increasingly dark and damp. It was strange that these trees, these odd flowering trees, had been the source of so many problems in my life, and yet I had never even seen a picture of one before.

Three hours later, we had only covered a very small part of the orchard, but Theo said we needed to go back for dinner.

"Theo," I began, "I didn't understand something you said before."

"Yes?"

"You said that the reason cacao became illegal was because it was difficult to grow?"

"Yes. This is true."

"Where I'm from, we're taught something different," I told him. "We're taught that the main reason cacao became illegal was because it was unhealthy."

Theo stopped and stared at me. "Anya, where do you hear such lies? Cacao is not unhealthy! The opposite! It is good for the heart, the eyes, the blood pressure, and just about everything else."

His face was turning red, and I feared that I had offended him so I backtracked. "I mean, obviously, it's more complicated than that. We're also taught that the big American food companies were under pressure to stop making such unhealthy food products, and so as a concession they all agreed to stop making chocolate. The reason being that chocolate was rich and calorie-filled and had addictive properties and so . . . Well, the public basically turned on chocolate. They thought it was dangerous. Daddy always said it was a wave of poisonings that set it off . . ." Yes, Daddy had said that. I hadn't even thought of that during the Gable Arsley fiasco. "And that this led to strict regulation of cacao as a drug, and then its eventual banning."

"Anya, even tiny little babies know that the chocolate poisonings were set up by the rich men who owned the food companies. The reason they stopped making chocolate was because cacao is hard to grow and hard to ship and the supply was becoming more and more expensive. It was easy for the food companies to get out of the cacao business because it was good for the bottom line. It was about *dinero*. It is always about *dinero*. It is as simple as that."

"No," I said softly. Still, I wondered if that was possible. Was it possible that chocolate wasn't dangerous, or even unhealthy? Was what I'd been taught in school propaganda, a history cobbled together out of opportunistic half-truths? And if that were the case, why hadn't Daddy ever said that to me? Or Nana?

Theo cut a pod off a tree. "Look here, Anya, this one is ripe." He set the pod on the ground, then split it in half with a blunt whack of his machete. Inside the pod were about forty white beans arranged in neat rows and stacks. He picked up half the pod and held it out to me in the palm of his hand. "Look inside," he whispered. "It is only a bean, Anya, and like you and like me, it is of God. Could there be anything more natural? More perfect?" He expertly removed a single ivory bean with his pinkie. "Taste," he said.

I took the bean into my mouth. It was nutty, like an almond, but underneath there was the faintest hint of the sweetness to come.

Early every morning, Theo and I and the other farmers would go out to the orchard to look for signs of mold and, also, any ripe cacao pods we could find. The unusual thing about cacao was that it didn't mature all at once. Some of the pods were early bloomers and some were late. It took practice to recognize just the moment when a pod was ripe. The weight of the pod, the size, the color, and the appearance of thick veins—all these signs could vary. We were careful with our tools (machetes for the pods close to the ground, and a long-handled hook for the ones higher up) because otherwise they could damage the tree. Our tools were blunt, and the bark was delicate. Though it was shady, I still got a deep tan. My hair grew out. My hands became worried with blisters, then thick with calluses. I had borrowed Luna's machete as she had no use for this part of the process.

The major harvest took place just before Thanksgiving, which no one at Granja Mañana celebrated anyway. Still, I could not help but think of Leo in Japan, and my sister and everyone back in New York. On the first day of the harvest, the neighbors arrived with baskets and for nearly a week, we collected the ripe cacao pods. After we had collected the pods and moved them to the dry side of the farm, the pod smashing began. We used mallets and hammers to open the pods. Theo could do almost five hundred pods an hour. My first day of pod-smashing, I think I managed ten in total.

"You're good at this," I told Theo.

He shrugged off my compliment. "I should be. It's in my blood, and I've been doing it all my life."

"And do you think you'll do this forever? Cacao farming, I mean."

Theo whacked another cacao pod. "A long time ago, I thought I'd like to be a chocolatier. I thought I'd like to study the craft abroad somewhere, maybe with one of the masters in Europe, but now that doesn't seem likely."

I asked him why, and he told me that his family needed him. His father was dead, and his siblings really had no interest in the family business. "My mother runs the factories, and I run the farms. I can't leave them, Anya." He smiled wickedly at me. "It must be nice to be able to go far away from home. To be free of obligations and responsibilities."

I wanted to tell him that I understood. I wanted to tell him the truth about myself, but I couldn't. "Everyone has obligations," I insisted.

"What are your obligations? You come here without a suitcase or anything else. You contact no one and no one contacts you. You seem pretty free to me and the truth is, I envy you!"

After all the beans were removed from the pods, they were scooped into ventilated wooden boxes. Banana leaves were placed over the beans, and then the beans were left to ferment for about six days. On the seventh day, we moved the fermented beans to the wooden decks, where they were spread out and left in the sun to bake and dry.

At this point, the least difficult part to my mind, Luna took over, freeing up Theo to go to Oaxaca to check on the Marquezes' factories. Occasionally, she and I had to rake the beans to make sure they were drying evenly. The entire drying process took a little longer than a week because every time it rained, we had to stop to cover the beans again.

"I think my brother likes you," Luna said to me as we raked through the beans.

"Castillo?" I had seen very little of him since that day he caught me in his arms, though my impression of him had certainly been favorable.

"Castillo is going to be a priest, Anya! I mean Theo, of course."

"As a sister maybe," I said.

"I am his sister, and I don't think so. He is always going on and on to Mama about what a good worker you are and how you are like him. How you have cacao in your blood! And Mama and Abuela and Bisabuela adore you. I do, too."

I stopped raking to stare at Luna. "I honestly don't think Theo likes me, Luna. The first day we met, he mentioned a girl he was in love with and he made a point of telling me how ugly he found me."

"Oh, Theo. My brother is so adorably awkward."

"Well, I sincerely hope he doesn't like me, Luna. I have a boyfriend back home, and . . ." And I chose not to complete the thought.

For a while, Luna said nothing, and when she next spoke, there was no small amount of outrage in her voice. "Why do you never talk about this boyfriend? And why does he never contact you? He can't be a very good boyfriend if he never contacts you." (*Readers, it was much commented upon at Granja Mañana that I didn't have a slate.*) Obviously, there was a good reason why Win never contacted me. I was a fugitive. But I couldn't very well say that to Luna.

"I don't even think you have a boyfriend. Maybe you are saying this to be nice, but you are not nice at all. Maybe you just think you are so much better than us!" Luna yelled. "Because you are from New York."

"No, it's nothing like that."

Luna pointed her finger at me. "You need to stop leading Theo on."

I assured her that I hadn't been.

"You are stuck to him like glue every day! He is a baby, so of course he gets the wrong idea."

"I honestly only wanted to learn about cacao. That's what I came here to do!"

Luna and I continued to turn over the beans in silence.

Luna sighed. "I am sorry," she said. "But he is my brother so I am protective."

I understood very well about that.

"Don't mention that I said anything to you," Luna said. "I don't want to embarrass him. My brother has much pride."

After the beans were dried, they were gathered up into burlap sacks so that Theo could drive them down the mountain back to the factories in Oaxaca. This took several trips. "Would you like to come with me?" he asked before the last of that season's drives.

I did want to go with him, but after my conversation with Luna, I wasn't sure if I should.

"Come, Anya. You should see this. Don't you want to see where the beans end up?"

Theo offered me his hand to help me into the truck, and after a moment's consideration, I accepted.

We drove for a while in silence. "You are quiet," he accused me. "You've been like this ever since I got back from the city."

"It's . . . Well. Theo, you know I have a boyfriend, don't you?"

"*Sí* . . ." He drew out the word. "Yes, you told me."

"So, I don't want you to get the wrong idea about me."

Theo laughed. "Are you worried that I like you too much, Anya Barnum?" Theo laughed again. "That is really very conceited of you!"

"Your sister . . . She thought you had a crush on me."

"Luna is a romantic. She contrives to set me up with everyone, Anya. You can't listen to a word that comes out of her ridiculous mouth. You should know that I don't like you at all. I find you just as ugly as the day we met."

"Now you're being hurtful." My hair was longer, and I knew I wasn't as sickly looking as when I had arrived.

"Who is being hurtful? What of my feelings? You could barely look at me when you thought you might have to reject me," he teased me. "Apparently, we are both completely repulsive to each other." Theo reached across the seat to ruffle my hair. "*Ay*, Luna!"

The beans were unloaded at the main factory in Oaxaca, where they began the process of becoming chocolate. "Let me give you a tour," Theo said. He led me through the factory, which was bright and terribly modern-looking compared to my dark and timeless farm. (Yes, I had begun to think of it as *my* farm.) The beans we delivered would be cleaned today, Theo explained, then they'd spend the rest of the week being roasted, winnowed, milled, cocoa-pressed, refined, conched, tempered, and last, cured. There were rooms for each step. At the end of this, you were left with the round hockey puck–like disks of chocolate that were the signature creation of the Marquezes. At the end of the tour, Theo handed me one of the disks. "And now you have seen the entire life story of *Theobroma cacao* from start to finish."

"Theobroma?" I asked.

"I told you it was a family name," Theo said. He went on to explain that he had been named for the genus of the cacao tree and that his was a Greek name given by a Swede who had been inspired by the Mayans and the French. "So you see, mine is a name from everywhere."

"It's a beautiful name . . ."

"If a bit feminine, didn't you once say?"

"Where I'm from, once they found out about your name, they'd probably think you were a criminal," I said without thinking.

"Yes . . . I have often wondered why a girl from a country where cacao cannot be grown and where the substance is banned would be so interested in its production as to stay with a family in Chiapas. How did you become interested in cacao, Anya?"

I blushed. I could feel we were beginning to tread on dangerous ground. "I've . . . Well, my father died, and chocolate was his favorite."

"Yes, that makes sense." Theo nodded. "*Sí, sí*. But what will you do with all your knowledge once you go back to your home?"

Home? When would I go back home? It was nearly 80° and I could feel the chocolate growing soft in my hand. "Maybe get involved with the legalize-cacao movement? Or . . ." I wanted to tell him about me, but I couldn't. "I haven't decided yet, Theo."

"Your heart drew you to Mexico, then. That is how it is sometimes. We do things without knowing entirely why, just because our heart tells us that we must."

Theo could not have understood less how it was with me.

"Come, Anya, we need to get back to the house. The night after the harvest is done, my grandmothers always make *mole*. It takes all day, and it is a *mucho* big deal so we can't be late."

I asked him what *mole* was.

"You have never had *mole*? Now I feel very sorry for you. You are so deprived," Theo said.

Mole was indeed a *mucho* big deal, and the farmers were invited to share the meal as were all the neighbors. Castillo even came home from the seminary. There must have been fifty people crowded around the Marquezes' long dining room table. I was seated near Castillo and Luna as they were the only English speakers aside from Theo and his mother. After Castillo said grace, the feasting began.

It turned out that *mole* was basically a Mexican-style turkey stew. It was spicy and rich and pretty delicious. I had seconds and then thirds.

"You *like*," Bisabuela said with her gap-toothed smile as she scooped out another portion for me.

I nodded. "What's in this?" I was imagining shocking my family by throwing it into my usual repertoire of macaroni and cheese.

"*Secreto de familia*," she said, and then she said something else in Spanish that was beyond my still-limited comprehension.

Castillo explained, "She says that she would tell you what's in it, but she can't. She doesn't believe in recipes and with *mole*, she especially doesn't believe in recipes. It is different every time."

"But," I insisted, "there must be general parameters. I mean, what makes the sauce so rich?"

"The chocolate, of course! Didn't you guess that's why my grandmothers make it after the harvest?"

Turkey with chocolate sauce? I had certainly never heard of that. "You couldn't serve this where I come from," I told Castillo.

"That's why I never want to go to America," he told me, as he finished another portion.

I laughed at him.

"You have sauce on your face," Castillo said.

"Oh!" I picked up my napkin and dabbed the corners of my mouth.

"Let me," Castillo said as he grabbed my napkin and dipped it into his water glass. "It is a more serious business than you think." He wiped my face roughly, like I was a little kid.

After dessert, which was *tres leches*, a sponge cake drenched in three kinds of cream, one of the farmers brought out his guitar and the guests began to dance. Theo danced with every girl that was there, including his sister, his mother, and both his grandmothers. I sat in a corner by myself, feeling heavy and satisfied and barely thinking of all the problems and the people I had left behind. And then the night was over. Luz, Theo's mother, packed up the extra *mole* in takeaway containers so that everyone could have what she called *"segunda cena,"* or "second supper."

After the guests had left, I started to move the chairs back into their places. "No, no, Anya," Luz said to me as she patted me on the hand, "we do all this tomorrow."

"I'm not good at putting things off," I said.

"You must, though. Come into the kitchen. *Mi madre* makes chocolate for the family." By chocolate, she meant the drink I had been served my first morning so I was eager to go into the kitchen to see if I could figure out what was in it. Theo, Luna, and Castillo were already seated around the kitchen table; Bisabuela must have gone to bed. The counters were piled high with pots and pans and dishes and cooking detritus. On the counter nearest Abuela sat the remains of a chili pepper, an orange peel, a plastic bear half-filled with honey, and what looked like the crushed petals of a red rose.

"No, no, no," Abuela said upon seeing me, just before she covered the counter with her arms. I could tell it was meant as a joke, so I wasn't offended.

"I won't look," I promised.

Then, as often happened, Abuela said something I couldn't understand in Spanish though I did catch my name. (As she pronounced it, *Ahhn-juh.*) A second later, Theo stormed out.

"Theo," Luz yelled. "Come back, *bebé*! Abuela was only joking!" Luz turned to her mother. "Mama, you shouldn't tease him like that!"

"What?" I asked. "What just happened?"

"*No es nada*, Anya. Grandma had a little fun at Theo's expense," Luna explained.

"I heard my name," I insisted.

Castillo sighed. "Abuela said that Anya can have the recipe when she becomes a member of the family."

I looked at Abuela. She shrugged, as if to say *What can I do?* Then she began furiously whisking whatever was in the pot.

I told them that I'd go talk to him.

I went out to the living room. He wasn't there, so I took a flashlight and went outside to the orchard, which was Theo's favorite place. Though it was dark, I knew he would be there and he was, machete in hand, checking his beloved cacao trees for signs of mold.

"Theo," I called.

"Just because the season is mainly over, you can never stop watching the crops, Anya. Hold that flashlight over here, would you?"

I redirected my beam toward him.

"Look here. *Monilia*. Unbelievable!" Theo hacked away at the baby pod. The incision was not clean. Had it been my cut, Theo would have done it again.

"Here," I said, taking the machete from him. "Let me." I swung the machete.

"Not bad," Theo admitted.

"Theo—" I began, but he interrupted.

"Listen, Anya, they are wrong. I don't love you." He paused. "I just hate them."

I asked him who he meant.

"My family," he said. "All of them."

I wondered how he could hate them. They had been so wonderful and kind to me.

"It is torture living in a house of women! They are a bunch of silly old gossips. And I can't escape them. Ever since I was born, they expect me to run this place. Even my name, Anya. They expect me to do all these things, but they never ask. No one asks. I don't love you, no."

"So you said," I joked.

"No, no, I do like you very much. But ever since you came here . . . I am jealous of you! I would like to see something other than this farm in Chiapas and those factories in Oaxaca and Tabasco. I want to be like you and not know what I am going to do next."

"Theo, I love it here."

"No, it is only fun for you because you don't have to be here forever. I'd like not to see the same people every day for the rest of my life. They think I love you and in some way, I guess I do. I am happy to know someone like you. I am happy to know someone who thinks I am knowledgeable and who doesn't talk like me and who hasn't known me since I was in short pants. And maybe I do love you, if love means that I dread the day you'll leave. Because I know my world will feel so much smaller again."

"Theo, I love it here . . . And this place, your family, have been incredibly good to me. Where I came from . . . It's not what you think. I didn't have a choice. I had to leave."

Theo looked at me. "What do you mean?"

"I wish I could explain, but I can't."

"I tell you all my secrets and you tell me none of yours. Do you not think you can trust me?"

I considered this. I did trust him. I decided to tell him part of my story. First, I made him promise never to speak of this to anyone in his family.

"I am like a safe."

"A pretty noisy safe," I said.

"No, you know me, Anya. I only talk nonsense. Nothing important ever comes out of these lips."

"You say you are jealous of me, but I swear, Theo, I have far more reason to be jealous of you." I told him about my father and mother being killed and my older brother being hurt and on the lam (I decided not to mention that I, too, was on the lam) and my grandmother dying last year and how the only one left was my baby sister and it was basically killing me that I couldn't be with her every hour of every day. "I only wish I had the problems you have."

Theo nodded. His eyes and the set of his jaw told me that he wanted to ask follow-up questions, but he didn't. Instead, he was quiet for a long time. "You have done it again—made me feel like a foolish, stupid thing." He took my hand and grinned at me. "You are going to stay through the next harvest, aren't you? There's so much more I could teach you. And I like having someone to talk to."

"Yes." Of course I was staying through the next harvest. I was every bit as stuck as Theo, if not more so. I would stay here until I got word that I could go back to New York or until the Marquezes wouldn't have me anymore, whichever came first.

VII

I RECEIVE AN UNEXPECTED VISITOR
WITH AN UNEXPECTED REQUEST

D ESPITE THE FACT that I was more or less a good Catholic girl, most of my life I have hated Christmas. Not the Christ-being-born-in-a-manger bit, but the holiday itself. At first, I hated it because my mother was dead, and it was awful to spend Christmas without my mother. Once my father died, the hate grew into a true abhorrence, though. This was followed by a brief period when Christmas became only mildly loathsome to me because of all the efforts Nana made. Among other things, she'd take us to see the Rockettes (*Oh yes, there were still Rockettes; there will always be Rockettes!*) and then she'd make fun of the dancing ladies and slip us orange slices and macaroons. After Nana got sick, of course, those traditions stopped, and I returned to hating Christmas as usual. This was the first Christmas since Nana had died, and my thoughts were with Natty in New York. I could only hope that

Scarlet, Win, and Imogen were making things bearable for my sister.

Christmas at Granja Mañana was a serious business. Food was prepared for days. Whatever space could be decorated with a bow or flower or nativity was. The Marquez chocolate factory even made Advent calendars with miniature chocolate figurines inside: a lamb, a heart, a snowman, a sombrero, an egg, a cacao pod, etc. The calendars would have delighted Natty, and how I wished I could have sent her one.

Because they were a large family, the Marquezes played Secret Santa—that way, each person only had to buy one present. I had drawn Luna's name. I bought her a set of paints I had seen when Theo and I had stopped for lunch in Puerto Escondido. Theo had insisted that he pay me something for all the work I had done. Initially, I had refused but I was glad to have the money so that I could buy Luna a gift. I would pay Theo back as soon as I could.

On Christmas Eve, Isabelle, the eldest Marquez sibling, arrived from Mexico City with her husband. She was very beautiful, tall and severe with a long nose. She looked like a painting of an angel, which is to say powerful and potentially wrathful. I could tell she didn't like me. "Mother, who is she?" I heard her ask Luz in Spanish. My Spanish was improving, and though I couldn't say everything I wanted to say, my comprehension was getting decent.

"Anya. She's come to learn cacao farming. She is friends with your cousin Sophia," Luz replied.

"Ugh, Sophia. I wouldn't like anyone on that girl's recommendation. Why is this Anya person here for Christmas,

144

Mama? Doesn't she have any people of her own?" Isabelle asked.

"She is staying with us through the next harvest," Luz said. "She is a very nice girl. Your siblings are fond of her. Give her a chance, my darling."

At night, we went to Midnight Mass. The service was in Spanish, but otherwise, it wasn't that different from being in New York.

Finally, it was Christmas morning, and we exchanged our gifts. Luna loved the paint set, as I knew she would. The thing I didn't know about the Marquezes and Secret Santa was that everyone cheated and ended up buying gifts for one another anyway. Though I had only bought for Luna, I received gifts from all the Marquezes (except Isabelle, of course): a blank recipe book from the *abuelas*, a sun hat from Luz, a red skirt from Luna, and my favorite, a machete from Theo. The machete was lightweight, but still solid, and had ANYA B. carved into the brown leather–covered handle. "I did the carving myself," Theo apologized. "I couldn't fit your last name. And I'll need to sharpen it before you use it the first time." I kissed him on the cheek and told him it was perfect.

In the evening, Isabelle left to go back to Mexico City. "Well, I will probably not be seeing you ever again in my life," Isabelle said just before she kissed me on both my cheeks. Those kisses felt like nothing so much as an order to leave. I wondered if enough time had passed that I could try to contact Simon Green.

All in all, it had been a beautiful Christmas. It was only at night in my bed that I began to feel lonely. Maybe I even cried a little, but if I did, it was very softly and I doubt that anyone heard.

The next morning, I decided to sleep in. I wasn't needed in the orchard or anywhere else. I was still sleeping when Luna knocked on my door. "Anya, there's a man downstairs who says he knows you."

My heart started to beat violently in my chest. Could it be Win?

But then again, what if it was Win's father? Or emissaries of Win's father, come to take me back to Liberty?

"A young man or an old man?" I tried to control the quaver in my voice.

"Young. Definitely young," she replied. "And very handsome."

I threw on the red skirt Luna had gotten me for Christmas as I hadn't bothered to put it away yet. I put on a white blouse and then a leather belt. I slipped my new machete into my belt, just in case, and then I threw a sweater on over that. I left my bedroom and went downstairs, loosely gripping the handle of my machete.

Yuji Ono stood by the door. Instead of his usual suit, he was wearing tan pants and a lightweight black sweater.

"Surprise!" Luna said.

I looked from Yuji to Luna. "You know Yuji?"

"Of course I do," Luna said. "He was engaged to Cousin Sophia before she married someone else. Yuji said that the three of you went to school together. Though Anya must have been a class or two behind you, right, Yuji?"

146

"Or three even," Yuji said. "Anya." He examined me from head to toe, then he offered me his hand to shake. "You are looking well."

I was grateful to see a familiar face. I pulled him in to me and I kissed him, though that wasn't something the two of us usually did. I could feel him react to the handle of my machete as it pushed into his thigh, and I pulled away. "How long are you staying?" I asked.

"Two days at most. I am considering switching my cacao supplier, and I thought I should come here to see the Marquezes' farms and factories before I made a decision. Though it is the day after Christmas, Ms. Marquez and her son were kind enough to meet with me this morning. I am an old friend of the family, as Luna mentioned, and I imposed upon the relationship, I am afraid. Imagine my surprise to find that my old classmate Anya Barnum was staying with the Marquezes.

"Theo said you might be good enough to give me a tour of the cacao orchard. He says you know nearly as much about the subject as he."

"He flatters me," I demurred. "I'm barely a beginner."

We left Luna back at the house, and I led Yuji into the cacao orchard.

"I told you I would come," he whispered.

"School friends, eh?"

"It seemed the simplest explanation."

"How is everyone?" I asked. "I haven't heard anything!"

"More of that soon, Anya. I've brought you a Christmas present, one I think you will most like."

I didn't care about Christmas presents. I just wanted news. "How is my sister?"

"Well, as far as I know."

"And my brother?"

"He"—Yuji paused—"is good."

"You hesitated. Why?"

"There's a story, Anya. I will tell it to you in a moment. But Leo is not in danger, if that's what you fear."

"*Is something the matter with Leo?*" I could see no one in the orchard and so I felt safe to yell.

"Your brother, it seems, has fallen in love."

Leo was supposed to be staying with monks. Who could he have fallen in love with there? "Who is she, Yuji?"

"She is no one. A fishing-village girl, I'm told. The family is not opposed to the match if the relationship should progress."

I considered this. "And the girl doesn't mind his deficit?"

"No. I am not sure she even knows that he has one."

I spotted a bit of mold on a cacao pod. I took my machete out of my belt and I sliced off the infected pod. "Pod rot," I explained.

"I've never liked you better, Anya Balanchine," Yuji said to me.

I had not heard my real name in months and it sounded almost foreign to my ears. I sat down in the grass and leaned against the trunk of a tree.

"Say you are happy to see me," Yuji ordered.

"Of course I am happy to see you."

"Tell me about your journey here. I want to know

everything. Besides, surely I will see your family again and they will crave news of you."

And so I told him about the container on the cargo ship and the loss of my hair and learning how to grow cacao and about all the Marquezes and especially Theo.

Yuji listened quietly. "You once told me that you hated chocolate. Do you still?"

"No, Yuji. Not anymore." Being here had changed me. I could feel it.

"And Win Delacroix? Do you think of him very much?"

The truth was, I hadn't—not because I didn't love him, but because I couldn't bear the thought of him. Still, the person my heart had raced for that very morning was Win. "I don't want to talk about Win," I said.

"Do you remember that I told you I would need a favor from you someday?" Yuji asked.

I nodded. How could I forget? It had been the night I had asked him to harbor my brother in Japan.

"Well, the time has come."

I did not hesitate to ask him what he needed.

He took my hand. "I want you to marry me."

"Yuji, I-I-I-I," I sputtered. "I can't marry you. I'm seventeen. I can't marry anyone!" As I shuffled to my feet, I dropped my machete. Yuji bent down to pick it up.

"No," I said. "I'll get it myself."

"I know you are only seventeen. That is why we don't have to marry yet. You only have to become engaged to me."

"Yuji, but I don't love you."

"I don't love you either. But we must be married. Don't

you see? It is the only way to secure Balanchine Chocolate. If I am to be your husband, I can help you organize the business and protect both our interests.

"I have put a great deal of thought into this matter. Originally, I hadn't known what I would do after the Balanchine poisoning incident. Should I eliminate Balanchine Chocolate entirely? Should I watch and wait for it to destroy itself? Or should I intervene? I believe I told you as much."

He hadn't said it quite so bluntly at the time.

"But then once I met you at the wedding, I thought, 'There is another way. This girl is formidable. She might have the makings of a good leader. How much better would it be for me to join interests with this person and have the potential to make both our companies bigger and better?' I began to formulate a plan."

"A plan to marry me?"

"No. At first, I thought I could just partner you with Mickey, that the two of you together might be enough to stabilize Balanchine Chocolate once his father died. But for many reasons, this plan was a failure. I am not blaming you, Anya. You were occupied with your boyfriend and your schooling and your legal troubles. Your obligations, I suppose. You are very young. And Mickey is older, but he is too much in his father's pocket. It was too much to ask of you." He paused. "Since you've been gone, you should know that the infighting among the Balanchines has only escalated."

"Why?"

"Who can say? The election of the new district attorney? The wails of the legalize-cacao people? Whatever the reason, the rank and file at Balanchine Chocolate are angry. My point is, Anya, the only way I can intervene is if I have the authority to do so. If I am to be the husband of Anya Balanchine, I will have that authority."

"What difference do I make, Yuji?" I asked. "I'm an outsider and now a fugitive. No one cares about me."

"That isn't true. You know very well that that isn't true. You are still the heir to Balanchine Chocolate. And, because of your notoriety, yours is the face people see when they think of Balanchine Chocolate." He took my hand, but I pulled it back.

Every kind word he'd ever said to me and every good deed he'd ever done for me, I questioned. I wondered whether I'd just been groomed, whether his plan had been to use me to gain control of Balanchine Chocolate.

And yet . . . .

It could not be denied that I was in debt to him. He had helped my brother when I needed to get him out of the country and Yuji had, in part, done the same for me. How much was this worth? Or rather, how much did I owe?

"Yuji," I asked, "what happens if I refuse you?"

Yuji cupped his hand over his chin. "I would rather you did not."

"Is that a threat?"

"No, Anya. I . . . Perhaps I have gone about this the wrong way. I should have started by saying how much I admire you and how much I see in you that I think is worthy of respect. If I don't say 'love,' perhaps this is because I don't think love is all that important."

"What is important?"

151

"In a marriage, shared sensibility, mutual interests, and a common goal."

"That isn't very romantic," I said.

"Do you want me to pantomime a schoolgirl's fantasy of romantic love? Should I get down on one knee? Should I tell you that I think you are beautiful? I should think you were past the need for such meaningless gestures."

The truth was, I think I would have preferred the show, but it was too late for that. I decided to repeat my question. "What happens if I refuse you?"

Yuji nodded. "Well, we would go our separate ways. I would not be your explicit enemy though I certainly could not forget that you would not grant me the favor you owed."

"Yuji, ask me for anything else!"

"There is nothing else you have that I want." His voice was calm as always, and I found this infuriating.

"What you ask is more than a favor. You know very well that you aren't playing fair when you make such a request."

"Why is it not fair?" Finally, he was beginning to sound as frustrated as I felt. "That I like you makes me want to join forces with you instead of destroy you. Isn't that enough for you? For people like us, marriages are business arrangements, nothing more. My father thought so and your father would have told you the same thing if he were still alive."

All he said sounded reasonable, except that he was completely wrong.

"Why is it not fair?" Yuji repeated.

"Because it is my heart!"

"Because you love someone else?"

152

"Why should that matter to you, Yuji? You don't want my love anyway. You just want my compliance." I started to walk back to the house. Yuji grabbed my shoulder.

"Anya, take the night to think about what I have asked you. Think of your situation. And the situation of your sister and of your brother. I do not mean this as a threat, but as a statement of fact. I have been your devoted friend, and I would like to be even more than that if you let me."

I shook my head.

"As I said, do take the night to think about it. I will come see you before I leave." He bowed his head, then reached into his pocket and pulled out a small stack of papers tied with a red ribbon. "Here. This is your gift."

"What is it?"

"Letters," he said. "From your family and your friends. Simon Green collected them for me to give to you."

I took the small bundle from him. I had never received a paper letter from anyone. "Thank you," I said. "Really, thank you so much."

"If you reply tonight, I can bring letters back to the United States. I'm not going back there for at least a month, though. I should see your brother very soon, however."

I didn't know if I could trust him anymore, but I thanked him for the offer.

Yuji had already started walking back to the main house to say goodbye to the Marquezes when I realized that I had left my machete against a cacao tree. I told Yuji I would see him later and I ran back out to the orchard. In the clearing was Theo. He was carrying my machete and he had a sheepish expression.

"Theo!" I yelled. "Were you back there the whole time?"

Uncharacteristically, Theo would not reply.

"Did you hear my entire conversation? Were you spying on me?"

"Listen, Anya, it is nothing like that. I just followed you out to the orchard to make sure you were safe. I don't know this Yuji guy very well."

"So you were spying on me!"

"*Perdóname.* It is none of my business."

"Theo!" My heart was racing. I honestly wanted to strangle him. "You know who I am then. You know my name."

Theo sighed.

"Say my name, Theo."

"Anya, I have known who you were for weeks now. Ever since you told me about your family being killed, I was able to piece it together. Why do you think I only engraved one initial on your machete handle?"

"Did you tell anyone else about me?"

"Of course not. I told no one. Do you think I have no honor? It is like I told you: Theobroma Marquez is a safe."

"But you heard everything just now?"

"*Sí. Lo siento.*" Theo paused. "You cannot marry this man, Anya. He is a bully, and in my opinion, he is no gentleman."

Despite the conversation I had had with Yuji, I could not see him the way Theo did. I told Theo I was tired even though the only part of me that was really tired was my mouth. I didn't want to talk anymore. I wanted to go up to my room to be alone with my letters so that was what I did.

12.7.2083
Dear Anya,

I hope these letters find you well and that your voyage to XXXXXX was not too difficult. Anticipating XXXX XXX's visit to XXXXXX, Mr. Green and I collected these in hopes that they would reach you before the holidays. For the record, I did debate the wisdom of assembling this package as, should it be intercepted the letters could potentially be incriminating. However, after strongly cautioning the writers, I ultimately decided that the benefits outweighed the risks. Your father, who I served before you, would have wanted you to know during the holiday season that your friends and family have noted your absence.

On to business.

Re: the matter of Nataliya's guardianship

I have filed the paperwork, and all is proceeding as we discussed.

Re: the manner in which you left New York
Though there was some interest in your disappearance in the days after, the official word from the city is that they have neither the resources nor the manpower to devote to tracking down Anya Balanchine.

Re: when you will be able to return
There is a new regime at the DA's office and I do not know if they will be sympathetic to our interests or not.

Re: your uncle Yuri
He is still alive.

Re: the Family business
Mr. Green believes that Fats may be trying to take a more active role in the company.
Know that you are often in my thoughts and Keisha's and Grace's as well.

Happy holidays,
S. Kipling, Esq.

December 5, 2083

Dearest Sister,

(Do you like the greeting? I saw it in one of Imogen's books.)

Well, it's been almost two months since you left. At first I was mad, but then Simon Green explained that you couldn't tell anyone where you were going or even that you were going and so I've more or less forgiven you. That's the nice thing about sisters, if I do say so myself.

Things have been tolerable—at first I wrote "okay," but I thought you'd prefer a better word here. The day after you left, they came to search the house but they didn't find anything.

School is tolerable, too.

Win comes to see me sometimes. He is so nice, Anya. Seriously, he is the nicest boy in the world. He walks me to class sometimes, too, and he even came over for part of Thanksgiving.

Oh, Charles Delacroix lost the election! Did you hear that where you are? I think Win was happy that he lost, but he stood by his dad's side at the concession speech.

The other thing that happened is that Scarlet is pregnant. I know she's writing you a letter so I guess you'll hear more about that from her. She isn't saying who the baby's father is, but everyone thinks it's Gable Arsley even though he isn't her boyfriend anymore. People are being kind of mean to Scarlet at school. I found her crying in the third-floor bathroom one day, and she said how much she missed you and wished you were here. She was so sad. (The funny thing is, I had gone up there to cry myself.)

Well, that's about it. I think about you all the time. I wonder where you are, and I hope everyone's being nice to you there.

Like I said before, I'm not mad, Anya, but I wish you had told me where you were going. I am your sister, and I would rather have decided for myself whether to come with you. I don't mean to complain.

Your Loving Sister,
Nataliya Balanchine

P.S. Are you okay with the plan to have Mr. Kipling become our guardian?
P.P.S. I don't want to bother you, but when will you be home?
P.P.P.S. Writing a letter is harder than I thought it would be.
P.P.P.P.S. I haven't had that many nightmares.

30 November 2083

Anya,

A brief note to let you know that Natty is fine. She misses you a great deal, but your friends Win and Scarlet have done their best to cheer her up. I admit that the apartment does feel large without you, and we consume peas at an even slower rate than before. We all hope you can return soon. I have not been told where you are, but I know it can be a disorienting experience to be away from home for the first time. Here is a quote from one of my favorite novels—I believe you will readily recognize which one: "It is a very strange sensation to inexperienced youth to feel itself quite alone in the world, cut adrift from every connection, uncertain whether the port to which it is bound can be reached, and prevented by many impediments from returning to that it has quitted. The charm of adventure sweetens that sensation, the glow of pride warms it; but then the

158

throb of fear disturbs it; and fear with me became
predominant, when half an hour elapsed and still I was
alone. I bethought myself to ring the bell." It seems to
me good advice, Anya. If all else fails, ring the bell.

Imogen Goodfellow

My Darling Annie,

My life has fallen into utter tragedy!

Do you remember how I threw up when you were in the hospital at Liberty? Well, I never got the flu, and I thought, Oh, Scarlet, how lucky you are! But then I kept throwing up every afternoon at exactly the same time, and it turned out that I, your silly, love-crossed friend, was pregnant! And by Gable Arsley, that monster. I haven't told him it's his, but he knows, I'm sure he knows. Actually, I haven't even spoken to him since the day we broke up. He tries to talk to me, but I ignore him. I don't care. I would never raise a baby with him. I wouldn't even raise a kitten with him. I wouldn't even raise a stuffed kitten with him.

As for being pregnant... The biggest tragedy is that I was cast to be Juliet in Fall Shakespeare and then that beast Mr. Beery threw me out of the play when I told him I was with child! Can you imagine, Anya? The show goes on without me.

Also, my breasts are now as big as yours. Where before I had kiwis now I have grapefruit! I am not terribly fat yet but soon I'll have to get a Trinity skirt with an elastic waist! Can you imagine? Scarlet Barber in an elastic waist?

159

Also, also, I have no friends. All the drama people are busy in the play, and everyone else is kind of ignoring me. Win is pretty much my only friend these days. He talks about you constantly. It would be incredibly boring if I didn't miss you so much myself.

Guess who almost joined you in the ranks of "girls expelled from Holy Trinity"? Apparently, getting pregnant is frowned upon by Catholic schools. Who knew? Since I'm a senior, they're letting me stay even though it has been made clear to me that I am little more than a walking cautionary tale.

While we are on the subject... How could I have been such a fool as to sleep with Gable Arsley? Yes, he said he loved me. But he said that to you, too, and you managed to keep your legs together, didn't you?

I'm sure there are a million other things I meant to say to you, but I am sleepy. All I want to do is nap lately. And eat chocolate if I could figure out where to get any.

Merry Christmas, Annie, my love.

Je t'aime! Je t'aime! Je t'aime!

Scarlet

Anya:

Mr. Kipling asked me not to write you about the business until we have more solid information but I feel that I must. I believe that your cousin Fats is making moves to seize the business from Yuri and Mickey. If that happens, Balanchine Chocolate will be left in utter disarray. Fats is a

160

small-time guy with no understanding of the larger organizational politics at play. I am at present trying to arrange for your return. I have meetings set with Bertha Sinclair in January to see what can be done. When the time comes, I will contact you.

Remember, Anya. You are still the <u>daughter of Leonyd Balanchine</u>. You have more claim than Yuri, Mickey, or Fats. The sooner you can come home, the better. Even an Anya Balanchine back in Liberty is superior to an Anya Balanchine that no one can see or talk to. Apologies if I have overstepped my place.

Your humble servant,
Simon Green, Esq.

Annie,

This is not a love letter.

I think you would laugh at me if I wrote you a love letter, so I'm not going to. If this accidentally becomes one, you have my permission to throw it in the fire.

So, here it is:

I ate an orange, and I thought of you.

I did a lab on tissue decomposition, and I thought of you.

I took the train to visit my sister's grave in Albany, and I thought of you.

The band played the Fall Formal, and I thought of you.

I saw a girl with dark curly hair on the street, and I thought of you.

I took your kid sister to Coney Island—she's the only one who is as blue as I am. Natty's the smartest kid in the world and good company. Still, I thought of you.

You have often said that you think the only reason I ever liked you was because of who my father is—that I liked you because my father wished I wouldn't. Well, it might interest you to know that Dad lost the election. He's out of politics, and I still like you.

There it is.

This is not a love letter.

Win

———◆———

I read my letters, then reread them. I put them to my face so I could feel where my friends' hands had been. I even tried to smell the letters, but they didn't smell like anything except ink and fresh paper. (If you've never smelled it, ink is oddly bitter, like blood almost.)

After so much time of hearing nothing, the news was overwhelming. When I left New York, I buried Anya Balanchine, and in Mexico, I had become this other girl. I liked this other Anya, but reading these letters reminded me that I couldn't be her forever.

A knock at my door. "May I come in?" Theo asked.

I stuffed the passel of letters under my pillow.

"Yes," I said. Theo entered, closing the door behind him.

"I was told boys weren't allowed in the girls' rooms at Casa Mañana," I said.

"This is a special case. I thought you might need to talk," Theo said.

He already knew my secret, and so I decided to unburden myself to him. It was the first time I had had a true confidant since Nana.

Theo didn't interrupt me and he was silent a while before speaking. "Here is what you do. First, you do not marry this Yuji Ono. He does not love you, Anya, and it is obvious that he is only interested in expanding his influence. Second, do not go back to New York"—he paused—"ever."

"But Simon Green said that everything is falling apart. And Yuji, whatever his interest, said the same thing."

Theo shrugged. "What difference does it make if the chocolate company falls apart? One set of crooks or another. What is it to you? Why do you care if it's the end of Balanchine Chocolate? This company has only brought you pain."

I considered what he said. "I . . . I suppose I care because my father built that company. And if Balanchine Chocolate dies, it will be like my father dies all over again."

Theo nodded slowly. "You love Balanchine Chocolate like I love cacao."

"I wouldn't say *love*, Theo."

"No, you speak the truth. Love isn't right. It isn't right for me either. Sometimes I hate cacao." Theo looked at me. "You don't love Balanchine Chocolate. You *are* Balanchine Chocolate."

"Yes. I suppose I am."

"You have to go back. But I also think it is no good if you are in too much of a rush. You should let your lawyers do the job of arranging your return. Until then, you can help me prepare the next harvest."

"Thank you, Theo." I did feel better having discussed this with someone.

"*De nada.*" Theo stood and walked to the door. Suddenly, he stopped. "Anya, tell me one thing."

"Yes?"

"Was there a letter from your boyfriend in that packet?"

I laughed at Theo. "*Sí*, Theo, and it was ridiculously romantic."

"Read it to me."

"I'm not going to do that."

"What? It is good for me to know. Don't you want me to learn from such a master Casanova as this Win?"

I shook my head at Theo. I walked over to the door, kissed Theo on the cheek, and then pushed him out the door. "You should go. Quick, Theo, quick! Before Luz catches us!"

In the morning, when I went outside, Yuji Ono was waiting for me. "Let's go speak in my car," he said.

The car was black with thick, tinted windows, possibly bulletproof glass. His driver was the same heavyset man I had seen in New York last spring when Nana died. Yuji asked the driver to leave, and then he opened the door for me so that I could join him in the backseat.

"Yuji," I began. I hadn't been able to sleep the previous night because I'd been going over what I would say to him so many times. My words came out sounding rehearsed. "Yuji, first I want to thank you for your friendship. I have had no better friend than you. My family has had no better friend than you either."

Yuji bowed his head slightly, but said nothing.

"I want to thank you very much for the offer of"—it was difficult for me even to say the word—"marriage. I know you wouldn't make it lightly, and I am truly honored. But, after much consideration, I want you to know that my mind hasn't changed. I am too young to marry anyone, and even if I weren't young, I wouldn't want to make a decision of this magnitude while I was away from home and while I have been out of contact with my advisers for so long." I had on purpose decided not to mention anything about *love*.

Yuji studied my face, and then he bowed his head. "I respect your decision." He bowed his head again, this time even more deeply.

I offered Yuji my hand to shake. "I hope we can still be friends," I said.

Yuji nodded, but he didn't shake my hand. What I thought at the time was that his feelings were too hurt. "I must go," he said.

He opened the car door, and I left. His driver got in, and then they were gone. I watched the car until I could no longer see it.

Although it was 70° that day, an uncommon wind swirled past, whipping my hair across my face, leaving me with goose-bumped arms and an unpleasant chill in my heart. I went inside to see if I could borrow a sweater from Luna.

I REAP WHAT I SOW

IMMEDIATELY AFTER NEW YEAR'S, we resumed work in the orchard. I'd wake before dawn, pile my nascent ponytail atop my head, and take my place beside Theo and the other workers. I was stronger than when I had arrived, so I found the January labors easier. I mentioned this to Theo, and he laughed at me.

"Anya," he said, "we are in siesta season."

"Siesta season?"

"Most of the last crop has already been harvested, and the second cacao season, which is always the lesser one anyway, is yet to begin. So, we work a little. Eat a big lunch. Take a nap. Work a little more. *Siesta season.*"

"It's not that easy," I protested. To prove my point, I showed him my hands, which had fresh blisters from using my new machete. Theo had sharpened it for me as promised.

"*Ay*, your poor hands." He took my hand and he held it up

against his own rough palm. "You will get calluses like these beauties of mine soon enough." Suddenly, he smacked his hand against mine.

I took the Lord's name in vain. "That hurt!" I yelled.

Theo found the whole thing hysterical. "I was trying to help your calluses along," he said.

"Yeah, that's hilarious. You're a jerk sometimes, you know that?" I walked away from him. Since the incident with his grandmother, Theo occasionally went out of his way to show me just how much he didn't fancy me.

Theo put his hand on my shoulder.

I shrugged him off. "Leave me alone."

"*Perdóname.*" He got down on one knee. "Forgive me."

"Siesta season or not, this work isn't easy, Theo."

"I know that," he said. "Yes, I know that very well. In other countries, they let little children work these orchards. The parents sell them off for nothing. I tell you, it disgusts me, Anya. So, if my cacao costs a bit more because I have to pay real farmers a real wage, I think it is worth it. Superior farmers make a superior product. My cacao tastes better and I do not have to hang my head at church, you know?"

In a low voice, I asked him if he knew what kind of cacao the Balanchines used.

"Not mine," Theo said. "I cannot know specifically what kind your family uses but most of the black market chocolate brands have to use the cheapest cacao they can get. It is the reality of running a black market business."

Theo was too nice to say what that reality probably meant for my family.

"I did meet your father once," Theo said. "He came to Granja Mañana to meet my parents about switching to our cacao. My parents thought he was going to do it, too. I remember Mama and Papa were even looking into buying more acreage. Supplying Balanchine Chocolate would have meant a lot of money to our family. But about a month later, we heard that Leo Balanchine had died and so the deal was off."

Theo had met my father! I lowered my machete. "Can you remember anything Daddy said?"

"It was a long time ago, Anya, but I remember him telling me that he had a son about my age."

"My brother, Leo. He would have been pretty sick back then."

"How is he now?" Theo asked.

"Better," I told him. "Much better. Yuji Ono even said that Leo was in love." I rolled my eyes.

"You don't believe this?"

I didn't have a reason not to believe Yuji Ono. It was something else. In the past several months, I'd come to realize how little I knew Leo. I'd always tried to protect him, but I think that had led me to not really see him. I shrugged. "If it's true, I'm happy for him."

"Good for you, Anya. The world needs more love not less. Speaking of which, I want to take you down to the factories to see the chocolate we make for Saint Valentine's Day. It's the busiest time of year for our factories."

I asked him why they made chocolate for Valentine's Day.

"Are you kidding, Anya? We make chocolate hearts and

candy boxes and just about everything else! What do they do in your country on Valentine's Day?"

"Nothing. It's not really a very popular holiday anymore." I remembered that Nana had told me that Valentine's Day used to be more of a big deal.

Theo's mouth dropped open. "So, no chocolates? No flowers? No cards? *Nada*?"

I nodded.

"How sad. Where is the romance?"

"We still have romance, Theo."

"You mean your Win?" Theo teased me.

"Yes, him. He's very romantic."

"I'll have to meet this Casanova when I go to New York."

I asked him when he was coming.

"Soon," he said. "As soon as you leave, I am following."

"What about the farm and the factories?"

"This? She runs herself. Let my sisters and brother do it for a change." Theo laughed. "Be ready for me, Anya. I'm staying with you. I expect nothing less than the red carpet."

I told him I'd be happy to have him anytime he wanted to come.

"Anya, tell me something serious now."

I already knew that this wouldn't be at all serious. "Yes, Theo."

"You cannot actually prefer this Win to me. You and I have so much more in common, and in case you haven't noticed, I really am adorable."

I ignored him and went back to my work.

"Anya, this Win . . . Is he very tall?"

The next day, Theo and I drove down to the factories, where they produced the products he had described and goods beyond that, too: hand creams and health powders and even a packet for making Abuela's hot chocolate.

By the time we'd returned to Granja Mañana, it was after sunset, and the workers had gone home. I accompanied Theo to make a quick check of the orchards. I was walking slightly ahead of him when I heard the sound of rustling leaves. It could have just been a small animal, but I felt for my machete anyway. As I was doing that, a pod with the telltale signs of *Monilia* distracted me. I bent down to slice it off.

A second later, Theo yelled, *"Anya, turn around!"*

I thought Theo might have been joking, so I continued what I was doing.

"Anya!"

Still squatting, I turned my head over my shoulder. Behind me was a large man. The first thing I noticed was that he was wearing a mask; the second thing I noticed was the gun. The gun was pointed at my head, and I was sure I was going to die.

Out of the corner of my eye, I could see Theo running toward me with his machete out.

"Don't!" I screamed. *"Theo, go inside!"* I didn't want Theo to end up dead, too.

My scream must have startled the masked man because for one second he hesitated. The masked man turned just as Theo struck him on the shoulder with the blade of his machete. The gun went off. There was a silencer, so it made very little sound. I could see the spark of the gunfire. I could tell that Theo had been hit but I didn't have time to figure out where. I picked up my own machete and I raised my arm. Without even thinking about it, I sliced off the masked man's hand. It was his right hand, the hand that held the gun. It was tough, but my machete had just been sharpened and I'd had so much practice with the cacao pods. (*Aside: In retrospect, it would feel like the moment I'd been training for since November.*) The only major difference between slicing off a human hand and a cacao pod was the blood. So much blood. The blood sprayed across my face and my clothes, and for a moment, all I could see were out-of-focus spots of red. I wiped my eyes. The man had dropped his gun (and his hand) and I could see him clutching his wrist as he ran deep into the rain forest, into the dark. We were miles away from a hospital. He'd probably bleed to death. "*Fffffiiiiick-errrrr,*" he howled. Or something like that, I couldn't quite make it out.

I turned to where Theo lay on the ground.

"Are you okay?" I asked him. The light was fading, and I couldn't see where he was bleeding.

"I'm . . ."

"Where were you hit?" I asked him.

"I don't know." He moved his hand weakly in the general direction of his chest area, and my heart began to petrify.

"Theo, I have to go inside to get help."

He shook his head.

"Theo!"

"Listen to me, Anya. Don't tell my mother what happened."

"You're being insane. I have to tell your mother what happened. I have to get you help."

Theo shook his head. "I am going to die."

"Don't be dramatic."

"Mama will blame you. It is not your fault, but she will blame you. Do not tell any of them who you are."

Theo saying that made me sure it was my fault.

"I'm going now!" I pulled my hand from Theo's grasp and I ran into the house.

The next several hours were a blur. Luz, Luna, and I put Theo on a stretcher we'd improvised out of bedsheets and then we dragged him to the truck and then we drove to the hospital, which was a half hour away. By that time, Theo had passed out.

I explained to Luz and Luna as best I could what had happened even though I couldn't understand it myself.

When we got to the hospital, I repeated the story to the local police, and then they asked me questions, which Luna translated for me. *No, I didn't know the man. No, I didn't see his face. No, I don't know why he was in the orchard. Yes, I cut off his hand. No, I didn't take it with me. It should still be on the ground with his gun.*

"And your name?" one of the cops asked.

I didn't answer right away so Luna answered for me. "She is Anya Barnum. She is staying with us in order that she might learn the cacao business. She is Theo's very good friend and a dear friend of our cousin, and I do not like the way you are questioning her."

Finally, the police left to go see if they could find the gun and the hand and the one-handed masked man.

Luna patted me on the arm. "It is not your fault," she said.

"We have many rivals in cacao. It's never turned to violence before but . . . I don't understand any of this!" Luna began to weep.

A doctor came out to talk to us. "The bullet ricocheted through his lung and his esophagus. Theo's condition is serious, but he is stable for now," the doctor said in Spanish. "You could go home if you like."

"Is he awake?" Theo's mother asked.

The doctor said that Theo's family could go in, so I went out to the lobby to try to place a call.

It was nearly ten, which meant it was nearly eleven in New York. I knew it was dangerous to call as it could potentially lead the authorities right to me, but I needed to talk to Mr. Kipling. I needed to go home.

I dialed Mr. Kipling's home number. Though it was late, he answered the phone immediately and I could tell he was completely awake. When I said who it was, he didn't even sound surprised to hear from me.

"Anya, how did you find out so quickly?"

For a second, I was confused. I wondered if he had somehow heard about Theo Marquez being shot. "How did *you*?" I asked.

"I . . . Your sister, Natty, called me. She's here with me right now."

"Why would Natty call you? Why is Natty with you? Why isn't Natty at home?"

"Wait," Mr. Kipling said. "I don't think we're talking about the same thing. Why don't you speak first."

"Theobroma Marquez was shot. And I think the hit man was trying to kill me."

173

Mr. Kipling cleared his throat. "Oh, Anya, I'm so sorry."

"I . . . I want to come home. I don't want to bring any more trouble to the Marquezes. Even if I have to go to Liberty," I added.

"I understand," Mr. Kipling said in a distracted way.

"What were you talking about before?" I asked.

"Anya, the situation here is very grave, and there's no nice way for me to put this. Imogen Goodfellow is dead."

I crossed myself. I could barely absorb this news. How could I be living in a world where Imogen Goodfellow was dead? Imogen, who loved paper books and who had taken such good care of Nana. Imogen, my friend.

"She died protecting your sister. There was an attack on the street outside the apartment, and Imogen came between Natty and a bullet. Imogen died on her way to the hospital. Natty was immediately brought to my house. She was hysterical, of course. She had to be sedated. Anya, are you still there?"

"Yes." I couldn't believe what I was hearing. "Do you think the attack on me and the attack on Natty are related?" As I asked the question, I knew it was true.

"I fear they could be," Mr. Kipling said. "Until I got your call, I had hoped the attack on your sister was just a random act of violence."

"Someone trying to dispatch the children of Leonyd Balanchine?" Suddenly, I thought of my brother in Japan.

"Leo," Mr. Kipling and I both said at the same time.

"I'll call Yuji Ono," I said.

I hung up with Mr. Kipling and immediately placed another call. This time, to Yuji Ono. He didn't pick up. I wanted to scream but I knew there were sick people trying to sleep in the hospital. How was it possible that I had no way of reaching my brother other than through Yuji Ono? I had put too much faith in this man, who—let's face facts—I had barely known.

I was about to try Yuji Ono again when Luna tapped me on the shoulder. "Anya, Theo wants to see you now."

I nodded and followed her into his hospital room. I could not help but be reminded of Win and of Gable. Everywhere I went, I brought violence.

Theo was hooked up to a ventilator. Despite his tanned skin, he looked gray and bloodless. He couldn't speak to me because of the tracheotomy but they had left a slate by his bed so that he could write messages. *Anya*, he wrote, *I love you like my sister . . .*

The stroke of his handwriting on the screen was weak.

I love you like my sister but you have to go. The man who did this . . .

I put my hand over his hand. I knew what he was trying to write. "The man who did this might come back to finish the job. Or a different man. You love me like your sister, but you love your family more. They aren't safe as long as I'm here," I said.

Theo nodded miserably. There were tears in his eyes.

"I'm so sorry, Theo. I'm so, so sorry. I'll get my things and I'll leave tonight."

He grabbed my hand and squeezed it. *Where will you go?* he wrote.

"Home," I said. "I'm not sure I ever should have come here.

I don't think you can really run away from things. They tend to follow you."

I am glad you came. Mi corazon es . . . The slate began to slip off the bed, and before I could catch it, it fell to the floor. Theo put his hand over my heart.

"I know, Theo," I said. "Promise not to think about me anymore. I just want you to get well."

Luz stayed at the hospital with her son. In the car, Luna barely spoke to me. I told myself she was tired.

When we arrived at Granja Mañana, Luna went to the kitchen to update her grandmothers on Theo's condition, and I went straight to my room to pack. I had arrived in Mexico with nothing and I was leaving with a mostly empty recipe book, a couple of letters, and a machete. I decided to burn the letters. I didn't yet know how I'd be traveling and I didn't want to implicate any of my friends if I should be arrested. I went down to the kitchen to ask for a match. Bisabuela was the only one there and she didn't seem at all surprised by my request. She just said I should burn the letters in the stove. I lingered over Win's letter but I still managed to burn it. The only one I decided to keep was Imogen's. Here, I started to cry.

Bisabuela put her arm around me. "What is it, *bebé*?" she asked. She didn't speak much English and I still didn't speak much Spanish.

"My friend died," I said.

"Theo is no dead. He is hurt, but will live." I could see the confusion in her eyes.

"No, not Theo, someone else. Someone from *mi casa*"—I paused—"and I need to go home."

At that moment, Luna walked into the kitchen. "Anya, you can't leave right now!"

I wanted to explain. I knew that if I explained, she would want me to go, too. But I had promised Theo. "I have to go."

Luna crossed her arms. "How can you go right now? You have become like family to us. And while Theo is sick, you could help so much on the farm. Please, Anya."

I told her that I had called home while we were waiting in the hospital and that someone in my family had died, and I needed to get back to New York immediately. All this was true, of course.

"Who in your family?" Luna demanded.

"The woman who watches my sister."

"So not even your real family, then!"

I said nothing.

"If you leave right now, I will never forgive you! Theo will never forgive you either!"

"Luna, Theo wants me to go."

"What do you mean? He would never say that. You're lying, Anya."

"I'm not . . . The thing is, Theo said he understood that I needed to get back to the city."

"You are a different kind of person than I thought you were," Luna said. Her face was covered with tears and snot. I went over to her and tried to embrace her, but she pushed me away and then ran out of the kitchen. Bisabuela followed after her.

I went down the hall to Luz's office to use her telephone. (I felt bad about the cost, but this was an emergency.) I called

Yuji Ono again. He still didn't pick up. Then I called Mr. Kipling. Simon Green answered the phone. "Anya, I've arranged for a private plane to meet you at the Tuxtla airport."

"A private plane? Isn't that expensive?"

"Yes, but there was no other way that was quick. You don't have identification and even if you did, the nearest airport to you doesn't have regular flights to the States, and honestly, this is the best I could do on short notice. You'll be flying into the airport on Long Island. When you land, I'll be there to meet you. If the authorities have become aware of your movements, you may be arrested, but I thought we had a better chance of avoiding that by flying into Long Island."

"Yes, of course. Have you talked to Leo? Or Yuji Ono?" I asked.

"I've been trying Yuji Ono but I haven't gotten him yet," Simon Green said. "I'll keep trying. Anya, how are you?"

"I'm . . ." I couldn't come up with an answer. "I want to see Natty."

I hung up with Simon Green and then I dialed Yuji Ono again. I was about to despair when Yuji finally answered. "Hello, Anya," he said. His manner seemed awkward but I didn't know if that was because of the conversation we'd had the last time we met.

"Why haven't you been picking up your phone?"

"I have been occupied with—"

I realized that I didn't care what he'd been doing. "I need to know if Leo is okay," I said.

For a second, Yuji didn't answer me. "There was an explosion."

"An explosion? What kind of explosion?"

"A car bomb. I am sorry, Anya. Your brother's girlfriend was hurt very badly, and—"

"What about Leo?"

"I am sorry, Anya. He is dead."

Oddly, I knew I was not going to cry. Some once fleshy part of me had turned to bone, and I was no longer capable of such displays. "Was it you, Yuji? Did you plan all of this? Just because I wouldn't marry you? Was it you?"

"It was not me," Yuji said.

"I don't believe you. No one else had the information. No one else knew where I was and where Leo was. No one except you!"

"There were others, Anya. Think about it."

I couldn't think. Leo was dead. Imogen was dead. Someone had tried to kill Natty and me. Theo was gravely injured because he had gotten in the way of a bullet meant for me.

"Say who you mean."

"I choose not to speculate. I can only say that it was not me," Yuji repeated, "but I did not intervene to stop these events from happening either."

"Are you saying that you let my brother die? That you would have let me die, too?"

"I said what I meant. I am very sorry for your loss."

I hung up on him. I was sorry, too. If it turned out he had killed my brother, Yuji Ono would have to die.

X I

I LEARN THE COST OF FRIENDSHIP; MONEY STILL MAKES THE WORLD GO 'ROUND

The plane was barely larger than a bucket, and the ride was bumpy. Though I hadn't slept for over twenty-four hours, my mind would not rest. I couldn't stop thinking of Leo and every time he'd ever asked to come with me and I'd refused him. I'd been the one to send him to Japan. Had that been a mistake? Why had I ever trusted Yuji Ono? How could Leo be dead when we hadn't spoken in almost ten months? None of this seemed possible.

My eyelids would begin to flutter shut, and it would seem as if unconsciousness might temporarily absolve my guilty conscience. That was when I'd start thinking of Imogen. When Nana had died, I had accused Imogen of unspeakable acts. Imogen, who'd done nothing but take care of Nana and Natty and me. And now Imogen was dead. Dead because of us.

I'd think of Theo. They'd said he was stable, but he could still die. What would they do on that farm without him? Theo ran that place, and because of me, he wouldn't be able to do that for a very long time. And then my thoughts would return to my brother. I began to feel as if I would never sleep again.

The plane touched down on Long Island around four in the morning. I looked out the window. The tarmac was reassuringly desolate. As I walked down the steps, I got my first whiff of New York air—filthy and sweet. Though I had loved Mexico and though I wished I were returning under better circumstances, I was happy to be restored to my city. It was freezing, by the way. I was still wearing the clothes I'd worn to visit the factories in Oaxaca, where it had been 72°.

A solitary car, black with tinted windows, was parked in the lot. On the driver's side, the window was rolled down about three inches, and I could see Simon Green sleeping. I tapped on the glass, and Simon started. "Annie, come in, come in," he said as he popped the locks.

"No cops," I pointed out once I was inside.

"We were lucky." He put the key in the ignition. "I thought I'd take you back to my apartment in Brooklyn. Imogen's murder has attracted a fair amount of attention as I'm sure you can imagine, and there are too many people around Mr. Kipling's apartment and yours."

"I need to see Natty tonight," I insisted. "If she's at Mr. Kipling's, that's where I need to be."

"I'm not sure that's such a great idea, Annie. Like I said—"

I interrupted him. "Leo's dead, Simon, and I don't want my sister to have to hear it from anyone but me."

For a moment, Simon was speechless. "I'm so sorry. I'm so, so sorry." He cleared his throat. "I honestly don't know what to say." Simon shook his head. "Do you think Yuji Ono was involved?"

"I don't know. He said he wasn't but . . . It doesn't matter right now. I need to get to Natty."

"Listen, Annie, you've experienced a very great loss. You're tired and you're overwhelmed, for completely understandable reasons, so please take my advice here. It will be much better for you and for Natty if you aren't apprehended by the police tonight. We should negotiate your surrender if that's something deemed necessary. Let me take you back to my apartment—no one will look for you there—and I promise to bring Natty to you as soon as it can safely be arranged. I don't want to compromise either of you."

I nodded my consent.

We didn't speak for the rest of the drive though I could tell Simon Green wanted to. "There's blood on you," he commented as we drove into Brooklyn. I looked at my sleeve: the blood was either Theo's or the masked man's. It had been that kind of day.

Simon's apartment was on the sixth floor of a walk-up with squeaky, steep stairs. After three flights, I wanted to give up. Sometimes, it's these little acts that seem the most unbearable. "I'll sleep on the landing," I told him.

"Come on, Anya." Simon pushed me onward.

Finally, we were in his apartment. It was large for a city place, the lone residence on the floor, but there was only one room. The ceilings were vaulted as the room was just below the roof. Simon Green lived in an attic. He told me that I could have his bed, and he would sleep on the sofa.

"Annie, I'm going to drive back to Mr. Kipling's now. Can I get you anything?" He stifled a yawn, then he took off his glasses and wiped them.

"No, Simon, I'm fine. I'm—"

(I told you that I would never cry again, and while I certainly believed that at the time, it turned out this was overly optimistic on my part.)

I fell to my knees and I could feel them bruise as they hit the wooden floor. "Leo," I sobbed. "Leo, Leo, Leo. I'm sorry. I'm sorry. I'm sorry . . ."

Simon Green put his hand awkwardly on my shoulder. It was not a particularly comforting gesture yet I felt grateful for the weight of him.

I had started to hyperventilate and I felt like I might choke. Simon helped me out of my bloody clothes like I was a toddler, and then he loaned me a T-shirt and helped me into bed.

I told him that I wanted to die.

"No, you don't."

"Everywhere I go, there is violence. And I can't escape because I bring violence with me. And I don't want to live in a world where my brother is dead."

"There are other people who love you and count on you, Anya. Think of Natty."

"I do think of her. All the time. And what I think is that maybe she'd be better off without me."

Simon Green put his arms around me. I had never been so close to him before, and he smelled of peppermints. He shook his head. "She wouldn't. Trust me, she wouldn't. Natty only gets to be Natty because you have to be Anya." Simon gently extricated himself from me. "Get some sleep. By the time I'm back, I'll have Natty with me, okay?"

I heard the door close and lock twice, and then I did fall asleep.

When I awoke, a white cat with a black spot on its side was looking at me. The cat was in my sister's arms. "Did you know that Simon has a cat?" Natty asked.

I had been too distracted to notice, though now that she mentioned it, his place did smell faintly of litter.

"She's a fighter," Simon Green reported. "She likes to go out during the night."

I looked at Natty. Her eyes were red from crying, and she looked even older and taller than the last time I had seen her. Natty set the cat down, and I stood and fiercely pulled my sister toward me. Her head banged against mine. That head was higher than I was used to it being.

"I knew you'd come," Natty said. "I knew it."

In order to give us some privacy, Simon Green said he was going on a walk.

"It was awful, Annie. We were on the street outside the apartment, and a man in a mask came out of nowhere, and Imogen tried to give him her purse. 'Take it,' she said. 'Just take it. I only have twenty-two dollars.' He grabbed the purse, and for a second, we thought he was going to leave, but then he threw it to the ground. All of Imogen's things spilled out—her books and her diary and everything! I remember thinking that it would be impossible to get everything back in the bag. The man started to point his gun at my head, but Imogen jumped in front of me. And this was when she got shot, but I didn't know where. It was weird because the shot was so close I didn't know if I'd been shot and I fell to the ground, too. I guess it was the sound of the bullet."

"You were smart to do that," I told her. "They thought they'd gotten you and so they left."

"What do you mean 'gotten me'?"

She didn't know that the attacks had been meant to kill the three of us. She didn't know about Leo. I told her what had happened to me in Mexico and then I told her about Leo.

She did not cry. She stayed completely still.

"Natty?" I moved to touch her arm, but she pulled away.

I looked at her face. She seemed thoughtful, not devastated. "If you don't trust Yuji Ono, how do you know for sure that Leo's dead?" she asked.

"I know, Natty. Yuji Ono would have no reason to tell us that Leo was dead if he wasn't."

"I don't believe it! If you haven't seen the body, you can't know that someone's dead for sure!" The pitch of Natty's voice had grown impossibly high. She sounded squeaky, hysterical. "I want to go to Japan. I want to see for myself!"

Simon Green returned from his walk. It had begun to rain, and his hair was damp. "Think about it, Natty," he said gently. "You and Anya were both attacked on the same night. You and Anya were both lucky to escape. Your brother wasn't."

Natty turned to me. "*This is your fault!* You sent him to Japan. If he was here, he might be in jail but at least he would be alive. He would be alive!"

Natty ran into Simon Green's bathroom and slammed the door behind her.

"It doesn't lock," Simon Green whispered to me.

I went in after her. She was standing in the tub with her back to me. "I feel stupid," she said tearfully. "But I didn't know where else to go."

"Natty, I did send Leo to Japan. It's true. If that was a mistake, it was also the best I could do at the time. We will go to Japan to bury Leo but we can't go right now. It's too dangerous and I have things to arrange here."

Slowly, Natty turned to me. Her eyes were furious and red, but dry. She opened her mouth to speak and that was when the tears started. "He's dead, Annie. Leo's dead. Leo's really dead." She took the wooden lion statue out of her pocket. "What will we do? No Imogen. No Leo. No Nana. No Mom and no Daddy. We have no one, Anya. We truly are orphans now."

I wanted to tell her that we had each other, but it felt too corny to say. Instead, I drew her closer to me and let her cry.

Simon Green knocked on the door. "Anya, I have to take Natty back to Mr. Kipling's now. He doesn't want to compromise my house as a safe place for you."

I took Natty's face in my hands and kissed her on the forehead, and then she was gone.

I sat down on Simon Green's bed, and the cat jumped onto my lap. I considered the cat, and she considered me with gray eyes that reminded me of my mother's. She wanted to be scratched so I obliged her. There were so many things I couldn't solve, but this cat's itch I could relieve.

I tried to imagine what advice Daddy would have given me for the situation I was in.

What would Daddy say?

Daddy, what would you do if your brother was dead because of decisions you made?

I came up with nothing. Daddy's advice only went so far.

The room got darker and darker, but I didn't bother to turn on the light.

Imogen's memorial service was two Saturdays away, and I felt Natty and I both needed to go to pay our respects. The problem was that I was still a fugitive, and so I decided it was time for me to resolve that situation. I couldn't very well spend the rest of my life holed up in Simon Green's attic studio. The six days I'd already passed there had been long enough.

The only person I was allowed to call from the apartment was Mr. Kipling.

"Three things," I told Mr. Kipling and Simon, who were at the office. "I want to go to Imogen's service. I want to surrender myself to the state. I want to arrange for Natty to go to a boarding school, preferably one in another state or abroad."

"Okay," Mr. Kipling said. "Let's take these one at a time. The boarding school is easy enough. I'll begin talking to that teacher of Natty's she likes so much."

"You mean Miss Bellevoir."

"Yes, exactly. And I agree that this is a good plan, though potentially one we won't be able to put into motion until next school year. Moving on. I fear that if you attend Imogen Goodfellow's service, you'll be arrested, which means that we have to arrange the terms of your surrender before that time."

"Even before the events of last Friday, I'd been talking to the new district attorney's office," Simon Green interjected.

"You do remember that Bertha Sinclair's staff people made the contribution to Trinity, don't you?" I asked.

"That was just politics," Mr. Kipling said. "It was nothing against you, and it's actually an advantage to us that Charles Delacroix lost because the Sinclair regime can basically disavow all the actions of the predecessor. The Sinclair people sounded amenable to arranging something with you. A short stay at Liberty and then probation, maybe. People are more sympathetic to you than you would think." Mr. Kipling said that he had planned to meet with Bertha Sinclair on Wednesday, but would try to get the meeting pushed up.

I asked if they had any leads on who had orchestrated the hits on my family.

"We've been discussing it. It was so complex," Simon Green began. "Three countries. Three hit men. It could only have been someone with the ability to arrange a multifaceted operation."

"And yet the mission was also 66 percent a failure," Mr. Kipling added.

"Maybe the person wanted to fail?" Simon Green suggested. "You said you didn't think it was Yuji Ono but when I think of the other obvious options, it doesn't seem like it could be anyone else. Jacks is in jail. Mickey doesn't have the skill set. If not Yuji Ono, the only person I can think of is Fats. He comes from the other side of the family but some people think he's making moves to overthrow Mickey. It would be to his advantage to have all the direct descendants of Leonyd Balanchine out of the picture."

I didn't think Fats would want to kill me. "But what if it *was* Mickey? He knew where I was and I'm pretty sure he knew where Leo was, too. What if after I lost favor with Yuji Ono, Mickey decided to avenge his father's shooting? Yuri Balanchine has been ailing a very long time, and it hasn't been a pretty decline."

"Lost favor with Yuji Ono?" Mr. Kipling asked.

"After he proposed marriage and she refused him," Simon Green explained.

"Marriage?" Mr. Kipling asked. "What's this? Anya's too young to marry anyone."

"I never told you about that," I accused Simon Green.

Simon Green paused. "When I gave Yuji Ono the letters, he informed me of his plans. I didn't know for sure that you had refused him. I just guessed that was what had happened."

"Simon," Mr. Kipling said in a hard voice. "If you knew that this proposal was going to happen, you should have told me. Maybe we could have arranged to get Leo out of Kyoto!"

"I apologize if I made a gaffe."

"Mr. Green, this is far more than a gaffe."

Mr. Kipling certainly had a point, but I decided to defend Simon Green. He had been kind to me since my return, and I knew that I had not been the easiest houseguest. (*Although I've chosen not to dwell on it in this account, I had been depressed and unable to sleep since my return.*) "Mr. Kipling, as of December twenty-sixth, I, too, knew about the proposal. I could have called you but I didn't think there was any need to move Leo. I honestly didn't think that what had happened with Yuji Ono was serious enough to merit a change. It is my fault much more than Mr. Green's."

"I appreciate you saying that," Mr. Kipling said. "But it is my and Mr. Green's job to advise you. It is our job to anticipate the worst-case scenario. We have been negligent in this duty once again. Simon and I will discuss this later." Mr. Kipling closed by saying they would call me once they had spoken to Bertha Sinclair's office.

I hung up with my counsel and looked at the clock. It was nine in the morning. The day stretched out ahead of me, everlasting and awful. I missed having the cacao farm to tend or a school to go to or friends. I was tired of Simon Green's apartment, which had begun to reek of cat litter. I was tired of not even being able to go for a walk.

I looked out the window. There was a park but no one was in it. I didn't even know what part of town I was in. *(Brooklyn, yes, but, readers, there are many parts of Brooklyn.)* Where did Simon Green live? I'd been staying there almost a week and I hadn't bothered to ask.

I needed to go out. I borrowed a puffy coat from my host's closet, making sure to pull the hood up. Since I didn't have a key, I couldn't lock the door, but what difference did it make? No one was going to rob a sixth-floor apartment. And even if they did, there was nothing worth taking. Simon Green's apartment was notable if only for its curious lack of personal effects.

I made my way down the flights of stairs.

Outside it was even colder than when I had landed. The sky was gray and it looked like it might snow.

I walked for maybe a half mile, up a hill and past bodegas and schoolchildren and vintage clothing stores and churches. No one noticed me. Finally, I arrived at the gates of a cemetery. Walk long enough in any direction and you'll usually find one.

The name on the gates was Green-Wood Cemetery, and though I hadn't been there since Daddy's funeral, I remembered that this was where the family plot was. My mother was buried here, too, and Nana, whose grave I still hadn't visited. *(Aside: This also solved the mystery of what part of Brooklyn Simon Green lived in—he lived in Sunset Park, where many of the Balanchines had lived before moving to the Upper East Side.)*

I made my way through the cemetery. I thought I remembered the general direction of the family plot, but I still had to backtrack a couple of times. Eventually, I realized I had no idea where I was going so I went to the information center. I typed *Balanchine* into the ancient computer and out popped a location on a map. I set out again. It was getting colder and grayer by the minute, and I didn't have gloves and I wondered why I had even come.

The plot was on the outer edge of the cemetery: five headstones and room for several more. Soon, my brother would join them here.

Nana's grave was the freshest. The stone was small and

simple, and the inscription read BELOVED MOTHER, WIFE, AND GRANDMOTHER. I wondered who had written that. I kneeled, crossed myself, and then kissed the stone. Though the custom of leaving flowers at gravesides had fallen out of fashion, I'd seen pictures of it and I wished I'd brought some. Even a couple of Nana's loathsome carnations. How else to say *I was here?* How else to say *I am still thinking of you?*

My mother's grave was next to Nana's. Her stone was heart-shaped and read I AM MY BELOVED, AND MY BELOVED IS MINE. No mention of the children she had left behind. How little I had known her, and how little she had known me. Some weeds were growing around the edges of her grave. I took my machete out of its sheath and sliced them away.

Daddy was behind my mother: ALWAYS LOOK ON THE BRIGHT SIDE. Atop his headstone, someone had set three green sprigs of what looked like an herb. The sprigs, weighted by a small rock, were fresh and had obviously been placed there recently. I bent down to smell them. It was mint. I wondered what the mint meant and who had placed it there. Probably one of the men who had worked for Daddy.

You might think me heartless, but I didn't feel all that much at the sight of these graves. Tears were not forthcoming. Leo's death, Imogen's death, Theo's shooting—I was wrung dry. The dead were the dead, and you could cry as much as you wanted, but they weren't coming back. I closed my eyes and mumbled the halfhearted prayer of a fledgling cynic.

When I got back to Simon Green's place, he was waiting for me. "I thought you'd been killed," he said.

I shrugged. "I needed to get out."

"Did you go to see Win?"

"Of course not. I took a walk."

"Well, we have to go," Simon Green said. "We have a meeting with Bertha Sinclair, but we have to be downtown in twenty minutes. She'll only talk to you in person."

I was wearing Simon Green's coat and also his pants and his shirt, but there wasn't time for me to change.

We raced down the stairs and then we were in a car. At reasonably great expense, Simon Green had borrowed one in the wake of the shootings so that Natty and I could avoid public transportation.

"Do you think there'll be paparazzi?" I asked him.

He said he hoped not but he wasn't sure.

"Do you think I'll be sent immediately to Liberty?"

"No. Mr. Kipling arranged with the Sinclair people for you to be under house arrest at least until Imogen's funeral."

"Okay." I leaned back in the seat.

Simon Green patted me on the knee. "Don't be scared, Annie."

I wasn't. I felt a certain sense of relief knowing that I wouldn't have to hide anymore.

The DA's office was in a part of downtown that I and everyone else in my family avoided—the whole area was dedicated to law enforcement. There weren't any press on the steps, but a legalize-cacao rally was going on in front of the district attorney's office. It was only about twelve people, but they were noisy enough.

"There've been a lot of these lately," Simon Green commented as he pulled up to the curb in front of Hogan Place.

"I'll drop you here. Mr. Kipling's waiting for you in the lobby."

I pulled up the hood of Simon Green's coat. "Why have there been a lot of pro-cacao rallies lately?"

Simon Green shrugged. "Times change. And people are tired of chocolate being so scarce. Your cousin Mickey isn't doing his job right. His dad's sick, and he's distracted. Good luck in there, Anya." Simon Green reached over me to open the car door, and I got out.

I pushed my way through the rally. "Take one," said a girl with braids. She handed me a pamphlet. "Did you know that cacao has health benefits? The real reason it was banned was because of the cost of production."

I told her I had heard something about that.

"If we didn't have to rely on unscrupulous mobsters to supply us with chocolate, there would be no risks at all!"

"*Cacao now. Cacao now. Cacao now,*" the throng chanted, and pumped their fists.

I, the spawn of the unscrupulous mobsters, pushed my way through the madding crowd and into the lobby where Mr. Kipling was indeed waiting for me.

"Quite a scene out there," he said. He pulled down my hood, then kissed me on the forehead. We hadn't seen each other since Liberty. "Annie, how are you, my dear?"

I didn't want to dwell on how I was because nothing good could come of that. "I'm eager to be through with this meeting. I'm eager to get on with things."

"Good," Mr. Kipling said. "Let's go in."

We gave our names at the desk, then took the elevator to the tenth floor. We gave our names again, then waited for what felt like forever in a nondescript lobby. Finally, an assistant escorted us into the office.

Bertha Sinclair was alone. She was in her late forties and shorter than me. She had metal braces on her legs and they squeaked as she maneuvered across the room to shake my hand. "Anya Balanchine, fugitive—welcome," she greeted me. "And you must be the persistent Mr. Kipling. Please, friends, have a seat."

She returned to her chair. Her knees didn't bend very well, so she had to fall backward into it. I wondered what had happened to Bertha Sinclair.

"So, prodigal daughter, your sister's nanny is dead, your brother has disappeared, and you have returned to the Isle of Mannahatta and laid yourself at my door. Whatever shall I do with you? Your lawyer thinks you should be given probation and time served. What do you think, Anya? Wouldn't that be a touch soft for a girl who shot someone and executed a jailbreak?"

"In my opinion," Mr. Kipling said, "Charles Delacroix had no right to return Anya to Liberty when he did. He was thinking of his campaign, not of what was in the public's best interest. Although Anya was wrong to escape, she escaped from a situation that was essentially unjust."

Bertha Sinclair massaged her knee. "Yes," she said. "I can't say I disagree with you if what you're *essentially* saying is that Charles Delacroix is an ambitious, arrogant prick.

"Really," Bertha Sinclair continued, "I should thank you, Anya. The luck of you being on that bus! My campaign staff and I beat that Anya-and-the-DA's-son story until it was dead, dead, dead. The irony is, I doubt the public cared nearly as much as Charles Delacroix thought they cared. And, in my opinion, it wasn't you but his misjudgment that cost him the election. Or, to put it another way, handed it to me." Bertha Sinclair laughed. "So, here's how I see it, friends. I don't care about chocolate. I don't care about Anya. I certainly don't care about Charles Delacroix's son."

"What *do* you care about?" I asked.

"Good question. The child doesn't speak much, but she does speak well. I care about my people and about doing what's right for them."

That seemed terribly broad to me.

"I care about getting reelected. And getting reelected takes many resources, Mr. Kipling."

Mr. Kipling nodded.

"The Balanchines were good friends of this office once. And I imagine that they could be again." At that moment, Bertha Sinclair took a tiny notepad out of her desk and scribbled something on it. She handed the note to Mr. Kipling. He looked at the paper. Out of the corner of my eye, I could see that it was a number with at least four zeros, maybe more.

"And what does this number buy us?" Mr. Kipling asked.

"Friendship, Mr. Kipling."

"Specifically?"

"Friends have to trust each other, don't they?" She began writing another note on a sheet of paper. "I never understood why paper fell out of fashion. It's so convenient to destroy. Put something down digitally and it's viewable by everyone and exists forever. Or at least it has the illusion of forever, but it's always potentially mutable. People had so much more freedom when there was paper. But that's neither here nor there." She set her pen on her desk and handed the second note to me:

> 8 ds Liberty
> 30 ds house arrest
> 1 yr probation
> 1 yr surrender passport

I folded the paper in half before nodding my consent. Even if we were paying for it, this still seemed more than reasonable. I'd need to go to Japan at some point but I imagined that could be worked out later.

"After you're released from Liberty, I will give a press conference where I say that I am prepared to let bygones be bygones. I will ridicule the way Charles Delacroix handled your situation—let me tell you, I'll enjoy that part very much. And then, as far as I'm concerned, that will be the end of it. You'll have your life back. And we'll all be friends for life unless you do something to irritate me."

I looked into Bertha Sinclair's eyes. They were so brown they were almost black. It was tempting to say that her eyes were as black as her heart or some such nonsense, but I don't believe that eye color is anything more than genetics. Still, there was no denying that the woman was corrupt. Daddy used to say that corrupt people were easy to deal with because they were consistent—you could, at the very least, count on them to be corrupt.

"I'll have someone arrange with Mr. Kipling when you'll return to Liberty," Bertha Sinclair said as we stood to leave.

"I'd like to go now," I heard myself say.

Mr. Kipling stopped. "Anya, are you sure?"

"Yes, Mr. Kipling." I had not been afraid of Liberty. I had been afraid of being left there indefinitely. The sooner I went back, the sooner I could get on with sorting the rest of my life out, and I had quite a bit of sorting to do. "If I go back now, I'll be out in time for Imogen's funeral."

"I think that's admirable," Bertha Sinclair said. "I'll escort you to Liberty myself if you'd like."

"The press will pick up the story if District Attorney Sinclair accompanies you," Mr. Kipling warned me.

"Yes, that's the idea," Bertha Sinclair said, rolling her dark, dark eyes. "Anya Balanchine has surrendered herself to me and, a week later, I show her leniency. It's a big, beautiful show, Mr. Kipling, and quite the coup de théâtre for my office, no?" She turned to me. "We'll go from here."

Mr. Kipling and I went to the lobby. When Bertha Sinclair was out of sight, I handed him my machete, which had still been attached to my (Simon Green's) belt.

"You brought this to the DA's office?" Mr. Kipling was incredulous. "It's lucky the city is too broke to fix those old metal detectors."

"I forgot I had it," I assured him. "Take care of it. It's my favorite souvenir of Mexico."

"Do you mind my asking if you've had opportunity to use

this . . . Is it a machete?" He held it with two fingers, like it was a fouled diaper, before slipping it into his valise.

"Yes, Mr. Kipling. In Mexico, it's what they use to remove the cacao pods from the trees."

"That's all you used it for?"

"Mainly," I told him. "Yes."

"Anya Balanchine! Anya! Look over here! Anya, Anya, where have you been?" The crowd of paps waited to pounce on us at the Liberty Island Ferry.

I had been instructed by Bertha Sinclair not to say anything, but I couldn't help turning my head. I was relieved to hear my name again. I was hustled into the boat, and Bertha Sinclair stopped to talk to the media.

Although she was a woman, Bertha Sinclair's voice carried every bit as much as Charles Delacroix's had, and from the boat, I could still hear her. "This afternoon, Anya Balanchine surrendered herself to me. I want it on the record that Ms. Balanchine's surrender was completely voluntary. She'll be detained at Liberty until we figure out what the best course of action is," Bertha Sinclair boomed. "I'll have an update for you all soon."

It was my fourth time at Liberty in less than a year and a half. Mrs. Cobrawick was gone, replaced by Miss Harkness, who wore athletic shorts all day long and in all weathers it seemed. Miss Harkness had no interest in celebrity, by which I mean my infamy. This made her an improvement over Mrs. Cobrawick. Mouse had also left—I wondered if she had ever gone to see

Simon Green—so I had a bunk to myself and no one to eat with in the cafeteria. The length of my stay was too short to bother with making new friends.

The Thursday before my scheduled release, I was sitting at a half-empty table in the back of the cafeteria when Rinko sat down across from me. Rinko was alone, and sans hench-women, she looked smaller somehow.

"Anya Balanchine," Rinko greeted me. "Mind if I join you?"

I shrugged, and she set her tray down.

"Clover and Pelham both left just before you came. I'm outta here next month."

"What did you do anyway?"

Rinko shrugged. "Nothing worse than you. I got in a fight with some dumb *beyotch* at my school. She started it, but I beat her until she was in a coma. So, like, whatever. I defended my-self. I didn't know she'd end up in a coma." She paused. "You know, we're not that different." She flipped her shiny black hair over her shoulders.

We *were* different. I had never beaten anyone into uncon-sciousness. "How so?"

She lowered her voice. "I'm from coffee people."

"Oh."

"Makes you tough," she continued. "If someone crosses me, I'm gonna defend myself. You're the same way."

"I don't think so."

"You shot your cousin, didn't you?" Rinko asked.

"I had to."

"And I had to do what I had to do." She leaned across the table and lowered her voice. "You look all sweet and innocent, but I know it's just a front. Rumor has it you sliced off someone's hand with a machete."

I tried to keep my face neutral. No one in the States knew what had happened in Mexico. "Who told you that?"

Rinko ate a scoop of mashed potatoes. "I know people."

"What you heard . . . It isn't true," I lied. Part of me wanted to ask who exactly she knew, but I didn't want to give myself away to a person I had never particularly liked or found trustworthy.

Rinko shrugged. "I'm not gonna tell anyone, if that's what you're worried about. Not my business."

"Why did you sit here today?"

"I've always believed that you and I should be friends. Someday, you might want to know someone who knows something about coffee. And someday, I might want to know someone who knows a thing or two about chocolate." She waved her hand around the cafeteria. "The rest of these kids . . . They'll go home, and maybe they'll be all reformed and crap. But you and me, we're stuck in it. We were born in it, and we're in it for life."

A bell rang, which meant it was time for us to return to afternoon exercises.

I was about to pick up my tray to put on the conveyor belt when Rinko intercepted it. "I'm going that way anyway," she said. "Be seeing you, Anya."

On Saturday morning, I was released. I had worried that something would happen to make our deal go bad, but Mr. Kipling made the campaign contribution and the corrupt Bertha

201

Sinclair kept her word. I took the boat back from Liberty, and Mr. Kipling was waiting for me at the dock. "So you're prepared, there's quite a crowd wanting to hear from Bertha Sinclair," Mr. Kipling informed me.

"Will I need to say anything?"

"Just smile at the appropriate times."

I took a deep breath and approached Bertha Sinclair, who shook my hand. "Good morning, Anya." She turned to face the press who had gathered. "As you know, Anya Balanchine surrendered herself to me a week ago. I've had these past eight days to reflect on the matter and"—she paused as if she hadn't known exactly what she would do the whole time—"I don't wish to cast aspersions on my predecessor but I think the way he handled Ms. Balanchine's situation was atrocious. Whether the initial sentence she received was just or unjust, my predecessor had no business returning Anya Balanchine to Liberty last fall. That move was politics, pure and simple, and in my opinion, everything that happened after should be forgiven. Unlike my predecessor, I think there is law and then there is justice. I want you to know that your district attorney is more interested in justice. A new administration is a good time for new beginnings. This is why I've decided to release Anya Balanchine, this daughter of Mannahatta, from Liberty, time served."

Bertha Sinclair turned to me and gave me a hug. "Good luck to you, Anya Balanchine. Good luck to you, my friend." She squeezed my shoulder with a hand that felt like a claw.

X I I

I AM CONFINED; REFLECT ON THE
CURIOUS NATURE OF THE
HUMAN HEART

THE MORNING OF MY RELEASE coincided with Imogen's funeral. We drove straight from the pier to Riverside Church,
where Mr. Kipling and I were to meet Simon Green and Natty.
Immediately after the funeral, I was to begin my month of
house arrest. I was wearing a black dress of Nana's that Mr.
Kipling had sent to Liberty for me. The dress was uncomfort-
ably tight across my shoulders. All that machete wielding had
bulked me up, I guess.

Riverside Church was about a mile north of the Pool, which
was where the New York branch of the Balanchine Crime
Family conducted its business. As we drove past the Pool, I
gripped the car door handle and wondered if the people in
there—my relatives—were the ones responsible for Imogen's
and Leo's deaths.

The church was next to the river (hence the name
Riverside), and the late January wind was sharp and brutal.

When we got there, a cadre of press stood shivering on the steps.

"*Anya, where have you been all these months?*" a photographer yelled at me.

"Here and there," I replied. I would never implicate my friends in Mexico.

"Who do you think killed Imogen Goodfellow?"

"I don't know, but I'm going to find out," I said.

"Please, folks," Mr. Kipling said. "This is a very sad day, and Anya and I just want to go inside to pay our respects to a beloved colleague and friend."

Inside, there were only about fifty people, even though the venue probably seated fifteen hundred or more. Natty and Simon Green were in the back. I wedged myself between them, and Natty squeezed my hand. Natty had a coat draped over her shoulders. The coat wasn't hers but I knew that coat all the same. I knew what it felt like to have my face pressed up against it. I knew what it smelled like—smoke and pine trees—and what it looked like when it hung on the shoulders of the boy I loved.

I looked down the row. On the other side of Natty sat Scarlet, with a slightly rounded belly and rosy cheeks. "Scarlet!" I whispered. Scarlet waved to me. I reached over Natty to set my hand on Scarlet's abdomen. "Oh, Scarlet," I said. "You're . . ."

"I know. I'm enormous," Scarlet replied.

"No, you're lovely."

"Well, I feel enormous."

"You're lovely," I repeated.

Scarlet's blue eyes grew glassy as a lake. "I'm so glad you're home and safe." She stood up and kissed me on the mouth. "My dear and best friend."

Scarlet leaned her head back so that I could see the person on the other side of her: Win. Natty hadn't just borrowed the coat.

I had known I would have to see him again, but I hadn't known it would be so soon. I hadn't had time to steel myself against him. My cheeks burned and I couldn't think. I leaned over Natty and Scarlet and found myself stupidly holding out my hand to Win.

"You want me to shake your hand?" Win whispered.

"Yes." I wanted to start the business of touching him. I wanted to touch his hand, then other things, too. But I figured we'd start with hands. "I . . . Thank you for coming."

He grabbed my hand and we shook. When he tried to let go, I didn't want to release him but I did.

During our separation, I had wondered if I even still liked him. This now seemed like little more than a pathetic coping mechanism. Of course I still liked Win. I more than liked him. The question was, could he possibly still like me? After all these things I'd done, I mean.

It was deeply wrong to have such concerns at a funeral, I know.

Win looked at me—his gaze was steady, if not overly warm—and he nodded formally. "Natty wanted us here," he whispered.

My heart started to pound in my chest. The *thrum* was so hard and loud that I wondered if Natty and Scarlet could hear it.

At that moment, the funeral began, and we had to rise, and

I reminded myself that Imogen, my friend, was dead, and that she had died saving my sister.

After the service, we went to the front of the church to pay our respects. "I'm so sorry," I said to Imogen's mother and sister. "Natty and I are both so sorry. Imogen took such good care of my grandmother and my sister. We'll miss her more than we can even say."

"I will always remember her books and how funny she was," Natty piped up in a soft but strong voice. "I loved her and I'll miss her so much."

Imogen's mother began to weep. Her sister pointed a finger straight at Natty and said, "You shouldn't be here, girly. You got Imogen killed."

At that point, Natty started to cry, too.

"You people!" Imogen's sister spat the words at us. "*You people* are criminals! I told Imogen about *you people*, but she would never listen. 'This family is a plague,' I said. 'It isn't safe. There are other jobs.' And look how she ended up!" the sister continued. "*You people* are the lowest, the worst."

"Hey, that's not called for," Win defended us.

The sister turned to Win. "You'd be wise to run, young man. Run as fast as your legs will take you. Or you'll end up just like Imogen."

"I'm very sorry for your loss," I said, in order to draw the focus away from Natty and Win.

The sister turned toward me. "There's a circus out there, thanks to you! Go now, and take your filthy circus with you."

I hustled Natty out of the church. Win put his arm around her. He leaned down and whispered in her ear, "You were very brave to come here. No matter what that woman said. It was the right thing to do."

The apartment was not altered in any material respect from how it had been the morning I had left it, and yet it wore its difference like a widow wears a veil. Imogen was gone, and Leo would never return. As for me, I felt years older, though not particularly wiser.

"Remember, Annie, you can't leave the apartment until February twenty-eighth without clearing it with me," Mr. Kipling said.

As if I could forget. A tracker had been injected into my lower calf just north of my tattoo that morning, and the area was swollen and pink, like overly kissed lips. Still, there was a relief to being confined. I had time to contemplate my next move.

Simon Green told me that security had been hired to stand guard outside the apartment (just in case anyone tried to finish off Natty and me) and then both he and Mr. Kipling left. Scarlet and Win had gone straight home after the funeral.

"Isn't it weird how quiet it is?" Natty asked.

I nodded. But it was also rather peaceful.

Early Sunday morning, before we even would have been up to dress for Mass had I not been confined, the doorbell rang.

Still drowsy, I stumbled down the hallway. I looked through the peephole. It was Win's mother of all people, and behind her, Win. I was about to open the door when I stopped. Maybe this will seem strange to you, but I wanted to watch him without him knowing I was watching him. I hadn't had the chance to really look at him at the funeral. He was still so handsome. His hair had grown out from the summer and he was wearing hats again—a red plaid wool hunting cap with furry earflaps! His coat was the same one from the funeral and from Fall Formal 2082. I loved that coat. I loved him in that coat. I wanted to unbutton it and crawl under the flap and button myself in and forget everything that had happened.

They rang the bell again, and I jumped back at the sound.

Natty came into the hallway. "Annie, what are you doing? Open the door!" She pushed past me and did just that.

Win and his mother were both carrying sacks. "Anya, hello!" Jane Delacroix said. "I hope you'll forgive me but I've brought you and Natty some groceries and other things. I know it's a difficult time for your family. And, in my small way, I wanted to help."

"Please," I said, "come in." I looked at the plump bags. "And thank you for this."

"It isn't much," Win's mother said. "The least I could do."

Natty took Win's bag, then she led Win's mother into our kitchen.

Win hung back, as if he didn't want to get too close to me. Maybe I was being paranoid though, maybe he was allowing me a respectful space. "I'm so sorry about your brother, and Imogen, too," he said.

I nodded. I kept my gaze directed at his shoulder. Now that I wasn't safely behind the door, I was almost scared to look into his eyes.

"My mother, she really did insist," Win said. "I wasn't planning to come until the afternoon."

"I . . ." I felt sure I was about to say something really incisive, but nothing came. I giggled—yes, giggled—and I put my other hand over my chest in an attempt to muffle the sound of my stupid, dogged heart. "Win," I said, "your father lost the election."

He smiled, and I could see his pretty, pretty teeth. "I know."

"Well, tell him when you see him that I'm not—" I giggled again; this giggling was getting embarrassing; I can only account for it by saying I was still not quite awake. "Say that Anya Balanchine isn't at all sorry!"

Win laughed, and his eyes softened a bit around the corners. He took the hand that was over my heart and he pulled me in close to him until my face was up against that wool coat I knew so well. "I've missed you so long, Annie. You barely seem real to me. I'm worried I'll turn around and you'll disappear."

"I'm not going anywhere for a while," I told him. "House arrest."

"Good. I'll like knowing where you are. I like this new DA already."

There were so many things to be sad and worried about, but at that moment, I couldn't be sad and worried. I felt brave and sturdy and better around Win. It would be so easy for me to love him again. Abruptly, I pushed him away.

"What is it?" he asked.

"Win . . . What Imogen's sister said at the funeral is true. The people around me do tend to get hurt. You know that." I

209

touched his hip with my fingertips. "We don't have to start this whole thing up again. Just because you met a girl you liked in high school doesn't mean you have to stay with her forever. I mean, no one does that. No one with any good sense at least. I"—I had been about to say something about how I considered myself to be a person with ample good sense but then I said something else—"I love you." I did; I was certain. "I love you but I don't want—"

Win interrupted me. "Stop," he said. "I love you, too." He paused. "You underestimate me, Annie. I'm not blind to your faults. You keep too many secrets, for one. You lie sometimes. You have trouble saying the things in your heart. You have an awful temper. You hold a grudge. And I'm not saying this next one is your fault, but people who know you have a disturbing tendency to end up with bullets in them. You don't have faith in anyone, including me. You think I'm an idiot sometimes. Don't deny it—I can tell. And maybe I was an idiot a year ago, but a lot has happened since then. I'm different, Anya. You used to say I didn't know what love was. But I think I learned what it is. I learned it when I thought I had lost you over the summer. And I learned it when my leg ached something awful. And I learned it when you were gone and I didn't know if I'd ever see you again. And I learned it every night when I'd pray that you were safe even if I never got to see you again. I don't want to marry you. I'm just happy to be near you for a while, and for as long as you'll let me be. Because there's never been anyone else for me but you. There will never be anyone else for me but you. I know this. I do. Annie, my Annie, don't cry . . ."

(Was I crying? Yes, I suppose I was. But I was still so awfully tired. You can't possibly hold this against me.)

"I know that loving you is going to be hard, Annie. But I love you, come what may."

I looked him in his eyes, and he looked me in mine. His eyes were not the blindly adoring ones that had looked on me a year ago. They were clear. So were mine except for the fact that tears were starting to make everything blurry.

"So, do you like anything about me?" I asked.

He considered my question. "Your hair," he said finally. "And you were a semi-decent lab partner last year. When you were around, that is."

"I had to cut most of my hair off. It's only half grown back."

"I know, Anya. It's a great loss."

"Hair's not much to build a relationship on anyway," I said.

I rose up onto my tiptoes and I kissed him on the mouth. The first kiss was soft, but then I kissed him again. The second was so hard, my teeth cut into my lip and I could feel myself start to bleed. I lapped up the blood with my tongue and laughed. Win moved in to kiss me again. "Stop, Win!" I said. "I'm bleeding."

"I didn't think there'd be bloodshed this soon," he commented.

I admitted that I'd hoped to avoid it.

"Maybe we should take it slow," he said, as he pulled me to him again. "Make sure no one gets hurt."

"Let's do that," I said. And then I took off his hat. He'd been wearing that silly hat this whole time. And I touched his hair, which was springy and silky and clean.

The heart is so very peculiar. How light and how heavy it can feel at the same time.

How light.

Re: the remaining twenty-nine days of house arrest. I couldn't go out, which meant I couldn't begin to address all the problems in my life. Win came over every day, and Scarlet came over most days, and the month passed quickly enough.

We played Scrabble, and Natty and I cried some, and I basically ignored everyone who tried to contact me. I didn't know what I wanted to say to anyone yet.

About three weeks in, there was a snowstorm, the kind that makes everything stop in the city. Win somehow made it uptown and he stayed for three days.

I had been having trouble sleeping at night, thinking of Leo and of Theo and of Imogen and even sometimes thinking of the man I'd likely killed in the grove, and I was glad for Win's company.

"Unburden yourself," Win insisted. "Confess."

"I can't."

"You'll die if you keep it all in, and I want to know these things."

I looked at Win. I could not visit a priest and I was tired of keeping secrets. And so I told him everything. I told him about growing cacao. I told him about the marriage proposal. I even told him about slicing off someone's hand with a machete. What it had felt like to slice through human bone. What the hand had looked like there, lying in the grass. What the man's blood had smelled like. I now knew that not everyone's blood was the same.

"Do you think Yuji Ono was behind the killings?" Win asked.

"He said he wasn't. And I think I believe him."

"So was it Mickey? Or Fats? Or someone else entirely?"

"I think it was Mickey," I said after a bit. "I haven't heard from him since I got back to New York. And I imagine once I lost favor with Yuji Ono, Mickey might have thought he was avenging his father's shooting by killing Leo."

"You think the other shootings were just meant to scare, not kill?"

"Yes," I said.

"Nothing has happened since then," Win said. "Maybe all of this is over."

But it wasn't over. If Leo was dead, I had to make someone pay. I furrowed my brow, and Win ironed it out with his fingers.

"I can read your mind right now, Annie. If you go after whoever you think killed Leo, they'll come after you or Natty. It won't ever end."

"Win, if I don't go after them, they'll think I'm weak. Why shouldn't they just come back at me and Natty to finish the job? I'll be holding my breath forever. I don't want to seem like a person who can be trifled with."

"What if you said you had no interest in the chocolate business? What if you said you were going back to school and then to college to become a crime scene investigator and good luck to everyone else?"

"I wish I could . . ."

"Why? Why can't you? I don't understand."

"Because . . . I'm a convict, Win. I have a record. I've missed tons of school. And no high school, let alone college, will want me. I'm stuck."

"There's one somewhere. We'll find one. I can help you, Annie."

I shook my head.

"Okay, what if we just go somewhere where no one knows us? We take Natty and leave. We could change our names, dye our hair."

I shook my head again. I had tried running and I didn't want that kind of life for Win, for Natty, or for me.

"It's more than that, Win. When I was in Mexico, something changed for me. I realized that I will never escape chocolate. And so there was no point in running away from it or even hating it anymore."

"Dad's always saying that it should never have become illegal in the first place."

"Really? Charles Delacroix says that?"

"All the time. Usually just before mentioning that it would be terribly convenient for him if I never saw you again."

I laughed. "How is my old friend?" I asked.

"Dad? He's awful. He's completely depressed. He's grown a beard. But who cares about him? Let's talk about me. I've never been happier in my whole life that Dad lost an election." Win paused to look at me. "You really sliced off that hit man's hand with a machete?"

"I did." I wondered if it had been a mistake to tell him

that, if he would love me less, knowing how violent I could be. "I don't regret it, Win. I don't regret shooting my cousin when he shot you either."

"My girl," he said, just before he took me in his arms.

I offered to show him my machete, and he said he'd like to see it, so I led him into my bedroom. After Mr. Kipling had returned it to me, I'd hidden the machete between my mattress and the box spring.

"Close the door," I told him.

"This is starting to feel like a trick," he said.

"Now, turn off the light."

On the final morning of my confinement, just as I was about to leave the apartment for tracker removal, I received a phone call from Mickey Balanchine.

"Annie, how are you?" he asked. "I'm sorry. I haven't had time to contact you, but I wanted you to know that I'm awfully sorry about what happened to you and Natty and especially Leo. Poor kid. It's insane is what it is."

I didn't say anything. I didn't know whether I believed him.

"That's not the reason I'm calling, however. I just wanted you to know that Yuri's dead." Mickey sniffled loudly. "I want to be able to tell you that Dad didn't suffer much, but I don't know. I just don't know. This last year since the shooting has been horrific, Annie.

"Dad mentioned you not long before he passed. He said that you were a fine girl. I think he liked you better than me." Mickey laughed weakly. "I think you reminded him of his little brother."

He meant Daddy.

"I know . . . I know that things are strange right now, but it would mean a lot to everyone if you came to the service."

I told him I would try and then I hung up the phone. Mickey did not sound as if he had just arranged for the murder of my brother. Then again, I did not sound like a girl who could slice off someone's hand with a machete either.

But I had been that kind of girl, and if the situation called for it, I knew I could be again.

XIII

I ENGAGE IN RECREATIONAL CHOCOLATIERING; RECEIVE TWO NOTES AND A PACKAGE

Mʀ. ᴋɪᴘʟɪɴɢ ᴡᴀꜱ ᴍʏ ᴅᴀᴛᴇ to the tracker-removal party at the East Ninety-Third Street police station. The police station had sentimental associations for me, as it was the same place I'd been detained after I'd been arrested for poisoning Gable Arsley. As for the tracker? Though it wasn't supposed to be painful coming out, it was. The officer said I should go to a doctor to have it checked out in case it was infected. "These little buggers are supposed to be thrown away, but," he apologized, "occasionally we do use them twice. Budget cuts, you know."

As I was leaving, another police officer handed me a note:

> *Congratulations on your release. Please come*
> *see me at Rikers. I have information for you.*
> *Fondly,*
> *Your Cousin*

I assumed it was Jacks, though—let's face facts—I probably had more than one cousin in prison.

Outside, the snow had melted, and the day felt positively tropical for the end of February in New York.

"So, now what?" Mr. Kipling asked me.

The prior evening, I had lain awake in my bed, thinking of the things I needed to do once I was free. The list was so long that I had to get up to write it on my slate:

1. Find a boarding school for Natty.
2. Find a school for me.
3. Find out who killed my brother and Imogen.
4. Avenge my brother's death.
5. Figure out how to get my brother's ashes from Japan.
6. Figure out what to do with my life post–high school (should I ever manage to graduate, that is).
7. Call Granja Mañana to see how Theo is doing (not from a traceable line, of course).
8. Get a haircut.
9. Go through Imogen's things.
10. Buy birthday present for Win (Saturday market?).

But I didn't want to do any of that just then. "Mr. Kipling," I said, "would it be all right with you if we walked around for a while?"

We went the long way, going west to Fifth, which took us past Little Egypt. Little Egypt looked as decrepit as ever.

"When I was a kid," Mr. Kipling said, "I thought this was the coolest place in the world. I loved the mummies."

"What happened?" I asked.

"Everyone and everything went broke. And no one thought the mummies were worth saving, I guess." Mr. Kipling paused. "And now it's this idiotic nightclub."

I knew it well.

In front of Little Egypt, I could already detect that there were more black market products being hawked out in the open than when Charles Delacroix had been acting as district attorney. I walked past a chocolate dealer. You wouldn't have known chocolate was being sold, as there was no product in sight. The table was covered with a dark blue velvet cloth and approximately one hundred matryoshka dolls sat atop it. Everyone knew what matryoshka dolls meant. I walked over to the table. Mr. Kipling asked me if I was sure I wanted to do that. "What if someone is watching?"

We'd paid off Bertha Sinclair so I thought I was pretty much in the clear.

"You have Balanchine Special Dark?" I asked the vendor.

The vendor nodded. He reached under the table and produced a single bar. I could tell from the wrapper that it wasn't real. The colors were off, and the paper had an unappetizing, gritty matte finish. It was probably some cheap, 1 percent cacao chocolate in a counterfeit Balanchine wrapper. I bought the bar anyway. Ridiculously, the vendor wanted ten dollars for this knockoff.

"Are you serious?" I asked. A bar of Balanchine Special Dark was usually three or four dollars, tops.

"Supply's been scarce," the vendor replied.

"You and I both know this isn't even Balanchine," I said.

"What are you? Some kind of expert? Take it or leave it."

I put the money on the table. Despite the cost, I was curious to see what was being sold in my father's name.

Mr. Kipling stood a bit away from me while I was making this transaction. He didn't want to be disbarred, I suppose.

I slipped the chocolate into my bag, and then Mr. Kipling walked me back to my apartment.

"Should we talk about schools?" Mr. Kipling asked.

What was there to talk about? "Homeschooling seems like the only option at this point. I'll study at home and try to get my GED before summer."

"And after that? College?"

I looked at Mr. Kipling. "I think we both know that I am no longer college material."

"That isn't true!" He argued with me for a while, and I ignored him. "Anya, your father wanted you to go to college."

If he'd lived, that might have been an option. "And Natty will," I replied.

"But you? What will you do instead?"

In the short term, I needed to find out who had killed Leo and ordered the hits on the rest of my family. As for long-term goals? It had begun to seem pointless for me to make any. "Mr. Kipling, I'm booked up," I said lightly. "I've got my uncle's funeral to attend, a cousin to visit in prison, and Win's birthday party is next Saturday. The only thing I wonder is how I ever had time for school at all."

Our walk had come to an end, and Mr. Kipling was giving

me an annoyingly tragic face. "Okay, my dear, I'll arrange to hire you a tutor."

Just outside the front door of the apartment, someone had placed a medium-size box and an envelope. I carried both inside and set them on the kitchen counter. The envelope had no postmark, but envelopes were unlikely to contain explosives, so I opened that first.

It was a note:

> Dear Anya,
>   Perhaps you remember me? My name is Sylvio Freeman. Syl. I had opportunity to meet you last fall when you interviewed at my school. I am aware that you are now back in the city, and for the moment at least, appear to have put your legal difficulties behind you. I had hoped you might speak at a Cacao Now meeting about your experiences. If this suits you, please come—

I tossed the note aside without bothering to finish reading it. I turned to the box. The postmark indicated Japan, and the return address was the Ono Sweets Company, which, of course, meant Yuji Ono. The box was surprisingly heavy. I debated whether to open it. There could be a bomb inside. And yet I doubted that if Yuji Ono wanted to finish me off, he would send a package with his own return address on it.

I retrieved my machete from my bedroom and sliced open the box. Inside was a gallon-size plastic bag filled with dust, and a small white card.

Leo.

Dear Anya,

    I am sorry I am not able to come to New York to deliver this myself. I am detained by both business troubles and poor health. I am also sorry about the way we left things. The timing was very poor. Someday, I hope I will be able to better explain my behavior. So you know, I did have opportunity to view Leo's body before cremation, but there was very little left of it. I do believe it was him. The corpse of his girlfriend, Noriko, was recognizable, and Leo has not been seen in Japan since.

                                    You are still in my thoughts,
                                      YUJI ONO

Oh, Leo.

Some part of me—my heart, I suppose—had hoped Leo's death might be a mistake, but now I knew it wasn't. The brain could not deny the evidence. Leo was dead.

I was glad that Natty was at school because I didn't know what I wanted to say to her yet.

I set the ashes on the coffee table in the living room and contemplated my next move. Leo needed a funeral, but if I gave him one—if I, say, had him buried at the plot in Brooklyn—it could potentially implicate me in his escape. I did not relish the idea of a fifth stint at Liberty. So, perhaps Leo's service could be informal: ashes scattered in the park on a sunny day, Natty reading a poem, etc. Did it really matter that Leo's remains shared space with my parents'? They were all dead anyway.

I wanted to cry over Leo. I could feel the rusty gears

turning behind my eyes and the tightening of my chest, but the tears would not come.

The longer I looked at Leo's ashes, the more I began to feel, oddly enough, embarrassed. The steps I'd taken to keep Leo safe had been just the wrong ones. Look at the outcome! My father, wherever he was, would probably be ashamed of me.

I hadn't moved for hours when Natty got home from school. Her eyes shifted from me to the bag to me. "Poor Leo," Natty said before she sat down on the couch.

Natty leaned over the coffee table and picked up the bag by one of its corners, as if she wanted to make as little contact with it as possible. "Does it seem like enough is here? Leo was so tall." She set Leo's ashes back on the table. "I dreamed of him last night."

"I didn't hear you scream or anything."

"I'm not a child anymore, Anya." She rolled her eyes. "Besides, it wasn't a nightmare. Leo was well and whole." She paused. "I don't think we should bury him. Leo wouldn't like that. He liked being home with us. He liked being here."

I told her I would pick out an urn next week.

I went into my bedroom. I took the chocolate bar out of my bag and set it atop my dresser.

The bar looked so sweet and harmless lying there. Not deadly in the least.

On Saturday, I put on my trusty black dress, which I couldn't have been sicker of wearing, and dragged myself to Uncle Yuri's funeral, which wasn't held at my church but at the Eastern Orthodox one that most members of the Family favored. I debated whether to take Natty but decided against it. Natty had known Uncle Yuri even less than I had, and I didn't want to put her in proximity of our nearest and dearest. I debated whether to take my machete, but decided against that, too. Since I would be frisked, there was really no point. I did take one of the bodyguards Mr. Kipling had hired to stand guard outside our place—a brick wall of a woman named Daisy Gogol. She was six feet tall, had arms as thick as my legs, and was in need of an eyebrow and upper-lip wax. She was Natty's and my favorite, though. Daisy Gogol had a melodious speaking voice. I once mentioned this to her and found out that she had studied to be an opera singer before moving into the more lucrative field of security. Natty reported that she had spotted Daisy Gogol feeding the birds on our balcony.

The funeral service was tedious as I felt almost nothing at Yuri Balanchine's death. Daisy, however, wept copiously. I asked her if she had known Yuri. She hadn't known him at all, but had been moved by the reading from Ecclesiastes. She clutched my hand in her meaty paw.

Since the night of the three attacks, I had not been in a room with anyone from the Family. In the front pew, Mickey sat next to his wife, Sophia. Fats was two rows behind them. The rest of the church was filled with employees of Balanchine Chocolate, some of whom were relatives I knew vaguely (but have found no need to mention in this narrative). It occurred to me that any of these people could have been responsible, or none of them. The world was very large, and at that age, I believed it to be filled with potential villains.

When it was my turn to view Yuri's body, I leaned over the casket and crossed myself. The mortician had managed to erase the effects of Yuri's stroke, and his face looked more symmetrical than it had the last time I'd seen him. His lips were painted an unnatural purplish hue, and I wondered what they had been trying to tell me that day in September. I thought of his other son, Jacks. He hadn't been let out of prison for the funeral, but Yuri had been his father, too. And despite everything Jacks had or hadn't done, on that day, I was able to manage a dust mote of pity for my poor cousin.

I went up to Mickey and Sophia to pay my respects. Mickey was wearing a dark suit as was to be expected. Sophia was wearing a shapeless maroon dress that was draped almost like a toga. An odd choice for a funeral.

Mickey's eyes were bloodshot. He took my hand and thanked me for coming.

Sophia smiled at me, but the smile was forced. "How are you, Anya?" She planted a kiss on each of my cheeks. Her cheekbones were sharp against mine. "We have been meaning to come see you since your return but we were much occupied with Yuri. How did you enjoy your time abroad?" Sophia lowered her voice. "With my cousins?"

"I loved them," I replied. "Thank you."

"You and I—we must really catch up," Sophia said. "Much has happened these past months."

On my way out, I was stopped by Fats. "Annie," he said. "You haven't been to my place since you've been back."

"No," I replied. "I haven't."

"You have nothing to fear from me," Fats said. "I wasn't involved in the attacks."

"Everyone I know says they weren't involved," I said. "And yet the attacks did happen all the same, didn't they?"

"Listen, Annie. I'm real sorry about Leo, but my interest here is business. Mickey is running Balanchine Chocolate into the ground. He's not a bad kid but he doesn't know what he's doing any better than his dad did. I work with a lot of the guys that actually sell the stuff. And they need to know that the supply will come on time and in good condition. With Mickey running things, no one believes that anymore. He's lost their confidence."

"Fats, I can't think about any of that until I know who was responsible for—"

"*Listen to me, Annie!*" I had never heard Fats raise his voice before. "That's what I'm trying to tell you. It doesn't matter who did it. There isn't time for you to track down the parties who were involved. Someone has to step in to organize Balanchine Chocolate, and I think that person should be me."

I said nothing.

"I'd like you to back me. Your support would mean a lot."

I chose my words carefully. "From where I'm standing right now, it looks like you tried to kill off Natty, Leo, and me so that you could take control."

Fats shook his head. "No. That's not what happened."

"So, who did it? Say it if you know."

"Kid, I am telling you I don't. I wish I knew. But what I think, what I think is that someone outside the organization wanted to inject chaos into it. Just like with the poisoning last year."

"Do you mean Yuji Ono?"

"Annie, I don't know. Could be."

"Why should I back you to run Balanchine Chocolate if you know so little?"

"All right . . . Here's one thought I had." He lowered his voice and looked across the room at Sophia. "What if *she* was involved? Her maiden name is Bitter, and Bitter is the perennial fourth-place chocolate distributor in Germany."

I looked across the room at Sophia Balanchine. It didn't seem likely that she would have sent me to hide in Mexico, potentially putting her mother's family in danger. At this point, it felt like Fats would point his finger at anyone to stop mine from pointing at him.

Daisy Gogol put her hand on my shoulder. "Are you copacetic, Anya?"

I nodded and told her I was ready to go.

Fats grabbed my arm. "I remember the day you were born. Your daddy bringing the pictures to the Pool for us to see. I would never have done anything to put you or your brother and sister in harm's way. You have to know that."

The only thing I knew for certain was that I didn't know anything.

227

XIV

I ENCOUNTER AN OLD FOE; ANOTHER PROPOSAL; WIN LOOKS UNDER THE WRAPPER

FOR WIN'S EIGHTEENTH BIRTHDAY, his parents hosted a party at their apartment. And by Win's parents, I mean his mother. Win's father was still "depressed," and according to Win, hadn't done anything to help plan the festivities.

Scarlet came over to my apartment so that we could all get dressed together. Natty and Daisy Gogol were also going.

Scarlet was about six months pregnant at this point and definitely showing. She wore an enormous black tulle skirt and a tiny pink velvet jacket she couldn't button. Her blond hair had grown almost to her bottom and was glossy. I found her as comely as ever and I told her so.

She kissed me on the cheek. "Why can't I marry *you*, Annie? You'd be the perfect husband to me." After seven years in a Catholic school, Gable Arsley was hell-bent on marrying Scarlet and making an "honest woman" of her.

Scarlet had been too exhausted to procure outfits for us, as she might have done in years past. She did approve our choices. Natty wore that red dress of mine (and my mother's), the one Win had always liked me in. I wore black pants—I was in a pants phase of my life—and a corset that Scarlet had worn to Little Egypt all those years ago. I was slutty on top and conservative on the bottom. But the thing was, I liked my arms and back after all that farming. As Daisy Gogol was coming with us, I resisted the urge to accessorize with my machete. Daisy was too large to borrow any of our clothes, but as it turned out, she had plenty of her own. She wore a crazy milkmaid dress and a helmet with horns. "Old opera costume," she said. "This is going to be so much fun!" She clapped her hands.

We rode the bus to Win's parents' apartment. The funny thing was, I had only been there two other times as, for an obvious reason—i.e., Charles Delacroix—Win and I had avoided the place.

Jane Delacroix was one of those people who could make everything beautiful. For decorations, she'd strung fruit from the ceiling. And there were candles everywhere to provide illumination. And of course a bar and a band. The truth was, I doubted Win even noticed all the pains she'd taken for him. He was a boy, and he'd never been without a mother.

Nearly everyone from what should have been my graduating class was there, with the exception of Gable Arsley—thank you, Win's mother. Most of these people I hadn't seen since the night of my ill-fated welcome-back-to-Trinity party. Chai Pinter came right up to me and started babbling. "Oh, Anya, you look fantastic! I'm so happy to see you!" She hugged me like we were best friends. "I was so worried for you all these months. Where were you?"

Like I was really going to tell the class gossip where I'd been. "Here and there," was my stock reply.

"Well, aren't you the cagey one! So, what are you going to *do* next year?"

Possibly arrange hits on some relatives of mine, I thought. "Stay here," I said.

"That's cool. I've already gotten into NYU so I'll be in the city, too! We should totally hang out."

NYU? My mother had gone to NYU. And the thought of stupid Chai Pinter going to NYU filled me with an inexplicable disgust. I knew I should be happy for her. Why wasn't I happy for her? Chai Pinter was a gossip, but she was a nice enough girl and a hard worker and . . .

"So, do you think you'll even bother finishing high school?" Chai asked me.

"I've got a tutor. I'm studying for my GED right now."

"Good for you! You'll probably ace it. You were always so smart."

I told Chai I needed to get a drink. I walked across the room and was immediately accosted by Alison Wheeler. "Annie," she said. "So, I guess you know that I wasn't the rebound girl after all." Alison Wheeler was wearing a skintight black dress and yellow spike heels. It was a new look for her.

I laughed. "You two had me fooled."

She leaned in to my ear. "I mean, I like Win, but he isn't really my type. You're much more my type."

"Oh!"

"Generally, yes. But specifically, I like your friend Scarlet. But Trinity's so boring and Catholic. I can't wait to be in college. Anyway, I was just trying to help the Charles Delacroix campaign. That Bertha Sinclair is a monster."

At least I wasn't passing my days at Liberty.

"She is, Annie. She's going to let the water run out, and she's in the pocket of all the big companies and she lets them pollute and not pay taxes, and she's totally corrupt. Charles Delacroix isn't perfect, but . . . he's good." She pointed across the room to Win, who was talking to an elderly woman. "He raised that, didn't he?"

"I suppose."

Alison started talking about college because apparently there was nothing else in the world worth talking about. She had gotten into Yale early admission and was planning to study political science and environmental engineering. I felt the same seething jealousy as I had with Chai—yes, that's what it was— rise up in me. I had to excuse myself again.

I was tired of hearing about all my classmates' plans for next year. I thought about going up to Win's room to lie down but when I got there I found it in use. The same with Win's parents' bedroom—gross. I went back downstairs. I knew that Win's father's office was supposedly off-limits. But I also knew that Charles Delacroix was out for the night, so that's where I decided to go. I removed the gold cord that had been tied around the door handles and let myself in.

I sat down on one of the leather couches. And then I took

231

off my shoes and lay down. I had just about dozed off when someone came in.

"Anya Balanchine," Charles Delacroix said. "So we meet again."

I struggled to sit up. "Sir."

He was wearing a red plaid flannel bathrobe, and he had, indeed, grown a beard. The combination made him look a bit like a homeless person. I wondered if he was going to throw me out of his office, but he didn't.

"My wife insisted on throwing this blasted party," Charles Delacroix said. "Now that I am unemployed, my opinions carry less weight than I would like. It is my hope that this infernal affair doesn't last long."

"You're being ridiculous. It's a birthday party. It's only one night."

"True. Little things do seem to weigh more heavily on me these days," Charles Delacroix admitted. "Look what a wonderful time you appear to be having."

"I like having your son to myself."

"That's the reason you broke into my office?"

"Moving a cord is not breaking in!"

"You would think that. You've always had—how to put this?—a flexible attitude toward the law." I was reasonably sure that Charles Delacroix was teasing me.

I told him the truth—that I was tired of hearing my peers talk about their plans for next year. "You see, I am plan-less, Mr. Delacroix. And you must admit that you had some part in my current situation."

Charles Delacroix shrugged. "A resourceful girl like you?

232

I bet you have a move or two up your sleeve. Avenging your brother's death and such. Taking the reins of your chocolate empire from the incompetents who currently run it."

I didn't say anything.

"Come now. Did I hit upon a sore subject?"

"You owe me an apology, Mr. Delacroix."

"Yes, I suppose I do," he said. "These months since we last saw each other have undoubtedly been worse for you than for me. But you are very young, and you'll recover. I'm old, or at least middle-aged, and the scent of failure clings longer to people in my time of life. And despite my machinations—and mind you, it was never anything against you—you and Win are still together. You've won, Anya. I've lost. Congratulations."

Charles Delacroix sounded bitter and hopeless, and I told him so.

"How can I be anything but? You met my successor. How did your release go down? Were you required to grease the wheels or did she just take her pleasure from humiliating me one last time?"

I admitted that wheels had been greased. "Do you know what she said about you?" I asked.

"Only awful things, I suppose."

"No. She said that her campaign kept hitting the story of Win and me because of how much it bothered you. The voters, she thought, cared much less about the matter than you did."

Charles Delacroix was silent for a while. He furrowed his brow and then he laughed. "Possibly. It's a good lesson come too late. So, where were you all these months anyway? Somewhere that was good for you, I see."

233

I told him I couldn't tell him that. "Someday you might use it against me."

"Anya Balanchine, we have always been candid with each other. Don't you know that I am nothing but a declawed tiger now?"

"For now, you are. But even a declawed tiger still has teeth, and I'm not counting you out yet."

"That's very kind of you," he said. "Aren't you angry at me for throwing you back in Liberty? Or have you just buried your anger deep inside the caverns of that ludicrously girlish heart of yours and one night I'll go to bed and there'll be a horse's head in it?"

"I like your wife and son too much for that," I said. "I have a long list of enemies, Mr. Delacroix. You're certainly on it, but you're nowhere near the top." I paused. "You know everything: What do you know about Sophia Bitter?"

Charles Delacroix furrowed his brow. "Your cousin Mickey's newish wife." He shook his head. "German, I think?"

"And Mexican." I asked him if there was any chance she was on his list of suspects for the Fretoxin poisonings.

"No. We suspected it happened at the manufacturing level, that it was someone outside the United States, but I wasn't able to allocate the resources to investigate beyond New York let alone outside the country. And then your cousin so conveniently confessed." Charles Delacroix rolled his eyes.

"You knew it was a lie?"

"Of course, Anya. But, for a variety of reasons, it was worth it to me to be able to close the books on the poisoning. Also, it gave me an excellent excuse to put away Jakov for a long period of time. He did shoot my son, I'm sure you'll recall."

I did.

"I'm sentimental, what can I say?" Charles Delacroix poured himself a drink. He offered me one, but I declined. "So, Sophia Bitter. I take it you think she arranged the poisoning. Seems like a reasonable enough guess. Her foreign interests coupled with excellent access to your family's business by way of her, at the time, fiancé."

I paused. "I think she killed my brother and tried to kill my sister and me, too."

Charles Delacroix took a good, long swig, and then poured himself another drink. He considered me for a moment. "When we're young we think everything has to be wrapped up in a month. But you should take the long view on this one. Before you make a move, be sure, Anya. And even once you're sure, tread carefully. And remember you don't have to do what they expect you to do."

But that was the problem. It was impossible to be sure. "How can I be sure? I'm surrounded by liars and criminals."

"Ah, that is a dilemma. If I were you, I'd put the question to Sophia Bitter directly. See what she says."

Seemed like good enough advice. "I like you better when you're not plotting against me."

At that moment, Win opened the door. "Dad." He nodded toward his father. "Annie," he complained, "I haven't seen you the whole night!"

"Anya," Charles Delacroix called as I was leaving, "come visit me again sometime."

Win grabbed my hand, and we went back out to the party. "What was *that* about?" he asked.

I kissed him, and he seemed to forget the question. "Isn't it nice that we can do that whenever we want in front of whoever?"

"You are a very strange girl," Win said.

Not long after, Scarlet, Natty, Daisy Gogol, and I took our leave. We were halfway down Win's street and a third of the way to the bus stop when a dark figure emerged from an alleyway.

"Scarlet! Scarlet!" A voice called.

Natty screamed, and Daisy Gogol got into a squatting position that I assumed had something to do with her Krav Maga training. Suddenly, she sprung up and had her arm around the figure's neck.

"What the Hell is this?" the figure said. I'd know that entitled voice anywhere. Gable Arsley.

"Oh, Gable, honestly. Just go away!" Scarlet said. "Why are you even here?"

"The guy at the door wouldn't let me into Win's stupid party. Like I'm so awful. Win's father did things a million times worse than anything I ever did, and he's in there. Can't bygones be bygones?" Arsley tried to free himself but Daisy Gogol was stronger. "Seriously, Anya, tell your beast to let me go."

Daisy Gogol looked at me. I shook my head. It was fine to let Gable Arsley struggle a little longer.

"That's rude, Arsley. Just because Daisy's stronger than you doesn't make her a beast," Natty said.

"Shut up, mini-Anya," Arsley said. "Seriously, Scarlet, I need to talk to you. Can't we please go somewhere?"

236

Daisy Gogol released Arsley as it had become all too obvious that we knew him.

Scarlet shook her head. "We can talk at school, Gable."

"Please! Give me one minute alone. One minute without your bloody entourage. I'm desperate here. I'm going to do something crazy!"

"Anything you have to say to me you can say in front of them," Scarlet said.

Gable looked from me to Natty to Daisy Gogol. "Fine. If that's the way it has to be. And I'm sorry. I'm so sorry. I'm sorry for everything. You have no idea how sorry. I wish I'd never taken those stupid pictures. I wish I could go back in time and do everything over again because I'm such an idiot."

"That's true," I added.

Gable ignored me. "But if I had to be poisoned and lose my foot just so I could meet you for real and fall in love with you, I'd do that again. You're perfect, Scarlet. You're freaking perfect. I'm awful. I do horrible things. I'm mean-spirited and vile."

"Also, true," I said. But no one was paying attention to me.

"Please, Scarlet, you have to forgive me. You have to let me in. You have to let me help raise our baby. You have to. I'll die if you don't let me."

I could not believe that this was Gable Arsley. He sounded like a girl. *(NB: By saying this, I meant no offense to girls—I counted myself among their number, after all.)* I very much wanted to look away from this pas de deux but I couldn't.

Gable was getting down on one knee. It was an awkward maneuver because of his prosthetic foot. Scarlet inhaled sharply. "Get off the ground, Gable," Scarlet ordered.

He ignored her. He began to reach into his pocket, and I knew what was going to happen. "Scarlet Barber, will you marry me?" The ring was silver and looked like a piece of twine tied into a bow.

I wanted to say, *She will not. Of course she will not.* But I didn't say anything.

"Last time, you said I couldn't be serious because I didn't bring a ring. This time, I came prepared," Gable continued.

Scarlet exhaled loudly. "Gable, go away. This isn't funny or romantic. It's just"—she paused—"sad. I can't love you ever again."

"But why can't you?" he whined.

"Because you really are awful. I thought you had changed but I was wrong. People like you can't change. You were awful before the poisoning and you're still awful. You sold pictures of my best friend—"

"But that wasn't you!" Gable insisted. "That was *her*! I'd never do anything to hurt you."

Scarlet shook her head. "Annie is me. Don't you know that? Please, Gable, just go. It's nearly eleven and I don't want to be out past city curfew."

Gable moved to take Scarlet's hand, but Daisy Gogol wedged herself between them. "You heard the lady," Daisy said, and then she growled at him like a bear.

On the bus, Scarlet and I were sharing a two-person row, and Daisy and Natty sat a couple of rows behind us. I had thought that Scarlet was sleeping as she had her head leaned against the window and hadn't said anything the entire trip. Three stops from my apartment, I heard a series of sniffles.

"Scarlet, what is it?"

"Nothing," she replied. "Hormones maybe. Ignore me." I had a handkerchief in my bag so I gave it to her. She blew her nose for half a city block. She paused and then she did it again. "I am so gross," she said. I told her she wasn't but I could tell she wasn't listening to me. "Oh Annie, what am I going to do?"

"About what?" I asked.

"I haven't wanted to bother you with any of it, because obviously, you have problems of your own. But everything is a complete disaster!"

The disaster of my best friend's life broke down in the following way:

1. Her parents were Catholic so there had been no question about her keeping the baby, but Scarlet wasn't even sure she wanted a baby.
2. Her parents were saying they didn't want to pay for college ("And certainly not drama school!") now that Scarlet had tarnished herself so.
3. Her mother really wanted her to marry Arsley and was threatening to throw her out of the house if she didn't.
4. Drama club wasn't going to let her be in the

239

photo. ("After everything I've done for them!" she said indignantly.)

5. If Scarlet didn't give birth before graduation, Holy Trinity was saying they weren't going to let her walk at commencement.

6. Arsley was harassing her constantly about getting back with him and she feared that he was wearing her down.

Here, Scarlet sighed.

I was trying not to be selfish, to think of things from Scarlet's point of view. I suggested that maybe she should get back with Arsley, if she still liked him.

"Annie, I loathe him! I honestly don't know what I was thinking." She paused. "I'm starting to believe that I really am the stupidest girl in the world."

"Scarlet, don't say that!"

"It's true. Sometimes I look at myself in the mirror and I'm so puffy and disgusting I have to turn away. I think, 'Scarlet Barber, you have done nothing but make horrible mistakes for the past year.'"

I told her that I had had the same thought about myself not that long ago.

"But I'm a million times worse than you! Because you had all of this thrust upon you. And I did this to myself." She paused. "I do hate Gable, but the thing is . . . The sad, awful, ridiculous truth is, I'm lonely. I'm so alone, Annie. And Gable sometimes feels like the only person in the world who is even a little pleased to see me."

I put my arm around her. "For the record, I'm always happy to see you," I said. "And if the worst happens with your parents, you can always come stay with Natty and me. You and the baby."

Scarlet planted a kiss on my cheek. "Really, Annie? Do you mean it?"

"Of course. That's the best part of having no parents or even a guardian. I make the decisions now. You do run the risk of being an innocent bystander in a violent crime. But we have more than enough bedrooms."

"I hate it when you're morbid," Scarlet said. "And I suppose I'm just surprised to hear you say that. You've always been so private. Even from me."

I had recently come to the realization that that wasn't the best method for living. "Nana used to say that 'family takes care of family.' And you are my family, Scarlet. Much more so than that band of criminals I'm blood-related to. We have been best friends since the day we were made to sit alphabetized in Miss Pritchett's class—"

"Balanchine, Anya. Barber, Scarlet."

"Natty and I love you. Leo loved you, too—"

Scarlet put her hand over my mouth. "Oh, please, please, please stop! I don't want to cry any more tonight. I've existed in a permanent state of tears for the last two years."

The bus arrived at Scarlet's stop. Between the combined volume of her skirt and belly and the height of her heels,

Scarlet was having trouble getting up out of the seat. I stood and offered her my hand.

Late that night, after the party, Win came over to the apartment. We'd just seen each other but I suspect his main reason in coming over was *because he could*—he was now officially over eighteen, which meant that city curfew didn't apply to him. We went into my room, so that we wouldn't wake Natty, who had already gone to bed. We were both hungry but there wasn't much to eat in the house. Win noticed the mongrel bar of chocolate on my dresser. "What's this?"

I told him I had bought it in the park. "You can have it if you want but it might be terrible."

I went into the kitchen to get water. For a second, the tap wouldn't start running and an awful breathy banging sound came from the pipes. I wondered if this would be the day the water ran out. But, finally, the water started.

When I got back to my room, I found Win studying the chocolate. He had taken off the jacket, and he was holding out the gold foil–wrapped bar. "Look, it's not Balanchine," he said. "The paper looks like it is, but underneath it's something else."

"Yeah, I thought that might happen," I said. "I bought it in front of Little Egypt. The jacket was off, so I thought it would probably be some generic brand underneath."

"It's not generic." Win held out the foil-wrapped bar so I could read it: BITTER SCHOKOLADE, HERGESTELLT FÜR BITTER SCHOKOLADEN GMBH, MÜNCHEN.

"At the funeral, someone was saying that they were the perennial fourth-place chocolate family in Germany," I said quietly. "Mickey's wife's family actually. You remember Sophia . . ." Sophia Bitter Balanchine. Sophia M. Bitter Balanchine. Sophia Marquez Bitter Balanchine. The former Sophia Marquez Bitter, who Theo's oldest sister hadn't liked. Sophia Marquez Bitter, who had once been engaged to Yuji Ono . . .

Everywhere I had been, she had been first.

Bitter Chocolate under a Balanchine wrapper.

Who would have had the ability to orchestrate supply-wide poisoning?

Who would have had the ability to execute a three-country hit?

Who would Yuji Ono have protected over me?

I dropped the bar on the floor. Because it was thin and stale and cheap, it broke into several pieces.

It was obvious. I had been so stupid.

Again.

I had to sit down.

"Annie, are you all right?" Win asked.

I was about to lie: to tell him I wasn't feeling well and that I'd see him tomorrow; walk him to the elevator; then, I'd go back into my room, close the door, and puzzle this out alone. But the truth was I hadn't done that well with this method—that is to say, solitude. Win knew plenty of appalling things about me, and he was still here.

I took a deep breath. "What if Sophia Bitter was the one who arranged the Fretoxin poisoning? That was about the time she came to New York to marry Mickey. And Theo's sister says that Sophia was once engaged to Yuji Ono."

Win nodded. "But Jacks confessed to it, didn't he?"

"No one really believes he did it, though," I said. "I think someone in the family convinced him to confess because he was going to jail for shooting the district attorney's son."

"Right, *him*," Win said. "He who thought he was going to prom. Him."

"Him—you." I paused to kiss him on the mouth. "The point is, Jacks would have had to go to jail either way. So it could have just as well been someone else."

Natty came into the kitchen. She was wearing her pajamas and rubbing the sleep out of the corners of her eyes. "If Bitter Chocolate is really the fourth-place chocolate company in Germany," Natty said, "maybe Sophia thought she could improve their standing by expanding the business into America. Listen—she marries Mickey, just to get close enough to destroy the Balanchines. Or at least, to take over the business herself."

"When did you wake up?" I asked her.

"Now. You two are loud. Hi, Win," she said.

"Natty, my gal," Win greeted her. "The question is, did Mickey help her, or will this be news to him, too?"

"And also, did she arrange to have Leo killed?" Natty added. "And did she try to kill Annie and me?"

"Aside from Yuji Ono, I think she was the only one who had the reach to arrange such a hit," I said.

Natty sighed.

"What are we going to do?" Win asked.

We. It was presumptuous of him, but I felt better all the same. "I'm not sure yet," I said. If she really was the one who had killed Leo, I might need to do some very hard things. But like Charles Delacroix had said, first I needed to make sure. And I needed to find out who her conspirators had been. Also, while it was pleasant to have Win and Natty to go over things with, I wasn't ready to admit to them that I might need to kill someone. "I'm going to visit Jacks," I said. "He might have some information and he's been bothering me to come see him for months."

I kneeled down and picked up the broken pieces of the Bitter Chocolate bar and threw them into the trash. I took the gold-foil wrapper. I was about to put it in my pocket when Natty took it from me. She folded it in half so that it was squarish and then she folded it several more times. When she handed it back to me, the paper had taken the form of a small, gold dragon.

"Hey, where'd you learn that?" Win wanted to know.

"Genius camp," she told him.

So you see, I thought. It hadn't all been for nothing.

X V

I GO TO RIKERS

There were no visiting hours at Rikers Island on Mondays and Tuesdays. I didn't go on Wednesday either, because the visitation schedule was determined by last name. After some research, I determined that Jacks's day was Thursday. I also read an exhaustively detailed dress code: among other things, no swimsuits, ripped or see-through clothing, spandex, hats, hoods, or uniforms. It also stated that "visitors to Rikers must wear underwear." *(NB: There had not been the remotest chance that I wouldn't.)*

The prohibition against uniforms put me in mind of the fact that I was no longer a student at Holy Trinity. Life had been so much easier with a uniform. As I was dressing that morning, it occurred to me that I would need to come up with a new uniform for myself. But, what? A uniform was meant to reflect your station in life. I was no longer college-bound or even a student. With a long list of offenses under my belt, I was not likely to become a criminologist. I was no longer an inmate at Liberty. I was no longer a cacao farmer. I was no longer my brother's keeper. Or my sister's either. Natty seemed increasingly able to keep herself.

At the moment, I was nothing more or less than a girl with an infamous last name and a vendetta or two.

But what to wear for avenging my slain brother?

I had to take two different buses to get to Rikers, and then I had to register, and finally I was led into a room with tables and chairs bolted to the floor. I would rather have visited Jacks behind a plastic screen with a phone like you see in those old movies, but I guess my cousin wasn't considered dangerous enough to merit such precautions.

I sat down, and about ten minutes later, Jacks was brought into the room.

"Thanks for coming, Annie," he said. My cousin's appearance was much altered since the last time I'd seen him. He had shaved his head. His nose had clearly been broken in multiple places, though it was healed for the moment, and one of his cheekbones had a disturbing flatness to it. He also had fresh stitches above his eyebrow. "I'm not the pretty boy I used to be, eh, cousin?"

"You were never that pretty," I said though I could not help but pity Jacks. He'd always been so vain about his appearance.

Jacks laughed, and he sat across the table from me.

I had things I wanted to know from him, of course, but the best way of dealing with Jacks was to let him talk.

"You finally came," he commented.

"You've only been begging me to for months," I said.

Jacks shook his head. "Nah, that's not why you came. No one loves Jacks. You're probably still holding a grudge 'cause I shot your boyfriend. You just want something."

I looked at the clock. "What could you possibly have that I want?"

"Like I wrote. Information," Jacks said.

True enough. "Your father's dead," I told him.

"Yuri, yeah, I heard. Who cares? That man was no type of father to me."

It seemed hard to believe that he could feel so little for his own father. "Back in September, you said that Natty and I were in terrible danger, and maybe you know that since then there have been attempts on both our lives and Leo is dead."

"Leo is dead?" Jacks shook his head. "It wasn't supposed to go down like that."

"What wasn't? What do you mean?"

"I had heard"—Jacks lowered his voice—"that someone in the Family was going to try to take you and your sister down. That way, there'd be no one from the Leonyd Balanchine side left to interfere in the business. No one was going to touch Leo though. Leo was gone to wherever you sent him. Leo was out of the picture."

"Who, Jacks? Say who you mean."

Jacks shook his head. "I . . . I'm not sure. Okay, see, here's the thing. See, I didn't poison everyone."

"I believe you."

"Really?" Jacks paused in surprise. "And I didn't mean to shoot your boyfriend either. What I said to you last year was true. I only wanted to wound Leo so that I could take him back to Yuri. But the unlucky thing that happened was me shooting your boyfriend. Because I would have served a couple of months if I had just shot Leo, but . . . Well, you know how it went down.

"So, Yuri had Mickey come to me. He said, 'City Hall wants a name to attribute to the Balanchine poisoning so that the Family can put it behind them.' And I took the fall."

"In exchange for what?"

"Mickey said he'd take care of me once I got out."

"But what does that have to do with Natty and me?"

Jacks rolled his eyes. "So I said, 'What happens when I'm out and Anya Balanchine and her sister are grown women? What stops them from shooting me right between the eyes in payback for all these things I've done?' And Mickey said he would handle you."

Jacks didn't know anything about Sophia Bitter. "Jacks, that's what you wanted to tell me? That doesn't mean Mickey was going to shoot me! I think he intended to partner with me."

"But you said there were attempts on you and your sister. So . . ."

"What about Mickey's wife?"

"Sophia, nah. I doubt she was involved. She's just a woman."

"That's sexist." I stood up. Talking to Jacks had always been a waste of time.

"Wait! Anya, don't go! Now that you mention it, the first time I met Sophia Bitter was right around the poisoning."

I slowly returned to the chair.

"She'd arrived in New York maybe a week or two earlier. I didn't think anything of it at the time, but maybe you're right. Maybe Mickey's cover-up was to protect her." Jacks's pale face was turning pinkish. "Maybe that *pizda* is the whole reason I'm in here!" He asked me what proof I had that Sophia Bitter had been involved and I told him about the wrapper and the fact that she had been one of the few people with knowledge of my siblings' and my whereabouts.

"She couldn't have done it alone," Jacks said. "She had to have had a partner."

I knew who the obvious choice was. "Yuji Ono?"

"Sure, him. But I mean someone on the inside."

"Her husband."

This conversation was going in a circle.

"Yeah, but the thing is, Annie, and maybe you don't get this, the poisonings hurt Mickey as much as anyone. He was next in line to run Balanchine Chocolate. The poisonings made everyone think he and Yuri were both weak." Jacks ran his fingers through his invisible hair. "What about Fats? No, Fats would never. He loves chocolate too much. And he loves you kids. What about that lawyer who works for you?"

"Mr. Kipling?" I asked.

"No, Simon Green."

That was the last name I'd expected to hear Jacks say. "How do you know Simon Green?"

"I met him years ago at the compound when he and I were both kids."

"At the compound? Where are you going with this?"

"Nothing. Just maybe I'm not the only bastard in this family."

"What are you saying?"

"Haven't you ever suspected?"

250

"Suspected what?"

"That Simon Green is, maybe, related to Yuri. Or even to your father. And if that's true, can you trust—"

I stood up and smacked Jacks across his ugly, broken face. I was strong from those months of manual labor, and I felt something in his cheek crumble under my hand.

A guard ran over to me and pulled me away from Jacks. At that point, I was asked to leave Rikers Island.

"It's okay, Anya! I'm sorry. I didn't mean any disrespect to your father," Jacks yelled desperately at my back. "I can't stay here! You know I didn't have anything to do with the poisoning, and I shouldn't be in here. You've got to help me. I'm gonna die in here, Annie! You can ask your boyfriend's father to help me!"

I did not turn around because a guard was pushing me toward the exit. Even if I had been physically able to turn, I wouldn't have.

That was the problem with Jacks. He would say anything. Daddy used to say that people who would say anything could be ignored entirely.

But what had Daddy known? Now that I was older, I was starting to wonder how much of what he'd told me had been fortune-cookie crap.

Look how successfully Jacks had injected poison into my mind.

Daisy Gogol was waiting for me outside the visitors' building.

On the bus ride home, it wasn't that cold but I began to shiver.

"What is it, Anya?" she asked.

I told her that the man I had gone to see had said something insulting about my dead father.

"This man—obviously, he is a criminal," Daisy said.

I nodded.

"And a liar?"

I nodded again.

Daisy shrugged her enormous shoulders. "I think you are safe to dismiss him."

Daisy put her heavy arm around me, pulling me toward her spectacularly muscular bosom.

She was right. What Jacks had implied about Daddy couldn't possibly be true. I didn't want to ask Mr. Kipling about it. I didn't want to have to repeat it. I didn't want my sister ever to have to hear it. I wanted to erase it from my brain. I wanted to put it in the section with all the stuff I'd learned for school that I was never going to need: Hecate's lines in *Macbeth* and the Pythagorean theorem and the subject of Daddy's fidelity. Gone, all gone.

(NB: If I had a daughter, the first advice I'd give her would be that willful ignorance is nearly always a mistake.)

When I got up to the apartment, I needed something to do to occupy my mind or at the very least, my hands. I decided to sort through Imogen's belongings. She didn't have much— books, clothing, toiletries—but I figured her sister would probably want them. Had it been Natty, I would have wanted her possessions. *(What had happened to Leo's things?)*

In Imogen's nightstand, I found the copy of *Bleak House*

Natty and I had given her for her birthday. How long ago that seemed. *Bleak House* was quite a lengthy novel, and Imogen was only about two hundred pages in. Poor Imogen would never find out what happened at the end of the story.

I was about to toss Imogen's handbag into a box when I noticed a leather-bound book inside. I opened the cover. The book was the diary Natty had mentioned. It was so like Imogen to keep a paper journal. I didn't want to snoop on her, but I also wanted to know what her last months had been like. She had always been a good friend to me, and well, I missed her.

I flipped through the pages. Her scrawl was familiar—a tiny, feminine slant.

This particular diary started about two years ago. She mainly detailed what she was reading. As I was not a reader, I found the whole thing rather boring. And then, an entry from a little over a year ago, February 2083, caught my eye:

G. getting sicker every day. Asked Mr. K. and me to help her die.
And then several weeks later:

It is done. G. sent the kids to the wedding. Mr. K. cut power to the building for an hour. I upped G.'s drugs so she wouldn't be in any pain & I held one of her hands & Mr. K. held the other & finally her eyes closed & her heart stopped. R.I.P., Galina.

I threw the book across the room, and when it landed, I could hear some of its delicate pages tear. Imogen Goodfellow had helped Nana commit suicide! And "Mr. K." could only be my Mr. Kipling.

I tossed the diary into a canvas bag and then I left the apartment and started walking down to Mr. Kipling's apartment. The sky had been a menacing gray all afternoon, but the evening had made good on that threat and a truly hard rain had begun to fall. Neither I nor Daisy Gogol, who had insisted she come with me, had brought umbrellas, and we were drenched by the time we reached Mr. Kipling's apartment at Sutton Place.

I rarely visited Mr. Kipling at his apartment. Most business could wait until the morning. I asked the doorman to call up but he recognized me and waved me toward the elevator. Daisy Gogol decided to stay in the lobby.

Mr. Kipling's wife, Keisha, answered the door. "Anya," she said, holding out her arms to me. "You must be freezing. You're soaked through. Come in. I'll get you a towel."

I walked into the foyer, where I dripped all over their marble floor.

After a minute, Keisha returned with a towel and Mr. Kipling.

Mr. Kipling's face was concerned. "Anya, what is it? Has something happened?"

I told him that I needed to speak to him alone. "Yes, of course," Mr. Kipling said. He led me into his home office.

One wall was covered in pictures. Mostly, they were of his wife and daughter, but there were pictures of my father and mother, and me, Natty, and Leo, too. I noticed one or two of Simon Green.

I took Imogen's journal out of the bag and set it on his wooden desk.

"What am I looking at?"

"Imogen's journal," I said.

"I didn't know she kept one," Mr. Kipling said.

I told him that I hadn't known either. "She says things in it"—I paused—"things about you."

"We were friends," Mr. Kipling said. "I can't know what you're talking about unless you tell me."

"Did you and Imogen kill Nana?"

Mr. Kipling sighed heavily and put his balding head in his hands. "Oh, Annie. Galina wanted us to. She was suffering so much. She was in pain all the time. She was losing her mind."

"How could you do that? Do you know what Nana's death led to? Leo getting in the fight with Mickey at the funeral, and Leo shooting Yuri Balanchine, and Leo getting shot himself. And me having to shoot Jacks. And me having to go to Liberty. And everything. Everything terrible that happened began with Nana's death!"

Mr. Kipling shook his head. "You're a smart girl, Annie. I think you know it started long before."

"What do I know? I know nothing! I've been in the dark for a year now. You left me that way." My face was flushed and my throat was raw. "You betrayed me! Nana and Imogen are probably in Hell! And you are going there, too!"

"Don't say that. I would never betray you," Mr. Kipling insisted. "The truth is, I worked for Galina before I worked for you. How could I deny her?"

"You should have come to me."

"Your nana wanted to protect you. She didn't want you involved."

"She wasn't in her right mind. She didn't know what she wanted. You said so yourself. You can't have it both ways."

"Annie, I love your family. I loved your father. I loved Galina. I love you. You must know that I did my best. That I did what I thought was right." He moved around his desk to put his arm on my shoulder but I shook him off.

"I should fire you," I whispered. My voice was husky, and I was on the verge of losing it altogether. I'd been yelling at people all day.

"Give me a stay of execution. Just this once," Mr. Kipling pleaded. "I love you, Annie. I love you like my own flesh and blood. There are other lawyers, maybe even better ones. But your business is not business to me. Your business is my life and my very heart. Your father was the best man I have ever known, and I promised him I would take care of you in any way I could. You know this. If ever I betray you again, even inadvertently, you have my permission to fire me immediately. God as my witness, I will fire myself."

I turned to look at Mr. Kipling. He was holding his arms out wide, a gesture of beseeching. I moved closer to him, and I let him embrace me. For a variety of reasons, I could not bring myself to mention Simon Green.

XVI

I ATTEND CHURCH

ASIDE FROM FUNERALS, I had not been inside a church since Christmas Eve. At first, I had had perfectly good reasons for my truancy—hiding, Liberty, house arrest—but even after I was free, I found that I didn't want to return. It is probably too strong to say that I had lost my faith but I can't think of another way to describe it. I had been pious for so long, and where had it gotten me? Leo was dead, and faith-wise, I might as well have been seasick in a cargo ship in the middle of the Atlantic.

(So, why was I going to church that Sunday? Did I hope to re-kindle the dying embers of my faith? No indeed, readers.) The reason I was going to church was decidedly ungodly. I hoped to run into Sophia Bitter. I had decided that Charles Delacroix, my foe, was right. The best way to settle the question of Sophia's involvement was to put it to her directly. Even if she lied

to me, that lie would tell me something. And she couldn't try to kill me in a church.

Natty had told me to wake her so that we could go to church together, but I didn't want her or anyone else with me. I set out early so that I could walk down to St. Patrick's instead of taking the bus.

I did not pay attention during the service. From the balcony, I had spotted Sophia Bitter. She sat about halfway toward the front and was wearing a red hat with a spiderlike ornament. Mickey was not by her side.

As soon as Mass was over, I ran down to the gallery to talk to Sophia Bitter.

"Sophia," I called.

She turned unhurriedly, like she was dancing a waltz. At eye level, I could see the hat wasn't a spider but two crimson bows sitting atop each other. "Anya," Sophia greeted me. "How lovely to see you. Forgive me. I was on my way to confession." Sophia moved closer to me and kissed me on both of my cheeks. Her lips were warm and sticky with lip balm. I asked her where Mickey was and she said that since Yuri's death, he'd been going to his father's church if not skipping Sunday Mass altogether. "Well," she said, "I must get in the confession line."

I asked her if something weighed particularly heavy on her soul.

Sophia cocked her head to the side and smiled a little. She paused to look me in the eyes, which I made sure to keep friendly and blank. "This is humor, yes?"

I made my voice as light as a butterfly. "Cousin Sophia, the strangest thing happened. I was on Museum Mile, and a man was selling chocolate. Of course, I asked him if he had Balanchine Special Dark. It's my favorite, you know. And since Nana died and Jacks went to prison, no one ever brings it by the apartment." I paused to look at Sophia. Her expression was as empty as my own, but I thought I saw her pupils dilate slightly. What had Dr. Lau said about dilated pupils? "So, I bought this bar and I forgot all about it until my boyfriend, Win—you remember him?—wanted chocolate. But when he took off the Balanchine wrapper, you'll never guess what was underneath. It was a Bitter chocolate bar. I thought, 'Bitter. That's Cousin Sophia's family. How strange that a Bitter bar should end up under a Balanchine wrapper.'"

Sophia opened her mouth to speak, and for a second, I even thought she might have a perfectly logical explanation for what had happened. Other churchgoers were passing us by. She closed her mouth decisively. She smiled more broadly than before. "All this honey," she said with a snort.

"What do you mean?"

"All this honey. There must be a bee, Anya." Sophia adjusted her ridiculous hat and then she appraised me with narrowed eyes. "So, we are seeing each other for the first time," she said. Sophia took off her gloves. "What a relief this is. Of course, I am aware of the oversight that you speak of. It has happened before. The workers are supposed to take off both layers of Bitter wrapping but they're lazy, Anya. Sometimes they forget."

"But why are you passing off Bitter chocolate bars as Balanchine?"

Sophia didn't answer my question. Instead she made a funny

clucking sound with her tongue, almost like the sound of a rattlesnake's tail.

"Did you arrange to have Natty and me killed?"

Sophia said nothing.

"Did you kill Leo?"

"A car bomb killed Leo. That is what Yuji Ono says. And I had nothing to do with that."

I tried to control my voice. "So you did arrange to have Natty and me killed?"

"What if I said that I had only arranged to have *you* killed? Would the insult be less? You are a silly girl, Anya Balanchine. Yuji Ono spoke so highly of you, and I have found you nothing but disappointing."

"I don't care if you like me. I just need to know whether to kill you or not."

Sophia let her bottom lip fall into an expression of mock horror. "It is Sunday, Anya. We are in church!" She paused. "No one died except Leo, so maybe you could take what happened as a warning."

"What about your own cousin? Theo is very sick."

"He shouldn't have tried to intervene. I have always hated that side of my family, and they have always hated me." It couldn't have been true. Why would they have been so kind to me, who they had been led to believe was Sophia's friend? "But all this is in the past, Anya. What are you going to do now? If you kill me, that would be a waste of your efforts. My relatives from Germany will come for you and Nataliya, and we Bitters will make you Balanchines look like bunny rabbits."

She put her arms around me and whispered in my ear, "I

had nothing to do with Leo's death. That was my husband. He is sentimental and an idiot. When you didn't agree to marry Yuji, Mickey took the opportunity to find out from Yuji where Leo was and he had him killed." Sophia took a step away from me, then she moved back in to kiss me on the mouth. "What a waste. Yuri Balanchine was an old man, and Leo wasn't bothering anyone in Japan."

"I don't understand. Why kill any of us? None of us are active in Balanchine Chocolate."

Sophia laughed. "Do you know what the problem with Balanchine Chocolate is? Not that it is organized crime but how very *dis*organized your family is. There is no reason that a company as disorganized as Balanchine Chocolate should enjoy such dominance in this market. Do you have any idea how difficult it has been for me? I thought if I married your cousin, I'd have some chance to get everything running again . . ."

Bitter Chocolate had been failing for some time, she said. The German market was too competitive and the only way to save the Bitter business was to move it into other territories. The perceived unrest in Balanchine Chocolate since my father's death had made America the obvious choice. She and her high school chum Yuji Ono had conceived of a plan where the two of them could create chaos in the American market and then swoop in to split up the results. She came up with the poisoning. Sophia's wedding to Mickey Balanchine had been another bit of strategy, devised by Yuji Ono. The tainted Balanchine supply would need to be replaced with something—why not Bitter brand? There were warehouses filled with uneaten Bitter chocolate.

There had only been one problem: at some point, Yuji Ono had changed his mind about wanting to destroy the Balanchines.

Here, Sophia rolled her eyes. "He saw potential in you. And he convinced Mickey to see potential in you, too. So instead of running Balanchine Chocolate into the ground, Yuji Ono became intent upon saving it. For you, Anya. As wrongheaded as I thought that was. And I was stranded here in this awful city, married to this dull man. And so I did what I could."

"You still haven't said whether you tried to kill Natty and me."

Sophia shook her head. "You are both alive, aren't you? So what difference can failed attempts possibly make? Bygones, I'd say."

"Your cousin was almost killed! My friend Imogen died! And for what?" I put my hands around her neck, but I did not squeeze and she did not scream.

"For all the usual things, Anya. For money. And a little bit for love." She paused. "What if I promised to leave? What if I went back to Germany and had my marriage to Mickey annulled? You can deal with him for the death of your brother without me. Or you can just decide to call it a day. One father for one brother. What if you and I never saw each other again?"

"Why shouldn't I just kill you?"

"Here? In St. Patrick's Cathedral? A good Catholic girl like you? I'll believe it when I see it." Sophia laughed. "You won't kill me because you are not a murderer. That is what I said to Yuji Ono after I met you the first time. The child may be brighter than her cousins but she doesn't have the stomach for our line of work."

262

"That isn't so."

"You think you're tough because you sliced off that assassin's hand. It isn't tough to injure someone when you really ought to have killed him."

"Right now, *liebchen*, the smart move would be to take that machete from under your coat and stab me through the heart, too. But you won't. I don't envy you. Daughter of a cop and a criminal. How your heart must war with itself. So, you'll let me go. You think you're still deciding but it's already done."

I took my hands from around her neck, and she began backing down the aisle away from me.

I ran to her and pressed the machete into her side, the blade only piercing her cashmere coat.

"Damn. I liked this coat," Sophia said.

"Just tell me one thing. Who helped you? You couldn't have arranged the poisoning by yourself. You must have had someone over here. Was it Fats?"

She shook her head no, and her spider hat bobbed up and down.

"Was it Yuri? Mickey? Jacks?"

She squinted as if that would help her see me better. Her lips came together for something like a smile. "The young lawyer," she whispered.

"Simon Green . . . Simon wouldn't."

"Simon did. He hates your father, Anya. And he hates you, too."

"I don't believe you. Simon Green doesn't hate me." I could not help but think of what Jacks had said to me.

"People have reasons for everything under the sun."

Sophia shrugged. "All our cards are on the table. Why would I lie?"

She turned and walked briskly out of the church. I wished I could have killed her, but Sophia was right: back then, I was still Catholic enough not to be able to do such a thing in church.

I hesitated. I wondered if maybe I could kill her on the steps instead.

I was about to chase after her when I felt something incredibly heavy hit me across the back of the head.

Despite my upbringing, I must admit to taking the Lord's name in vain.

I turned in time to see a Bible coming straight at my forehead.

Just before the smack, Sophia Bitter laughed.

I awoke in a hospital bed. What I felt was a mild amount of pain and an incredible amount of annoyance. I had let Sophia Bitter go. Who knew where she was or what trouble she would cause next? Also, I was nearly as tired of hospitals as I had been of Liberty.

I needed to get going. I stood, feeling a bit woozy. I hadn't been at the hospital long, so I was still in my clothes. I found my shoes (though not my machete) in the closet. I went into the bathroom to take stock of my injuries. There was a huge bump on my forehead and another one on the back of my head. I couldn't see the second one as it was covered by hair. Other than that, I seemed to be in one piece.

I poked my head out the doorway. There didn't seem to be any nurses around, so I made my move. I walked down a hallway, then past the reception area. No one noticed me. In the waiting area, I could see Daisy Gogol and Natty. My sister's face was red and tearstained while Daisy's was pale and tense. I didn't want to be stopped, but I also didn't want them to be too concerned.

I went up to them. "Shh," I said.

"Annie, what are you doing out of bed?" Natty yelled.

"I'm okay, but I have to go," I told them.

"You're not making any sense," Natty said. "Who hit you? What happened?"

"I'll explain everything later. I'll be fine."

"You don't look fine," Natty insisted. "You don't look *at all* fine. If you don't go back to that hospital room, I swear to God, Anya, I am going to scream."

I looked at the reception desk. Despite my sister's increasingly hysterical tone, we still hadn't aroused much interest. It was a busy hospital in a crime-filled city, and the staff was used to filtering out the cries of the agitated.

"Natty, I have something I need to take care of, and it absolutely cannot wait." I turned to Daisy. "Would you happen to have my machete?"

Daisy Gogol did not choose to answer my question. Instead, she looked from me to my sister. "I feel awful, Anya. I shouldn't have let you go to church without me. I thought you'd be fine. It is church after all."

"It's fine, Daisy."

"I understand if you need to fire me," Daisy Gogol said.

I didn't want to fire her, but I did want to know if she had my weapon.

265

"I do, Anya," she said. "But I can't give it to you."

"Oh, for God's sake," I said.

"I'm sorry. My job is to protect you, not facilitate you." Daisy Gogol lifted me off the ground, as if I weighed nothing—and trust me, I did weigh something; I may have been small, but I was also dense (yes, occasionally in the other sense of the word, too)—and carried me back to the desk. "This girl has had a head trauma, and she's gotten out of her room," Daisy Gogol said to the nurse.

The nurse looked insufferably bored with us, as if giant women toting around smaller women was a regular occurrence. She instructed Daisy to carry me back to the room, where a doctor would be in to see me shortly. As we were traveling down the hallway, I weighed my options. I could not overpower Daisy Gogol, but I was fairly confident that I could outrun her.

She placed me on the bed gently, like I was a beloved doll. "I am sorry, Anya."

"I understand."

"But I do know a thing or two about head traumas, and you need to be monitored for the next day at least. Whatever has happened can surely wait until you're thinking more clear—"

I sat upright and pushed her as far as I could. I didn't make much of an impact, but she was stunned enough that I had time to run out of the room. "Take Natty home!" I called as I fled.

Since I didn't have my machete, the first place I went was Fats's speakeasy. I'd need backup before going to deal with Mickey and Sophia. "Annie, what brings you?" Fats asked.

I had run from the hospital and I was scant of breath. "You were right. Sophia Bitter planned the hits. And I think she was responsible for the poisonings," I said.

Fats poured himself a shot of espresso. "Yes, that makes sense. Do you think Mickey was in on it?"

"I'm not sure. Sophia says he was the one who killed Leo in retaliation for what Leo did to Yuri. The truth is, she might have just been lying to get the heat off her for Leo's death."

"And the easiest way to do that is to point the finger at her husband." He paused to look at me. "Jesus, kid, what happened to your forehead?"

"I got between a sinner and her Bible," I explained. "I want to go confront Mickey, and I need you with me."

Fats nodded. "I'll get my gun."

When we got to Mickey's brownstone, a servant answered the door. "Mr. and Mrs. Balanchine just left. They said they were going to visit her relatives."

I said to Fats that we should go to the airport, but he shook his head. "We don't even know which one. Maybe the best thing that could possibly happen is the two of them leaving town. Think of it, Anya—if the two of them stayed, we'd have an internecine war on our hands. With them out of the picture, it's back to business as usual and that's a very good thing."

"But I want to know for sure if Mickey killed my brother!"

"I understand that, Annie. But what would knowing really matter? Sophia said he did. And Mickey is gone. You drove them out of town, so you got to take some comfort in that because that is all the truth you're going to get for now."

This seemed incredibly naïve to me. Just because they had

left town didn't mean they'd be gone forever. "We need to go see Simon Green," I told him.

"The lawyer? Why?" Fats demanded.

I told him that Sophia had said that he was involved in the poisoning. "Fats, have you ever heard a rumor that Simon Green might somehow be related to us?"

Fats cocked his head and screwed his mouth into a skeptical ball. "Annie, there's always rumors about us. And most of them you don't got to bother paying no mind to."

But I wouldn't be deterred.

At Simon's building, we walked up the six flights of stairs. My head was starting to pound and I was wishing I'd had the foresight to ask someone at the hospital for an aspirin before I'd run out.

We found that the door was open, and Mr. Kipling was standing in the center of the room. He must not have been there too long, because he was still out of breath from the stairs. "He's gone," Mr. Kipling said. "Simon Green's gone."

"How do you know?" I asked.

Mr. Kipling nodded to Fats, then held out a slip of paper to me:

Dear Mr. Kipling,

I am about to be accused of a crime, and I must now leave in order that I may clear my good name.

You have been like a father to me.

Please forgive the short notice.

Please also forgive me.

Simon Green, Esq.

268

"Do you have any idea what this is about?" Mr. Kipling asked me. "Anya, what happened to your head?"

I answered him with a question of my own. "Mr. Kipling, why are *you* here?"

"Simon Green told me to come, and I did. I should ask the same question of you, I suppose."

I told him what Sophia Balanchine had said about the poisoning and Simon Green hating my father and his children.

Mr. Kipling looked at Fats. "Would you mind giving us a moment alone?"

Fats nodded. "I'll be in the hall if you want me."

Mr. Kipling shook his head. "No, Anya. She's wrong. Simon Green loves you. And I love Simon."

I reminded him of the day of his heart attack. "Did you ever wonder if it was a setup?"

"No, I didn't. I didn't watch what I ate and I didn't take care of myself."

"You should have heard Simon Green in court that day. What if he was being incompetent on purpose? What if he *wanted* to get me sent to Liberty?"

Mr. Kipling said that I sounded paranoid, insane.

"He knew the most intimate details of my business. He knew where all of us were. He knew everything, Mr. Kipling! If he was in partnership with Sophia Bitter the whole time . . . !"

"No! He would never have partnered with Sophia Bitter."

"Why?" I asked.

"He would never have partnered with her because of who he is."

269

"Who is he, then?" I demanded. "Mr. Kipling, who is Simon Green?"

"My ward," Mr. Kipling replied.

"Who was Simon Green to my father?"

"Before he was my ward, he was your father's ward."

"Why was he my father's ward?"

"Anya, I promised," Mr. Kipling said.

"Is he my . . ." I couldn't say it. I couldn't bring myself to say it. "Is he my half brother?"

"It's so long ago. What difference can dredging up any of this make?" Mr. Kipling said.

"Tell the truth!" I shrieked.

"I . . . You see, Anya, there's a very good reason Simon Green could never have been involved in anything that would harm you." Mr. Kipling took his mini-slate out of his wallet. He turned on the slate and showed me the screen. On it was a picture of my father standing next to a little boy. The boy was Simon Green. I recognized the eyes. Light blue like Leo's and Daddy's. "Your father . . . Well, you could say he adopted Simon. He took him under his wing."

"I don't understand what 'you could say' means. He either adopted him or he didn't. Why would he have adopted him and never told any of us about it?"

"I . . . Maybe he planned to someday, but he didn't live long enough. The story I was told was that Simon Green's father had worked for your father. The father died on the job, and when the mother died, too, your father thought it was his responsibility to take care of him. He was a good man, your father."

"Why do you say 'the story'? Stop being vague, Mr. Kipling." I was covered in sweat and my head felt like it might explode. Something fierce and terrible was beginning to burn within me.

Mr. Kipling walked over to the window. There was a distant look in his eyes. "The day you met Simon, he had been wanting to meet you for so long. But I always kept him from you."

"Why? Why did he want to meet me? Who was I to him?"

"Have you never noticed the resemblance?" Mr. Kipling turned. "The eyes and the skin. Does he not look like your cousin Mickey, your cousin Jacks? Does he not look like your brother? Your father? Green was his mother's name."

"Is he my father's son?"

"I don't know for sure, Anya. But I have arranged everything for Simon. His schooling. This apartment. And I did these things because your father told me to."

I felt ill. "You had no right to keep this from me." I've always thought it was preposterous in a story or a movie when someone throws up upon hearing dramatic news, but I really did feel like I might. (Of course, it might also have had something to do with the blow I'd taken to the head.)

"Sophia Bitter says that Simon Green helped plan the poisoning last fall," I said to Mr. Kipling.

"Simon is a good boy," Mr. Kipling said. "He would never do something like that. I've known him his whole life."

I looked at Mr. Kipling's threadbare head. I loved that head. It had been one of the few constantly good things in my life. That is to say, what I needed to do next wasn't easy for me.

"I believe that you have made an inexcusable lapse in judgment, Mr. Kipling, and I can't have you working for me anymore."

Mr. Kipling thought about what I had said. "I understand," he said. "Anya, I do understand."

At that moment, Simon's cat came into the room. "Here, Koshka," Mr. Kipling called. The cat approached him warily, and Mr. Kipling lured her into a pet carrier that was sitting on Simon's bed. "When he called, Simon asked me to take care of the cat," Mr. Kipling explained.

I left Simon Green's apartment. Mr. Kipling did not try to stop me.

"So, what's next?" Fats asked me on the trolley ride across the Brooklyn Bridge to Manhattan.

I shook my head. The sun was going down on what had been a fruitless afternoon, and I was discouraged. I had wanted a big scene where I confronted Mickey and Simon, and maybe only one of us came out alive. Instead, they had both disappeared. "I'm surprised Mickey left," I admitted.

"We don't know what Sophia told him," Fats said. "And you haven't been around to follow it, but the Balanchine distributors are pretty frustrated with him at this point." Fats looked at me. "Kid, don't be blue. As far as these things go, this is a pretty happy ending. You sniffed out the bad eggs, sent them packing, and everyone lived."

"Except Leo."

"God rest his soul." Fats crossed himself. "I'm telling you, your dad would have been proud. He didn't believe in violence."

I may have snorted.

"Sometimes he had to use it, but it was only ever a last resort for him."

"Just because Mickey is gone, I don't want Balanchine Chocolate to die. I don't want Daddy's company to die," I said. I knew that Mickey and Sophia's departure had made Balanchine Chocolate even more vulnerable.

"The key thing now is to establish a new leadership as quickly as possible. We can't have any appearance of dissent."

"Fats, do you think you'll really be able to do a better job running Balanchine Chocolate than Mickey did?"

"No one can say for sure, Annie. But, if you back me, I'll do my best. I'm honest, and I know the tribulations of chocolate better than anyone."

It was true. Fats had run his speakeasy successfully for years, and he knew all the players. I realized now that Yuji Ono and Yuri and Mickey had probably just been flattering me to suggest that I should run Balanchine Chocolate. Because I was young and ignorant, they had been able to use me for their own ends. I had allowed myself to be flattered and had ended up being foolish yet again. "Why do you even care if I back you?"

"You don't know the chocolate business, but the rank and file still care what you think. They remember your daddy, and they've seen your face in the news, and I would appreciate your support."

"If I do back you, what happens to me?" I probably sounded childish or at least teenage-ish.

We were just about over the Brooklyn Bridge and back into Manhattan. Fats put his hand on my shoulder. "Look, Annie. See that city. Anything can happen there."

"Not for me," I said. "I'm Anya Balanchine. First Daughter of the chocolate mob. I have the name and the rap sheet to go with it."

Fats stroked his goatee. "It's not as bad as all that. Finish school, kid. Then come back to me. I'll set you up with a job if you still want one. You can learn the ropes. Maybe even find out what it is they do in Moscow."

At that point, I had to get off the trolley to switch to the bus that would take me back uptown. Fats said that there would be a meeting at the Pool the next day, and that he would really appreciate it if I would come.

"I'm not sure I want to back you," I said.

"Yeah, I can see that. Here's what I think you should do. Get a good night's sleep, and when you wake up in the morning, ask yourself what it would be like to be free of Balanchine Chocolate forever. Your brother's dead, and the players are gone. You back me tomorrow, and I'll make sure that no one ever messes with you or your sister again."

I arrived at the apartment around ten o' clock. Daisy Gogol and Natty and Win were waiting for me, and no one looked pleased.

"We should take her immediately back to the hospital," Natty said.

"I'm fine," I replied as I collapsed onto the couch. "Exhausted, but fine."

Daisy Gogol shot me an evil look. "I could have stopped you, but I didn't want to hurt you. I'm not accustomed to being pushed by people I'm supposed to be protecting."

I apologized to Daisy.

"At the hospital, they said someone was supposed to watch her to make sure she didn't go to sleep." Natty stood up from the couch and crossed her arms. "I'd watch her but I don't even want to look at her."

"I'll do it," Win volunteered, though he didn't sound particularly enthused about the task.

"Listen, Natty, don't be cross. I think I found out who tried to kill us." And then I told them what I had learned that day.

"You can't keep going on like this," Natty lectured me. "Running around and not telling anyone where you're going or what happened. I'm tired of it. And, for the record, I don't want to end up with no brother and no"—her voice broke a little—"sister either, Annie." I stood to embrace her, but she pulled away, then ran down the hallway to her bedroom. A second later, I heard the door slam.

I turned to Daisy. "You can go home now, if you want."

Daisy shook her head. "I can't. Mr. Kipling called to tell me I should stay on guard overnight. He was extremely concerned about your safety."

"Fine, but you should know that I had to dismiss Mr. Kipling this afternoon."

"Yes," Daisy replied, "he said that, too. He told me that he would be personally covering my salary."

Daisy went to the hallway to stand watch.

I sat back down on the couch. Win went into the kitchen and came back with a bag of frozen peas for my head.

"It's probably too late for that," I said.

"It's never too late for frozen peas," Win said cheerfully.

"Aren't you angry at me, too?" I asked.

"Why? Just because you put your life in danger and didn't tell anyone what you were doing? Why should I care? I don't worry about you at all."

He set the peas on my forehead as I had done so many times to Leo. I winced a bit at the cold. I stretched up to kiss him, but my head started to pound. I lay back down on the pillow. "Sorry," I said.

"Do you think I even want to be kissed by you? You're pretty much horribly deformed at this point." He leaned down to kiss me lightly, sweetly. "What am I going to do with you?" His voice was gentle and low.

Because I still needed to make sense of it myself, I decided to describe for him the baffling events of the day, ending with Fats's request that I abdicate any leadership position in Balanchine Chocolate.

"Would it be so awful?" Win asked. "What he was essentially saying to you is that you could walk away."

"But what about Leo?" I asked. "What about Daddy?"

"Nothing you do for Balanchine Chocolate will bring either of them back, Annie."

It was good advice. The truth was, the quickest way for me to destroy Balanchine Chocolate and my father's legacy—such as it was—would be to get into a war with Fats over leadership. Besides, what did I know about running a chocolate business anyway?

I moved the bag of peas so that it covered my eyes, too. Even my eyes were starting to hurt. It felt peaceful to be in the cold and in the dark.

—◇—

I hadn't been to the Pool since I'd made my speech before going to Liberty the prior year. Aside from Fats, so many of the people I had known were dead, gone, or in prison, and while everyone was vaguely and literally familiar, I didn't really know any of them personally. That was the thing about organized-crime families—you shouldn't bother getting too attached to anyone.

Fats had asked me to explain about Mickey's disappearance and Sophia's involvement in the poisoning and in the hits on my family, which I did. Then I stated that I supported Fats in his desire to be the interim head of the Balanchine Family. Lukewarm applause followed this sentiment. Fats himself gave a brief speech regarding his vision for the Family. His vision didn't seem to be markedly different from any of the previous heads of the Family: mainly things about ensuring the quality of the product and limiting supply delays, etc. Finally, Fats opened up the room to questions.

A man with a curly mustache and round eyeglasses turned to me and said, "Anya, I'm Pip Balanchine. I wonder what your dealings with the new district attorney have been like. Does she seem anti-chocolate?"

"Not particularly," I said. "The only things she cares about are money and advancement."

The men laughed at my assessment.

A black man with reddish hair piped in, "You're a good guy, Fats, but you run a restaurant. You really think you're up to heading the Balanchine *semya*?"

"Yes," Fats said, "I do."

" 'Cause personally I am tired of the unrest. It doesn't make for good business and it certainly doesn't make for good chocolate. I think we sell ourselves short. The poisoning should have been an opportunity to overhaul the business, not . . ."

The meeting went on a while longer though my presence barely seemed necessary. Daisy Gogol stood behind me as was the convention at these meetings, and occasionally, she would nudge me. But what was I to say? The truth was, some part of me really was happy to let Fats run the company. Maybe I'd learned something about cacao but there were still so many other aspects of the business I didn't know. And the endless garbage Yuji Ono had fed me about my being "a catalyst"—well, maybe I didn't have it in me to be a catalyst. I had tried to call Yuji Ono the day before to confront him about everything that Sophia Bitter had said. I still had so many questions. Had he helped plot Leo's murder out of love for Sophia or hate for me, or had there been other reasons entirely? Had he ever really believed anything he'd said or had he just preyed on me because I was young and susceptible to flattery? What had he known about Simon Green? But the number I had for Yuji Ono had been disconnected. He was as much a mystery to me as he had ever been.

Sitting at the bottom of the empty pool, my mind drifted. I thought of Mexico. The water there had been so blue. I wondered how Theo was. I had been too embarrassed to contact him. Had I done it over the phone, I would have had to confront one of the mighty Marquez women. A letter seemed impossible—I wasn't good with words.

A man in a purple suit turned to me. "Anya, are you

planning to consult with Fats? I like knowing that at least one of Leo Balanchine's children is in on things."

I promised to keep tabs on my cousin. Then, out of respect, I bowed my head toward Fats.

"Anya knows my door is always open to her," Fats replied. "And when she's a little older and knows more, I imagine her involvement in the business can be even greater, if that's something she desires."

Not long after, the meeting was over. My abdication was brief and bloodless. As Mr. Beery might have said, *The Merchant of Venice*, and not *Macbeth*.

XVI

I HAVE DOUBTS

Just before Easter, we heard news of Sophia and Mickey. They had landed in Belgium, where they planned to open a new branch of Bitter Schokolade. In the photo that Natty located, I noticed that their entourage included a one-handed giant. It seemed safe to assume that the man I'd maimed at Granja Mañana hadn't bled to death in a Mexican rain forest. I did not yet have the black mark of murder on my soul.

Easter Sunday, Natty and I went to church. Even for a semilapsed Catholic having a crisis of faith, Easter was too big a holiday to skip. Daisy Gogol had gone home for the weekend, but security hardly seemed necessary anyway with Sophia and Mickey in Belgium and Jacks still in prison. Natty and I were safe, if only because we were the last women standing. Hadn't Daddy once said that "he who survives, wins"? Who cared what Daddy had said, though.

I had always loved the Easter liturgy. I loved the candle

lighting and that renewal was the theme of the day. But that year, I felt disconnected from the entire thing. I did not, could not, could no longer make myself believe. It was during the renewal of baptismal vows that I felt this most strongly. The priest asked the congregation, "Do you turn to Christ?" Easy enough. Yes, I thought, of course I did. Then the priest asked, "Do you repent of your sins?" This one was more difficult. My list of sins was long, and most of them I'd committed knowingly. For instance, could I honestly say I repented cutting off that man's hand? If I hadn't, he would have murdered Theo and me. Despite everything, I was glad to be alive. And I was definitely glad that Theo was alive. And, toward the end of the liturgy, when we were all meant to say "I believe and trust in Him" over and over again, I said it because everyone around me was saying it, but I could not honestly say that I did believe and trust in Him. I had prayed and been devout but where had that led me? Leo was dead. My parents were dead. Nana was dead. Imogen was dead. I wouldn't be graduating. I had a criminal record. Sometimes it seemed as if my whole life had been decided from the moment of my birth, and if that was the case, why bother with religion or prayer or any of it? You might as well just do what you wanted. Sleep with whomever you wanted on Saturday. Sleep in on Sunday.

At that moment, Natty looked at me. "I love you, Annie," she said. "And I am so grateful for you. Please don't be bitter."

I shook my head. "I love you, too," I told her. That was about the only thing I knew to be true.

———◇———

After church, we took our time walking back home. The late-March afternoon was humid and gray, though there was a lackluster patch of sun poking through a thin spot in the sky. I was warm in my spring coat so I unbuttoned it.

"I want to go back to genius camp this summer," Natty announced when we were about halfway home.

"Good. You should go."

"But you seem . . ."—she searched for a word—"adrift, Anya, and angry, and I'm worried about leaving you alone."

"Natty!" Had I become Leo to her? Someone she felt she needed to watch? "Natty, I have friends. And interests. Go to your destiny. Go to genius camp."

"By interests, do you mean fulfilling various vendettas?" Natty asked.

"No!"

"Listen, Annie," Natty said gently. "Leo is dead. And the people who planned it are gone. Win will be in college, and he's the nicest boy in the world, but you have to be prepared that he might meet someone new. Scarlet is having this baby and she might even marry Gable Arsley. You've fired Mr. Kipling and Mr. Green. Everything is about to change, and you need to be ready to move on."

Of course my wise little sister was right. But what was I to do? I didn't want to spend my whole life on the opposite side of the law—in and out of Liberty until I was too old to go there, then in and out of Rikers or whatever the age-eighteen-and-up equivalent was for female habitual criminals. I didn't want to end up like Jacks or Daddy, which is why I had agreed to let Fats take over. Still, the truth was, I wasn't suited for anything else. I knew a little bit about chocolate and a little bit about organized crime and I had an infamous last name. What did all these things add up to?

"So," Natty continued, "if you want me to stay and help you out this summer, I will—"

"Natty, I want you to go! Of course I want you to go."

Natty looked me in the eyes, and then she nodded. "Maybe you should go see Dr. Lau?"

I shook my head.

"She asks about you every time I see her."

I shook my head again. "She's just being nice."

Natty and I rode up in the elevator. When we got to our floor, the door was slightly ajar.

I held out my arm. "Stay," I told Natty. I took my machete out from under my coat.

Natty's eyes grew wide. "Maybe we should run?" she whispered.

I was not a person who ran. I ordered her to stay in the hallway, in the area where the fire escape was. "If you hear me scream, I want you to go down the stairs as fast as you can. Run to Win's house. Don't talk to anyone until you get there."

Natty nodded.

At that moment, the front door swung wide open.

Standing there was a ghost.

I felt like I was losing my mind.

"Annie," the ghost said, and then he put his arms around me.

The ghost was made of flesh and bone.

"Leo," I said. "Leo, Leo." My head began to throb, and I couldn't breathe. I grabbed at his cheeks and his arms, pinching and poking him to make sure he was real. "But how?" I mumbled. "How?" I looked into Leo's light blue eyes. I pulled his wavy black hair. I buried my face in his chest to smell him.

"I faked my death so I could come back to New York," Leo said.

"You *what*?" It was such an extraordinary thing for him to say.

"I was so homesick, Annie. I missed you and Natty so much. And I was bored, too. I couldn't stay there anymore. Please don't be mad."

I was really having trouble breathing. I was on the verge of passing out.

"Oh, Leo, you shouldn't have." This was going to cause more problems for me than I could even begin to imagine, but still my heart was full. "Natty!" I yelled. "Come here!"

Natty emerged from the fire-stairs door. "Leo?" she asked. And then Natty fainted.

Leo and I picked her up and brought her inside.

In the living room were Simon Green and a Japanese girl I didn't recognize.

I glowered at Simon. "What are you doing here?"

"He helped me plan everything," Leo said. "I contacted Simon Green in the fall after Yuji Ono said you were going away. I didn't want Natty to be all alone."

That meant that the hit on Leo had been a fake? And yet I knew that the hits on Natty and me had been real. Why coordinate a fake hit on the same day as two real hits? What did this mean?

I sat down on our couch. "Simon, why didn't you tell me that Leo was alive?"

Simon took off his glasses and wiped them on his shirt. "I suppose because I didn't think you'd believe me. Not with the awful coincidence of the attempted murders of you and Natty. I realized that Sophia had somehow become aware of Leo's and my plan and had used that fact to her advantage."

The Japanese girl smiled pleasantly at me. Though she was clearly a woman, she was about the size of a child, with no breasts to speak of and limbs like twigs. "I'm sorry," I said. "Who are you?"

"This is Noriko," Leo said. "She doesn't speak much English yet but she's learning. She is Yuji Ono's niece. And she is also my wife."

"You're married?" This was too much to process. "Leo?"

Noriko held out her hand. On it was a single silver band.

Natty woke up. "Leo?" she asked. "Leo?" Natty had begun to cry.

"Oh, Natty, please don't." Leo wiped her tears on his sleeve. He sat down next to her on the couch, and they held each other for the longest time.

I stood to give them some space. Although I was overjoyed to find that Leo was still alive, I could not afford to be overcome in this moment. I had too many things to figure out. I walked to the balcony, and Simon Green sidled up next to me. "You must see, Anya, that I never could have planned anything that would have hurt you or Natty or Leo."

"Sophia Bitter says that you helped her plan the poisonings," I told him.

"I did not!"

"Why would she say that if it weren't true?"

"She's a liar, Anya, and I suppose she was just trying to cover her bases. Point fingers at whomever she thought was vulnerable."

I looked into Simon Green's eyes, eyes like Leo's and Daddy's. "Who are you?" I whispered.

"I don't know for sure, Annie. But I can tell you what I have come to believe." He took my hand. "I believe that I am your half brother. I believe that is why your father provided for my care."

"Does he know?" I indicated Leo.

Simon Green shook his head. "No. You are the head of this family, and it is your decision when to tell Leo and Natty."

I told him I appreciated that. "So why did Leo know to go to you about faking his own death?"

"He didn't come to me." Simon Green said that he had started making plans to get Leo out of Japan as soon as he had found out that I had refused Yuji Ono's proposal. "I didn't think it would be safe for him there anymore."

I wondered if I had somehow misunderstood what Leo had said to me—Leo had explicitly stated that he had decided to fake his own death, hadn't he?

I asked Simon if Mr. Kipling had known.

Simon Green shook his head no.

"Why didn't Daddy ever tell us about you?"

"Think of it, Anya. I'm eight years older than Leo. I don't think your father even knew about me until my mother died."

Daddy should have told us.

"Your father was a good man," Simon Green continued. "But he was just a man."

I turned away from the city and looked back through the glass doors into the living room, where Leo was introducing Natty to his wife. *Wife!*

Simon Green took my hand. "I want you to trust me, Anya. I want to be your partner. I want to be the brother that Leo doesn't have the ability to be. I want you to feel free to lay some of your burden on my shoulders."

I shook my head.

"Why not? Can't you see that I've risked everything to save Leo? You must know that I did that for you."

"It's just a lot for me to take in right now. Give me a little time," I pleaded. "We'll have to do something about Leo's legal situation," I told him. "It won't work to hide him in this apartment. And we certainly can't leave him as a fugitive forever."

Simon Green agreed. "I'll go to Bertha Sinclair as soon as the Easter holiday is over."

"Maybe Mr. Kipling could help?" I suggested.

"Yes, I think that could be arranged."

After Simon Green had left and everyone else had gone to bed, I went into the kitchen. I could not sleep. It was too late to call Win (he had been in Connecticut visiting a college with his mother), and even if it hadn't been, I could not begin to explain about the events of the day.

I got a glass of water from the tap and sat down at the table. The kitchen seemed oddly bright. The room was different than it had been that morning. There were more colors somehow, and my mind felt overwhelmed with sensation. There were so many things for me to solve now that Leo had returned.

I clasped my hands and bowed my head. *Thank you, God, for returning my brother to me. Thank you.* "I believe and trust in Him," I whispered.

At that moment, Leo came into the kitchen, wearing his pajama bottoms and a white T-shirt.

"Annie," Leo said. "I thought you were up." He sat down across from me at the table.

I told him that I hoped I hadn't woken him.

"You always wake me," Leo said. "Just like that night with Gable Arsley. I always listen for you."

I smiled at him. "Leo, how did you and Noriko get back to America?"

"By plane," Leo answered. "Simon Green came to get us."

I still had so many questions but I didn't want to overwhelm Leo with them. "Leo, can you explain something for me? Yuji Ono told me that your wife was from a fishing village and that she had been killed along with you. He never said that she was his niece."

Leo shrugged. "Noriko *is* from a fishing village," Leo said. "I went to stay with her family around October after Yuji Ono said it wasn't safe for me with the monks anymore. Noriko is the daughter of Yuji Ono's half brother."

Yuji Ono had had Leo moved? He had certainly never mentioned anything about that. And if that were true, it didn't necessarily make sense with Simon Green's depiction of Yuji Ono, i.e., that Leo had been unsafe in Japan once I'd refused Yuji Ono's proposal. And whose ashes had we been sent? And why had Yuji Ono lied about seeing Noriko's dead body? I shook my head. I needed to talk to Yuji Ono but he was still unreachable, and he hadn't tried to contact me.

I took my brother's head in my hands and kissed him on both cheeks. "Leo, let me ask you something. Do you think Yuji Ono is a good man?"

"Yes," Leo said. "But I haven't seen him in a very long time. Around January, he went into seclusion. Noriko thinks he might have caught a sickness during his travels. No one in his family knows, and Yuji Ono is very private."

I grabbed Leo's hand. I was still surprised to see the silver band around his ring finger. "Leo, are you very much in love with Noriko?"

"Yes!" Leo said. "I love her more than anyone I ever met except for you and Natty."

"Why?"

"Well, I think she is the prettiest girl in the world except for you and—"

I interrupted him. "Me and Natty, I know. And I agree. She is very pretty. What else, Leo?"

Leo's face grew solemn. "The thing is, Annie, she doesn't treat me like I am stupid. You probably won't believe this but she thinks I'm really smart." There were tears in the corners of Leo's eyes. "I'm sorry, Annie. I'm sorry for all the trouble I caused you last spring. I know everything you did for me. Yuji Ono said you even went to jail for me."

289

I told him that I'd do it again. He was my brother and I'd do anything for him. "Leo, Yuri's dead now and Mickey's gone. But we'll need to arrange something with the authorities so that you and Noriko can live here in peace."

Leo nodded.

"You might even have to go to jail for a little bit yourself."

"Okay," Leo said with such equanimity that I could not help but wonder if he'd understood what I'd said. "As long as Noriko can stay here with you and Natty. You'll have to take care of her."

"Of course, Leo. She's my sister now," I said.

The world was a remarkable place, really. I had started the day with one sister, and I had ended the day with a sister, a sister-in-law, a brother, and a half brother.

I had started the day with no faith and now my heart was full.

XVIII

I ATTEND A SCHOOL DANCE;
NO ONE GETS SHOT

In exchange for another modestly sized bribe to the Campaign to Reelect Bertha Sinclair, Leo was given a seven-month sentence to the Hudson River Psychiatric Facility and two years of probation. He'd be out in time for Thanksgiving.

The third Saturday in April, Mr. Kipling, Daisy Gogol, Noriko, and I drove Leo there. He kissed his wife (*wife!*), waved to the rest of us, and that was that. Noriko cried the whole three-hour trip back. We tried to comfort her but she spoke almost no English, and we spoke no Japanese, so I doubt we were much help.

Coincidentally, that evening was prom. I hadn't wanted to go, but Win had convinced me that we should, if only to re-deem the previous year's disaster. "Do you think they'll even let me on campus?" I had asked him. He reminded me that technically I had not been expelled this last time.

I had not bothered to shop for a dress so I went digging

around in Nana's and my mother's old clothes. I picked out a navy blue dress with capped sleeves, a high neckline, and a low back. I thought the dress fit well, but upon seeing me, Noriko screamed, *"No!"*

"No?" I asked.

"Bad," she said as she unzipped the back. "Old lady."

Noriko went into Leo's room and returned with a white dress. The dress was covered in lace and might have been a decent length on Noriko, but would be short on me. I would look like an insane bride. "You wear this," Noriko said. She was smiling. It was the first time she had smiled all day, and I thought of my promise to Leo to take care of his wife. I really didn't care about the matter anyway so I agreed to put on the dress.

I looked in the mirror. The dress was a bit tight on top, but otherwise, it fit surprisingly well.

Noriko came up behind me to adjust the sash, which tied in the back. "So pretty," Noriko said.

I shook my head. Natty came out of her room to examine me. "You look . . ."—Natty paused—"mad but attractive. Attractive mad." She kissed me on the cheek. "Win's going to love it."

Win met me at the apartment. He attached an orchid corsage to my wrist. I waited for him to make a joke about my crazy dress but he didn't seem to notice that anything was amiss. "You look beautiful," Win said. "Let's hope no one gets shot this year. It'll be hard to get blood out of that dress."

"Technically, I think it's still too soon for that kind of joke," I told him.

"Oh." He asked, "When will be the right time?"

"Probably never," I told him. "Interesting jacket choice, by the way." The jacket was white with black piping. Summery. Tacky.

"By 'interesting,' you mean you don't approve? Because people in glass houses, by which I mean people going to prom dressed like brides, shouldn't—"

"I didn't say that. It's, um, unexpected."

He said that his old tux jacket had gotten misplaced at the hospital the year before. I told him I was pretty sure it had been cut off him. "That explains that then," Win said. "This jacket's my dad's. He had white-tie and black-tie options. I picked white so no one will mistake me for anyone else."

At prom, my classmates seemed pleased to see me and the administration tolerated me. The theme was "The Future," but the organizing committee's world-building skills were lacking, and they hadn't really come up with a way to depict said theme in decorative terms. There was a handful of decorations with reflective surfaces and clocks, and a large digital banner that said WHERE WILL YOU BE IN 2104? Their vision of the future was vague at best, and I found the whole thing rather anxiety-producing. I had no idea where I'd be next year, let alone twenty years from now. Truthfully, the first answer to occur to me upon reading that banner was, *Dead. In 2104, I'll probably be dead.*

I was interrupted from my morbid thoughts by Scarlet. She was nearing eight months pregnant, and she looked pretty and miserable in her huge pink dress. She had come alone. Keeping her company was another tactic Win had used to convince me to go to this ridiculous dance in the first place.

"Annie, I love the dress!" Of course she did. Scarlet and Noriko would probably get along famously once I introduced them. Scarlet kissed me, and Win went to get us drinks. "I'm so glad you made it. Did Leo get to Albany all right?"

I nodded. "How are you?" I asked.

"Awful," she said. "I probably shouldn't have come. There's nothing sadder than a massive pregnant girl at prom. I hate what I'm wearing, and I'm too unwieldy to dance."

"That isn't true."

"Well, no one wants to dance with me except Arsley anyway."

I told her that I would dance with her, but Scarlet shook her head. "We aren't twelve anymore, Anya."

"Don't feel too sorry for yourself. Headmaster keeps shooting me awful looks, and this 'future' theme is making me nervous," I said.

Scarlet laughed halfheartedly.

Win returned with drinks. "I'll dance with you," Win said to Scarlet.

"What am I? That spinster aunt everyone takes pity on?" Scarlet asked in mock horror.

"No. She hates dancing." Win indicated me. "And you're the knocked-up girl *I'm* taking pity on. Come on." Win offered Scarlet his hand. "Seriously, it would be nice to dance with someone I don't have to cajole."

"I should throw this at you," Scarlet said to Win as she handed me her drink. I watched them make their way out to the dance floor.

Even as pregnant as she was, Scarlet still moved pretty well. I watched them with some degree of amusement though I could not help but feel wistful. I looked at Scarlet, and the size of her belly reminded me of the whole year I'd missed while I'd been . . . Well, you know what I'd been doing. Let's just say, the year I'd missed while I'd been otherwise engaged. I was still marveling at the bittersweetness of it all when Gable Arsley sat down in the chair next to me.

"Anya," Gable greeted me.

I nodded and tried not to look at him. As with animals in the wild, I hoped that if I didn't make eye contact, Gable would go away.

"I didn't expect to see you here," Gable said.

"I was invited," I said.

"I didn't mean any offense," Gable said. "I . . . You have to talk to Scarlet for me."

I looked at him out of the corner of my eye, then raised my eyebrow. "Why in the world would I ever do that?"

"Because she's carrying my baby! Because she is being unreasonable." He paused. "I know if she thought you approved she might forgive me."

I shook my head. "I don't approve, Arsley. You sold pictures of me. And that was just your latest move in a long line of offenses."

"I only did that because I needed the money," Gable protested.

"As if that makes it okay."

Gable grabbed my hand.

"Don't touch me," I said as I wrested my hand from his. "Seriously, don't."

Gable took my hand again. I could feel his metal fingertips through his glove.

"I don't want a scene here." I took my hand back again.

"You have to make Scarlet marry me," Gable said insanely.

"I can't do that."

"Tell her you've forgiven me!"

"But I haven't, Arsley."

Arsley slumped back into his chair. He crossed his arms. "I could still sue you, you know. I wish I had. Then I'd never have to work again. And I'd have loads of money to take care of Scarlet and the baby."

"How noble of you. Listen, Gable. If you really want to sue someone, you should sue Sophia Bitter. She was the one responsible for the poisonings."

"Sophia Bitter?" Gable asked. "Who's that?"

Win and Scarlet returned to the table. "Hello, Arsley," Win said in a hard voice.

"Is he bothering you?" Scarlet asked me.

It was adorable the way my friends thought that Gable Arsley could be anything other than an annoyance to me now. Strapped to my thigh, under Noriko's outrageous dress, was my favorite souvenir of Mexico.

Gable got up and limped back to whatever corner he had come from.

A slower song came on, and Scarlet insisted that Win and I dance at least once. "It's senior prom, you guys!"

On the dance floor, Win pulled me close to him and briefly, I could imagine what this whole year might have been like if everything had been different.

I felt him stiffen as his thigh pressed into my machete.

"Do you always have to have that with you?" Win asked.

I felt myself blush. "I'm sorry. But this is me, Win."

Win nodded. "I was only teasing. I know that." He brushed a curl off my forehead.

"It was the machete or Daisy Gogol," I joked. "No one is shooting my boyfriend at this year's prom."

Win tapped the machete through my dress. "I wondered why you were so insistent that we come in through the back."

"Metal detector," I said.

"Well, I do appreciate this. I'd like to be in your life a very long time and that'll be somewhat easier to do if I'm alive."

The song dissolved into a faster song, at which point Win agreed that we had both suffered through enough of prom. Scarlet was planning to spend the night at my place so we went to fetch her before going outside to catch the crosstown bus home.

Outside, there were many boys in black jackets, but mine was the only one in white.

297

XIX

I GRADUATE; YET ANOTHER PROPOSAL

Eᴀʀʟʏ ɪɴ ᴍᴀʏ, while Natty was studying for finals and my ex-peers were being fitted for caps and gowns, I took the New York State GED. The test was administered at the New York City Department of Education on West Fifty-Second Street. Out of sentimentality, I wore my old Trinity uniform. In the windowless testing room, I snuck glances at the faces of the other test-takers. They didn't look particularly stupid or downtrodden or even old, so I could not help but wonder what in their lives had led them to this room. What mistakes had they made? Who had they trusted that they shouldn't have? Or had they just been born to the wrong parents at the wrong time? Maybe I was being negative though. Maybe finishing high school in a classroom with no windows and a broken-down air conditioner wasn't such a bad thing. At the very least, these people had survived whatever missteps they had taken and come out the other side.

Mr. Kipling had hired me a tutor, and though I'd only been semiconsistent in my studies, the test was easy enough. I wouldn't find out for another three to four weeks if I had passed, but effectually and if all went well, this marked the end of high school for me. A bit anticlimactic, no? Then again . . . I had had plenty of climax in the past year and certainly more than my share of conflict and rising action. I could stand for a bit of denouement. No one tended to get shot during the denouement. *(The GED had a section on literary terms, if you were wondering.)*

At home, an e-mail was waiting for me. When I saw the domain mark was Mexico, I felt ashamed. As I was at least partially responsible for Theo's injuries, I'd been too embarrassed to call or write the Marquezes. Still, a good person would have found some way to send word.

Dear Anya,

Hello. I hope you have not forgotten your very best pal, Theo. I am writing to you because you have not written to me. Why do you stand on circumstance? Do you not know that your good friend Theo misses you? Do you not care at all about him?

You will like to know how I am faring, I think. But maybe you are too ashamed to ask. Well, you should feel very guilty, Anya, because I have been very sick. I did almost die. And I was not allowed to go back to the orchards until just last week. I am almost better now. My sister and my mother and the *abuelas* are being unbearable as you can imagine. We did here learn that Cousin Sophia was responsible for the attempt on your and my lives. She has always been a strange woman and never a favorite in our family for a variety of reasons that I would be glad to detail for you in person. (This is an invitation if you choose to take it as one.) But the reason I am writing you today is because the *abuelas* feel responsible for the attempts on your life. They think that they did not love Sophia enough. (But then they do think that all the problems in the world can be attributed to lack of love.) To make amends, they have asked me to pass on the recipe for Casa Marquez Hot Chocolate. I translated it for you, but it is not a literal translation. I embellished it where I thought it might amuse you (see attachment). Abuela wants me to remind you that it is a very powerful and ancient recipe with many, many health and spiritual benefits. "Please, Theo," she begs, "make sure she knows not to let it fall into the wrong hands."

Anya, when we were together, I know I spent much time complaining about my responsibilities to the farm and the factories. How I longed for my freedom. It is strange because in all the months I was sick, the only thing I wanted was to get back to the factories and the farm. So, maybe it is a good thing that I was nearly fatally shot. (This is me, joking. I am still the funniest person you know, I bet.)

I hope you will come back to Chiapas someday. You're a natural at cacao production, but I still have much I can teach you.

Besos,
Theobroma Marquez

I read the recipe, then I went into the kitchen. We didn't have rose petals or chili pepper but it was Saturday market, so I decided to take the bus down to Union Square to shop for the ingredients. It was Daisy's morning off, and Natty was occupied with her studies, so I decided to go by myself.

The roses were easy enough to come by, but I had trouble finding the chili pepper and I had just about given up when I spotted a stand selling, according to its sign: MEDICINAL HERBS, SPICES, TINCTURES, & MISCELLANY. I pulled back a striped curtain and went inside. The air smelled of incense. Rolling wooden shelves were lined with rows of hand-labeled glass jars.

The proprietor quickly located a small glass jar of chili peppers. "Is that all you need, girl?" the proprietor asked. "Have a look around. I have many other enticing products, and if you buy two, the third is free." The proprietor had a glass eye and a velvet cloak and a walking stick, and he looked rather like a wizard. The glass eye was a very good one. The only hint that it wasn't a real eye was that it didn't track me around the store like the other eye did.

On the lowest shelf sat a small jar with cacao nibs. As I took the jar in my hand, I felt a rush of nostalgia for Granja Mañana. I held it up to the stall-keeper. "How are you able to sell these? Without getting arrested, I mean?"

"It's perfectly legal, I assure you." He paused to give me the evil eye. (Literally, just the one.) "Do you work for the authorities?"

I shook my head. "The opposite."

He looked at me questioningly but I didn't feel like telling him my entire life story. Instead, I told him I was a chocolate enthusiast, and he seemed to take me at my word.

The stall-keeper used his walking stick to point to the word *medicinal* on his sign. "Even in this corrupt country of ours, you can sell all the cacao you want as long as it's for medicinal purposes." He snatched the little glass jar from me. "But I'm afraid I can't sell that particular product to you unless you have a prescription."

"Oh," I said. "Of course." Out of curiosity, I asked him what kind of condition would get me a prescription.

The stall-keeper shrugged. "Depression, I suppose. Cacao is a mood enhancer. Osteoporosis. Anemia. I'm not a doctor, miss. I do have an acquaintance who uses it to make skin creams."

I stood up from the squatting position I'd been in, and handed him the glass jar of chili peppers. "I guess I'll just take this then."

The stall-keeper nodded. As I was paying him, he said, "You're the Balanchine girl, aren't you?"

Paranoid mobster daughter that I was, I made sure to scan the store before answering. "I am."

"Yes, I thought so. I've been following your case closely. It's all been very unfair to you, hasn't it?"

I told him that I tried not to dwell on it.

On the bus back home, the aroma of roses was pervasive. I looked in my bag and found that the not-a-wizard had slipped the cacao nibs in with the chili peppers.

Since the crash, I was still a bit on edge during bus rides, but the rose-scented air suffused me with a sense of calm and— dare I say—clarity. My mind relaxed. My brain became soft and empty and then it began to fill with a picture. First, I saw Our Lady of Guadalupe, and I knew it was her because of the roses that haloed around her and because her image had featured so prominently at Granja Mañana. But then I saw that she wasn't a real person, but a painting on a wall and underneath the painting were the words, *Do not fear any illness or vexation, anxiety or pain. Am I not your Mother? Are you not under my shadow and protection? Am I not the fountain of life? Is there anything else you need?* And the wall was the back wall of a smallish store. And Balanchine chocolate was stacked on the dark-stained mahogany shelves. And the chocolate was right out in the open, even in the front display windows. And the sign on the store said:

Balanchine's Medicinal Cacao Bar
Chocolate For Your Health — By Rx Only — Doctor On Premises

I sat up in my seat.

I was not my sister. No one had ever suggested sending me to genius camp nor should they have, and I was not given to brilliant ideas. If I had a genius, I'd say it was probably one for survival, nothing more. But this seemed like it could almost work. Cacao might never be legal, but what if there were legal ways around that? Things Daddy and Uncle Yuri and now Fats had never even considered.

The bus was about a block away from Win's house. I didn't want to wait. I wanted to know what he would think. I pushed the tape to indicate that I wanted the bus to stop, and I got out.

Outside Win's apartment, I rang the bell. Charles Delacroix answered. Win and Mrs. Delacroix were still out, but he expected them back any minute if I wanted to wait. Mr. Delacroix hadn't shaved but at least he had dressed for the day.

Charles Delacroix led me into the living room. I was still thinking about my vision.

"How are you?" Charles Delacroix asked me.

"Mr. Delacroix, you're a lawyer."

"You're very businesslike today, Anya. Yes, I am a lawyer. An unemployed one at present."

"Have you ever heard of anyone selling medicinal cacao?" I asked.

Charles Delacroix laughed at me. "Anya Balanchine, what have you gotten yourself into now?"

"Nothing," I insisted. I could feel myself blushing. "I only wondered if a person could sell medicinal cacao legally in the city. I'd heard that you could sell it with a prescription."

Charles Delacroix studied me for a moment. "Yes, I suppose a theoretical person could."

"And if that were true, could a proprietor sell a customer a chocolate health bar or, say, a hot-chocolate vitamin shake as long as there was a prescription?"

Mr. Delacroix nodded. "Yes. Though I'd have to research the matter in greater detail."

"And if you were still acting as district attorney, would you have gone after a person who was selling medicinal cacao at a store in Manhattan?"

"I . . . Such a person might have aroused my interest, yes, but if they had a good lawyer who made sure everything was in order, and all the prescriptions were legitimate, I doubt we would have bothered with them. Anya, you're looking terrifyingly bright-eyed at the moment. Don't tell me you know such a hypothetical proprietor."

"Mr. Delacroix . . ."

Win and his mother got home. "Aren't you two looking chummy," Mrs. Delacroix said.

Win kissed me. "Were we supposed to meet? I thought you'd still be at the GEDs."

"I was at the market, and I thought I'd stop by to see if you were home." I was still carrying my roses and the bag with the chili peppers and cacao nibs. I told him how my friend from Mexico had sent me a recipe that I'd been planning to try. Win's mother wanted to know what it was. While it was one thing to pose hypothetical legal questions to Win's father, it was another thing to admit to recreational cacao consumption in front of him. "An ancient family health drink from Chiapas," I said.

Charles Delacroix raised an eyebrow. I wasn't fooling him.

"It's almost dark," Win said. "I'll walk you the rest of the way uptown."

"Goodbye, Anya," Charles Delacroix said.

Once we were outdoors, Win took my bag in one hand and I linked my arm through his.

"What were you and my father talking about?" Win asked.

I had stopped by Win's house with the full intention of telling him my idea, but now that he was standing next to me, I couldn't bring myself to do it. I didn't want to see his eyebrows furrow and his lips purse if he thought it was pure folly. I'd only been thinking of this for the last hour or so, but in that brief span, I'd already grown incredibly attached to the concept. It felt big to me, the kind of idea that might just change my life. I felt, for the first time in a very long time, hopeful.

"Annie?"

"It wasn't anything." I was emphatic. "I was waiting for you."

He stopped walking and looked at me. "You're lying. You're awfully good at it, but you forget—I know what you look like when you're being deceitful."

What did I look like when I was lying? I'd have to ask him sometime. "I'm not lying, Win. It's only an idea I had, but I'm not ready to talk about it yet," I said. "While I was waiting for you, I thought I'd run a couple parts of it by your dad because it has a legal component to it."

"Well, he certainly owes you the free advice." He took my arm again, and we resumed walking. At some point, we got to talking about our plans for what was left of the weekend.

"Win," I asked, "would you mind if we went to a legalize-cacao rally some time?"

"Sure . . . But why would you want to do that?"

"Mainly curiosity, I suppose. Maybe I'd like to see what it's like on the other side."

Win nodded. "Does this have anything to do with what you were talking to my dad about?"

"I'm not sure yet," I admitted.

When I got home, I found out the next Cacao Now meeting was Thursday night.

The tough part was that I didn't want to be recognized. I wanted to check it out without making a spectacle of myself. Noriko lent us wigs and dispensed makeup advice. I had a stick-straight blond wig and red lips. (I had abandoned my mustache in Mexico, of course, not that I would have wanted to unveil my mustachioed look in front of Win.) Win wore dreadlocks and a mesh cap, a modified version of what he'd worn to visit me at Liberty.

Win and I took the bus downtown to the abandoned library building where the meeting was being held.

We were a little bit late so we slipped in at the back.

About one hundred people were there. Standing behind a lectern in the front of the hall was Sylvio Freeman, who was in the middle of introducing a speaker. "Dr. Elizabeth Bergeron will speak about the health benefits of cacao."

Dr. Bergeron was a pale, skinny woman with a high-pitched voice. She wore a long tie-dyed skirt down to her ankles. "I am a doctor," she began. "And it is from this perspective that I will speak tonight." Her lecture dealt with many of the same things Theo had said to me in Chiapas. I looked at Win to see if he was bored. He didn't seem to be.

"So why," she concluded, "if there is so much enrichment to be found in natural cacao, should it be illegal? Our government allows the sale of plenty of things that are completely toxic. We should be using common sense and not money to determine what we consume."

The Cacao Now people did not overly impress me. They were disorganized, and their main plans seemed to involve standing outside government buildings and passing out leaflets.

On the way back uptown, Win started talking about next year. "I've been thinking I want to do premed," he said.

"Premed?" I'd never heard anything about that before. "What about your band? You're so talented!"

"Annie, I hate to tell you this, but I'm only okay." He looked at me shyly. "The band still doesn't have a name and, had you been around, you'd know that we've barely played this year. At first, because I was hurt, and then I just wasn't all that interested. And, well, a lot of guys who have bands in high school would be better off not making a life of it. I'm into other things, too, you know. I'd never want to do what my dad does, but I would like to help people. That doctor at the rally. I was watching her and thinking how great it would be to do that."

"Do what exactly?"

"Help people be less ignorant about their health, I guess." He paused. "Plus, if I do stay with you, medical skills would probably come in pretty handy. Everyone's always getting hurt when you're around."

"*If . . .*"

While the bus was stopped at a traffic light, I studied Win out of the corner of my eye. The streetlights lit up different parts of his face than I was used to seeing.

From two rows behind us, Daisy Gogol, who'd been trailing us the whole night, chimed in. "I thought I was going to be a singer, but I'm so glad I know Krav Maga."

"Thanks for the support, Daisy," Win said. "What should the pro-cacao people do instead?" he asked me.

"I know that they think too small. They need lawyers. And money, lots of it. Standing in front of a courthouse with dirty hair and pamphlets isn't going to do anything. They need ads. They need to convince the public that they deserve chocolate and that there was never anything wrong with it to begin with."

"Anya, you know I support you, but aren't there bigger problems in the world than chocolate?" Win asked me.

"I'm not sure, Win. Just because something is a small problem doesn't mean it shouldn't be addressed. Small injustices conceal larger ones."

"Is that something your father used to say?"

No, I told him. It was my own wisdom, and something I had learned through experience.

Sunday after church, I went to talk to Fats at the Pool. His stomach was distended and his eyes were red. I worried that he might have been poisoned. "You feeling all right?" I asked.

"I look that bad to you?" He chuckled, then patted his gut. "I'm an emotional eater."

I asked him if anything specific was bothering him.

He shook his head. "Nothing to concern your pretty little head with. Been working nights at the speakeasy and here in the days. Let's just say there's a reason guys in my position don't live that long."

Fats punctuated that remark with a laugh so I suppose it was meant as a joke. I reminded him that my father had been "a guy in his position."

"Didn't mean any disrespect, Annie. So what's on your mind?" Fats asked.

"I've got a proposition," I said. "A business proposition."

Fats nodded. "I'm all ears, kid."

I took a deep breath. "Have you ever heard of medicinal cacao?"

Fats nodded slowly. "Yeah, maybe."

309

I described what I had learned from my discussions with Mr. Delacroix and the man at the market.

"So what's the big idea?" Fats asked.

I took another deep breath. I had not wanted to admit to myself how invested I was in this idea. Before she whacked me over the head, Sophia Bitter had called me the "daughter of a cop and a criminal" who would always be at war with herself. It was a cruel thing to say, but it also happened to be true. It was cruel *because* it was true. I felt it in my every impulse, and I was incredibly tired of living that way. This idea, for me, was a way to end the war. "Well, I was thinking that instead of selling Balanchine chocolate on the black market, we could open a medicinal cacao dispensary." I looked at Fats to see what he thought of the idea, but his face was blank. "Eventually, maybe even a chain of them," I continued. "It would all be aboveboard. We'd hire doctors to write the prescriptions. And possibly even nutritionists to help us come up with recipes. And the only chocolate we'd use would be Balanchine, of course. We'd also need pure cacao, but I know a great place we could import that from. If the dispensaries were a success, maybe this could even go a long way toward changing public opinion and convincing the lawmakers that chocolate should never have been illegal in the first place." I snuck another glance at Fats. He was nodding a little. "The reason I came to you is because you know all about the restaurant business and, of course, you're the head of the Family now."

Fats looked at me. "You're a good kid, Annie. You've always been a good kid. And I can tell you put a heck of a lot of thought into this idea. And it's definitely an interesting one.

I'm glad you came to me. But I got to tell you, from the *semya* side of things, this will never work."

I was not yet ready to let this go. "Why won't it work?"

"It's real simple, Annie. The machinery of Balanchine Chocolate is set up to service a market where chocolate is illegal. If chocolate became legal or there even became a popular way to get around its illegality—à la the medicinal dispensaries you propose—Balanchine Chocolate would be out of business. We exist to serve a black market, Anya. The only way I know how to run a restaurant, if you want to call it that, or any sort of business at all is under the conditions of illegality. Chocolate is legal, Fats is obsolete. Maybe someday chocolate will be legal again, but I honestly hope I'm dead by then."

I didn't say anything.

Fats looked at me with sad eyes. "When I was a kid, my senile old grandma used to read me vampire stories. You know what a vampire is, Anya?"

"Kind of. I'm not sure."

"They're like these superhuman beings that enjoy drinking human blood. I know, it doesn't make any sense, but Grandma Olga was mad for them. So, okay, there's this one vampire story I remember. Maybe the only reason I remember it is because it's the longest. This human girl falls for this vampire boy, and he loves her, but he kind of wants to kill her, too. And this goes on for a really long time. You wouldn't believe how long! Should he kiss her or kill her? Well, he ends up kissing her a lot—you wouldn't believe how much! But ultimately, he kills her and turns her into a vampire anyway—"

I interrupted him. "What is your point, Fats?"

"My point is, a vampire is always a vampire. We Balanchines are vampires, Annie. We will always be vampires. We live in the night. In the dark."

"No, I disagree. Balanchine Chocolate was around before the chocolate banning. Daddy wasn't always a criminal. He was an honest businessman, dealing with obstacles." I shook my head. "There has to be a better way."

"You're young. It'd be wrong for you not to think that," Fats said. He reached out his hand across the table. "Come see me with your next big idea, kid."

I walked home from the Pool. It was a long walk, past Holy Trinity and through the park. The park looked about the same as the last time I'd been there—sere, seedy. I jogged across the Great Lawn, and I had just about hit the south side of Little Egypt when I heard the sound of a little girl screaming. She was standing by a graffiti-covered bronze statue of a bear. She didn't have shoes on and her only clothing was a T-shirt. I went up to her. "Are you okay? Can I help you?"

She shook her head and started to cry. That was when a man jumped me from behind. I felt his arm around my neck. "Gimme all your money," he said. Obviously, he and the little girl were a team. It was a shakedown. I can only attribute my imprudence to the fact that I had been preoccupied and dejected because of Fats's rejection of my idea.

I only had a little money on me, which I gave to the man. I did have my machete but I wasn't going to kill someone over a small amount of money.

"*Stop,*" a brassy voice called. "*I know her.*"

I looked in the direction of the voice. A girl with mousy brown hair cut short looked at me. My old bunkmate, Mouse.

"She's okay," Mouse said. "We were at Liberty together."

The man loosened his grip. "Really? Her?"

Mouse came up to me. "Yeah," Mouse said to her colleague. "That's Anya Balanchine. You don't want to mess with her." Mouse smelled foul and her hair was matted and dirty. I suspected that she had been sleeping outside.

"Mouse," I said. "You talk now."

"I do. I'm cured, thanks to you."

I didn't need to ask her what she'd been up to. She was obviously a member of some kind of band of juvenile criminals.

I asked her if she had ever called Simon Green.

"Yes," she told me. "But he didn't know who I was so he basically blew me off. I don't blame you. You had a lot on your hands."

"I'm sorry for that," I said. "If there's ever anything I can do to help . . ."

"How about that job?" Mouse asked.

I told her I was out of the family business, but maybe I could help her financially.

Mouse shook her head. "I don't take handouts, Anya. Like I told you at Liberty, I work for my keep."

I definitely owed her. "Maybe my cousin Fats could give you a job."

"Yeah? I'd like that."

I asked her how I could get in touch with her. "I'm here," she said. "I sleep behind the statue of the bear."

"It's nice to talk to you at last, Kate," I said.

"Shh," she said. "The name's classified."

When I got home, the first thing I did was contact Fats at the Pool. He said he was surprised to hear from me so soon, but that he'd be happy to give my friend a job. Despite the fact that he'd abjectly rejected the idea I thought was going to save us all, Fats was a good guy.

Win came over that night. "You're quiet," he said.

"I thought I'd come up with something really smart," I said. I described my idea to him, and then I told him the reasons Fats had said it wouldn't work.

"So that's what the cacao rally was about and why you've been so secretive," Win said.

I nodded. "I really wanted it to work."

Win took my hand. "I hope you won't take this the wrong way but I'm kind of glad that it didn't work. Even if there were a legal way to justify selling chocolate, you'd end up in court all the time. You'd be fighting City Hall and public opinion and even your own family, it sounds like. Why would you want to take on all of that? Not having anything to do after high school is not a good enough reason."

"Win! That's not the reason! How stupid do you think I am?" I shook my head. "It might sound silly to you, but there's some part of me that always wanted to be the person who returned Balanchine Chocolate to the right side of the law, I guess. For Daddy."

"Look, Annie. You gave the business to Fats. Sophia and Mickey are gone. Yuji Ono, too. You really can be free of this now. It's a gift, if you choose to see it that way."

He kissed me, but I didn't feel like being kissed.

314

"Are you angry at me?" Win asked.

"No." I was.

"Let me see your eyes."

I turned them on him.

"My father's the same way."

"Don't compare me to him."

"He's done nothing for the past six months because he lost the election when really, losing the election was a gift to all of us. Me. You. My mother. And especially him, if the bastard could just open up his eyes and see it."

I didn't say anything for such a long time that Win finally changed the subject.

"Graduation is next Wednesday. Are you coming?" Win asked.

"Do you want me to?" I replied with a question of my own.

"I don't care," Win said.

But obviously he did want me to come if he was bringing it up.

"I'm giving the salutatorian speech if you're interested," Win continued.

"That's right. You're smart. I forget that sometimes."

"Hey." Win smiled.

I asked him if he knew what he planned to say.

"It'll be a surprise," he promised.

That was how Natty, Noriko, and I found ourselves at Trinity's high school graduation.

Win's speech was, I think, in part directed at me and in part directed at his father. It was about questioning what society tells you and standing up to authority and other things that have probably been said at countless other graduations. He had acquired his father's gift for oration, so in terms of the crowd's response, it barely mattered what he said. I clapped as much as anyone else.

Did I feel a twinge at the sight of my classmates walking across the stage? Yes, I did. More than just a twinge actually.

Scarlet waved to us as she accepted her diploma. After some amount of back-and-forth, the administration had allowed her to walk at graduation while pregnant. Cap-and-gown was basically like a maternity dress, so Scarlet didn't stick out much anyway. And from the point of view of Trinity, it was far worse *not* to keep one's baby than to keep it. Gable met her on the other side of the stage to help her down the steps.

When they reached the bottom, Gable got down on one knee.

"Oh no," Natty said. "I think Gable's proposing again."

I dismissed her. "Gable wouldn't do that here."

"He is. Look, he's taking a little jewelry box out of his pocket," Natty said.

"Romantic," Noriko said. "So romantic." And I imagine it did look romantic if you didn't know either of the parties involved.

"Poor Scarlet," I said. "She must be so embarrassed."

At that moment, a cheer went through the gymnasium. We were sitting toward the back, so I could no longer see Scarlet or Arsley. "What?" I asked. "What just happened?" I stood.

Scarlet and Arsley were kissing. He had his arms around her.

"Maybe she's letting him down easy?" I said. But even as I said it, I knew that she wasn't.

After graduation was over, I scrambled to the front to find Scarlet but she'd already left. I spotted Scarlet and her parents outside. They were standing in a coven with Gable Arsley's parents. I grabbed Scarlet's hand and pulled her away.

"What is *wrong* with you?" I asked as soon as I'd gotten her alone.

Scarlet shrugged. "I'm sorry, Annie. I knew how you'd feel but . . . with the baby coming, I just got worn down." She sighed. "I'm worn out. I even wore flats to graduation. Can you imagine me—"

"I told you that you could stay with me!"

"Could I really? It's a nice offer, Annie, but I don't think I could. Leo's wife is there. And Leo will be back. And there won't be any room for me and a baby."

"Yes there will, Scarlet! I'll make room."

She didn't say anything. Even in flats, she was taller than me. She looked over my head. She didn't seem to be looking at anything specific other than *not at me*. Her expression was even and the set of her mouth was firm.

"Scarlet, if you seriously marry Gable Arsley, you and I won't be friends anymore."

"Don't be dramatic, Annie. We'll always be friends."

"We won't," I insisted. "I know Gable Arsley. If you marry him, your life will be ruined."

"Well, then it's ruined. It was already ruined," she said calmly.

Gable came up to us. "I assume you're here to congratulate us, Anya."

I narrowed my eyes at him. "I don't know how you've

317

fooled her, Gable. What you did to make her change her mind."

"This isn't about Scarlet. It's about you, Anya. Like it always has to be," Gable said calmly.

Not for the first time, I wanted to smack him across his face. Suddenly, I felt Natty's hand in mine.

"Let's go," she whispered.

"Goodbye," Scarlet called.

My jaw wobbled like a three-legged stool, but I did not cry.

"Anya, we aren't children anymore!" Scarlet said.

In that moment, I hated her—for implying that the reason I objected to her marrying that sociopath was because I was somehow stunted and pathetically suspended in childhood. As if I hadn't been forced to do away with childish things years ago. "Do you mean because we graduated or because you're knocked up?" Even as I said it, I knew it was cruel.

"*We* didn't graduate!" Scarlet yelled back. "*I* graduated. And for the record, my job title is not Professional Best Friend to Anya Balanchine!"

"If it were, you'd be fired!"

"Okay," Natty said. "You two really need to stop now. You're both being awful." Natty went up to Scarlet and embraced her. "Congratulations, Scarlet for . . . um . . . making a decision that you're happy with, I guess. Come on, Annie. We need to get going."

After graduation, Natty and I went to a celebratory brunch at Win's parents' place. I was still preoccupied from my argument with Scarlet, and I spent the whole meal brooding. Just before dessert, Win's father tapped his knife against his glass and stood to make a speech. Charles Delacroix liked making speeches. I'd heard more than enough of them in my life so I didn't feel the need to pay attention to this one. Finally, it seemed like we'd stayed long enough that it wouldn't be rude to leave.

"Don't leave yet," Win said to me. "You'll just go home and brood over Scarlet and Arsley."

"I'm not brooding."

"Come on," he said. "Don't you think I know you a little bit?" He smoothed out the furrow that must have formed between my eyebrows.

"That's not the only thing I'm brooding about, you know," I objected. "I'm very deep and my problems are vast."

"I know. At least one of them isn't that your boyfriend is moving away to go to college."

I asked him what he meant.

"Didn't you pay any attention to my dad's speech? I've decided to stay in New York for college. It means going to Dad's alma mater, which pleases him. I'd rather not do anything to please him, but . . ." Win shrugged.

I took a step back. "You can't mean that you're staying here on my account?"

"Of course that's what I mean. A school is a school."

I didn't reply. Instead, I fidgeted with my necklace.

"You seem less pleased than I'd hoped."

"But Win, I didn't ask you to stay here. I just don't want you to do anything you don't want to do. These past two years have taught me that it's best not to make too many plans beyond the present moment."

"That's crap, Anya. You don't think that. You're always thinking about your next move. It's one of the things I like about you."

Of course he was right. The real reason I didn't want him to stay was too hard to say aloud. Win was a decent guy— maybe the most decent one I'd ever known—and I didn't want him to stay in New York because he felt sorry for me or out of some misplaced sense of obligation. If he did that, he'd only end up regretting it later.

Since I'd learned about Simon Green, I'd done a bit of re-flecting over my parents' marriage. My mother and father had fought constantly the year before she died. One of the major points of contention between them was that she resented leav-ing her job at the NYPD and had wanted to go back to work— which obviously was impossible, considering what Daddy did for a living. My point was, I didn't want Win to end up resent-ing me that way.

"Win," I said, "it's been a good couple of months for us, but I can't know what's going to happen to me next week let alone a year from now. And neither can you."

"Guess I'll have to take my chances." Win studied my face. "You're a funny sort of girl," he said, and then he laughed. "I'm not asking you to marry me, Anya. I'm just trying to put my-self in your neighborhood."

At the mention of marriage, I winced.

"And I'd done so well distracting you from the news of Scarlet's nuptials."

I rolled my eyes. "What is *wrong* with her?"

He shrugged. "Nothing. Except that life is hard. And complex."

I asked him if he was taking her side, and he said there were no sides. "The one thing I do know about Scarlet Barber is that she is your friend."

Scarlet Barber may have been my friend but soon she would be Scarlet Arsley.

Win's mother dragged him away to talk to some of the other guests at the brunch. He made me promise to stay a little longer. Natty seemed to be enjoying herself—she was talking to a cute cousin of Win's—so I wandered up to the garden. The day was unseasonably hot so no one was out there. The last time I'd been in that garden was that long-ago spring day when I had ended things with Win.

I sat down on the bench. Mrs. Delacroix was using a trellis to grow peas, and the plants made little white flowers, which reminded me of the blooms on the cacao plants in Mexico. I was glad to be in New York—not to be in hiding—but I also missed Mexico. Maybe not the place itself, but my friends there and the feeling that I was part of something worthwhile. Theo and I had both been raised in chocolate yet his life had been totally different from mine. Because chocolate wasn't illegal in Mexico, he had lived his whole life in the open whereas I had always been hiding and ashamed. I suppose that was why I had been so drawn to the idea of medicinal cacao.

I was about to leave when Charles Delacroix came out to the garden.

"How do you stand the heat?" he asked me.

"I like it," I said.

"I would have guessed that about you," he replied. Mr. Delacroix sat next to me on the bench. "How goes the medicinal-cacao business?"

I told him I'd run the idea by the powers that be at Balanchine Chocolate and that it had been roundly and unceremoniously rejected.

"I'm sorry to hear that," Charles Delacroix said. "I thought it was a good concept."

I looked at him. "You did?"

"I did."

"I would have thought you'd think it was a cheat."

He shook his head. "You don't understand much about lawyers. We live for the gray areas." He nodded and stroked his beard. "We live in them actually."

"You ever gonna shave that thing off? It makes you look like one of those park people."

Charles Delacroix ignored me. "I imagine the idea was threatening to your cousin Sergei, or 'Fats'—word on the street is that he's the one running the *semya* now? I'm horribly out of touch, but I do try to keep up. And he probably said that the Balanchine business model was based on the idea of illegal supply which, of course, is true."

"Something like that." I paused. "You always think you know everything, don't you?"

"I don't, Anya. If I did, I'd be giving speeches downtown instead of at a graduation party. As for your cousin? I can predict his response because it's thoroughly predictable. He's a guy who was promoted through the ranks, a guy with his own speakeasy. Yes, I know about that. Of course I do. What you said would terrify a guy like that."

None of it mattered much now.

"Do it anyway," Charles Delacroix said.

"What?" I stood up from the bench.

"It's a big idea, maybe even visionary, and those don't come along every day. It's a chance to really change things, and I believe it could make money, too. You're young, which is a good thing. And thanks to me, you know a thing or two about chocolate. You'll have to tell me all about that trip to Mexico someday."

He knew about Mexico? I tried to keep my face expressionless, but I must not have succeeded. Charles Delacroix smiled at me.

"Anya, please. I practically put you on the boat, didn't I?"

"Mr. Delacroix, I . . ."

"Make sure you hire a good security team—that wall of a woman is a fine start—and an even better lawyer. Mr. Kipling won't do. You'll need someone with an expertise in civil law and contracts and such—"

At that moment, Win came out to the garden. "Is Dad boring you again?"

"Anya was telling me about her plans for next year," Charles Delacroix said.

Win looked at me. "What plans exactly?"

"Your dad's kidding," I said. "I don't have any plans."

Charles Delacroix nodded. "Well, that *is* a shame."

323

Win defended me. "Not everyone goes to college right after high school, Dad. Some of the most interesting people don't go to college at all."

Charles Delacroix said he was aware of that fact and that there were many ways in life to get an education. "International travel, for instance."

After Charles Delacroix went back inside, Win commented, "I'm amazed you can even be civil to him after everything he'd done to us last year."

"He was just doing his job," I said.

"You really think so? You're more forgiving than I thought."

"I do." I stood on my tiptoes and leaned in to kiss him. "Worst mistake I ever made, falling for the acting DA's kid." I pulled away. "But you were wrong to pursue me."

Win kissed me. "Very."

"Why did you anyway? Pursue me, I mean. I'm pretty sure I kept telling you to go away."

Win nodded. "Well, it's simple really. The first time I saw you, you were dumping that tray of spaghetti—"

"It was lasagna," I interjected.

"Lasagna. Over Gable Arsley's head."

"Not my finest hour."

"From where I was sitting, I liked the looks of you. And I liked that you stood up for yourself."

"That simple?"

"Yes, it was. These things usually are, Annie. It had become clear to me that you and your boyfriend had parted ways. I knew you'd be in Headmaster's office at the end of the day so I contrived a reason to go there myself."

"Admirably duplicitous of you."

"I am my father's son," he said.

"Was it worth it? You did end up shot." I put my arms around his waist.

"That was nothing. A flesh wound. Was it worth it for you? All the trouble I caused you. I feel almost"—he paused— "guilty sometimes."

I thought about this.

Love.

There were so many kinds of love. And some of them were forever like the kind I had for Natty and for Leo. And other kinds? Well, you'd be a fool if you tried to guess how long they'd last. But even the ones that weren't necessarily everlasting were not without meaning.

Because, when it came down to it, who and what and that you loved was your whole life. And when it came to love, it could not be denied that I'd received more than my portion: Nana, Daddy, my mother. Leo, Natty, Win, even Theo. Scarlet. *Scarlet.*

I furrowed my brow.

"You're making a face," Win said.

"I just realized that I'm going to have to forgive Scarlet."

I looked at Win, and he looked at me.

"What I mean to say is, I'm going to have to ask her to forgive me."

"I think that's sensible."

"I liked your speech today," I said.

"I appreciate that," he said. "You really don't want me to stay in New York?"

"Of course I want you to stay . . . I just don't want you to end up hating me."

"I couldn't end up hating you. It's as impossible for me as slamming a revolving door. I'll walk you and Natty home." He picked a bloom from the trellis and then he tucked it into my hair. Summer was here.

I PLAN FOR THE FUTURE

My FATHER HATED THE SUMMER because summer was the worst time of year for dealing chocolate. The heat made distribution like running a gauntlet. A train delay or a malfunctioning refrigerated truck could mean that entire shipments were spoiled, i.e., melted. Daddy always said that people lost their taste for chocolate in the summer anyway—that chocolate was a cold-weather food, that people would rather have ice cream or even watermelon in the heat. The cost of shipping, expensive at all times of the year, was even more exorbitant in the summer. According to my father, the one thing that could have significantly eased the summer months was if it had been legal to create chocolate stateside: "Sure, we can't sell it here, but why do they care if we make it?" I knew that Daddy often fantasized about Balanchine Chocolate going on hiatus from May through September. But as soon as he'd said this, my father would shake his head: "Not to be, Annie. If we force people to go three months without chocolate, they might lose their taste for it altogether. The American buying public is as fickle as a teenager's heart." I was not yet a teenager, so I didn't bother taking offense at this analogy.

Though it was June, I was not thinking of any of this. My most immediate concern was helping Natty pack for her second summer at genius camp. I was in the middle of rolling a T-shirt when the phone rang.

"Did you hear the news?" He didn't bother to introduce himself but I was more practiced at recognizing Jacks's voice than I had once been.

"Phone calls are expensive, Jacks. You shouldn't waste your weeklies on someone who doesn't want to hear from you."

Jacks ignored me. "Word on the street is that Balanchine Chocolate isn't going to supply chocolate in the summer anymore. Fats thinks it's too costly. He's saying that he thinks chocolate should be a seasonal business. The dealers are about ready to kill him."

I told him that Daddy had often said the same thing, and that seasonal or not, it wasn't *my* business.

"You can't be serious. Fats is running the business into the ground, and you don't think it's your business. Let me tell you, you backed the wrong guy with Fats. The only thing that guy cares about is his speak—"

"I'm finally out, Jacks. What do you want me to say?"

"You know I got no one else to call, right? Now that Mickey's unreachable and Yuri's dead, no one else will even take my call. And I'd like to have a job to go back to when I'm out of here."

"Maybe you should consider a different line of work?"

"You finding it real easy to move on, Annie? It'd be about a million times harder for me, you know."

"You're not my problem," I said, and then I hung up the phone.

I went back into Natty's room, where she was folding up a raincoat. She wanted to know who had been on the phone. "No one," I said.

"No one?" she repeated.

"Jacks. He's worried that Fats is . . ." I let my voice trail off. If Fats was running Balanchine Chocolate into the ground, it wasn't necessarily my problem, but it could definitely be my opportunity. "Excuse me, Natty. I have to go make a call."

I went back out to the kitchen. If I were to make a go at this, I'd need a lawyer. I thought about calling Mr. Kipling, but we hadn't been on the best of terms since Simon Green's return. I thought about calling Simon Green, but I didn't trust him. The greater problem with Mr. Kipling and Simon Green was that both men had spent their whole careers defending people from the wrong side of the law and what I needed right now was someone who played for the angels.

I thought about calling Charles Delacroix. In terms of drawbacks, he had thrown me in a reformatory twice, and also, Win would hate it.

It really did make the most sense to call Mr. Kipling. Maybe we'd had some hard times, but he was a good man and he was always on my side. At the very least, Mr. Kipling would be able to point me in the direction of the kind of lawyer I thought I needed.

I picked up the phone. I was about to dial Mr. Kipling when I found myself pressing the numbers for Win's apartment instead. Win answered the phone. "Hello," he said.

I didn't reply.

"Hello," Win repeated. "Is anyone there?"

I could have abandoned the idea right then. I could have just asked Win if he wanted to come over. I could have at the very least told him what I was thinking. But I didn't do any of these things.

This might sound low to you, but I decided to disguise my voice. I made it deep and husky and a bit New York. "I'm calling for Charles Delacroix," I purred. I was no vocal chameleon and part of me expected Win to burst out laughing and say, *Annie, what are you playing at?*

"*Dad!*" I heard Win yell. "*Telephone!*"

"I'll take it in the office!" Charles Delacroix called back.

A second later, Charles Delacroix picked up the phone, and I heard Win hang up. "Yes?"

"It's Anya Balanchine," I said.

"Well, this is a surprise," Charles Delacroix replied.

"I'm going to do it," I said. "I'm going to open the medicinal cacao dispensary."

"Good for you, Anya. That's terribly industrious," he said. "What changed your mind?"

"I saw a window—an opportunity that was too good to pass up," I said. "I'm thinking that you should be my business lawyer."

Charles Delacroix cleared his throat. "Why would I ever do that?"

"Because you have the expertise in city government and because you have nothing else to do and because I know you think it's a good idea."

"Let's meet," Charles Delacroix said finally. "I don't have an office other than at home, and it would appear that you're keeping this information from your boyfriend, my son, so . . ."

We agreed to meet at my apartment. Although I'd met with Charles Delacroix many times and under far more trying circumstances, I was still nervous. I took a while deciding what to wear. I didn't want to look like a schoolgirl, but I also didn't want to look like a little girl playing dress-up. I finally picked a pair of gray pants that might have been Daddy's though I couldn't say for certain and a black tank top that Scarlet had left at some point. The pants were too big so I belted them below the waistband. I looked at myself in the mirror behind the door and concluded that the outfit was silly. The doorbell rang—too late to change.

I invited Mr. Delacroix into our living room. He still hadn't shaved, but it looked like his beard might have been trimmed.

"Tell me about your plan." Charles Delacroix sat down on the couch and crossed his legs.

"You, um, already know the basic idea. I've done a little research since then." I turned on my slate. I had made notes there, but as I scanned them, they looked less thorough than I had thought they would. "So, you'll obviously know that the Rimbaud Act of 2055 banned cacao and specifically choc—"

"I can remember when it happened, Anya. I was a little younger than you and Win are now."

"Right. But, well, the law was designed to stop the food

companies from producing chocolate. Most cities, including this one, still allow the sale of pure cacao in small quantities as long as it's for medicinal purposes. I guess this includes beauty products but it can also include anything health-related. So, what I thought is, I could start with a small store, less than five hundred square feet, maybe somewhere uptown, so that I wouldn't compete with Fats. I'd hire a doctor, and a waitress, and I'd sell medicinal health drinks, made from cacao and chocolate. But where it would be different from Fats is that everything would be in the open. I wouldn't have to be underground."

"Hmm," he replied. "It's clever, as I already told you, but you're thinking too small."

I asked him what he meant.

"I've worked in government a very long time. Do you know the way to get the city to leave you alone? Be the biggest business out there. Be an elephant right smack in the middle of Midtown. Be popular. Give the people a product they want, and the whole city will be on your side. They'll be grateful to you for making legal what they thought should never have been illegal in the first place." He paused. "Also, medicinal cacao dispensary has no ring to it. People won't even know what you're talking about. Hire your doctors and your nutritionists, but you need to make the whole enterprise sound sexy."

I considered his words. "What you're describing could cost a lot of money." I had Natty and Leo to think of.

"True, though it could also make you a lot of money. And as for the space, that'll be cheap as the city has more mammoth abandoned spaces than it knows what to do with. How do you think those criminals who run Little Egypt manage it? You should have dancing, too, by the way."

"Dancing? Are you saying I should open a nightclub?"

"Well, that makes it sound tawdry. How about a lounge? Or just a club. I'm thinking out loud here. If it were a club, all the members would need to have prescriptions before they could join. It would be a requirement of membership. Yes, then you wouldn't even need the doctors on-site."

"Those are, um, interesting ideas. You've certainly given me a lot to consider."

Charles Delacroix didn't say anything for a while. "I've been thinking about this ever since you called me and I want to help you do this. Because I respect you, I'm going to be completely candid about why I want to help. It isn't because I like chocolate or you, although I do. The fact of the matter is, I'm a failure right now. However, if I give chocolate back to the people, I'll be a hero. What better platform for me to run for DA or even some other, higher office?"

I nodded.

"So, why do you want me to help you?" Charles Delacroix asked.

"Don't you already know? You always know everything."

"Humor me."

"Because you have a reputation for being ethical and always on the side of the good, and if you say this is legal, people will believe you. What I learned during those months I was away is how much I don't want to spend my whole life in hiding, Mr. Delacroix."

"Fine," he said. "That makes sense." He offered me his

hand to shake and then he pulled it back. "Before we agree on this venture, I need you to know something. I don't think anyone knows what I'm about to say, but if it came out later, I don't want you to be shocked—I poisoned you last fall." He said this as if he'd been asking me to pass the sugar.

"Excuse me?"

"I poisoned you last fall but I don't see this as any reason we shouldn't work together. I assure you I had perfectly good intentions, and you were never in any real danger. Perhaps it was wrongheaded of me but I wanted to get you out of the girls' dormitory at Liberty and into the infirmary, a venue that I believed you would find more accommodating to escape."

"How?" I sputtered.

"The water I gave you when we had our discussion in the Cellar was spiked with a substance that can emulate a heart attack."

Though I was surprised, I was less shocked than you might have thought. I looked at him. "You're ruthless."

"Only a bit. I'll be the same way for you."

Had there been an official villain for my last two years on earth, it would have been Charles Delacroix. What had Daddy once said? "Games change, Anya, and so do players." I offered this man my hand, and he shook it. We began to make a list of all the things we needed to do.

In the morning, I put Natty on a train bound for genius camp, and in the afternoon, Charles Delacroix called me. He said that although it might have been too early to be making such decisions and although this may have fallen outside of his purview, he'd become aware of a potential venue in Midtown. "Fortieth and Fifth," he said.

"That's right in the middle of town," I said.

"I know," he replied. "That's the idea. I'll meet you outside."

Other than its capaciousness, the most notable feature of the exterior was the pair of graffiti-covered statues of reclining lions. "Oh, I know this place," I said to him. "It used to be that nightclub the Lion's Den. None of us ever liked to go there because it was awful and Little Egypt was closer."

Charles Delacroix said that apparently it was awful enough that it had just closed for good.

We walked up a grand flight of steps, then through a set of columns. A Realtor met us inside. She was wearing a red suit and had a sickly-looking carnation tucked into her lapel. The Realtor looked at me dubiously. "This, the client? She looks like a kid."

"Yes," Charles Delacroix said. "This is Anya Balanchine."

The Realtor started at my name. After a beat, she offered me her hand. "So, we can't lease out the whole place on your budget, but we have this one room that might meet your needs."

She led us up to the third floor. The room was about eighty feet wide and three hundred feet long and probably fifty feet high. Arched windows lined both sides of the space, so that the overall feeling was one of openness. The ceiling was vaulted, with dark wooden moldings. The part I liked best were the murals that had been painted on the ceiling: they were of blue skies and clouds. The effect of the room was such that it was like being outside while you were inside. I loved it immediately because it was private enough to accommodate my business, but it also said *Chocolate can and should be sold in the open*. It felt sacred to me, like being in church.

Much was in disrepair—broken panes of glass, holes in the plaster—but none of it seemed impossible to fix.

The Realtor said, "The old tenant had a kitchen just outside. And there're bathrooms somewhere around here, too."

I nodded. "What used to be here?"

"Lion's Den. Some kind of club." The Realtor made a face.

"Before that," I specified. "What was the original purpose?"

The Realtor turned on her slate. "Um, let me see. It was a library, maybe? You know, paper books, something like that." She wrinkled her nose as she said "paper books." "So, what do you think?"

I wasn't necessarily a believer in signs but the lion statues outside made me think of Leo, and paper books of Imogen, of course. I knew this was the place for me, but I wanted to get a good deal so I kept my face blank. "I'm going to sleep on it," I said.

"Don't wait too long. Someone might snap it up," the Realtor warned.

"I doubt that," Charles Delacroix said. "You can't give these old ruins away. I used to be in government, you know."

Charles Delacroix and I walked out into the sticky New York June.

"So?" he said.

"I like it," I said.

"The location is good, and it has some kind of historical significance, for what that's worth. But the main thing is the gesture of it—if you take a space, it becomes real to people,

336

more than just an idea. I doubt you'll have much competition for the lease."

"I'm going to speak to Mr. Kipling," I said. Mr. Kipling was managing my finances until August 12, when I turned eighteen. As yet, I had not felt any need to run my business plans past him.

Upon returning home, I slate-messaged Mr. Kipling that I needed to talk to him at his office. I had not seen him since Simon Green's return.

When I arrived at his office, he greeted me warmly, and then he embraced me. "How are you? I was about to call. Look what came yesterday."

He passed an envelope across the desk. It was my GED. I must have used my business address. "I didn't know it would be paper," I said.

"Important things still are," Mr. Kipling said. "Congratulations, my dear!"

I took the envelope and slipped it into my pocket.

"Perhaps we could talk about your post-graduation plans?" Mr. Kipling cautiously suggested.

I told him that that had been exactly why I had come and then I described the business I planned to open and the space I wanted to rent in Midtown. "I'll need you to arrange two payments for me. The first is a retainer for the business lawyer I've hired"—I purposely didn't mention who the business lawyer was—"and the second as a deposit on the space I'd like to rent."

Mr. Kipling listened carefully and then he said exactly what I'd feared he would say: "I'm not sure about any of this, Anya." Although I didn't ask him to, he began listing his objections:

mainly that the idea could potentially anger the *semya* and that a business of any type was a financially risky venture. "A restaurant is a money pit, Anya."

I told him it was a club, not a restaurant.

"Can you really say you know what you're getting into?" he asked.

"Can anyone?" I paused. "You honestly don't think this is a good idea?"

"Possibly. I don't know. What I think is a really good idea is you going to college."

I shook my head. "Mr. Kipling, you once told me that I would never escape chocolate so there was no point in hating it. That's what I'm trying to do. I believe in this idea."

Mr. Kipling didn't say anything. Instead, he ran his fingers through his imaginary hair. "I may not be your lawyer anymore, but I am still the keeper of the trust, Anya."

"In two months, I'll be eighteen and I won't need to ask your permission," I reminded him.

Mr. Kipling looked at me. "Then I think you should wait two months. That'll give you more time for research."

I informed him that I had already drawn up a detailed business plan.

"Still, if it's such a good idea, it'll be good two months from now, too."

Two months. I didn't have two months. Who knew what the situation at Balanchine Chocolate would be two months from now? Who knew where I'd be? Now was the time. In my heart, I knew it.

"I could take you to court," I said.

Mr. Kipling shook his head. "That would be foolish. You'd eat up money in legal fees, and it wouldn't be settled by August anyway. If I were you, I'd wait."

Mr. Kipling put his hand on my arm. I shook him off.

"I'm only doing this out of love," he said.

"Love? That's why you killed Nana, too, right?"

I left Mr. Kipling's office, feeling despondent but also determined. I tried to come up with someone who could lend me the money I needed for the deposit on the lease. It was only five thousand dollars to hold on to the room, and I didn't want to lose the space. I couldn't think of anyone, or at least not anyone to whom I wished my brand-new business to be indebted. I thought of whether I had anything worth selling, but nothing was worth much in those days.

I was on the verge of despair when Mr. Kipling called me. "Anya, I know we've had our struggles this year, but I've thought about it. I'll draft you the payments if that's something you really want. You're right when you say it'll be your money in two months anyway. In the meantime, though, I want you to sign up for some extension school classes in business or law or restaurant management or medicine. That's the price of me drafting these payments or any others."

"Thank you, Mr. Kipling." I gave him the name of the Realtor and the amount.

"You mentioned a business lawyer? Does this person have a name?"

"Charles Delacroix. I suppose you don't need me to spell it."

"Anya Pavlova Balanchine, have you lost your mind? You have to be kidding!"

I told him that I had thought about it, and for a variety of reasons, Charles Delacroix was the person who best met my needs.

"Well, it's a very bold choice," he said after a bit. "Certainly unexpected. Your father would probably approve. You'll need to open a corporate account."

"Mr. Delacroix said the same thing."

"Of course, I'm glad to help you with that or anything else you need, Annie."

On my way to the nightclub formerly known as the Lion's Den, the place where I was meant to meet Charles Delacroix to sign the lease, I walked past St. Patrick's Cathedral. I decided to go in to say a quick prayer.

It wasn't that I was having doubts exactly. But I knew that once I signed that paper, everything would start to become real. I guess I thought it would be a good idea to ask for a blessing for my new venture.

I knelt down at the altar and bowed my head. I thanked God for the return of Leo and for keeping Natty safe. I thanked God that my legal problems were behind me. I thanked God for the time I'd spent in Mexico. I thanked God for my father, who had taught me so many things in the short time we had known each other. And I thanked God for my mother and Nana, too. I thanked God for Win because he had loved me even when I was pretty sure I was unlovable. I thanked God that I was Anya Balanchine and not some other girl. Because I, Anya, was made of pretty sturdy stuff, and God had never given me more than I could bear. And then, I thanked God for that, too.

I stood up. After depositing a small offering in the basket, I left the church, then went southward to sign the lease.

The second Friday in June, I decided to throw a small gathering at the new venue to tell my friends about what I'd be doing next year. Before I even invited anyone, I knew I would have to tell Win about his father's involvement.

That summer, in an attempt to show that New York City wasn't so awful, the mayor was screening ancient movies outside in Bryant Park. Win wanted to go, in the way rich, privileged people liked to do things that were potentially dangerous. I told him I'd come, but as was to be expected, I had my machete with me.

No one accosted us at the screening—police presence had been fairly impressive for a recreational event. Still, I could barely pay attention to the movie because I kept thinking about what I had to tell Win.

On the walk home, Win was still talking about the movie. "That part where the girl rides the horse across the water? That was amazing. I want to do that."

"Yeah," I said.

Win looked at me. "Annie, were you watching at all?"

"I—I have something I need to tell you." I told him about the business and the lease I had signed and finally the name of the lawyer I had hired. "I'm having a sort of party to kick the whole thing off next week. I'd really like it if you came."

Win did not speak for an entire city block. "You don't have to do this, Anya. Just because you signed a lease doesn't mean you have to do this."

"I do have to do this, Win. Don't you see? It's a way to redeem my father. It's the way I could change things in the city. If I don't do this, I'll always be living in the dark."

"You think you have to, but you don't." He grabbed my hand and turned me roughly toward him. "Do you have any idea how hard this is going to be?"

"Yes, I do. But I have to anyway, Win."

"Why?" he said in a sharper voice than I had ever heard him use. "Your cousin took over Balanchine Chocolate. You are out!"

"I'll never be out. I am my father's daughter. And if I don't do this, I will always regret it."

"You are not your father's daughter. I am not my father's son."

"I am, Win." I told him that to deny this was to deny who I was at my core, that I could not change my name or my blood. He wasn't listening, though.

"Why did you have to hire my father?" he asked in a quiet voice that was more frightening than his loud one had been.

I tried to explain but he just shook his head.

"I knew you were headstrong, but I never took you for a fool."

"I have reasons, Win."

Win cornered me against the wall. "I have been loyal to you. If you do this, I won't be by your side. We can be friends, nothing more. I will go as far away from you as possible. I will not watch you destroy yourself."

I shook my head. My cheeks were wet, so I suppose I was crying. "I have to, Win."

"I mean that little to you?"

"No . . . But I can't be anyone other than who I am."

Win looked at me with an expression of disgust. "You know he poisoned you last year, right?"

Win knew. "He told me."

"You know exactly what kind of a man he is and you go and do this anyway! If he's helping you, it's because he sees some kind of angle for himself."

"I know that, Win. He's using me, and I'm using him."

"You deserve each other then." Win shook his head. "We're done," he said.

"Don't do this, Win. Not here. Not now. Take a little time to think." Embarrassing as this is, I fell to my knees and clasped my hands together.

He said he didn't need to think. "I will not be my mother. I will not be long-suffering."

And then he left. I got up to run after him, but I tripped and skinned my knees against the pavement. By the time I stood up, a bus had arrived, and Win was on it.

As soon as I got home, I tried calling Win. "He's already gone to bed," Mrs. Delacroix said coolly. "Would you rather speak to Charlie instead?"

I told her that wouldn't be necessary. I saw Charles Delacroix all the time.

This went on for several days (fill in excuses appropriate to whatever time of day it was) until finally Mrs. Delacroix said that Win had gone to visit friends in Albany.

Maybe I should have gotten on the first train to Albany,

but I just couldn't. I didn't know what I would say. The truth was, he was probably right. I had disregarded his feelings in pursuit of whatever this was, and I couldn't explain to him why. Or rather, if I did explain, I suspected he wouldn't like the answer: Win had been steadfast, loyal, kind, and everything good, but all that was not enough. For better or for worse, the desire I had to succeed where my father had failed was greater than the love I had for Win.

So, no, I did not chase my boyfriend to Albany. I was occupied with arranging for my business and finishing preparations for the prelaunch party on Friday.

The phone rang. Despite myself, I hoped it was Win, but it wasn't.

"Are you not happy to hear from your old friend?" Theo asked.

I had messaged him several days earlier for advice from the *abuelas* about what could be used as a substitute for cacao in frozen hot chocolate, the drink I planned to serve at the party.

"The *abuelas* say that nothing can substitute cacao! They want to know why you would want to commit such a blasphemy."

I told him about my business. "We're having a prelaunch party, but my business partner doesn't think it's a good idea to serve anything illegal since the whole idea is for it to be aboveboard."

"I see. Well, then perhaps you might try carob powder? It is a pale substitute but . . ."

I thanked him.

"Let me know what else I can do to help," Theo said.

"How about a good deal on Granja Mañana cacao?" I suggested. "I'm going to need a supplier."

"The best deal I have," Theo said. "I am proud of you, Anya Barnum-Balanchine. You seem to have made peace with everything."

"*Gracias*, Theo. You know you are the only person to say that to me."

"It is because I know you, Anya. In our hearts, we are the same." Theo paused. "How is your boyfriend?"

"He's mad at me," I said.

"He will get over it."

"Maybe." But I wasn't really sure if he would this time.

We talked for a while longer, and Theo promised to come and see me when he could. I asked him if they'd be able to spare him at Granja Mañana, and he said that Luna had been much more help since he'd been sick. "I guess I should be grateful to you for getting me shot."

"Unfortunately, you aren't the first boy to say that to me."

Friday came, and with it, the party. Still I had not heard from Win. I spent the day having the space cleaned and setting up samovars for the frozen hot chocolate along the sides of the room. I'd invited everyone in my circle—though no one from the *semya*—and Charles Delacroix had invited people, too, including potential investors.

Scarlet and Gable were among the first people to show up. She was about a million months pregnant at this point and I hadn't been sure if she'd come at all. When I messaged her though, she had replied in about a second: *Really happy to have a reason to get out of the house and really happy for the invitation! P.S. Does this mean we aren't mad at each other anymore? I am so lonesome without you.* When she arrived, she hugged me.

"You two married yet?" I asked them.

"We're thinking about waiting until after she gives birth," Gable said.

Scarlet shook her head. "I couldn't get married without you, Anya."

"This is a terrific place," Gable said. "What are you planning to do with it anyway?"

"You'll hear all that soon enough," I said. "Hey, Gable. You planning to take any pictures tonight?" I asked.

Gable snarled that Scarlet had taken away his camera phone. "Where's your boyfriend?" he wanted to know.

I pretended I didn't hear him and I moved on to other guests.

Once most everyone had arrived, I went to the podium at the front of the room. I looked around to see if Win perchance had shown. He hadn't. Without him or Natty or Leo, I felt a bit unmoored, and it certainly was not the best speech of my life. I ran through the bullet points about the club I was planning to open, and what I planned to serve, and the reason all of this would be perfectly legal. As I described the business, I could feel the room grow deathly quiet, but the quiet did not scare me. "Tonight, you'll be drinking carob versions of the medicinal health drinks I'll be serving in the fall. They're going to taste a lot better then, I promise." I raised my mug, but I hadn't remembered to have it filled before starting my speech. Because it seemed awkward not to, I pretended to drink. "Someone once told me that last year's enemy could very well be this

346

year's friend, so with that in mind, I'd like to introduce you to my new legal counsel."

Charles Delacroix took the podium. He had shaved for the occasion, a gesture I appreciated. "Forgive me if I'm a bit rusty. I'm out of practice," Charles Delacroix began, with a falsely modest chuckle. "Seven months ago, my career in politics, for lack of a better word, ended. We don't need to go into the reasons why." He shot a look over at me, which made the crowd laugh. "Tonight, I'm here to talk about the future, however." He cleared his throat. "Chocolate," he said. "It's sweet. It's pleasant enough. But it's not worth dying over and it's certainly not worth losing an election over. Well, I've had a lot of time to think about chocolate this past year for obvious reasons"—he looked at me again—"and here's why chocolate matters. Not because I lost or because organized crime is bad. The reason it matters is because the legislation that banned chocolate is and has always been bad legislation.

"How does a city in decline become a city of tomorrow? It's a question I've asked myself nearly every day for the last ten years. And the answer I've come to is this: we must rethink the laws. Laws change because people demand change or because people find new ways of interpreting old laws. My friend—and I think I can call her that—Anya Balanchine has come up with a novel way of doing both.

"Ladies and gentlemen, you are at the start of something larger than just a nightclub. I see a future where New York City is a shining city once again, a city of laws that make sense. I see a future where people come to New York City for chocolate because it is the only place in the country that has had the good sense to legalize it. I see an economic windfall for this city, this chocolate city." He paused. "Even when we aren't elected to serve, we can still find ways to serve. I believe that this is so, and that's why I have agreed to help Anya Balanchine in any way that I can. I hope you, my friends, will join us."

It was a far better speech than mine, though it should be noted that Charles Delacroix had had far more practice with such matters. It should also be noted that my colleague's goals were a bit loftier than my own. He'd never said anything to me about a chocolate city. The term struck me as absurd.

I made my way through the crowd, stopping briefly to talk to Dr. Lau. And then I saw Dr. Freeman from Cacao Now. He shook my hand. "I can't thank you enough for inviting me. You *must* come speak to us this summer. This is visionary, Anya. Visionary!"

Just as I had reached the banquet table, a waitress I had hired for the evening told me there was someone who was asking for me outside. I would be lying if I told you I wasn't hoping for Win.

I went into the hallway, which was deserted. I walked down the stairs. On the landing stood my cousin Fats. He was sweaty and red-faced. Needless to say, he had not been invited. A flight down, I could see his security. That was new. Fats usually traveled alone.

"Fats," I said lightly. When I was close enough, he kissed me. His lips smacked almost violently against my cheeks. "What brings you here?"

"Heard there was a party," he said. "Hurts my feelings when

I don't get an invite after all the time you and your friends spent in my joint over the years."

"I didn't think you'd be interested," I said lamely.

Fats craned his neck up the stairs. "This where the—what did you call it?—health cacao place is gonna be?"

"I came to you. You didn't like the idea."

"Maybe so. Guess I didn't think you'd go and do it anyway," Fats said. He pulled me in to whisper in my ear. His breath was moist and hot against my skin. "You sure about this, Annie? You sure you want all this brought down on you? There's still time for you to change your mind. You got your brother to think about. Your little sister, too. And I know you already have plenty of enemies. Yuji Ono. Sophia Bitter. Mickey Balanchine. You really want me to be one more?"

I pushed him away. He was bluffing, I was certain. And even if he wasn't, there were months before the club would open, which meant there were months left for me to broker some kind of peace between us if that proved necessary. Maybe it was foolish of me, but I truly believed that I could convince him to my way of thinking. Fats had loved my father, and I knew I was doing what Daddy would have wanted. I just didn't want to make this case to Fats tonight. "It's done," I said. "Have a good night. I really must attend to my guests."

I ran up the stairs and I did not look back.

At long last, I made it over to one of the samovars. I turned the spigot to fill my glass, and Charles Delacroix sidled up next to me. "You did well," he said. "This is a great night. This is where it all begins."

"So you said. 'Chocolate city,' huh?"

"I thought it had good drama to it. People like drama, Anya. They remember drama."

I tasted the drink. I'd followed Theo's instruction to the letter, but the flavor was strong, if ever so slightly sour. Though no one at the party seemed to notice, something had gone bad in the mix. Maybe Theo was right when he had told me that there wasn't a good substitute for chocolate. Yet half the samovars were already empty, so perhaps I was being an overly sensitive hostess. I took a second tentative sip. When I looked up, I saw Win, standing across the room next to Scarlet and Gable. I hadn't seen him arrive. Despite everything, he had come for me. At that moment, my heart, my lowly, amnesiac heart, could not recall the things that had been more important than those eyes, those hands, that mouth. *Forgive me,* I wanted to say to him, *I knew I would hurt you and I did it anyway. I don't know why I am the way I am. I don't know why I do the things I do. Please, Win, don't give up on me. Love me a little, even though I'm flawed.*

"Thank you," was what I did manage to whisper. He couldn't have heard, but I was sure he saw my lips. He did not cross the room to me. He did not reply or even smile. I was not forgiven, not yet. After a moment, he raised his glass. I imitated his gesture before draining that bitter drink to its lees.

Author GABRIELLE ZEVIN
discusses the Birthright series

© Hans Canosa

Miss Print

Emma Carbone has been blogging as Miss Print since 2007. An avid reader and writer, she resides in New York City, where she is working on her first novel. Visit her on the Web at missprint.wordpress.com.

Miss Print (MP): In addition to being a catchy, clever twist on dystopian futures and organized crime, *All These Things I've Done* was one of my favorite reads this summer.

Gabrielle Zevin (GZ): Thanks very much! I'm so pleased.

MP: Can you tell us a bit about your path as a writer? How did you get to this point?

GZ: I was an avid reader who became a writer because it turned out I had an aptitude for both lying and solitude. In terms of my career, I think I got to this point through willful self-delusion and lots of caffeine. Seriously though, there's much discussion about the end of conventional publishers in the wake of e-books. I can honestly say that I probably wouldn't be a writer if there hadn't been conventional publishers when I was starting. I learned my craft by working with professionals at the top level who knew more than I about everything from content to design to promotion. Some writers, by the way, have no gift for self-promotion, but they still write beautiful and worthy books. In fact, it could be said that the kind of introspection it takes to write a really original novel can be in direct opposition to the ability to self-promote. My point is, I'm lucky that I came up when I did. I've had a lot of support. It takes a village to raise a child, but it also takes a village to publish a book.

MP: *All These Things I've Done* is your third young adult novel. You have also written two novels that were marketed to adults, as well as the screenplay for *Conversations with Other Women*. What is it like writing for these different audiences and formats?

GZ: I suspect I would have quit writing a long time ago if I hadn't been able to move among genres, kinds of characters, styles of writing. There's nothing as creatively freeing as trying something you haven't done before. In terms of process? It is just as difficult and painful to write a young adult novel, a screenplay, or a "serious" work of literary fiction.

MP: *All These Things I've Done* is the first book in a series. Do you have a set arc for Anya's story?

GZ: I absolutely have a set arc. Anya is going to grow up and go through so much and travel to so many places, I'm kind of dying for readers to get to *Because It Is My Blood*. (The one thing I want readers to know is that sometimes when a boy looks too good to be true, it's because he is. And, for the record, most of us don't end up marrying the boy we loved in high school.)

MP: The book is set in 2083 and a lot of things are scarce (like paper) and some are illegal (most notably chocolate and coffee). Did you always know chocolate would play such a big part in the story? What are your favorite kinds of chocolate and coffee?

GZ: The weird thing is, I'm not the biggest chocolate person. I've grown an appreciation for it from all the research I did for the book, but I don't crave it and I could live without it. If it were a society that banned bread, I'd be a lot more upset! I once read an interview with Ralph Fiennes (who plays Voldemort) in which they asked him if he was a big Harry Potter fan. He replied that he wasn't, but that the man who played Voldemort probably shouldn't be. I guess it's like that for me and chocolate. I do love coffee, however—I'm an espresso girl. Don't know how to write a book without it.

MP: Did your vision for Anya's New York start with a specific place or aspect?

GZ: I've lived in New York City most of my life, but this is the first novel I've set there. So writing the world was easy, or as easy as these things ever are. I just imagined what would happen if the economy never picked up, if we stopped funding the arts and the parks, and if everything got a little worse each year instead of a little better. I think it might have started with a docent at the Metropolitan telling me that I should give more than the suggested ticket price because the museum needed it. Despite how bad the economy was and is, I really had never thought that an institution like the Metropolitan Museum of Art would ever be in jeopardy. But you start looking into it and things are bad everywhere, and especially for the things that are considered nonessentials like, you know, culture.

MP: One of the things that I really enjoyed about *All These Things I've Done* is that it is set in New York City—albeit a New York of the future

where a lot of things are different. How did you decide what details to include in Anya's version of the city? Are you particularly fond of any details? (I was especially struck by Little Egypt and Liberty Island.)

GZ: I guess I probably chose the places I thought I'd miss the most if they weren't there any longer. Little Egypt definitely came from that museum trip. Liberty Children's began from a news story I read about the cost of maintaining the Statue of Liberty. In terms of favorites? The New York Public Library (referred to as the Lion's Den) makes a very brief appearance in the book, but it ends up being extremely important in the series.

Book Probe: Observing Worlds Of Fiction

Braiden Asciak is an enthusiastic reader, writer, and blogger. It is in his blood to tell people all the latest in books and stories. Visit him on the Web at bookprobereviews.com.

Braiden Asciak (BA): Was there an issue or "big question" that you wanted to solve and answer, which may have inspired you to write *All These Things I've Done*? Or was it just strings of information and visions that came together for you from the beginning to the end?

Gabrielle Zevin (GZ): Oh, Braiden, I have loads of issues! Luckily, I've always found writing books to be a cheap form of therapy. The truth is, every book I've written really has been me attempting to answer some sort of major life question for myself. For *All These Things I've Done*, the main question is: How do we escape the circumstances of our birth when so much in life seems to be determined from the moment we set foot on the planet? How do we escape a legacy of violence? These are big questions, I know, and ones that will play out across all the characters in the story. But yeah, *All These Things . . .* incorporates a variety of my obsessions—everything from why certain things in society are legal and others are not, to the fate of conventional publishing.

BA: All that we know within the society of *All These Things I've Done* so far (the illegality of chocolate, this mafia situation, etc.) seem to have been an influence on and dictator of Anya's decisions in her life and that of life in general. Was there a reason for this? Will we find out more about this modern-futuristic society in later books of the Birthright series?

GZ: Yes, absolutely. When coming up with Anya's voice and point of view, I'd often find myself thinking of a certain quote from the movie *The Truman*

Show: "We accept the reality of the world with which we've been presented." My thinking was that I didn't want to write the future like it was the future. Because if you are a person living in the future, you're not thinking how amazing and odd everything is, and you're not going to explain the world as if the reader is living in the past. I absolutely didn't put anything in the book that wouldn't come plausibly through Anya's point of view. Anya is not a history teacher or a political scientist, and her knowledge of how the world works is pretty shallow in a way, especially in the first book. This is to say, yes, you will definitely find out more about the world as the books go on. As Anya learns more and becomes more entangled in the family business, she's able to guide us through her world with sharper eyes and true expertise. Above all else, this is a character-driven story.

BA: What can we expect from the sequel, *Because It Is My Blood*?

GZ: International travel and intrigue! For a while, the second book was called *All the Kingdoms of the World,* and that title reflected one of my larger goals for the series. I am an American, but my mother was born in Korea, and I very much wanted to write a series that took place in a world greater than just America, that put my main character in contact with a culture and viewpoints greater than just her own. The other thing you should know is that the second book is neither a high school story nor particularly a love story.

BA: Why the year 2083? What makes it so special?

GZ: Among many things, I imagined a sixteen-year-old reader of *All These Things I've Done* in 2011. She'd be born in 1995, which as we learn on page one is the same year Anya's grandmother was born. The reader, like Nana, knows what OMG means, even if Anya doesn't. My hope had been that this would establish an empathy between Nana—who at eighty-eight years old is a sick, largely forgotten, bed-bound woman—and the reader. I had been thinking a lot about grandmothers and what it is to get old because my own had been slowly dying of Alzheimer's. So, in a way, it was a tricky thing about point of view. I wanted readers to relate to Nana because she is of their generation, but also to Anya because she is the same age as them. I wanted the reader to have an uncomfortable sense of divided empathy.

BA: There are many references within *All These Things I've Done* to the works of Shakespeare and Charles Dickens. Was there a specific reason why such classic texts are still learned in your 2083?

GZ: That's a funny question, really. I'll give you my personal, writer answer first. I was going through a Dickens phase, and he was one of the first series writers. All his books were serialized in newspapers, of course. (A novel like *Bleak House* is something like one thousand pages in all, and would probably be published in three books or more these days.) And what I found when I reread Dickens was the sort of possibilities for series writing. I had never been particularly interested in writing a series. Many contemporary series I've read sort of mark time—which is to say, the plot doesn't turn much past the first book. What we end up with quite often is a promising first book that doesn't really go anywhere narratively in subsequent installments. If readers are attached enough to the characters, they tend not to notice these things. With Dickens, the plot is turning the whole length of the series—it had to be to keep readers coming back to those newspapers—and the characters are growing and developing the whole time, too. And that's the kind of series I wanted to write. A series that, if you put all the books together, at the end you would have a master—by which I mean, planned—narrative that made sense from page one to page twelve-hundred. In addition, of course, to books that held up on their own.

The shorter story answer is this: Anya is not a reader, nor does she come from a society that cares a whit about books. The stories she's heard are the ones she happens to have read for school or the ones Imogen has read to Nana. Her ideas of novel writing are classic and old-fashioned because that really is all she's been exposed to.

BA: Do you think in our reality and our foreseeable future such literary classics (and classical music could be fitted to this as well) would be forgotten? Will they ever be?

GZ: No, I don't think literary classics will really be forgotten. Because all those writers are dead and don't need to be compensated for their work. That is to say, a Dickens novel can live forever in Google Books, and it will. It has already been canonized as classic. I think the problem will come with allowing truly great new writers and new voices to also join the classics party. The annoying thing about a living writer is that she or he needs to eat and be paid. But—from a publisher and an author standpoint—it's hard to compete with all the great writers that are dead and thus have work available for free. It's also hard to compete with writers that only value their work at $.99. Now, I'm not saying all $.99 e-books are awful, but it's worth thinking about why self-published authors, for instance, might choose to value themselves so cheaply. I could go on, but this is a long answer that invokes things like self-publishing, what publishers really do, e-books, bookstores, newspaper review sections, and what it means to be a reviewer of taste and expertise.

BA: Author or screenwriter? Book writing or screenwriting? Page or screen? What's better in your opinion?

GZ: Stories are stories, friend. Though I will say that I think some of the best writing going on right now is on television—shows like *Breaking Bad*, for instance. Here's an anecdote, though. I'm sure you've come across the phrase "show, don't tell" to indicate bad writing in novels. Well, the funny thing about that is it actually comes from Syd Field's (and Robert McKee's) screenwriting classes and books. And yes, this advice makes perfect sense for movies—movies are a visual medium. But books, and quite often the best books, have always been a great deal "tell." It deeply matters what the voice of the narrator is, what the narrator feels, and what the narrator thinks. Novels do not play out in movie scenes. Novels are interior. Consider *The Great Gatsby*! Consider *The Catcher in the Rye*! The "tell" is what I love about novels, actually. So, I kind of laugh any time I see a reviewer who thinks they have a little bit of knowledge flogging some poor book with the "show, don't tell" rule.

BA: What are a few of the challenges you come across when starting a new idea or novel? What is your writing process like? Do you start with an outline or do you just start typing and see where it leads you?

GZ: The biggest challenge is probably choosing the right idea. There are so many things to be inspired by, but it's hard to commit to just one, to truly convince myself it's going to be the right thing. In terms of process, I spend a long time thinking before I start. I spend more time thinking than writing. The first half of a book is super slow for me, and the second half is usually much quicker. If you've done the early work right, then the ending ought to be inevitable.

Reading Writing Breathing

HD Tolson is a full-time student who shadows as a YA book blogger in his spare time. Visit him on the Web at readingwritingbreathing.com.

HD Tolson (HT): What interests you most about the genre of dystopian?

Gabrielle Zevin (GZ): Forgive me, HD, if I come at this answer through the side door. Though I'm not surprised that people are calling *All These Things I've Done* dystopian, I never really thought I was writing dystopia! I don't see the government in the story as particularly more oppressive or corrupt than our government today, and I think the concept of what is "good" or "legal" (especially with regard to what we consume) tends to shift with each generation. Consider that when Coca-Cola was launched in the 1880s, its two key ingredients were caffeine and cocaine—and this was perfectly legal! Consider Prohibition in the 1920s. Consider the current ban on high fructose corn syrup in Europe. Consider the fact that it certainly seems possible that marijuana may become legal in our own country in the next decade.

From my point of view as a reader, I am drawn to "dystopian" because of the way it can potentially hold up a mirror to our own society. (I'm certainly not the first person to say this.) And in general, I think readers' fascination with dystopia is a great deal about their dissatisfaction with today's economy and government. The Ancient Greek translation of the word "dystopia" is simply "bad or ill place." One could argue that that describes many places today. By the way, I imagine that Anya Balanchine wouldn't think she was living in dystopia. It's just a topia—i.e., the world—to her. Aside: Does anyone living in a dystopia really think it is a dystopia?

HT: Chocolate and coffee are contraband in your dystopian society of *All These Things I've Done*. Why did you make that so?

GZ: Okay, I'm about to sound like PBS. Chocolate appealed to me because cacao, the plant from which all chocolate is derived, is a truly fascinating crop. The Mayans believed cacao had healing properties and even used it as currency. The DSM doesn't go so far as to classify it as a drug, but they do note that it is one of the few foods from which people experience with-drawal-like symptoms. I also found it interesting that chocolate is sometimes packaged with a cacao percentage on the label, not unlike the way alcohol is packaged with a proof number. Finally, and this is probably the most impor-tant reason, cacao is extremely difficult to grow and only thrives in a handful of places around the world. In fact, it's not really possible to grow cacao in North America. It was easy for me to imagine a scenario in which, as fuel and transportation costs continue to rise, it would become financially difficult for big corporations to produce chocolate in the United States.

HT: Did you read other dystopian YA for inspiration while or before writing your book?

GZ: My inspirations were more Dickens or Dostoevsky than dystopia! But I've definitely loved several of the dystopian (or at least dystopian-ish) novels of the last decade or so: *How I Live Now* by Meg Rosoff; *Catching Fire* is probably my favorite of the Hunger Games series (I even reviewed it for the *New York Times*); *Bumped* by Megan McCafferty; and this isn't YA, but I adored *Never Let Me Go* by Kazuo Ishiguro. As a reader, I generally prefer my novels to be character-driven as opposed to world-driven. I can't bear to read one more story of a sullen girl in a humorless, post-apocalyptic world where everyone is wearing brown clothes and the government is controlling personal freedoms in a way that is administratively impractical.

HT: Anya, the main character of *All These Things I've Done*, is the heir to a large chain of "drug" dealing, dealing chocolate. Why did you choose to tell a story in a society through her eyes, and why did you decide to write a mafia chain?

GZ: The reason I love mafia stories is because they are about families, good and evil, social justice, religion, love, honor, money, and basically all the greatest literary subjects. In most mafia stories, however, the women characters are reduced to wives, girlfriends, or hookers. I wanted to write a story where the girl had a chance to rise to power. In terms of character, I was attracted to Anya's point of view because she is smart but, in many ways, ignorant. She doesn't know why everything in the world is the way it is, and in many ways, she's too busy living her life to care.

HT: What was your favorite part about writing *All These Things I've Done*?

GZ: I've really loved creating all the international chocolate mafia families: the Balanchines/Balanchiadzes in the U.S. and Russia, the Marquezes in Mexico, the Onos in Japan, the Bitters in Germany, and a handful of others. (You'll see more of them as the series continues.) I've had fun watching Anya grow as she interacts with cultures and viewpoints different from her own.

HT: What was your least favorite part about writing *All These Things I've Done*?

GZ: I'm about to cheat here. I'm going to talk about something that isn't exactly writing but is still an important part of the process—promotion. The truth is, I've found it difficult to explain this book to people. I think when people hear the word "dystopia," they have a certain expectation for what the book is going to be based on what other dystopian books have been like in the past. But this really is a book about a girl and a family, not a book about a world.

CLASSIFIED

Name: Anya Pavlova Balanchine

DOB: 08/12/2066

Weight: 118 lbs.

Hair: Black   Eyes: Green

Height: 5' 3"   Sex: F

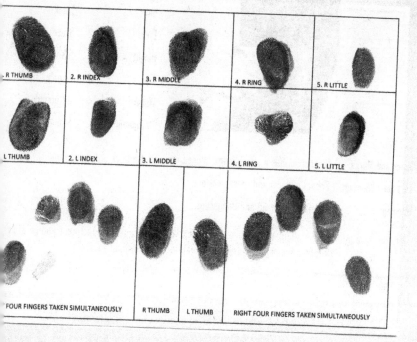

| R THUMB | 2. R INDEX | 3. R MIDDLE | 4. R RING | 5. R LITTLE |
| L THUMB | 2. L INDEX | 3. L MIDDLE | 4. L RING | 5. L LITTLE |

| LEFT FOUR FINGERS TAKEN SIMULTANEOUSLY | R THUMB | L THUMB | RIGHT FOUR FINGERS TAKEN SIMULTANEOUSLY |

WANTED

POSSESSION OF A BANNED SUBSTANCE, ATTEMPTED MURDER
ANYA PAVLOVA BALANCHINE

ALIASES/NICKNAMES: no known aliases at this time; the chocolate princess

DESCRIPTION:

DOB: Aug. 12, 2066

Place of Birth: New York, NY

Hair: Black

Eyes: Green

Height: 5'3"

Sex: Female

Weight: 118 pounds

Occupation: Student

Scars and Marks: Balanchine has a small, heart-shaped mole on the back of her left hand.

Last Seen Wearing: School uniform and cross necklace

Warning: Considered Armed and Dangerous

If you have information about this individual, contact your local police department immediately. Do not attempt to apprehend or detain this individual yourself.

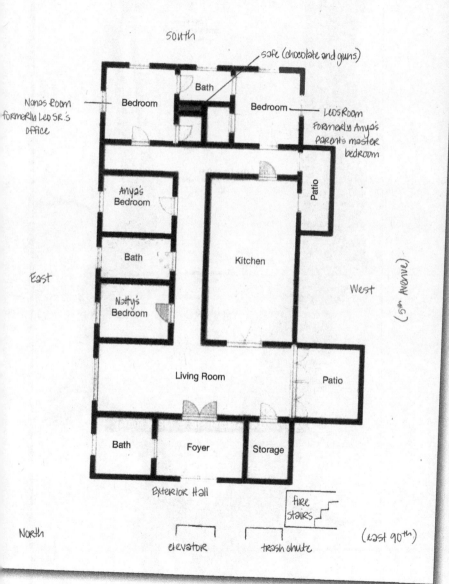

Balanchine Apt. Floor Plan

south

safe (chocolate and guns)

Bath

Nana's Room
formerly Leo Sr.'s
office

Bedroom

Bedroom — Leo's Room
formerly Anya's
parent's master
bedroom

Anya's
Bedroom

Patio

Bath

Kitchen

East

West

(5th Avenue)

Natty's
Bedroom

Living Room

Patio

Bath

Foyer

Storage

Exterior Hall

fire
stairs

North

elevator

trash chute

(east 90th)

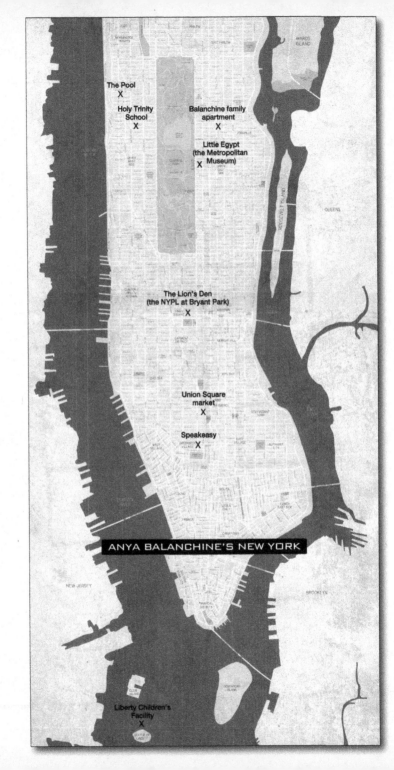

The Pool
X

Holy Trinity
School
X

Balanchine family
apartment
X

Little Egypt
(the Metropolitan
Museum)
X

The Lion's Den
(the NYPL at Bryant Park)
X

Union Square
market
X

Speakeasy
X

ANYA BALANCHINE'S NEW YORK

NEW JERSEY

BROOKLYN

Liberty Children's
Facility
X

BRATVA PRINCESS AND ASST. DA'S SON FIND LOVE IN THE CITY

Guess which buxom mafiya daughter had lips flapping again this weekend? If you said Anya Balanchine, ding ding ding ding, you win the teddy bear. The daughter of Leonyd Balanchine was spotted at Grand Central Terminal holding hands with none other than – wait for it – Goodwin Delacroix. Yes, *that* Delacroix. (Turns out Charles Delacroix isn't the only lady-killer in the family.) I'd watch out if I were Goodwin. The boys Anya dates have a disturbing tendency to end up in the hospital. (Gable Arsley, anyone?) Who wants to place bets on whether Goodwin Delacroix finds himself in mortal peril before 2083 is over? The good people of Charles Delacroix's office had no comment. Even more annoying than that, I can't for the life of me come up with a decent nickname for the new match. Goodanya? Winya? You know where to send your suggestions.

Jennifer Snarkwell, Gossip Columnist

ANYA BALANCHINE:

A COLLECTION OF FAN ART

ALL THESE THINGS I'VE DONE

BECAUSE IT IS MY BLOOD

CREDITS:

LEFT:
© SIMINI BLOCKER

RIGHT:
© JANIE MULONE/OXYDERCES.DEVIANTART.COM

Life has been hard for Anya Balanchine. Now, for the first time ever, she's experiencing success. Her nightclub is a hit. Nothing can possibly go wrong. Nothing, that is, until Anya finds herself fighting for her life—and reckoning her choices. Maybe this time Anya needs help.

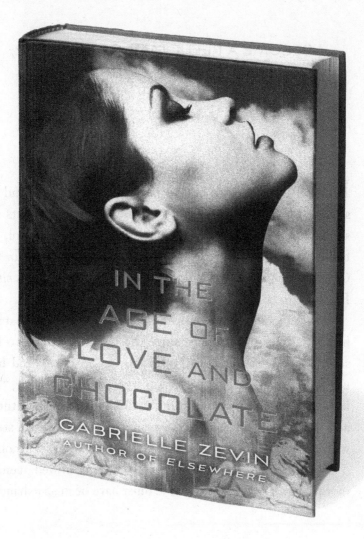

Read Anya's story in the breathtaking conclusion to the Birthright series.

I BECOME A RELUCTANT GODMOTHER;
ON THE BITTERNESS OF CACAO

I HADN'T WANTED to be godmother, but my best friend insisted. "I'm flattered," I tried to demur, "but godparents are
supposed to be Catholics in good standing." In school, we
had both been taught that a godparent was responsible for the
Catholic education of a child, and I hadn't been to mass since
Easter or to confession in over a year.

Scarlet looked at me with an aggrieved expression that she
had acquired in the month since she had given birth to her
son. The baby was beginning to stir, so Scarlet picked him
up. "Oh, sure," she drawled in a sarcastic baby talk voice, "Felix and I would positively adore a fine, upstanding Catholic
as a godparent, but *malheureusement*, the person we are stuck
with is Anya, who everyone knows to be a bad, bad Catholic."
The baby cooed. "Felix, what could your poor, unwed, teenage
mother have been thinking? She must have been so exhausted

and overwhelmed that her brain must have stopped working. Because no one in the entire world has ever been worse than Anya Balanchine. Just ask her." Scarlet held the baby toward me. The baby smiled at me—it was a happy, apple-cheeked, blue-eyed, blond-haired creature—and wisely said nothing. I smiled back, though truth be told, I was not entirely comfortable around babies. "Oh, that's right. You can't talk yet, little baby. But someday, when you're older, ask your godmother to tell you the story of what a bad Catholic—no scratch that—bad person she was. She cut off someone's hand! She went into business with a terrible man and she chose that same business over the nicest boy in the world. She went to jail. To protect her brother and her sister, but still—who, when presented with other options, wants a juvenile delinquent for a godparent? She poured a steaming tray of lasagna over your daddy's head, and some people even thought she tried to poison him. And if she'd succeeded, you wouldn't even be here—"

"Scarlet, you shouldn't talk like that in front of the baby."

She ignored me and continued chattering to Felix. "Can you imagine, Felix? Your life will probably be ruined because your mother was so thick as to choose Anya Balanchine to be your godmother"—she turned to me—"do you see what I'm doing here? I'm acting like it's a done thing that you're going to be the godmother, because it *totally* is"—she turned back to Felix. "With a godmother like her, it's probably straight to a life of crime for you, my little man." She kissed him on his fat cheeks, and then she nibbled him a bit. "Do you want to taste this?"

I shook my head.

"Suit yourself, but you're missing out on something delicious," she said.

"You've gotten so sarcastic since you became a mother, you know that?"

"Have I? It's probably best if you do what I say without argument then."

"I'm not sure I'm even Catholic anymore," I said.

"OMG, are we still talking about this? *You are the godmother.* My mother is making me have a baptism so you're the godmother."

"Scarlet, I really have done things."

"I know that, and now Felix does, too. It's good that we go into this with our eyes open. I've done things myself. *Obviously.*" She patted the baby on the head, then gestured around the tiny nursery that had been set up in Gable's parents' apartment. The nursery had once been a pantry, and it was a tight squeeze for the three of us and the many items that make up a baby's life. Still, Scarlet had done her best with the miniature room, painting the walls with clouds and a pale blue sky. "What difference does any of that make? You're my best friend. Who else would be godmother?"

"Are you honestly saying you won't do it?" The pitch of Scarlet's voice had shifted up to an unpleasant register, and the baby was beginning to stir. "Because I don't care when the last time you went to mass was." Scarlet's pretty brow was furrowing and she looked like she might cry. "If it's not you, there's no one else. So please don't get neurotic about this. Just buy the christening gown and stand next to me in church and when the priest or my mother or anyone else asks you if you're a good Catholic, lie."

On the hottest day of summer, in the second week of July, I stood next to Scarlet in St. Patrick's Cathedral. She held Felix in her arms, and the three of us were sweating enough to solve the water crisis. Gable, the baby's father, was on the other side of Scarlet, and Gable's older brother, Maddox, the godfather, stood beside Gable. Maddox was a thicker-necked, smaller-eyed, better-mannered version of Gable. The priest, perhaps conscience of the fact that we were about to pass out from the heat, kept his remarks brief and banter-free. It was so hot he did not even feel the need to mention that the baby's parents were unwed teenagers. This was truly the boilerplate, no frills baptism. The priest asked Maddox and me, "Are you prepared to help these parents in their duties as Christian mothers and fathers?"

We will, we said.

And then the questions were directed to the four of us: "Do you reject Satan?"

We did, we said.

"Is it your will that Felix be baptized in the faith of the Catholic Church?"

It is, we said, though at that point we would have agreed to anything to get this ceremony over with.

And then he poured holy water over Felix's head, which made the baby giggle. I can only imagine that the water must have felt refreshing. I would not have minded some holy water myself.

After the service, we went back to Gable's parents' apartment for a baptismal party. Scarlet had invited a couple of the kids we had gone to high school with, among them my recently coronated ex-boyfriend, Win, who I had not seen in about four weeks.

The party felt like a funeral. Scarlet was the first one of us to have a baby, and no one seemed to know quite how to behave at such an affair. Gable played a drinking game with his brother in the kitchen. The other kids from Holy Trinity chatted in polite, hushed tones among themselves. In the corner were Scarlet's and Gable's parents, our solemn chaperones. Win kept company with Scarlet and the baby. I could have gone over to them, but I wanted Win to have to cross the room to me.

"How's the club coming along, Anya?" Chai Pinter asked me. Chai was a terrible gossip, but she was basically harmless.

"We're opening at the end of September. If you're in town, you should come."

"Definitely. By the way, you look exhausted," Chai said. "You've got dark circles under your eyes. Are you, like, not sleeping because you're worried you'll fail?"

I laughed. If you couldn't ignore Chai, it was best to laugh at her. "Mainly I'm not sleeping because it's a lot of work."

"My dad says that ninety-eight percent of nightclubs fail in New York."

"That's quite a statistic," I said.

"It might have been ninety-nine percent. But Anya, what will you do if you fail? Will you go back to school?"

"Maybe."

"Did you even graduate high school?"

"I got my GED last spring." Need I mention she was starting to annoy me?

She lowered her voice and cast her eyes across the room toward Win. "Is it true that the reason Win broke up with you is because you went into business with his father?"

"I'd rather not talk about that."

"So it *is* true?"

"It's complicated," I said. That was true enough.

She looked at Win, and then she made sad eyes at me. "I could never give up *that* for any business," she said. "If that boy loved me, I'd be, *What business?* You're a way stronger person than me. I mean it, Anya. I totally admire you."

"Thanks," I said. Chai Pinter's *admiration* had managed to make me feel horrible about every decision I'd made for the last two months. I pushed out my chin with resolve and pulled back my shoulders. "You know, I think I'm going to step out onto the balcony for some fresh air."

"It's like one-hundred degrees outside," Chai called after me.

"I like the heat," I said.

I opened the sliding door and I went outside into the sweltering evening. I sat down in a dusty lounge chair with a cushion that was bleeding foam. My day had not begun in the afternoon with Felix's baptism, but hours before that at the club. I'd been up since five that morning and at some point I must have fallen asleep. Though I have never been much of a dreamer, I had the oddest dream in which I was Scarlet's baby. Scarlet held me in her arms, and the feeling overwhelmed me. All at once, I remembered what it was to have a mother, to be safe and to be loved by someone above anyone else in the world. And in the dream, Scarlet somehow transformed into my mother. I could not always remember my mother's face, but in this dream, I could see her so clearly—her intelligent green eyes and her wavy reddish brown hair and the hard pink line of her mouth and the delicate freckles that were sprinkled across her nose. I had forgotten about the freckles, and that made me even sadder. She had been beautiful, but she didn't look like she took guff from anyone. I knew why my father had wanted her even though he should have married anyone *but* her, anyone but a cop. "Annie," my mother whispered, "you are loved. Let yourself be loved." In the dream, I couldn't stop crying. And maybe that is why babies cry so much—the weight of all that love is simply too much to bear.

"Hey," Win said. I sat up and tried to pretend I hadn't been sleeping. (Aside: *Why do people do that? What is so embarrassing about being asleep?*) "I'm leaving now. I wanted to talk to you before I went."

"You haven't changed your mind, I suppose." I did not look him in the eye. I kept my voice cool and even.

He shook his head. "You haven't either. My dad talks about the club sometimes. Business proceeds, I know."

"So, what do you want, then?"

"I wondered if I could stop by your place to get a few things

I left there. I'm going to my mother's farm in Albany for the rest of the summer and then I'll be back in the city for a couple of days before I leave for college."

My tired brain tried to make sense of this statement. "Leave?"

"Yes, I decided to go to Boston College. I didn't have a reason to stay in New York anymore."

This was news to me. "Well, good luck, Win. Have a *fantastic* time in Boston."

"Was I supposed to have consulted you?" he asked. "You certainly never consulted me about anything."

"You're exaggerating."

"If you're honest with yourself, you'll know I'm not."

"What would you have said if I told you I was going to ask your father to work for me?" I asked.

"You'll never know," he said.

"I do know! You would have told me not to do it."

"Of course I would have. I would have told Gable Arsley not to work with my father, and I don't even like him."

I don't know why, but I grabbed his hand. "What things of yours do I have?"

"You have some of my clothes and my winter coat and I think Natty might have one of my hats, but she can keep that. I left my copy of *The Great Gatsby* in your room, and I might like to read that again some day. But mainly, I need my slate back for college. It's under your bed, I think."

"There's no need for you to stop by. I can put the stuff in a box. I'll bring it to work, and your dad can bring it to you."

"If that's what you want."

"I think it would be easier. I'm not Scarlet. I don't crave pointless, dramatic scenes."

"As you like, Anya."

"You're always so polite. It's irritating."

"And you always keep everything inside. We're a terrible match really."

I crossed my arms and turned away from him. I was angry. I wasn't quite sure why I was angry, but I was. If I hadn't been so tired, I feel quite sure I would have been better able to keep my emotions in check. "Why did you even come to the launch party for the club if you weren't going to at least try to forgive me?"

"I *was* trying, Anya. I wanted to see if I could get past it."

"So?"

"So, it turns out I can't."

"You can." I didn't think anyone could see us, but I wouldn't have cared anyway. I threw my arms around him. I pushed him into the sidewall of the balcony and I pushed my lips against his. It only took me a couple of seconds to notice that he was not, in fact, kissing me back.

"I can't," he repeated.

"So, that's it. You don't love me anymore?"

For a moment, he didn't reply. He shook his head. "Not enough to get past this, I guess. I don't love you that much."

To restate: *he had loved me, just not enough.*

I couldn't argue with that, but I tried to anyway. "You're going to regret this," I said. "The club is going to be a huge success, and you're going to regret that you didn't stand by me. Because if you love someone, you love them all the way.

You love them even when they make mistakes. That's what I think."

"So I'm meant to love you, no matter how you act, no matter what you do. I couldn't respect myself if I felt that way."

He was probably right.

I was so tired of defending myself and of trying to convince him. I looked at Win's shoulder, which was less than six inches from my face. It would be so easy to let my neck drop and ease my head into that cozy space above his shoulder, which seemed designed specifically for me. It would be easy to tell him the club and the business with his father were terrible mistakes and to beg him to take me back. For a second, I closed my eyes and tried to imagine what my future would look like if Win were in it. I could see a house somewhere outside the city—Win has a collection of antique records, and maybe I learn to cook a dish besides macaroni and frozen peas. I could see our wedding—it's on a beach and he's wearing a blue seersucker suit and our rings are white gold. I could see a dark-haired baby—I call him Leonyd after my father, if it's a boy, and Alexa after his sister, if it's a girl. I could see everything and it was so very lovely.

It would have been so easy, but I would have hated myself. I had a chance to build something, and in the process, do what my father had never been able to do. I couldn't let that go, even for that boy. He, alone, was not enough.

So, I held my tired neck erect and kept my eyes fixed forward. He was going, and I would let him go.

Inside, I could hear baby Felix start to cry, which the kids took as a sign to leave the party. Through the glass door, I could see them as they left. I don't know why, but I made a joke. "Looks like the worst prom ever," I said. "Maybe the second worst if you count junior year." I lightly touched Win's thigh where my cousin had shot him at the worst prom ever. For a second he looked like he might laugh, but then he repositioned his leg so that my hand was no longer on it.

Win pulled me to his chest. "Goodbye," he whispered in a gentler tone than I'd heard from him in a while, "I hope life gives you everything you want."

I knew it was over. In contrast with the other times we'd quarreled, he did not sound angry. He sounded resigned. He sounded as if he were already somewhere faraway. Maybe he had sounded that way the entire time?

A second later, he released me and then he really did leave.

I turned my back and watched the city as the sun went down. Though I had made my choices, I could not bear to know what he looked like when he was walking away.

I waited about fifteen minutes before I went back into the apartment. By that time, the only person left was Scarlet. "I love parties," Scarlet said, "but this was a miserable party. Don't say it wasn't, Annie. You can lie to the priest, but it's too late for you to start lying to me."

"I'll help you clean up," I said. "Where's Gable?"

"Out with his brother," she said. "Then, he has to go to work." Gable had a truly wretched-sounding job as a hospital orderly, which involved changing bedpans and cleaning floors.

It was the only work he could find, and I suppose it was a little noble of him to have taken it. "Do you think it was a mistake to invite the kids from Trinity?"

"I think it was fine," I said.

"I saw you talking to Win."

"A little," I said. "Nothing has changed."

"I'm sorry to hear that," she said. We cleaned up the apartment in silence. Scarlet started to vacuum, which is why I didn't notice right away that she had begun to cry.

I walked over to the vacuum and turned it off. "What is it?"

"I wonder what chance any of the rest of us have if you and Win can't make it work?"

"Scarlet, it was a high school romance. They aren't meant to last forever."

"Unless you're stupid and get yourself knocked up," Scarlet said.

"That's not what I meant."

"I know." Scarlet sighed. "And I know why you're opening the club, but you're certain Charles Delacroix is worth this trouble?"

"I am. I've explained this to you before." I turned the vacuum cleaner back on, and vacuumed. I was pushing the vacuum in long, mad strokes across the rug: angry-vacuuming. I turned the vacuum off again. "You know, it's not easy to do what I'm doing. I don't have any help. No one is supporting me. Not Mr. Kipling. Not my parents or my nana because they're dead. Not Natty because she is a child. Not Leo because he is in jail. Not the Balanchine family because they think I'm threatening their business. Certainly not Win. No one. I am alone, Scarlet. I am more alone than I have ever been in my entire life. And I know I chose this. But it hurts my feelings when you take Win's side over mine. I'm using Mr. Delacroix because he is the connection I have to the city. I need him, Scarlet. He has been part of my plan from the beginning. There is no one else who could replace him. Win is asking me for the one thing I can't give him. Don't you think I wish I could?"

"I'm sorry," she said.

"And I can't be with Win Delacroix just so my best friend doesn't give up on romance."

Scarlet's eyes were tear-filled. "Let's not argue. I'm an idiot. Ignore me."

"I hate when you call yourself stupid. No one thinks that of you."

"I think it of myself," Scarlet said. "Look at me. What am I going to do?"

"Well for one, we're going to finish cleaning this apartment."

"After that, I meant."

"Then, we're going to take Felix and go to my club. Lucy the mixologist is working late and she has a bunch of cacao drinks for us to sample."

"And then?"

"I don't know. You'll come up with something. But it's the only way I know how to move forward. You make a list and then, you go and do it."

"Still bitter," I said to my recently hired mixologist as I handed her the last in a series of shot glasses. Lucy had white blond hair cropped short, light blue eyes, pale skin, a big bow of a mouth, and a long, athletic body. When she was in her chef's coat and hat, I thought she looked like a bar of Balanchine White. I always knew when she was working in the kitchen because even from my office down the hall, I could hear her muttering and cursing. The dirty words seemed to be part of her creative process. I liked her very much, by the way. If she hadn't been my employee, maybe she would have been my friend.

"Do you think it needs more sugar?" Lucy said, furrowing her brow.

"I think it needs . . . something. It's even more bitter than the last one."

"That's what cacao tastes like, Anya. I'm starting to think you don't like the taste of cacao. Scarlet, what do you think?"

Scarlet sipped. "It's not obviously sweet, but I definitely detect sweetness," she said.

"Thank you," Lucy said.

"That's Scarlet," I said. "You're always looking for the sweet."

"And maybe you're always looking for the bitter," Scarlet joked.

"Pretty, smart, and optimistic. I wish you were my boss," Lucy said.

"She isn't as sunny as she seems," I told Lucy. "An hour ago, I found her crying and vacuuming."

"Everyone cries when they vacuum," Lucy said.

"I know, right?" Scarlet agreed. "Those vibrations make you emotional."

"I'm serious, though," I said. "In Mexico, the drinks weren't this dark."

"Maybe you should hire your friend from Mexico to come make them, then?" My mixologist had trained at the American Culinary Institute and at Le Cordon Bleu, and she could be touchy when it came to criticism.

"Oh Lucy, don't have hard feelings. You know I respect you enormously. But the drinks need to be perfect."

"Let's ask the heartbreaker," Lucy said. "With your permission, Scarlet."

"I don't see why not," Scarlet said. She dipped her pinky into the pot, and then she held it out to Felix to lick. He tasted tentatively. At first he smiled. Lucy began to look intolerably smug.

"He smiles at everything," I said.

Suddenly, his face crumpled into the shape of a dried out rose.

"Oh, I'm sorry, baby!" Scarlet said. "I'm a terrible mother."

"See?" I said.

"I suppose cacao is too sophisticated a flavor for a baby's palate," Lucy said. She sighed and dumped the contents of the pot into the sink. "Tomorrow," she said, "we try again. We fail again. We do better."